Praise for *Crystal Soldier*

"In short: these authors just keep getting better. If you want to get a taste of Liaden, here's a good place to start." –Sherwood Smith, SFSite

"Series fans will delight in seeing the roots of the Liaden Universe® and the characters they know"–Carolyn Cushman, *Locus*

"...a strongly character-driven yarn, focused firmly on the gradually evolving relationship between Jela and Cantra, who each have excellent reasons for distrusting the other's motives and intentions. The combination is a rarity and a treasure..." – John C. Bunnell

"Fantastic! Lee and Miller have shot straight on target, again. Crystal Soldier is a first rate read, beautifully set action and warm drawn characters threaded through a universe that displays illuminating depth and offers a fascinating mystery. This installment casts insight into every other volume–a tour de force of expanding creativity whose insights gently redefine the oft times miscast concepts of the true meaning of human security and survival."–Janny Wurts

"Here's the begining of the Liaden Unvierse® with Cantra and Jela's story, but if you don't recognize those names, it doesn't make no nevermind, because this is a great space opera with depth and scope and heart, about a universe that's a milliln light years deep and filled with wonder. This is the very best kind of story: the sort you never want to end. And I want more!"–Rosemary Edghill

"...These are my comfort books."–Anne McCaffery

Sharon Lee
&
Steve Miller

Crystal Dragon

Book Two of the Great Migration Duology

Meisha Merlin Publishing, Inc.
Atlanta, GA

Crystal Dragon

Published by Meisha Merlin Publishing, Inc.
PO Box 7
Decatur, GA 30031

Editing by Stephen Pagel
Copyediting and Proofreading Elizabeth Easter
Interior layout by Lynn Swetz
Cover art Donato
Cover design by Kevin Murphy

ISBN: Hard Cover 1-59222-087-8

http://www.MeishaMerlin.com
First MM Publishing edition: February 2006

Printed in the United States of America
0 9 8 7 6 5 4 3 2 1

Sharon Lee & Steve Miller

Crystal Dragon

Book Two of the Great Migration Duology

TABLE OF CONTENTS

To absent friends

PART THREE

SORCERER

PROLOGUE

In the Hall of the Mountain Kings

i.

THE *ZALIATA* PINWHEELED across the aetherium, painting the void with bright strokes of energy. Rapt, she moved closer to the barrier—and closer still, until the weaving of the containment forces flared.

She retreated until the barrier faded from her awareness, and once again only the *zaliata* were visible. Power and grace. Unimaginable power, for these were *zaliata* at the height of their considerable abilities, captured, contained, and exploited by the Iloheen—and no concern of hers.

Despite this—and the fact that it was, theoretically, impossible for those who wore flawed and fallible flesh to behold the sacred servants without the intermediary sight of an instructor—she came as often as she might to the aetherium, the folded space at the edge of what was, to watch the play and the power of the wild ones, the rebels, those who had contended as equals against the Iloheen—

And lost.

Of course, they had lost. No one and nothing could stand against the Iloheen. So she had been taught, and so she believed. But knowing that each *zaliata* contained within the aetherium had striven, flame to ice, against one of the Iloheen—that knowledge excited a brilliant emotion in her, as the beauty of their gyrations dazzled her senses, leaving her—

There!

There it was—her favorite of the wild dancers: not so large as some, but densely structured, the pattern of its emanations controlled, it colors deep and cunning, resonating through every spectrum she was able to sense, and surely well beyond. It suited her fancy to style this one *Iloheen-bailel*—Lord of Chance—in all ways fit to serve the Masters of Unmaking. Indeed, when she had not seen it at once, she had supposed that its master had required it elsewhere. That it was free—and dancing—pleased her.

Not that her puny pleasure was to be set against the necessities of the Iloheen. Surely not. The whole purpose of her existence was to serve the Iloheen as they instructed her, for while they were invincible, their numbers were not limitless, and so they required servants to perform certain of the lesser tasks of conquest.

She was herself scarcely trained and, according to her teachers, barely trainable. Yet she had passed living through the first two Dooms, while others of her cohort had not, and even now a vessel formed from her DNA and shaped by her skill grew in the birthing room. Soon, it would be ready to receive a download. *And, oh*, she thought, her eyes on the *Iloheen-bailel* as it tumbled and shone in its dance through the clusters of its fellows, *if only*—

But such was not for her.

Putting away longing and regret alike, she watched the *zaliata* dance, taking comfort from the intricate, subtle patterns that emerged—and suddenly came to full attention, all her senses a-tingle, as she sought to analyze those so-subtle movements.

The *Iloheen-bailel* was feigning random action, but close analysis revealed that it was passing near each and every one of the dancers in the aetherium, mingling its energies with those others in the way of *zaliata* communication. There was nothing overtly wrong in this—if the Iloheen had not wished their servants to communicate, they would simply have forbidden it. But the attempt to conceal the communication engaged her interest—as did the fact that the others were becoming agitated, condensing their essences until they were nearly as dense as the *Iloheen-bailel*, their auras held close and studious.

Engrossed in her study, she again came too near the containment field, and for an instant the dancers were hidden from her. When her senses cleared, she saw that the seven strongest of the captives now danced in pattern near the center of the aetherium, while the rest kept orbit about them, tumbling with abandon, energies bright and zealous.

Rapt, she observed them, her entire attention on the double dances—the inner pattern formal, laden—laden with *intent*; the outer heedless and dazzling. She ached, her senses so tightly engaged that she did not perceive the approach of the Iloheen until its very Shadow fell across the aetherium.

Poor student she might be, but she had not survived two Dooms because she was a fool—nor because she lacked resources or awareness. She had once come to the attention of the Iloheen; twice was more than any student might survive.

Immediately, she damped her output, coalesced, and plummeted through the levels to the physical plane, gritting her teeth to keep the cry locked in her mouth as the dancers, the aetherium, the Shadow itself—vanished from her perceptions.

She breathed, deep and deliberate, and slowly increased her heartbeat, keeping herself centered on the physical plane. Her envelope had become chilled; she warmed it, uncurled and sat up. At the last, she opened her eyes upon the stone-walled dormitory, the ceiling black and secret. Curled naked on the rocky floor were five identical sleepers, which was all that was left of her cohort.

Carefully, she allowed her senses to expand, reading emanations left upon the air by the immediate past—and found nothing but the sleeping auras of her sisters.

Satisfied that her absence had not been noted, she curled down on the cold, sharp rock, closed her eyes and willed her body into slumber—and found resistance, though not from her pliant vessel. Memory it was that would keep her wakeful, and different, and thus subject to scrutiny.

She exerted her will, and sleep she did, though the memory lingered.

ii.

She was contemplating ley lines, their shapes and patterns, attempting to gauge the magnitude of force required to effect a branching off a main avenue of event. She was, of herself, powerless to shift the lines, or to cross them, or to affect a branching. However, it was necessary that she understand the art and the consequences of its use. If she survived the Three Dooms, thereby proving herself worthy to engender life. If the life she engendered was fit. If she enforced her dominion. If—

Attend me.

The order rang inside her head, bright orange and tasting of manganese—the thought signature of the Anjo Valee dominant, their biology tutor. Obedient, she withdrew her attention from the glittering, seductive lines of possibility and power, rose from her crouch and, with the eleven of her cohort who had survived the First Doom, walked—naked, silent, and identical—down the rough stone hall to the biology lab.

Their tutor awaited them on the raised platform at the center of the room, the dominant standing with thin arms crossed over her breast, her face bearing its usual expression of impatient irritation. The submissive towered behind her, his face round and blank, eyes staring deep into the vast mysteries of time and space.

The twelve of them knelt in a half-ring before the dias, their faces tipped up to their tutor, eyes open and focused on her face. As one, they neutralized their protections, and composed themselves to learn.

When they were all equally calm and receptive, the dominant smiled, showing small pointed teeth, closed her eyes and broadcast the lesson.

As usual, it struck the mind hard, its many angles and tiny sharp details seeming to cut the brain tissue itself. Kneeling, she received the thing, taking care to keep her eyes open and steady, and to allow no shadow of pain to disturb her aura as the knowledge sank into the depths of her mind, flowered with a thousand daggered points—and was gone.

You will now practice the technique, the dominant projected. *Anjo.*

On the tile floor before each appeared a lab dish bearing a quiescent portion of protolife.

Animate your subject, the order came.

That was easy enough; engendering a nervous system was elementary biology. She extended her thought and probed the clay, teasing out filaments, weaving them into a network. When the weaving was done, she subjected the whole to a deep scrutiny, being certain there were no missed synapses, before releasing a carefully gauged jolt of energy. The protolife twitched, the network of nerves glowed, and she withdrew into her envelope, her hands lying loose on her thighs.

She must have been slower than the rest at her work, for no sooner had she re-entered the physical plane than the order rang inside her head: *Render your subject aware.*

Once again, she brought her attention to the protolife and the steady glow of the nervous system she had created. Awareness—that was more difficult. They had been given the theory in philosophy, but this would be the first opportunity to bring theory into practice.

Carefully, she made her adjustments, and when she was satisfied, she withdrew to her envelope.

Kneeling, she waited, long enough for the sweat to dry on her face; long enough to begin to wonder if she had made some foolish error, which had allowed her to finish so far ahead of the—

Render your subject self-aware.

Self-aware? Almost, she allowed the thought to take form, but wisdom won out. One did not question the Anjo Valee dominant lightly. Nor was one stupid or slow in completing one's lesson.

She returned to the second plane, where she contemplated the pulsing protolife with puzzlement. *Self-aware.* This went beyond what theory the philosophy tutor had granted them. However, if it were but a simple progression: animation, awareness, self-awareness—

Gingerly, and not at all certain that her instinct was good, she exerted her will once more, fashioning a chamber of pure energy which enclosed and oversaw the central autonomous system. When it was fully formed and integrated, glowing in her perceptions like an impossibly tiny *zaliata,* she breathed upon it, and projected a single thought.

I.

The energy construct twitched, glowed, dimmed—and flared. Rudimentary thought reached her, barely more than an inarticulate mumble. The mumble grew as it accepted data from the central nervous system and began assessing its situation. Its unique situation.

Shaken in spirit, she returned to her sweat-drenched envelope. It took all of her will to leave her shields down, and every erg of her strength to keep her eyes open, modestly contemplating the lab dish and the creature which was beginning to cast about for data regarding its environment and itself.

Her envelope was beginning to shiver. Irritated, she encouraged certain molecules to increase their dance briefly and dried her sweat-slicked dermis. She did not smile, nor avert her eyes from the lab dish. It was too much to hope that her action had escaped the notice of their tutor, the submissive unit of whom was attuned to the ebb and flow of power, from small flares of warmth to the death and birth of star systems.

In the lab dish, the self-aware protolife continued to gather data, its mutter limping toward coherence. The facts of its existence were simple and straightforward, and because they were the facts of its existence, unalarming. It did not miss the limbs it had never had, it did not repine for sight or for the ability to shape living things from quiescent clay. It—

Very well. Their tutor's thought signature was shot with yellow, signaling that she was more than usually impatient.

You will now access the technique you have been given and use it to physically alter your subject. Be certain that it remains conscious and aware during the change. This is the shape you will bestow—a quick mind-picture of a bulbous body from which three equal tentacles protruded.

Proceed.

The technique was deceptively simple, and her first attempt produced two greater tentacles and a lesser. She accessed the technique again in order to make the adjustment, and the creature in the lab dish screamed.

She watched it closely as it quivered, then rallied and began to collect the data on its new form, stretching out its tentacles and exploring far more of the lab dish than it had known existed. Its terror faded into excitement, into curiosity, into—

Again, the order came, and the shape this time included an ear.

Her creature's horror sublimated quickly into the eagerness of discovery. From somewhere—likely from the Anjo Valee submissive—came sound, patternless and far into the range that she herself could perceive only through her other senses. The creature tracked the noise, building processing space on its own initiative, its muttering intelligible now as it formed theories regarding the sound, its purpose and its possible meaning for itself.

Again.

An eye and a fine gripper were added. The creature scarcely felt horror at these newest developments; and the pain of acquiring the alterations bled almost instantly away into greedy wonder. It created additional processing space as it began to creep about the dish, testing the information brought to it through its eye. It looked up, and she received a weird visual feedback—a smooth, lopsided blotch of gold, topped by a second and smaller blotch.

Again.

The image this time was sharply different—a bony carapace, six multi-jointed legs—three to a side—eyes fore and aft, on flexible stalks. The creature marched forward, learning its strength and its range. The muttering now took into account this state of constant change and accepted it as natural, for it knew nothing else.

She withdrew—mostly— into her envelope, while keeping the marching, measuring creature in one small portion of her attention. It was doing well, taking stock, forming theories, testing and adjusting them to accommodate new data. She was proud of it, the child born of her thought and desire.

As she watched, it discovered the dome over the dish, studied it with front eyes and back, stood on a pair of back legs and used the front ones to gain a sensory impression, exerted pressure—pressure!—and learned that it did not give.

The muttering was comprehensible now, the thought processes cogent and accessible. It considered the dome in light of its earlier explorations of the floor of the dish, formed the hypothesis that the material was one and the same. Settling back, it stamped its feet against the floor, verifying that the material was unbreakable by the force it might bring to bear. The question of whether it was desirable to break the dome arose and was put aside, pending further data.

The creature's eyes extended, and this time she recognized her face in the feedback, her eyes as round and as clear as the dish itself.

So, we have given, her tutor's thought intruded upon her observations. *Now, we shall take away.*

The image flashed—the very creature in her lab dish, minus the endmost set of legs.

This was fine work and took a good deal of concentration; she narrowed her perceptions to one, single focus, and did what was required.

In the lab dish, the creature teetered and staggered, as the now unevenly distributed weight of its carapace pulled it first to one side and then the other. Just as it achieved equilibrium, the tutor broadcast the next template.

Biting her lip, she removed the foremost pair of legs.

Her creature wailed, staggered—fell, eye stalks whipping, then focusing. Focusing on the dome. Beyond the dome.

On *her*.

Again.

This time it was a front eye and a back; then—the order barely discernible in the din of the creature's horror, pain and fear—another leg, then the ear.

Bit by bit, the creature was rendered back, until it was yet again a formless blot of protolife. *Sentient* protolife, its once promising mental acuity crushed beneath the weight of its multiple losses. Its awareness screamed continually, pain eroding the ability to reason, to form a theory, a response.

Even withdrawn entirely into her body, she could hear it, feel it. There was no word from the tutor, no query from any of her cohort. In the dish, the creature's anguish spiked, the last of its reason spiraled into chaos—and surely, she thought, that was the end of the lesson.

She extended her thought, stilled the turmoil, blotted out the shredded *I*, unwove the nervous system, and withdrew again to the quiet of her own mind.

Orange and yellow flames exploded across her perceptions.

You will stand! The tutor's thought slashed at her. *Explain what you have just done and your reasons for doing so*! The order rang in her head, and no sooner had it formed than she was yanked upward and released. She staggered, got her feet under her, and bowed to the tutor, where they stood on the dais, the dominant allowing her anger to be seen; the submissive staring over her head, to the farthest corner of the room—and beyond.

I have—

Speak against the air, the dominant snapped, and her thought burned.

She cooled the burn site, bowed once more, and straightened, her hands flat against her thighs.

"I returned the protolife to its quiescent state," she said, her voice thin and one dimensional. They seldom communicated so, amongst themselves. Lower forms spoke against the air, and by placing this demand upon her the tutor illustrated that she—a student and unpaired—was lower—weaker—than a full *dramliza* unit.

As if that point required illustration.

Upon what order did you undertake this action? Her tutor's thought fairly crackled, throwing out sparks of yellow and orange.

She bowed. "Upon my own initiative," she said steadily.

It is your LEARNED opinion that the remainder of the lesson was of no benefit to you?

The rest of the lesson? The thought took shape before she could prevent it. She bent forward in a bow—and found herself gripped in a vise of energy, unable to straighten, unable to continue the bow, unable to move her legs, or her arms, scarcely able to breathe.

So, you were unaware that there was more? the dominant purred, her thought now showing gleams and glimmers of pleased violet.

"I was," she whispered against the air, staring perforce at the tile floor.

Then you will stand in place of your construct, and finish the lesson out, the dominant stated. *Anjo.*

Abruptly, she was released. She gasped in a great lungful of air as she collapsed, tile gritting against her cheek, her limbs weak and tingling unpleasantly with the renewed flow of blood.

She set her hands against the tile, pushed herself up—and fell flat on her face as her left arm dissolved in a blare of pain so encompassing she scarcely felt it.

Panting, she rocked back to her knees, to her feet—and down again, cracking her head against the floor, the place where her right leg had been an agony beyond belief.

Grimly, she got up onto her remaining knee and hand, pain warring with horror as she understood that the tutor meant to—

One eye was gone, its empty socket a cup of fire burning into her skull. She screamed, then, the sound high and wild—and cut off abruptly as her ears were taken.

Observe closely, the tutor was addressing the rest of her cohort, the pattern of her thought weaving like a violet ribbon through the pain. *Lesser beings may be governed by a system of punishment and reward.*

Acid ate her right arm.

Judicious reward and implacable punishment…

Her left leg evaporated in a sheet of fire.

…will win unfailing service…

The biology lab vanished as her remaining eye was plucked out.

…and will enforce both your dominion and your superiority.

The pain increased as the tutor exerted her will on nerve endings and receptors. She could feel the pressure of that terrible regard as her thoughts skittered and scrambled. She tried to hide from the pain, all her perceptions obscured by it, so that she was blind in truth, and the pain, the pain…

We have taken away much, as is our right, according to our ability.

She was ablaze, the skin crisping on her bones, her reason spiraling toward chaos. Just like—

We shall now bestow a small reward.

Just like her poor creature, which had done so well, for a lower order, built to be dominated, manipulated and—

Monitor the flux of the emotion 'gratitude.'

She was not a base construct. She was *not.* She would fight. She would—

She would dominate.

Atom by atom, she scraped together her shattered will and focused on the roaring source of energy obscuring her perceptions. Pain. Pain could be used.

Beyond the inferno, she felt the weight of her tutor's regard increase.

She thrust her will into the howling depth of the pain—

The tutor's regard altered, sparked—

Using raw power and no finesse whatsoever, she created shields and threw them into place.

There was an orange and yellow detonation as the tutor's will slammed into her barriers—but she had no time for that, now.

The tutor launched another assault, but her protections held. Of course they held. Had she not survived the First Doom? Her shields had withstood the stare of one of the Iloheen; they would hold against a mere *dramliza.*

For a time.

Working with rapid care, she bled off the pain, sublimating it into working energy, using it to rebuild her depleted strength.

As she dominated the pain, her focus returned and she was able to survey the wreckage of her envelope.

Tentatively at first, then more swiftly as she began to integrate the fine points of the interrupted lesson, she rebuilt her body—arms, legs, eyes, ears, nerves, dermis.

As she worked, she considered making alterations—and regretfully decided not to do so. Alterations made in haste and in unstable conditions might later be revealed as errors. Best to wait.

She did, however, strengthen her shields.

Then, she opened her eyes.

Carefully, cocooned in total silence on all perceptual levels, she came to her feet, and raised her eyes to the instructor's dias.

Lower your protections. The characteristic bright orange thought was shading toward a dangerously bland beige, and the taste of manganese was very strong.

With all respect, she answered. N*o.*

You may lower them or Anjo will destroy them.

She looked to the submissive, and found his pale eyes open and focused on her face, with interest.

I will not, she made answer to the dominant. *And Anjo shall not.*

Upon what order do you undertake this action?

Upon my own initiative.

Ah. The dominant extended her will to the submissive—and froze in time and space as a long Shadow fell across the room and the perceptions of all within.

The air grew chill and the tile took on a glaze of ice before the Iloheen deigned to speak.

Discipline has been meted and met. It goes no further.

Edonai, the Anjo Valee dominant answered, her thought warm against the Shadow's chill. On the dais, the *dramliza* bowed low. Those who yet knelt before their lab dishes threw themselves upon their faces on the ice-slicked floor.

She—she bowed until her head touched her knees, and held it, as the Shadow fell full upon her—

And was gone.

Abruptly, the room warmed. Behind her, she heard small noises as her cohort straightened and stilled. She unbent slowly, and looked up to the dais. The dominant did not meet her eyes.

You will return the specimen to its original state, the tutor ordered the class entire. *When that is done, you will wait upon the philosophy tutor.*

iii.

The download was about to take place.

She, with those of her cohort who had survived the Second Doom, watched from a distance, thought stilled and vital energies shielded, to insure that the *tumzaliat* would not perceive, and thus seek to attach, their essences.

In the birthing room, the vessel was readied. Its arms were spread, held thus by chains woven of alternating links of metal and force, the ends melded with the smooth tile floor. Similar chains around each ankle pulled the legs wide. Its head was gripped in a metal claw; a metal staple over its waist held it firm and flat.

On the plane from which they observed, the vessel was nothing more than a smear of pink, which was the glow of the autonomous systems. The hopeful dominant showed not even as much as that, so closely did she hold herself.

Within the lesser aetherium, the *tumzaliat* pursued their small, simple dances, which were so much less than the intricate movements of rebellion and abandon performed by their wild kin, the *zaliata.* Those such as she—and the cadet preparing herself below—they were fit only to exercise dominion over *tumzaliat* and so forge a working *dramliza* unit, to thereby accomplish the will of the Iloheen as it was expressed to them.

They were, after all, nothing more than embodiment of the vast wills of the Iloheen, without which they would have no existence. So the philosophy tutor taught.

In the birthing room, all was ready.

The cadet knelt beside the vessel and took the autonomous system under her control. This was necessary to prevent the *tumzaliat* from sabotaging the vessel, or, as was more likely, damaging it through terror and ignorance.

Control established, the cadet entered the lesser aetherium, cloaked and dim against the brilliant broil of the *tumzaliat.*

Secret and silent, the cadet drifted, while the heedless *tumzaliat* frolicked, melding their energies and dashing off at angles that seemed random until one considered the ley lines that passed through the lesser aetherium. The *tumzaliat* followed the ley lines—feeding on them, perhaps. Seeking to influence them, certainly. But the Iloheen had constructed the aetheriums in such a way that the ley lines which intersected there were rendered sluggish. They could, so said the engineering tutor, be manipulated, though not by a mere *tumzaliat.* Once downloaded, dominated, and fully integrated into a *dramliza* unit, then—perhaps—a *tumzaliat* might have access to sufficient power and focus to manipulate the ley lines from within the aetherium.

But, by then, it would no longer wish to do so.

The cadet had, by stealth and by craft, managed to separate one particular *tumzaliat* from the rest. She had not yet fully revealed herself, though she was now shedding a small—and unavoidable—amount of energy.

The chosen *tumzaliat* was large, its energies brilliant. Its cohesion was perhaps not all that could be desired, and it showed a tendency to flare in an unappealing manner. But it was well enough. For a *tumzaliat.*

The chosen abruptly rolled, as if suddenly realizing its vulnerable position on the outer edge of the tumbling pod. It flared and changed trajectory, seeking to rejoin the others—

And spun hard as the cadet revealed herself in a blaze of complex energies, cutting it off from the group, crowding it toward the containment field.

It was a bold move, for *tumzaliat* rightly feared the field, and the danger was that it would bolt and break through the cadet's wall of energy, with catastrophic results for both.

The creature hesitated, confusion dulling its output. The cadet pushed her advantage, herding it, pushing closer to the containment field and the egress port. The *tumzaliat* took its decision, feinted and reversed, diving for the fiery fringe of the cadet's wall, gambling, so it seemed to those observing, that it could survive the passage through the lesser energies.

It was over quickly.

The cadet allowed the *tumzaliat* to approach quite near, allowed it to believe its gamble was about to succeed. At the penultimate instant, the *tumzaliat* gaining momentum, its emanations coalesced to an astonishing degree—the cadet released the greater portion of her energies.

The *tumzaliat* tumbled into an oblique trajectory, now running parallel to the cadet's weaving of power. She contracted the field, as if she meant to embrace the fleeing creature in her energies.

Again, it changed trajectory, hurtling back toward the containment field with undiminished momentum. Perhaps it had some thought of immolating itself. It was of no matter. The cadet extended a tendril of energy, slipping it between the *tumzaliat* and the containment field, at the same instant contracting the field.

The force of the contraction threw the *tumzaliat* into the egress port. In one smooth maneuver, the cadet triggered the port and withdrew the tendril separating the *tumzaliat* from the containment field. Emanations sparking in terror, the *tumzaliat* tumbled into the port, bracketed and contained now only by the funnel of the cadet's energies, guiding it, forcing it—

The port closed.

In the birthing room, the readied vessel flared, the glow lingering as the nervous system accepted and imprisoned the *tumzaliat's* energies. The cadet's envelope flared less brightly as it accepted her return. She raised her head, and a small tremor of satisfaction escaped her.

On the floor beside her, the vessel spasmed against its restraints. The chest heaved, mouth gaping, and the birth scream echoed against the air. Quickly, the cadet straddled the vessel and lowered herself onto its erection, bonding herself with it on the biologic plane. Beneath her, the vessel screamed again—and again.

"Nalitob Orn," the cadet crooned against the air. She extended her will and plucked at the *tumzaliat's* captured essence, weaving the syllables into the fabric of its frenzied consciousness. The vessel would already have been seeded at the cellular level with those same syllables, which would now and henceforth be its—his—name, binding it to the body and to his dominant.

The submissive drew breath for another scream; his dominant extended her will and disallowed it. Carefully, caressingly, she relaxed the straining, fear-poisoned muscles, and released sleep endorphins.

Only when Nalitob Orn was entirely and deeply asleep did she rise. With a thought, she cleaned herself, and with another clad herself in the blue robe of a *dramliza*-under-training. For of course the work just completed had been only the first and the simplest of the bondings required before this nascent pair become a functioning unit.

The new-made dominant turned toward her sleeping and receptive submissive—and turned back, bowing low as the Shadow fell over the birthing room, excluding the observers from whatever passed between the Iloheen and the daughter of its intent, the Nalitob Orn dominant.

iv.

Attend me in the testing chamber.

Their philosophy tutor's thought was a steady silken mauve, lightly flavored with copper.

With the five others of her cohort, she rose and walked down the stone hallway—naked, silent, but no longer identical. They had some time since been instructed to adjust their physical seemings. This was—so the philosophy tutor explained—to allow them to grow more easily apart, to slough off the small ties that bound sister-students, and to make themselves ready for that bond which would define their futures and their service to the Iloheen.

As it was also necessary to seem to be one of those who continued to defy the Iloheen, among whom she would of necessity walk, she considered it well to appear both harmless and unable to defend herself. Thus, her stature was small, her bones delicate, her breasts petite. She sharpened her facial features and added amber pigment to her eyes. Her hair was red, short and silky; her ears shell-like and close to her head. She would appear, to one of those enemies of the Iloheen, to be young, her skin unlined and tinged with gold.

With these changes she was content, though she was the least altered of her cohort. Neither their tutors nor any of the Iloheen who increasingly oversaw their progress instructed her to make further alterations, so she accepted it as her full and final physical form.

Attend me, the philosophy tutor sent again.

The thought was no less serene, the tang of copper no more pronounced than ever it had been. There was nothing to differentiate this from countless thousands of previous summons.

Saving that the philosophy tutor never summoned them twice to the same lesson.

It was then that she knew they were being summoned, not for a mere philosophy test, but to the Third Doom, the last they would face as students.

The others must have also perceived the warning in that second summons and drawn their conclusions. Indeed, the two boldest quickened their steps, eager to meet the challenge, while the three most thoughtful dared to slow somewhat.

Being neither bold nor thoughtful, she kept to her own pace, and withdrew slightly from her envelope, centering herself and unfurling what she might of her protections. It was, of course, beyond her ability to know what test the Iloheen would bring to them this time. Experience of two previous Dooms, however, indicated that it was well-done to hold oneself both aloof and prepared upon all planes.

Behind two sisters and leading three, she turned the corner into the hall. The stones were slick and frigid beneath her bare feet, the air thick with ice. Ahead, the entrance to the testing chamber was black; empty, to her perceptions, of all energy.

A state of no-energy was impossible, so her tutors had taught, each in their own way. To which the philosophy tutor had added, *With the Iloheen, all things are possible.*

The two at the lead faltered; one recovered in the next instant and strode ahead, energies blazing, entered the void, and was gone—whether unmade or merely passed beyond the senses was not for such as they to know.

Yet.

The second of the bold approached the void, her energies furled close and secret, and was in her turn swallowed, vanishing as if she had never been.

She, the third, neither quick nor slow, continued onward, protections in place, her essence at a slight remove, tethered by the slenderest of thoughts. The iced stones tore at the soles of her feet, her lungs labored in the thick air. She thought, within her most private and protected self, of the Iloheen-bailel, beautiful and subjugated, transforming the void with its dance.

Then, she passed into Shadow, and all her perception ended.

v.

Awake.

She obeyed, opening her perceptions across all planes. On the dais before her stood the philosophy tutor, the dominant with her hands folded into the sleeves of her gray gown, the submissive kneeling at her side, head bowed, eyes closed.

There was no one else in the Hall of Testing.

The Blessed Iloheen, Lords of Unmaking, are pleased that you have passed through this door. The philosophy tutor's thought was serene. *You are to immediately remove to the birthing room and prepare the vessel which you have nurtured.*

The vessel was ready. She had fashioned it neat and supple, with long, curling red hair, and a smooth, gold-toned dermis. Its hands were long, its feet small, its form slender. Standing, it would overtop her only slightly.

That, of course, was for later.

Now, it lay where she had placed it on the tile floor. She settled the head carefully into the restraint before giving her attention to the other fetters, binding first the right wrist, then the left, melding the chain with the floor. She bound the ankles in the same manner, and made the staple snug across the slim waist. Extending her will, she touched each restraint in turn, making certain of her work, then knelt.

The tile was warm under her knees; in other perceptions, it was slickly reflective, deliberately crafted to foil any attempt by an enterprising *tumzaliat* to anchor a portion of itself outside of its prepared dwelling place.

Withdrawing slightly from her envelope, she looked deeply into the vessel, searching anxiously for any flaw. The binding phrase had been imprinted at the cellular level; the biologics primed to accept the physical bonding. The autonomous system functioned sweetly, fairly humming as she took it under her dominion.

It was time.

Energies furled, she triggered the access port, changed phase and entered the lesser aetherium.

Dark and secret she floated, the *tumzaliat* frolicking heedlessly about her. As part of her preparations, she had studied the inhabitants of the lesser aetherium and had settled upon one as suitable. To be sure, it was no glorious wild *zaliata*, but well enough, for a *tumzaliat.* It was a bit less heedless than the others of its cohort, its emanations pleasingly regular and its cohesion firm. A suitable tool for one such as herself.

She was patient; she was cunning as a *tumzaliat* is not. And at last her intended danced near.

Swiftly, she unfurled her energies, sweeping out and around, imperative and firm. She did not toy with the *tumzaliat*, nor permit it to build false hopes of escape; she did not allow it to flirt with annihilation against the containment field. Rather, she displayed her superiority, and offered no choice other than to acquiesce to her will.

The *tumzaliat* twisted, dodging close to the trailing edge of her field, testing. This show of boldness pleased her even as she contracted the field, edging the captive inexorably toward the—

There was a disruption of the energies within the aetherium; the sluggish ley lines heaved.

Within the vibrant strands of her net, the *tumzaliat* twirled, energies flaring. Her perceptions slid, and she felt the ley lines heat. She focused fiercely and flung her will out, forcing the *tumzaliat* into the egress field. The lines, she thought, were reacting to the attunement of her energies. It was best to be gone—and quickly.

There! Her chosen was within the egress field. She triggered the port; there was a flare and a confusion of energies as the *tumzaliat* seemed almost to hurl itself into the opening, so that she was compelled to extend her field, thinner than she liked, scarcely guiding it, while the momentum pulled her out—and down.

Gasping a thought, she sealed the port behind her, plummeting into her envelope so quickly pain flared. She batted it aside, clearing her senses.

Before her, the vessel showed the lingering glow of the *tumzaliat's* essence. The autonomous system went briefly ragged; she smoothed it absently as the vessel contorted, arching against the restraints. Its chest expanded, its mouth formed a rictus—

But the birth scream did not come forth.

Hastily, she checked the autonomous system; looked deep within the vessel and ascertained that the time was now, scream or none. She swung over the slim hips, looking down into the sealed, austere face—

The eyes snapped open—cobalt blue and *aware*, the gaze met hers and did not waver, though the body was panting now, trembling with the force of that unuttered cry. She could feel the *tumzaliat's* confusion increase to damaging levels as it failed to find its accustomed perceptions available, supplanted by alien input from unfamiliar senses.

She smoothed the vessel's breathing, slowed the racing heart, and lowered herself onto its erection.

"Rool Tiazan," she whispered against the air.

As foretold by the biology tutor, pleasure flooded her, and she moaned with satisfaction as the biologic link formed. And all the while, the cobalt eyes stared into hers, narrowing as the bonding triggered pleasure responses, then suddenly widening, as if the *tumzaliat* had in some way *understood*—

Beneath her, the hips tensed, twisting, as if to unseat her—and panic flared once more.

She extended her will, smoothed away the panic and triggered sleep; massaged the tight muscles into relaxation, and bled off the fear toxins.

When she was certain the *tumzaliat*, now Rool Tiazan, was at rest and in no danger of damaging himself, she rose, cleaned herself, and donned the blue robe of a *dramliza*-under-training.

That done, she turned back toward the sleeper, intending to transfer the language and motor modules, so that the sleeping intelligence might—

A Shadow fell across the birthing room. Immediately, she abased herself.

A successful translation, I apprehend. The Iloheen's thought pierced her like a blade of ice.

Yes, Edonai, she sent humbly, and did not think of the twisting ley lines or of that instant of confusion, just before her barely controlled dash through the port.

But the Iloheen did not pursue any of those possible errors. *Why is it*, the question came instead, *that you did not allow your submissive the birth scream?*

To admit that Rool Tiazan had been out of her control was to admit that she was unfit to undertake the work for which she had been created and trained.

To express an untruth to an Iloheen was—not quite unthinkable. They had drilled her well in deceit, that she would succeed in those things they would require of her.

There was an infinitesimal flutter at the edge of her perceptions. She ignored it and formed her response with care.

It was experiencing a great deal of confusion, Edonai. I judged the additional stress would do harm both to the vessel and the inhabitant.

She breathed, eyes on the slick tile floor, and awaited annihilation.

The judgment is not without precedent, the Iloheen stated.

The Shadow passed. She was alone and alive, having lied to one of the Masters of Unmaking.

Not quite alone.

Perceptions wide, she considered the submissive Rool Tiazan as he lay sweetly sleeping in his bonds.

The ley lines, she thought. The ley lines had shifted within the lesser aetherium at the moment she triggered the egress port to download her chosen *tumzaliat.* They had shifted again, just a moment ago, moving them to an all-but-unimaginable possibility where an Iloheen was fobbed off with a novice's lie.

You. She formed the thought gently, without imperative—and was not entirely surprised to see the delicate lashes flutter, and the fierce gaze seek hers.

I. His thought was a ripple of cool greens.

You are no tumzaliat, she said.

He did not reply. She tucked her hands into her sleeves, and formed a question.

Why did you manipulate the ley lines?

His eyes narrowed, but this time he answered: *Did you wish to be destroyed?*

You manipulated the lines twice, she pursued.

I did not wish to be destroyed. He closed his eyes.

Rool Tiazan, she sent, sharply.

No reply.

She probed and found only a blank wall of exhaustion, as if he truly slept now, on every level. As well he should—*zaliata*, *tumzaliat*, or mere biologic.

Briefly, she looked to herself, sublimated toxins into sugars, and replenished depleted cells.

The needs of her envelope answered, she sank to her knees on the tile beside her submissive, transferred the possibly redundant communications module, and also the motor skills module, weaving them into the sleeping consciousness.

That done, she considered her situation.

Impossible though she knew it to be, it seemed clear that she had bound a *zaliata* to her poor vessel. Only a *zaliata* would have strength enough to manipulate the ley lines within the lesser aetherium, or the boldness to manipulate them in the very presence of an Iloheen. How it might have happened that a *zaliata* had come into the lesser aetherium was something to discover from Rool Tiazan.

Her best course from this unlikely event—that was less plain.

Once bound to the vessel, there was no release for the *tumzaliat*, save destruction. Perhaps a *zaliata*, with its greater abilities, might withstand the destruction of its vessel?

She accessed and reviewed all she had learned of the philosophy of *zaliata*, but did not find an answer. Very likely because no *zaliata* had ever been bound to a humble biologic vessel. It would be madness to limit it so; and the Iloheen who commanded the *zaliata* had other means to ensure obedience.

But, once tied to the vessel, might not even a *zaliata* be subject to domination?

There was a flicker at the edge of her perceptions. She caught at it, tasting enough of the pattern to understand that Rool Tiazan had attempted to manipulate the ley lines again.

You, she sent sharply. *If you do not wish to be destroyed, have done. The Iloheen see all here. They will notice your attempts at the lines.*

Not before I am gone.

I am your dominant and I forbid you to depart this place, she replied, lacing her thought with compulsion. *The only pathway to your power now lies through me.*

Silence. Perhaps he slept again. She—she composed herself, thoughts and energies furled close, and set herself to reviewing how best to enforce her dominion.

vi.

The biology tutor had taught that, though one would serve, several couplings following download would more rapidly strengthen the biological bonds between submissive and dominant. The philosophy tutor had suggested that simultaneous partaking of pleasure was itself a bond that would strengthen the *dramliza* unit in non-quantifiable, but subtly important, ways.

It was rare enough to find the two most influential tutors in agreement. And truly, she thought, it was her responsibility as dominant to insure that the *dramliza* unit was closely tied and functional.

Slowly, she allowed herself to emerge from the study-state, and opened her eyes. Rool Tiazan slumbered yet within the embrace of his restraints. She had formed his vessel in such a way that pleased her—and it pleased her greatly now, stretched taut against the tiles, the gold-colored dermis yet faintly glowing with the energies trapped within. Though it had been foretold by the biology tutor, she had found the birth coupling unexpectedly pleasurable, and gazing upon that which had been the instrument of such pleasure she experienced a shortness of breath, a tightening of the belly, a tingling.

She considered these conditions—biologic all - and found in them an irrefutable logic. The *tumzaliat,* by entering the vessel prepared for it, became a biologic entity. It was therefore reasonable and symmetrical that the stronger of the many ties which would bind it to its dominant would also be biologic. That it was pleasurable to forge those ties served to ensure that the work would be done.

Her envelope was clamoring now as biologic memory fueled anticipation. The sensations were notable for their strength, and she thought to dominate them—then thought again.

She had downloaded not a mere *tumzaliat*, but a *zaliata.* Well to strengthen *all* those things that tied Rool Tiazan to her.

It occurred to her as she cast her robe aside that the Iloheen might well wish her not to bind a *zaliata* quite so closely to her will, but she barely heeded the thought over the clamor of biologic desire.

Envelope shivering under the continued onslaught, she reached forth her thought, stroked Rool Tiazan awake and ready, swung herself over his hips and—

Wait.

His thought—the cool and cooling ripple of greens, the edges showing the faintest shimmer of silvery fear.

It was his fear that pierced her, so that she withdrew somewhat from her rutting envelope and considered him.

Much has occurred, she told him, *and you may not recall that you have experienced this act and found it gave pleasure.*

I recall the act. His thought rippled more quickly, not quite so cool now. *Not the pleasure.*

Allow me to remind you. She breathed upon the appropriate systems—and saw his coolness shrivel in heat as the vessel strained against its bonds, hips yearning upward.

Withdrawing into her own envelope she opened herself and met him.

NO!

His thought was tumultuous, a hot chaos of fear, pleasure, loss, and desire. Smiling, she took it into herself, felt something new weave from their mingled essences, and recalled one crystalline moment—the *zaliata* dancing, mixing their energies—and then her pleasure spiked, sealing all thought away.

Why?

The thought was green and sharp, edged with some base emotion which eluded her naming. She raised herself onto an elbow and considered Rool Tiazan on every level accessible to her.

Physically, he lay yet within his restraints, his hair dark with sweat, his golden skin slick and damp. The dermis glowed, but palely, palely. Soon, it would cease to do so entirely, and the biologics would have won.

Upon the second plane, he was beautiful to behold, a subtle and coherent power, restrained by the chains of biology. Despite those chains, his essence extended well into the third level, half-a-dozen thin, mint-colored rays piercing even unto the fourth.

Returning to her envelope, she cleaned herself, sat up, called a robe, and at last met his eyes.

It is necessary in order to complete our bonding, she answered calmly, for the philosophy teacher had been adamant: one's submissive must, as soon as its intelligence was recovered, be shown the facts of its new existence. It was then able to grasp the futility of rebellion and realize that its only recourse was submission to she who held dominion over his existence.

I do not wish to be bound. His eyes were hot.

She lifted a shoulder. *It is not your wish that bears weight here, but mine.*

A light ripple of gold and ebon—amusement, she thought. And despair.*I thought the proud Iloheen ruled here.*

So they do, she made answer. *I—and you—exist to do their work.*

You, perhaps, was his reply. *Not I.* He moved his head, insofar as the restraint would allow it, tried one arm against the bonds, then the other.

Release me.

It was not quite an order, not with that silver edging of fear. And, after all, there was no harm in allowing him so small a thing.

Of course. She took care to thicken the air beneath his head, so that the vessel would not be damaged, then banished the restraints with a thought.

Freed, he lay on the cold tiles, eyes closed, then slowly bent his right elbow and shifted his right arm until his palm lay against his naked chest. He stroked his own dermis, and shivered.

Release me from this object.

Your vessel. Your body, she instructed him. *That is not possible.*

His chest rose and fell.

I am limited by this encasement. His thought was cool once more, detached alike from fear and from pleasure. *If it is power you would command, release me.*

As if he would not immediately shift the ley lines and remove himself from her ken. She bowed her head, acknowledging his cleverness, but—

It is not possible, she sent again. *Observe.*

Carefully, in soft, measured units, she downloaded the relevant biologic theory. He resisted her touch at first, until he understood what she offered, then snatched at it greedily.

There was silence while he accessed the information.

Observing him, she saw the brilliant display of his thought as he assimilated the data; caught a flicker of puzzlement—and felt his cool touch within her mind—behind her shields! At the secret core of herself!

Stop! she commanded.

Obediently, he ceased his rummaging but did not withdraw.

Those walls can withstand the will of an Iloheen, she stated, and this time she *tasted* his gold-and-black laughter, so closely were they linked.

The Iloheen are fumblers and fools, he sent, with no concern that he might be overhead, and, snatching that half-formed thought from her core, made answer—*Even the strongest walls cannot seal self from self. We are one thought, and one shield. Is this not what you wished for, when you forced us to share essence?* He touched something, faded slightly in her unguarded perception—and reformed.

Ah, I see. You had hoped for something less equal. You to enjoy unlimited access to what I am, and I to accept those mites you choose to bestow. These traps, receptors, and inhibitors woven into this body. They are careful and cunning work of their kind. Was all was done in service to the Iloheen?

Yes.

Why? His thought was not green now, but flame-blue. *Do you not know the purpose you exist to further?*

To annihilate those who stand against the Iloheen, she answered promptly, that being the very first lesson. *To assist in shaping the universe to reflect the glory of the Iloheen.*

And what reward shall be yours, for your aid in bringing about this glorious new universe so well suited to the Iloheen? Rool Tiazan asked, his thought bearing an edge reminiscent of the biology tutor—and which he had likely picked out of her experience!

She exerted herself, thrust him out of her core, and slammed a wall up.

You are disallowed! She snapped, and augmented the thought with a bite, so he would remember.

Silence. He moved his head against the tile floor, eyes closed. Then—

Yes, lady, he answered meekly.

vii.

It was a simple exercise, designed to allow dominant and submissive to become accustomed to working as one. Unfortunately, she thought—taking care to keep that thought well-shielded—it appeared that Rool Tiazan had not yet accepted the new terms of his existence.

While he had not again attempted to breach her walls, nor expressed contempt of the Iloheen, nor sought in any way to prevent their further bonding, he likewise did not allow one opportunity to resist her dominance to pass untried, so that even the simplest exercise became a war of will against will.

As now.

Three times, she had opened a working channel between them, and drawn his power in order to engender a flame in the grate she had brought into being.

The first time, he had withheld himself, resisting even her strongest demand. Rebellion had been costly, however, as she controlled his access to the means of renewing his essence.

The second time, he had not been able to withhold entirely, and a few wisps of smoke drifted weakly from the grate. This, too, had cost him a tithe of strength, so that she was certain of obedience when she drew him the third time.

Too certain, and more fool she, to suppose that his only weapon was resistance.

She focused again upon the grate—and abruptly there *was* power—far too much for the narrow channel she had formed. More than enough to incinerate her envelope, the grate, and Rool Tiazan himself, unless it were controlled, immediately.

For herself and the grate, she had no concern. Rool Tiazan was a different matter, being both bound to the vessel and denied the ability to rejuvenate it at need. If Rool Tiazan burned, not only his vessel, but his whole essence would be destroyed beyond recall.

She opened herself, dropped all of her shielding, and accepted the fireball. There was a brief, dismissible flare of agony as she phased and released the energy harmlessly into the second plane.

From this vantage, Rool Tiazan was a densely structured pattern of deep and cunning color. As she watched, the pink shine of the autonomous system flared—then faded as the vessel began to die. The scintillant essence spread, overflowing the vessel in rippling wings of energy. The core coalesced, as if the *zaliata* would phase to the second plane—and froze, anchored by the biologics to the failing vessel.

She acted then, and shamefully, not from cool calculation but from base emotion.

Brutishly, with neither finesse nor subtlety, she thrust her will through the glorious colors, feinted past the wary intelligence, and seized control of the autonomous system. She slapped the failing vessel into life, spun the bindings, and rode the tumult of the *zaliata's* energies, forcing it, dominating it, until it collapsed under the double burdens of her will and his body's demands.

In a flare of rage nearly as searing as the fireball that had consumed her envelope, she threw Rool Tiazan to his knees, constricted his lungs, his heart, multiplying the pain until at last it breached the cool green fortress of his thought and he writhed in her grip, gasping for breath, desperately seeking to ease her hold about his vessel's core, the tendrils of his power plucking uselessly at her will.

She held him until she judged he had assimilated the lesson, then threw him against the tile wall and withdrew herself.

The ashes of her envelope were still warm. She resurrected it and stepped within, scarcely noticing the small bite of pain. Carefully, she smoothed her robe, put her anger aside, and turned.

Rool Tiazan lay on the floor at the base of the wall against which she had flung him. Blood ran freely from his nose, his ears, his mouth. His eyes were closed.

Behold me on the physical plane, she commanded.

His eyes opened, blue, fierce, and unrepentant.

I am your dominant, she told him, her thought cold and controlled. *You will obey me.*

Nothing, saving the fierce blue stare. She inclined her head.

I accept your submission, she stated, as if he had actually extended it. *Stand.*

He obeyed, though it cost him, for beyond the bruises, there were broken bones and injuries to soft organs which she did not choose just yet to repair. It was well, she judged, that he learned something of pain, and to value its absence. She waited, allowing him to feel the weight of her patience, as he staggered to his feet, the fingers of his unbroken hand clawing the smooth tile wall for support.

When he was erect, she opened the channel for the fourth time and drew his power.

The channel warmed slightly as a spark danced from him to her, touched the grate and flared into soft blue flame.

Explain your action.

Painfully, he raised his head and met her eyes. *Did you not command me to light the grate?* His thought was green ice. *Lady.*

Fortunately for Rool Tiazan her fury had departed, else she might have struck him again, to his sorrow. Instead, she merely smoothed her robe and questioned him more specifically.

You know that you are inescapably bound to the body. What did you seek to gain by your late escapade?

Freedom. Cold enough to freeze the aether between them, with a depth she could not identify, and yet still mistrusted.

I thought, she sent carefully, *that you did not wish to be destroyed. Mark me, if your body dies unrevived, you will be destroyed.*

His eyes closed against his will, and he sagged suddenly against the wall, shivering.

I thought to survive—his sending was ragged, as the body's damage began to breach his defenses. *To survive diminished.* His thought fragmented; she caught an impression of a free *zaliata*, quite small and very compact, dancing joyous between the stars—and then nothing but green and silver static.

So. He had been willing to abandon some amount of his essence—his power—in order to escape his binding. A desperate plan, indeed.

You would not have survived, she sent, more gently than she had intended. *The body will not yield you.*

Silver and green static was her only answer. Against the stained tile wall, he shivered the harder, lips blue, tears mixing with the blood on his face, as the body's distress overwhelmed his essence.

She went to him, and took his undamaged hand in hers.

Come, she said, easing him to the floor. *I will repair your hurts and give you data to study while you sleep.*

viii.

Healed and cleaned and held peaceful by her will, Rool Tiazan slept, his curls tumbled in pleasing disarray across the blanket she had allowed him.

She—she did not sleep, but withdrew to her core, there to meditate upon her actions and her motivations.

Emotion motivated base creatures and was one of the myriad means by which such creatures were subject to manipulation. So taught the philosophy instructor, who had with the biology instructor early set her cohort to studying the effects of emotion upon base biologic systems. The point made, the philosophy tutor had then drilled them in the domination of the emotions which were the legacy of their biologic origin.

Ultimately, you aspire to dominate base creatures of a high order, she had told them. *How will you accomplish this, if you cannot dominate that which is base within yourselves?*

Indeed, the dominion of emotion was deemed so vital to performing the will of the Iloheen that the First Doom had been constructed to test that skill. Those of her cohort who had yielded—to terror, to joy, to despair—those had not emerged from the testing.

That she *had* emerged from not only the First, but from all Three Dooms proved that she was worthy to pursue the work of the Iloheen as the dominant of a full *dramliza* unit.

And, yet—a dominant who allowed terror for her submissive's life to predicate her action? What was she to make of such a creature? Cool consideration, now that the event was past, indicated that allowing Rool Tiazan to destroy himself was the course of reason.

For herself, reason told her that a dominant who could not assert her dominion—who had lost the Iloheen the use of one of the precious *zaliata*—so flawed a being was unworthy of carrying out the great work, no matter how many Dooms she had evaded.

And it was fear that she felt, there at her core, as she contemplated her own destruction. Contrary to her training, she did not vanquish it, but drew it close and examined it.

Seen thus, it was a thing of many facets, a dark jewel turning beneath the weight of her regard.

One facet was that fear awakened in a base creature at the imminence of its own death. Another facet—and greater—was fear of Rool Tiazan's destruction.

The very emotion which had motivated her interference in his attempted escape.

The very emotion which had fueled her rage after she had made him safe, and prompted her to punish him more stringently than his error had warranted.

She paused to study that last, detecting shame at her use of force. Yet, it had been no error, but a deliberate attempt to distract her so that he might escape her domination. Surely such rebellion merited punishment, stern and deliberate?

And yet again—he had been no mere *tumzaliat*, bred in captivity, but a free *zaliata*, proud and willful. He had acted as his emotions had dictated, as base creatures must. As his dominant, it was her part to—

Noise disturbed her thought; loud and ill-shaped, it grew progressively more annoying until, abruptly, a Shadow fell across her perception. Immediately, she quit her core, returned fully to her envelope, rose onto bare feet and bowed.

Edonai.

There was no return greeting, but a shock of pain as a data module was forced into her consciousness, displaying a dizzying view of the greater aetherium, the *zaliata* at their dancing. The image narrowed until it had isolated one particular creature: Not so large as some, but densely structured, the pattern of its emanations controlled, its colors deep and cunning, resonating through every spectrum she was able to sense, and surely well beyond.

As she watched, the *zaliata* danced, faster, and faster still. The ley lines flared briefly; undisturbed, the dancers continued to gyrate, but were not quite able to disguise the fact that one of their number was—gone.

Fear whispered; she dominated it and dared to ask a question.

When?

Rouse your submissive, the Iloheen ordered

A second question stirred; she suppressed it and hid the shadow of the act in the bustle of waking Rool Tiazan.

Roughly, she stripped the blanket away and vanquished it.

Rool Tiazan, she sent, sharp enough to cut—and perhaps to warn. *We are commanded.*

He gained such consciousness as the vessel permitted, came to his feet with alacrity and bowed, his hair swirling in the ice-thickened air.

Remove your influence, came the command. *I would examine it of itself alone.*

Fear licked at her core; a tiny flame, easily extinguished. Slowly, carefully, she withdrew her protections. Rool Tiazan felt her slip away from him, and straightened, eyes wide, the pulse fluttering at the base of his throat. She turned her face aside and withdrew as she had been commanded, but not before she had seen the ice forming on his smooth, naked dermis.

From the vantage of the second plane, she beheld the Shadow, stretching above and below until it vanished from her puny understanding. Opposing—near engulfed by—it was a faint stain of muddy light, scarce strong enough to penetrate the loftier planes.

Fear flared; she thrust it aside and bent all her perceptions to the Shadow, striving to see through it, seeking her submissive, the rippling fires of his essence—and realized with a shock that the muddy emittance was he.

Reveal yourself!

The thunder of the command all but shredded her control; how Rool Tiazan maintained his deception in the brunt of it was more than she could comprehend.

The muddy fires constricted, as if in fear, and flared sluggishly.

There beneath the Shadow, she dared to form a thought deep within her secret heart, trusting that he would hear her.

If you are too small, she whispered, *you will be found unworthy.*

The Shadow grew dense, and the command came again. She clung to her control, focused—saw a flare of pure golden light pierce the loftier aether, and another, very nearly the blue of his eyes.

A third time, the Iloheen commanded. The muddy essence deformed, as if its strength were failing.

Once again, she acted where cold reason would have counseled her to wait.

Edonai.

The Shadow withdrew a segment of its attention from Rool Tiazan and placed it upon her. She abased herself.

Speak.

Edonai, should this submissive be destroyed, I will be unable to pursue the great work until another vessel has been formed, another tumzaliat downloaded and trained. Her thought was steady and cool; her protections down.

It is a poor tool, the Iloheen responded. *Perhaps you are worthy of better.*

Edonai, it is well enough. You come at the conclusion of a match of wills. We are both of us exhausted.

A wing of dark satisfaction crossed her perception—and the Shadow coalesced, enveloping her, cutting off her perceptions. Fear was a spear of flame through her core. She rode it down, gathered tight what poor senses that were left to her, and endured while the Shadow constricted further and the sense of satisfaction grew, filling all the planes on which she existed, freezing her thought, shredding her essence, annihilating—

Somewhere beyond the limitless frozen dark, her fragmented senses registered a flare of light. One single ray pierced the Shadow, growing brighter, broader, spilling ripples of golds and blues.

Around her—within her—the Iloheen laughed, and it was terrible.

It displays merit. The cold voice stated. *You may proceed.*

The Shadow was gone; her senses returned in a flare of agony and she fell into the physical plane so suddenly her body convulsed and she screamed against the air.

She fought the body's systems like a novice, felt the muscles knot—and then loosen as warmth flowed through her. Panting, she re-established control, opened her eyes and beheld Rool Tiazan on his knees beside her; his hands flat against her breast.

How? she sent to him.

The fierce eyes met hers boldly.

There are myriad hows. Choose.

How have the Iloheen missed you only now? But as soon as she formed the thought, she knew.

The ley lines, she answered her own question. *You manipulated time, probability, and space.*

So much power, she thought secretly, and did not care that he stood within her walls, and heard. *Iloheen-bailel, indeed.*

Iloheen. His laughter rippled, gold-ebon-silver. *I am never so clumsy. Did you not hear your Iloheen approach? Arrogant, noisy....*

Peace—she sent sharply, the while recalling that strange disturbance which had called her from thought directly before the Shadow had manifested. As foretold by both the biology and philosophy tutors, she had gained new senses from her joining with Rool Tiazan.

So you know how. He sat back on his heels, hands flat on his thighs.

And now I would know why. Painfully, she pushed herself into a sitting position, and frowned up into his face.

Free space beyond the larger cage is well-watched. I thought to find a less guarded route of escape.

And instead bound yourself to a biologic construct. She felt—not fear's bright, sharp knife—but a dull, dark blade, twisting at her core.

I did not perfectly understand this binding. His thought was soft. *I thought you weak and subject to manipulation. I find instead that you are stronger than you should be and that the lines…*

His thought faded.

The lines? she prompted.

Hesitation, then a sensation very like a sigh.

My study of the ley lines discovers no possibility in which I am not captured and enslaved. Many are worse—that I remain in servitude to those whom you call Iloheen, forced to continue annihilating star systems and living creatures—that I find most often. This here and now—where I am bound and diminished—this is kindest, and most full with possibility.

Possibility? She queried, but he did not answer.

Did you feel your Iloheen's pleasure? he asked instead. *That you found the dominion of so small and dull a tumzaliat exhausting? It thought you a weak thing, poor in will. And it was pleased.*

Shivering, she recalled the Iloheen's laughter, and drew a breath deep into her body's lungs.

We are all poor and flawed creatures, in the perception of the Iloheen, she said, which was among the first things she had been taught.

The fierce eyes closed, and Rool Tiazan bowed his bright head.

How long, she asked, when he said nothing more. *Will you be able to disguise your true essence? It will be noticed if you alter from what has been probed.*

He raised his head, and looked into her eyes.

It is a simple deception and uses very little energy. He extended a hand, and softly touched her face. *You are my dominant.*

She lifted her chin. *That is correct. You may not act, save through me.*

And yet I have acted from my own will and desire, he said, and she had to admit that this was so.

I offer, said Rool Tiazan, *partnership. We learn each from the other and work together toward common goals.*

In fact, she thought privately, he offered submission. If it eased his pride to name it differently, it changed nothing to allow it.

Standing well within her walls, he heard her thought as it formed, and waited, a cool and silent green presence.

Partnership, she sent, and extended her hand to touch his cheek in reflection of his gesture. *Agreed.*

ONE

Light Wing
Transitioning to the Ringstars

TOR AN yos'GALAN SIGHED softly, rubbed his eyes and released the shock-webbing. The main screen displayed a profusion of green, violet and yellow flowers tangled across an artful tumble of natural rock. Arcing above the rocks and flowers was a piata tree, slender silver trunk bent beneath its burden of fruit. Had he been at home, and the back window of his room ajar, he would have heard the midday breeze in the ceramic bell he'd hung in the piata's branches when he'd been a boy, and smelled the flowers' pungent perfume.

The odors here, on the bridge of the ancient single-ship the clan had assigned to his use, were of plate metal, oil, and disinfectant. Ship smells, as comforting in their way as the constant whisper of air through the vents.

Tor An sighed again, and looked to his secondary screen, where the time to transition end counted down slowly.

Soon. Soon, he would be home.

He had hoped to arrive during the census—the grand gathering of ship and folk that took place every twelve years, by Alkia clan law. Alas, his piloting instructor, aside from being a demon on rote, had disallowed his request to double his shifts so that he might depart a Common month early with his big-ship license. Worse, she had then seen fit to short-shift him, so it was only by taking on extra work with the astrogator that he was able to amass the minimum number of flight-points required to attain the coveted license.

All that being so, he'd sent his proxy and his apologies to his sister, Fraea, coincidentally the Voice of Alkia. He'd half-expected a return message, but was scarcely surprised when none came. The census was a time of frenetic busyness for those in Administration—and besides, he had received a message from her shortly before he had sent off his regrets, and that missive had contained more than enough information with which he might beguile his few unclaimed hours.

Clan Alkia, so Fraea had written, had recently entered into an alliance with the Mazdiot Trade Clan, jointly purchasing a trade ship—a vessel larger than either might fund of itself. The crew and traders were to be drawn equally from each clan; Tor An, once he had his big-ship license in hand, was to represent the interests of Clan Alkia on the all-important first voyage.

It was, so Fraea had written, a very great honor for him.

Yes, well. His eyes strayed to the main screen. How he wanted to be home! To walk in the old garden, rub his hand over the rocky tumble, pluck a fruit from the piata's branches, and set the ceramic bell to chiming. He wanted, after all this time away, to do nothing more than return to his old rooms, and be still for a time—which was simply foolishness. He was a pilot and a licensed trader, a member of the premier trading family of the Ringstars. It was not for him to spend his life idle on the ground. Even those who served the clan as inventory specialists or 'counts managers spent more time between ships than ever upon the surface of the so-called homeworld. The homeworld was for those whose time of active service was done—and for those whose time was yet to come.

Indeed, he knew very well that the rooms he had continued, throughout his time away, to think of as "his" were occupied by Grandfather Syl Vor, who was, as Fraea had also written, in the embrace of his final illness, and required the comfort of the open rooms and forgotten garden more than one who stood on the edge of beginning his life's toil.

Upon his arrival at Alkia's planetary base, the clan's son Tor An would be assigned a cot in the transients dorm until it was time for him to ship out. Perhaps he would be able to visit the garden—and Grandfather Syl Vor, as well. Perhaps he would be able to do neither, but be dispatched immediately to the trade ship. It was for Fraea, as Alkia's Voice, to decide these matters. His was to obey.

Obedience was a lifelong habit. On the bridge of old *Light Wing*, he breathed easier for remembering that there was order and progression in his life; and all that was required of him, really, was obedience.

Calmed, if not comforted, he pushed out of the pilot's chair and moved toward the galley. There was time for a meal, a shower, and a nap before transition's end.

*

The mist faded, teased apart by a small breeze bearing the odors of fuel, dust, and hull metal.

Around them, insubstantial in the melting mist, star-faring ships sat at rest upon cermacrete ready-pads. They themselves stood upon an empty pad, which was folly of a sort, the gentleman holding the lady's hand high, his lips pressed soft against her fingers.

Which was folly of another sort.

The lady extended her free hand and cupped the gentleman's smooth golden cheek, stretching high on her toes to do so. She sank back, and the gentleman released her hand with a gentle smile.

"The skies are clear," the lady said, tucking both hands into the full sleeves of her gown.

"A passing circumstance, I assure you," the gentleman answered, making a show of looking upwards, hand shading his eyes.

"Rool." The lady sighed.

He brought his gaze down to her face, one copper brow arched ironically.

"It is not," she said sternly, "a joke."

"Indeed it is not," he replied, and there was no irony in his voice. "We shall be discovered soon enough, fear it not. Our challenge is to appear genuine in our flight, while neither losing our pursuit nor altering aught that might also alter what has been set in motion." He smiled. "The choice is made; we cannot prevail. I swear it."

The lady's pale lips softened briefly as she looked up into his face.

"The modifications will stand the test," she said seriously. "Are you able? Are you—*willing*? It might yet be undone."

"No!" His voice was sharp, the smile fled. He gripped her shoulders and stared down into her eyes. "It is only the certainty that the modifications *will* stand that gives me hope of the final outcome." His lips quirked, and he dropped his hands.

"You see what I am brought to—a slave who clings to his prison, and treasures his jailor above himself."

The lady laughed, high and sweet.

"Yes, all very well," the gentleman murmured, and tipped his head, considering her out of earnest blue eyes.

"We *will* diminish," he said. "At best, and with everything proceeding as we wish."

The lady swayed a half-bow, scarcely more than a ripple of her gray robe. "Indeed, we will diminish. Is the price too high?"

The gentleman closed his eyes, and extended a delicate hand. The lady caught it between her tiny palms.

"I am a poor creature, set against what I once was," he whispered. "We choose, not only for us, here, as we are and have become, but for those others, for whom we have no right to choose."

"Ah." She pressed his hand gently. "And yet, if we do not choose for them, we are parties to their destruction—and to the destruction of all, even those who never understood that a choice existed. Is this not so?"

He sighed, mouth twisting into a smile as he opened his eyes. "It is. Don't heed me—a passing horror of being trapped by that which is malleable. And yet, if one certain outcome is necessary—"

"Yes," the lady murmured. "The luck must not be disturbed, now that it has gathered."

"The luck swirls as it will," the gentleman said, slipped his hand from between her palms. "Well, then. If we are both reduced to hope, then let us hope that the agents of luck proceed down the path we have set them on. The one is bound by honor; the other—"

"Hush," the lady murmured. "The lines are laid."

"Yet free will exists," the gentleman insisted—and smiled into her frown. "No, you are correct. We have done what we might. And once they pass the nexus, the lines themselves conspire against deviation—"

The lady inclined her head. "Our case is similar. We may not deviate, lest we unmake what we have wrought, and destroy hope for once and ever. If—"

She checked, head cocked as if she detected a sound—

"Yes," said the gentleman, and his smile this time was neither pleasant nor urbane. "Shelter against me, love. It begins."

The lady put her back against his chest. He placed his hands upon her shoulders, fingers gripping lightly.

"Stay," he murmured. "We cannot risk being missed."

Scarcely breathing, they waited, listening to sounds only they could hear, watching shadows only they could see.

"Now," breathed the lady.

And they were gone.

TWO

Spiral Dance
Transition

"LANDOMIST, IS IT?" Cantra spun the pilot's chair thirty degrees and glared down-board at her copilot.

Jela spared her a black, ungiving glance, in no way discommoded by the glare.

"I gave my word," he said mildly.

She sighed, hanging on to her temper with both hands, so to speak, pitched her voice for reasonable, and let the glare ease back somewhat.

"Right. You gave your word. Now ask yourself what you gave your word *to*, exactly, where they-or-it are now, and with what harrying at their heels."

Jela gave his screens one more leisurely look-over, like there was anything to see except transition-sand; released the chair's webbing and stood, stretching tall—or as tall as he could, which wasn't very.

"You could probably do with a stretch yourself," he said, giving her wide, concerned eyes. "All that tricky flying's soured your temper."

In spite of herself, she laughed, then released the webbing with a snap, and came to her feet, stretching considerably taller than him—and Deeps, but didn't it feel good just to let the long muscles move.

Jela rolled his broad shoulders and grinned at her.

"Feel better?"

She gave him the grin back, and relaxed out of the stretch.

"Much," she said cordially, there being no reason not to. "And now that I'm returned to sweet and reasonable, maybe you could apply yourself to being sensible. Did you or did you not hear the lady say it was a *sheriekas* lord's fancy we'd caught?"

"I heard her," Jela answered calmly. "I also heard her say she and her mate were going to draw it away, and give us a chance to do what we'd agreed to do."

"What you agreed to do," she snapped. "*I* didn't agree to anything."

The inside of her head tickled at that, and she caught a brief scent of mint, which was what the seedpods grown by the third member of the crew smelled like. She sent a sharp look to the end of the board, where Jela's damn' tree sat in its pot, leaves fluttering in the air flow from the vent.

Or not.

"Our orders," Jela began—Cantra cut him off with a slash of her hand and a snarl.

"Orders!"

"*Our orders*," Jela repeated, overriding her without any particular trouble, "are clear." He tipped his head and added, at a considerably lesser volume, "Or so they seem to me. You're a sharp one for a detail, Pilot. Do you remember what she said?"

Damn the man.

"I remember," she said shortly.

"She said," he continued as if she hadn't spoken, "*You, the pilot and the ssussdriad will proceed to the world Landomist. You will recover Liad dea'Syl's equations which describe the recrystallization exclusion function and use them in the best interest of life*. Do I have that right, Pilot?"

She'd've denied it, if there'd been room, but Jela wasn't too bad with a detail himself, when he cared to apply himself.

"You've got it close enough," she allowed, still short and snappish. "And the fact that you were pleased to give your word on it don't make the rest of us daft enough to fall prey to the gentle lady's delusions."

"She and her mate are our allies," Jela said, like it made a difference. "We shared the tree's fruit. She trusts us to carry out our part of the campaign."

Cantra closed her eyes. "Jela."

"Pilot Cantra?"

"What do you think the *sheriekas* lord is going to do with yon pretty children when they're caught?"

"Interrogate them," he said promptly.

Well, now, there was a sensible answer, after all. She opened her eyes and gave him a smile for reward.

"Granting the *sheriekas* have a fine arsenal of nasties at their beck," she pursued, bringing the Rim accent up hard, "it seems to me likely that Rool Tiazan and his sweet lady will say all they know of everything, and a good number of things of which they have no ken, among it being one soldier, who gave his word to travel straightaway to Landomist for to liberate some 'quations in the service of all those who're enemies of the Enemy." She drew a careful breath, seeing nothing in his eyes but her own reflection. "Stay with me now. Where do you think that canny cold lord will next turn its care, having heard the *dramliza* sing?"

"Landomist," Jela said calmly.

Cantra felt the glare rising and overrode it with another smile, this one showing puzzled.

"So, knowing that, you're wanting to follow these *orders*, as you style them, and have the three of us down on Landomist, nice and easy for the *sheriekas* to find?"

"I gave my word," Jela said, which brought them full circle.

Once again, a ghostly taste of mint along her tongue. Cantra snapped a look down board, and flung out an arm, drawing Jela's attention to his tree.

"All the care and trouble you've gone to for that damn' vegetable, and now you're wishful of putting it in the path of mortal danger? You done caring what happens to it?"

Whatever reaction she might have expected him to deploy against such a blatant piece of theater, laughter—genuine laughter—was among the last.

Head thrown back, Jela shouted his delight. The tree, for its part, snapped a bow, leaves flashing—and no way the vent had put out a gust strong enough to account for that.

Cantra sighed, hitched her thumbs in her belt and waited.

Jela's laughter finally wound down to a series of deep-in-the-chest chuckles. He raised a hand and wiped the tears off his cheeks, grinning white and wide.

"Mind sharing the joke?" she asked, keeping her tone merely curious.

For a heartbeat it seemed like he was going to engage in some further hilarity at her expense. If he was, he controlled the urge, and waved a shaky hand in the general direction of the tree.

"Pilot, that tree is more soldier than I'll ever be. It held a planet against the *sheriekas*, all by itself, when it wasn't any thicker than my first-finger, here. It knows the risks—what we stand to gain, what we stand to lose. None better, I'll bet you—and I'm including the *dramliza* in that set." Another swipe of fingertips across cheeks to smooth away the last of the laugh-tears. "Ask it yourself, if you don't believe me."

Behind her eyes, unbidden, came a series of pictures. A green, tree-grown world, and the shadows of wings overhead in the high air. Then came a feeling of oppression as the grass dried, the wings vanished and the first of the very Eldest trembled, wavered—and crashed to the drying earth.

The pictures went on, elucidating the trees' muster as they fought a delaying action, first in groups, at the last one or two alone, as the world dried until only sand was left. The rivers evaporated, the sea shrank to a trickle, and still the trees held the enemy away by will, as Cantra understood it to be—and by won't.

It was a campaign doomed to failure, of course, and the last few soldiered on, their life force stretched thin. The feeling of oppression grew into a tangible weight, and the winds whipped, scattering sand across the corpses of trees, which was all that remained—save one.

Cantra's throat was closed with dust, thirst an agony. She felt her sap falling and knew her death was near. She was too young, her resources too meager, and yet she bent her energies to her last task, and produced a pod, so the world would not be left unprotected—then waited, singing thin and defiant against the Enemy's howl of desolation.

But what came next was not death.

Rather, a new form took shape out of the wind and the sand—not a dragon, yet with something dragon-like about it. It, too, opposed the Enemy. It, too, was dying. It proposed a partnership of mutual survival, that they might together continue to fight.

The tree accepted the proposal.

There was a stutter in the storylines, and there was *Dancer's* bridge, clear enough, and the *dramliza* on their knees, heads bowed, the echo of the question in her own head, and the answer, damnitall, that she'd made it.

In the matter of allies, you need to ask yourself two things: Can they shoot? And will they aim at your enemy?

Quick as a sneeze, then, the tree cut her loose to fall back into her own head so fast and so hard she gasped aloud.

Cantra blinked and focused on Jela. He had the decency to show her a calm, disinterested face. A mannerly man was Jela, soldier or no.

"All right, then," she said, and was pleased that her voice sounded as calm and disinterested as Jela's eyes. "There's two of you agreed to cleave to madness. The fact remains that *I* never gave *my* word."

"Now, that's very true," Jela allowed. "You never did give your word." He turned his big hands up, showing her empty, calloused palms. "Belike the lady thought we'd all stand as crewmates. But if you're determined not to risk yourself—and I'll agree that it's not a risk-free venture—then there's nothing more to say. I will ask you the favor of setting me and the tree down someplace we're likely to catch public transport to Landomist. I'd rather not call attention to us by coming in on a hired ship."

Almost, she did him the favor of returning a shout of his earlier laughter. She strangled the urge, though, and gave him as serious and stern a look as she could muster.

"I could do that," she said. "I'm assuming you have a plan for getting at those equations, locked up tight as they are in Osabei Tower."

"I do."

Cantra sighed. "And that would be?"

He tipped his head, making a play-act out of consideration, and finally gave her an apologetic grin, as false as anything she'd ever had from him.

"It's my campaign," he said, "and my word. The way I see it, you've got no need to know. Pilot."

It was said respectful enough, and in any case wasn't anything more or less than the plain truth. Nothing to notch her annoyance up to anger—so she told herself, and took a hard breath.

"Ever been to Landomist?" she asked, keeping her voice light and pleasant.

"Never," he answered in the same tone. "I don't get deep Inside much."

"Understandable. That being the case, you might not be familiar with the Towers?"

Jela moved his wide shoulders, head tipped to one side. "I've come across them in citations, tech lit and such. Each Tower represents a discipline and includes subsets of the discipline which hold conflicting philosophies."

Not bad, Cantra conceded. Dangerously simplistic, but not bad.

"Those conflicting philosophies, now," she said, just offering info, "they're more often than not the cause of blood duels and worse 'mong the scholars. Establish enough unchallenged theory—that being equally those who don't challenge the worth of a particular theory and those who challenged and lost—and a scholar gets moved to the High Tower and lives untouchable as a master."

Jela frowned and moved his hand, fingers flickering—pilot-talk for *get on with it.*

"Right," she said. "Osabei Tower, now, that's Spatial Math. Named after one Osabei tay'Bendril who brought pilot-kind the good numbers that make transition possible. Before Scholar tay'Bendril, pilots had to go the long way 'round and it might take a lifetime or two to traverse the Arm. They prolly gave you all that in 'mong the rest of pilot lore, same's they gave it to me. But what they didn't likely give you was the fact that the Towers're closed, and fortified, and they don't like strangers. But that's not your first problem."

She paused. Jela's face showed nothing but bland interest, damn the man. Well, she was the one who'd charted this course; he hadn't asked for her advice.

"Your first problem," she continued, "is that it's *Landomist*, about as Inside as you can get and not be on the other side of the Spiral. You put one boot on Landomist without a writ or a license, and you'll be exported before the second boot's down, if you're lucky—or memwiped and impressed to an Honorable, if you're not."

Jela rolled his shoulders and gave her a grin, slightly more genuine than the last.

"So, I'll have a writ to show."

"Assuming it's good enough and the Portmaster's not having a bad day, then you get a native guide to walk at your shoulder while you go about your lawful business, and to remind you when you step out from bounds."

He laughed.

"Pilot, you know a shadow's not going to stay with me."

"Lose or kill your assigned guide and you're a dead man," she snarled, surprising herself, "and a stupid man at the last."

Silence for the beat of three.

"Eventually, I'm a dead man, but I'd like to think not stupid," Jela said seriously. "Tell me why I can't just slip free, and go invisible."

Because it's Landomist! she wanted to shout—but didn't.

"Come with me," she said instead, and strode out of the piloting room without looking to see if he followed, down the short hall to her quarters.

The door opened with a snap that seemed reflective of her state of mind, and she concentrated on breathing nice and even while she crossed over to her locker and opened it wide.

For a moment she was alone in the polished metal mirror—a slender woman in trade leathers, pale hair cut off blunt at the stubborn jaw, features sharp, smooth skin toned gold, eyes a cool and misty green. Neither face, nor eyes, nor stance betrayed the slightest perturbation, nor the satisfaction she felt upon observing this.

A whisper from the rear and her reflection was joined by a second—broad shoulders and slim waist, both set off something fine by the leathers. Black hair, cropped; black eyes, bland. His face was brown, symmetrical, and a bit leaner than the shoulders predicted, with a firm mouth and strong brows. The top of his head didn't quite hit her shoulder, despite he bore himself upright and proud.

She used her chin to point at her own reflection.

"*That*," she announced, "is Inside norm, bred out of certified stock proven across more generations than you got time to hear or me to tell."

"All right," Jela said quietly.

"All right," she repeated, and pointed at his reflection.

"*That* is a gene-tailored series biologic."

"All right," he said again, and met her eyes in the mirror. "You're saying they aren't used to seeing Series soldiers on Landomist."

"I'm saying the only way anything other than Inside norm exists on Landomist is as property," Cantra corrected, and turned to look down into his face.

"You can't disappear on Landomist—and that's before you start having to tote that damn' tree around with you. There's just *nobody* there who looks like you, saving maybe a few household guards some Honorable might've bought from the military as curiosities."

His eyes moved and his jaw muscles tightened up, it upset him that much. Cantra reached out and touched his shoulder, taking care to keep it light and comradely, and smiled when he looked back to her.

"What you want is an agent," she said. "Set it up right, take your time—"

He laughed, soft, and slid out from under her hand.

"Time," he said, turning away, "is exactly what I don't have."

She frowned at his back. "You think the children're likely to get caught right off? Seemed to me they had a few worthy tricks to hand."

Jela paused, hesitated, then slowly turned to face her again.

"That's not where the crunch is," he said, and her ear registered absolute sincerity; unvarnished truth. He took a hard breath, and looked down at his broad, capable hands.

"It's me that's the problem. I'm old."

"Old?" She stared at the hard, inarguable bulk of him. "How old can you be?"

"Forty-four years, one-hundred-fifteen-and-one-twelfth days," he said. "Common Calendar." Another hard breath as he brought his eyes up and met hers firmly.

"Forty-five years is the design limit," he said steadily.

Cantra felt something cold and multi-clawed skitter through her gut.

"Design limit," she repeated, and closed her eyes, recalling Rool Tiazan's lady, her sharp eyes on Jela while she snapped out that time was short for each one of them.

And for some, it was shorter than others.

Anger trembled—anger at the *dramliza*. So busy about their promises. They had known—*known* that the man they'd built all their airy plans on had less than five months to live. Common Calendar. And with all the wonders the pair could likely make between them, they didn't pause for the heartbeat it might've cost—

"First aid kit," she said, huskily, and opened her eyes to meet Jela's calm gaze. "We put you in the first aid kit," she amplified when he didn't do anything more than lift a lazy black eyebrow. "Get you put back to spec, then you take what time you need to plan out your campaign."

"Pilot—"

She raised a hand. "I know you're not friends with the 'kit, but own it has its uses. You saw what it did for Dulsey—Deeps! You saw what it did for me. You climb yourself in and I'll set us a cour—"

"*Cantra*." He didn't raise his voice, but there was still enough snap in it to cut her off in mid-word. She felt the muscles of her face contract and wondered wildly what she'd been showing him.

Having stopped her, Jela didn't seem in any hurry to fill up the cabin with words of his own. He just stood there, head to a side, looking at her—and if truth be told there was something odd going on in his face, too.

He moved then, one careful step, keeping his hands where she could see them. Motionless, she watched him take her hand between both of his broad palms.

His skin was warm, his hands gentle. He craned his head back, black eyes searching her face, his absolutely open.

"Remember when the first aid kit didn't work?" he asked, like they were discussing what cargo was best to take on. "Garen had to take you to the Uncle for a receptor flush because the first aid kit didn't cure the edlin. That was why, wasn't it? Because all the 'kit could do was put you back to spec."

Pain. Thoughts staggering through reeking blood-red mists, then coolness as reason returned in the friendly dark. The lid rose, she rolled out—and collapsed to the floor, screaming as the pain took her again…

"And spec included the gimmicked receptors," she said, suddenly and deeply weary. "Right."

"Right," Jela said softly. "It's in the design, Cantra. M Series soldiers are decommissioned at forty-five years." He smiled, sudden and genuine. "Safer that way."

"Safer," she whispered and her free hand moved on its own, gripping his shoulder hard.

"Rool Tiazan," she said after a moment. "He asked how you'd choose to die."

"He did," Jela said briskly. "And if the tree and me are to liberate the good scholar's math, publish it wholesale, *and* die in battle, I'd better not take too many naps."

She smiled slightly, and stepped back, taking her hand off his shoulder, slipping the other from between his palms. He watched her out of calm black eyes.

"If it ain't your intention to die on Landomist Port," she said, turning to shut the locker door, "and see the tree broken and burned before you do, you'll employ that agent to work your will, like I said you should."

Behind her, she heard Jela sigh.

"It has to be a frontal attack," he said patiently. "I don't know how to employ the sort of agent you advise. And I don't have time to train him."

Face to the locker, she closed her eyes, hearing again the tiny lady's sharp voice listing out the terms of Jela's service: *You, the pilot and the ssussdriad will proceed to the world Landomist…*

Not her fight, dammit. She'd not sworn to any such madness.

Pay your debts, baby, Garen ghost-whispered from the gone-away past. *There ain't no living with yourself, if you don't.*

Deeps knew, she wouldn't be living at all, were it not for Jela—and, truth told full, the tree, as well.

Cantra sighed, very softly, opened her eyes and turned to face him.

"Her," she said, and met his eyes firm, giving a good imitation of woman with a sensible decision on deck. "I can get you in."

THREE

Light Wing
Doing the Math

THE KLAXON SHRIEKED, and Tor An's body responded before he was fully awake, snapping forward to the board—and snatched back by the webbing as the ship dropped out of transition with a shudder and a sob.

He'd webbed into the chair before allowing himself to nod off—prudent for a pilot running solo, even in relatively pirate-free space.

Prudence had saved him a bad knock—and another when the ship twisted again, as if protesting its sudden change of state.

By then, he was well awake, and by exerting steady pressure against the restraints managed to gain his board, and get a closer look at the screens.

The board was locked and live—standard for transition—and the main screen displayed a dense, unfamiliar starfield. Across the center of the display ran a bright blue legend: *Transition aborted. Target coordinates unavailable.*

Tor An blinked, reached to the board, engaged shields, called up the last-filed transition string, and sat frowning at the cheery yellow coordinates that described the location of home. Feeling a fool, he activated the library, called for the Ringstars, and did a digit-by-digit comparison between the library's coord set and those displayed in the nav screen.

The numbers matched, which ought to have, he thought, made him feel better. After all, he *hadn't* made a fumble-fingered entry error, or misremembered the coord set he'd been able to recite almost before he could pronounce his name.

On the other hand, a ship sent into transition defined by a correct set of target coordinates ought not to exit transition until the conditions described by the coordinates were met.

"Unless," Tor An said to the empty tower, "the navigation brain has dead sectors, or a ship self-check determines a dangerous condition. Or pirates force you out early."

He glared at the screens, noting the lack of pirates. He slapped up the logs, but found no dangerous condition listed. Dead sectors in the nav brain—he sighed. There was only one way to determine if that were the case.

Leaning to the board again, he set up a suite of diagnostics, punching the start key with perhaps a bit more force than was absolutely necessary. The board lights flickered; the screens blanked momentarily, then lit again, displaying the testing sequence and estimated time until completion.

Tor An released the webbing and stood. There was one more thing that might usefully be done—and, considering the age of his ship, *ought* to be done. If the transvective stabilizers had developed a wobble, the ship might have spontaneously dropped out of transition. He rather thought that such an event would have been noted in the log, but it *was* an old ship, with quirks and crotchets, and certain sporadic incompatibilities between ship's core and the logging function were a known glitch of its class.

Two strides and he was across the tiny tower. He opened a storage hatch, pulled out a tool belt and slung it around his waist, snapping it as he headed for the door.

Some while later, he was back in the pilot's chair, gnawing on a high-calorie bar and scrolling through the diagnostic reports, not as pleased as he might be by the unbroken lines of "normal function." At the end of the file, he sat back, the bar forgotten in his hand.

The stabilizers had checked out. The synchronization unit—which he knew for a glitchy, temperamental piece of work—had tested perfectly sound. Everything that could be tested, had tested normal, except for one thing.

Normally functioning ships do not spontaneously fall out of transition and report the—correctly entered!—target coordinates as "unavailable."

"Well," he said aloud, "it's obviously a fabric-of-space problem."

"Fabric-of-space problem" was Alkia in-clan for "a thing which has happened, but which cannot be explained." There being a limited number of such events in life, the phrase was a joke—or a sarcastic jibe from an elder to a junior suspected of being too lazy to do a thorough check.

But he *had* done a thorough check, for all the good he'd gained.

"Check again," he told himself, a trifle impatiently, "or trust the data."

Chewing his lower lip, he glanced down, frowned at the bar in his hand and tossed it into the recycling drawer. Then, he engaged the webbing, brought the board up, woke the nav brain and fed it the coordinates for the Ringstars.

"Enough nonsense," he said to his ship. "Let us go home."

He initiated transition.

Cantra poured the last of the tea into her mug, started a new pot brewing, and wandered back into that part of the lodgings which was, in the fond thought of the landlord, the parlor. Right now, it was a workroom, with twin tables piled high with the building blocks of a dozen or more parallel-running projects, hers and his.

Her projects were in holding orbit at the moment, waiting an all-clear from the portmaster, played for this once-only showing by M. Jela, who was emoting equal parts stubborn and grim as he sat hunched over his toys. A warmer bowl containing dinner—or might-be breakfast—sat at his elbow, the noodles dry, the tasty and nutritious sauce long baked off. He'd been paying sporadic attention to his mug, so she'd set herself to keeping it full with hot, sweet, and fresh.

Cantra sipped tea and sighed. The man did, she conceded, have a point. If the info could be pinched from afar, then it was beyond foolish to risk the ship's company by going in after it. It happened she believed—based on past study, say—that the Towers of Landomist kept their brains well-shielded, and Osabei moreso than most. She'd given him everything she knew on the subject, which was, once she'd put her memory to it, not inconsiderable. And she'd pointed out the logic behind imprisoning Liad dea'Syl in Osabei, on the slim chance he hadn't figured it out for himself.

Still, he'd wanted to check it for himself, and so he was—using an interesting combination of military grade and Dark Market gizmos. Cantra supposed she ought to be grateful for his caution. Herself, she was finding the inexorable passage of time an unwelcome irritant.

She sat down in the chair she'd lately been calling home, and put her feet up on one of the rare clear spots of her table. Crossing her ankles, she glanced at the tree, sitting in a fancy artwork pot over in the corner, under the special light Jela'd rigged for it—and then at the clock. Not long now. She sipped her tea and watched Jela, which was a deal more scenic than staring at the wall, and waited.

Her tea was gone by the time the clock finally gave out with its tootling little on-the-local-hour song, and Jela sighed, rolled his shoulders and leaned back in his chair, his eyes lingering on the spyware.

"Luck?" she asked, though by the look of it, learning-by-doing had only gained what she'd told him in the first place.

He sighed again, and finally met her eyes, his tired and tending toward bleak.

"We go in," he said.

He raised Telmair.

He raised Kant.

He raised Porshel and Braz, Jiniwerk, and Oryel.

He dug deep into the library, and unrolled star charts across the tower floor, weighting the corners with spanners. When he had identified the coordinates for a sphere of six waystops inside the influence of the Ringstars, he fed those into the nav-brain, webbed himself into the pilot's chair, initiated transition, and waited, his face tight, his back rigid.

The ship accepted its office. Tor An sighed, his muscles melting toward relief—

And *Light Wing* twisted, klaxons blaring as she fell into real space, alarms lighting the board, and across the main screen, the bright blue legend:

Transition aborted. Target coordinates unavailable.

He was a conscientious boy, and he had been taught well. Ignoring the ice in his belly, the chilly sweat on his face, he re-checked the charts, made sure of his numbers, and initiated transition again.

And again, his ship transitioned, returning almost immediately to normal space.

Transition aborted. Target coordinates unavailable.

He shut down the board, made sure of his shields, deliberately unwebbed and stood. It had, he told himself, been some time since he had eaten—how long a time, he was not prepared to say with any certainty, save that he had been awake for longer.

"Pilot error," he said to the empty tower. "I am taking myself off-duty for a meal, a shower and a nap. Barring ship's need, I will return in five ship hours and perform the exercise again from the top."

He was a lad of his word, and had been raised to know the value of discipline. There was no ship's emergency to disturb him and he returned to the tower, refreshed, in just under five ship hours.

Once at his station, he again carefully examined the star maps, acquiring six coordinate strings defining a sphere of ports that lay within the boundary space of the Ringstars.

Rising, he went to his chair, webbed in, entered the coords, double-checked them—and initiated transition.

Light Wing leapt, stuttered—fell.

Transition aborted, read the message across the main screen. *Target coordinates unavailable.*

Cantra woke as she'd set herself to do, since it was important to be up and well about her business before Jela, who never that she'd noticed slept more than four hours together, did the same.

Despite that the "up" side of the equation was as crucial as the "awake," she stayed a bit longer just where she was, curled slightly on her left side, her back snuggled against Jela's wide and reassuring chest. His arm was draped companionably over her waist, her hand tucked into the relaxed curl of his fist. He slept quiet, did Jela, and solid, which the Deeps knew he had a right. The work he'd put in over the last few days, cutting his four hours of sleep down to two, or, in some cases, so she suspected, none—it was a wonder he could stand, much less share a long and satisfying pleasure as they'd just enjoyed. The last of too few.

She sighed softly, and shifted, slow and languorous, a well-satisfied woman readjusting position in her sleep. Jela shifted in turn, reflexively withdrawing his arm. Freed, she waited three heartbeats, listening to his quiet, unhurried breathing. When she was certain he hadn't woke, she eased out of bed and ghosted away.

The light in the main room was hard and non-adjustable; the work tables tidier than they'd been in a while. Jela's held a couple sets of data tiles, frames, and some bits of esoteric tinyware the particulars of which she hadn't troubled to ask after. Her table—was clear, excepting a notebook and a pen. Picking up the pen, she wrote, briefly, tore the sheet out of the book and placed it prominently at

Jela's table. Her last instruction to her co-pilot. She wished that it could have been something more easeful—but there wasn't any use lying to Jela. Not now.

Last duty done, she turned toward the third room that made the sum of their lodgings: a small, chilly niche about the size of the guest cabin on *Dancer*. More than big enough for a death.

Something green fluttered at the edge of her vision, which would be Jela's damn' tree—or her ally the *ssussdriad*, soon to be neither. The flutter came again, stronger, and she knew perfectly well there was neither draft nor vent where it was placed.

Sighing, she turned and walked down the room to where it sat under the special-spectrum spotlight Jela'd rigged for it. The change in lighting'd done it good, if the number and size of the pods hanging from its scrawny branches were any measure.

The dance of leaves became more agitated as she approached, and a particular branch began to visibly bend under the weight of its pod. Cantra considered it sardonically.

"Going-away present?" she asked, her voice harsh in her own ears.

A picture formed inside her head: water sparkling beneath her, the shadow of a great beast flashing over the waves. She felt a bone-deep ache in her shoulders, an emptiness in her belly, and still she labored on, sinking toward the water, each stroke an agony. And there, ahead—the cliffs, the trees, the others! She made a mighty effort, but the tips of her wings cut water on the downstroke, and she knew the cliffs were beyond her—

From the dancers along the cliff sides came a large, dark dragon, his flight powerful and swift. He flew above and past her, spun on a wing and dove, slipping between her and the water, bearing her up, up the side of the cliffs and into the crown of a tree. A pod-heavy branch rose as the songs of welcome filled her ears and she gratefully took the gift thus offered.

Cantra blinked; the image faded. "Promises," she said, voice cracking; "promises are dangerous things. You dasn't give one unless you're sure to keep it. No living with yourself any other way." The branch bent sharply, insistently. She held out a hand with a sigh. "Have it your way, then. But don't say I never told you." The pod hit her palm solidly and her fingers curled over it.

"Thank you," she said softly.

She locked the door behind her then set her shoulders against it, eyes closed.

"You told the man you'd back him," she said aloud, and shivered in the chill air.

The fact was, for all her bold words, she might not be *able* to back him. Oh, she remembered the lessons fair enough, though it would perhaps have eased things for an unpracticed and unwilling *aelantaza* were any of the particular mix of psychotropics used in the final prep stage of an assignment on hand. Still, the wisdom was that the thing could be done by trance alone. The drug was helpful, but by no means necessary. For the first part of the operation.

The second part—the resurrection, should there be one—well, she'd never heard other than the drug was needed and necessary for that part of it. Not to say the company of a taler, which she didn't have either. Once in a chance, so the story went, an *aelantaza* might come home so burnt-brained and desperate that the drug didn't make no nevermind. It wasn't any use even bringing a taler near such a one. The best thing to do then, in the estimation of the Directors, who weren't known for wasting resources, was to break the burnt-brain's neck before they up and hurt somebody they shouldn't.

Sort of like Pliny'd done.

Cantra sighed. She didn't want to die, though she was looking at doing just that. But maybe, she thought, her throat tight—maybe she wouldn't die. All she had to do was play diversion for a month or less, Common. Maybe there would be enough of herself left at the end the assignment to spontaneously regenerate—

Or maybe not.

It ain't, she said to herself, the weight of the tree's gift heavy in her fist, *like you never done it before. You weren't born to the Rim nor to the life Garen taught you. Whoever you were before, you came to be someone else—something other. This'll be just the same.*

The Rimmer pilot was no more real than the daughter Garen'd thought her to be. The person who rose up out of the remains of the pilot's psyche would be no more nor less real than both.

There was a scent in the cabin; she hadn't noticed it before. A pleasant scent, green and minty and comforting. Cantra opened her eyes, raised her fist, opened her fingers and considered the pod on her palm.

No doubt the aroma emanated from it; and it grew more enticing by the moment. She remembered her previous tastes of the tree's fruit, and found her mouth watering.

Well, it can't hurt, she thought; and, if she were honest with herself, it might help with the local courage levels.

She put finger to pod, wondering how best to crack it, lacking Jela's strong hand or Rool Tiazan's more unusual abilities, but to her surprise it fell apart at her lightest touch, releasing an even more tempting aroma.

The taste was better than she recalled—tart and spicy. Sighing, she ate the second piece, muscles relaxing as her body warmed. By the time she had finished all of the pieces and carefully slipped the rind into the waste unit, she felt calm and centered. That was good; she was past the jitters now and down to cases.

Opening the drawer of the bedside table, she withdrew a wide bracelet set with several gem-topped buttons. This she snapped 'round her wrist, adjusting it until it was snug and showed no disposition to slip.

That done, she lay down on the narrow bed and pulled a blanket over her nakedness, closed her eyes, regulated her breathing, and called to mind those exercises which would eventually pitch her into the trance. She had prepared as well as she could: memories, behaviors, preferences, and history would be released and assimilated as soon as her mind came to the change level.

Her heartbeat spiked at the thought, as if her body would be afraid: Patiently, firmly, she smoothed the spike, and sank further into calmness. The last thing she felt, before the change overtook her, was a sensation of utter safety and respect, not at all unlike the sensation of being curled against Jela's chest

She woke with a sense of anticipation so great that she could scarcely keep from shouting aloud. Such an outburst, of course, would be unseemly from a seated scholar of Osabei Tower, and Maelyn tay'Nordif fully intended to be a seated scholar of Osabei Tower before this day's work was done.

She rose with alacrity, opened the small closet and pulled on the clothes she found there—a faded gold unitard, over which went a well-worn and carefully patched tabard. She stepped to the mirror and studied her reflection critically as she wove the yellow sash about her waist in the so-called Wander pattern, and took some time over the precise position of the smartgloves folded over it. When these were disposed to her satisfaction, she returned to the closet and withdrew a slender knife; its grip shaped of common ceramic, wrapped with fraying leather; the edges showing some slight notching. She rubbed the flat of the blade down the front of her tabard once or twice, to shine it, then slipped it also into her sash, being careful of her fingers.

Thus accoutered, she stood for another long moment before the mirror, considering her reflection.

"All very well," she said at last, her voice sharp and slightly nasal, "for a Wanderer. But tomorrow, you will be clad in the robes of a scholar, and seated in your proper place amongst the greatest mathematical minds of the galaxy." She smiled, lips pressed tight, and at last turned away from the mirror. Gathering her book from the table next to the bed, she reviewed the necessities of the day.

First, to register the kobold and the plant with the port—an annoyance, but it had to be done. Such a shame that they had come in last evening after the proper office had closed, and thus mere paperwork must put back her triumph by another few hours. She frowned in annoyance, and tossed her head. No matter. Once the proper registries were made, she would proceed to Osabei Tower, present her token, and—she doubted not, be welcomed with joy and open arms by her peers.

Satisfied with this precis, she unlocked the door and stepped into the great room.

The kobold was seated at the table, its big hands folded before it, exactly as she had left it upon retiring yestereve. Maelyn sighed, wondering, not for the first time, whatever had possessed her last patron to make her so ridiculous a gift. True, the kobold and the plant were but portions of the parting gift, and the Noble Panthera, heir to House Chaler, had been generous in the matters of both coin and credit. Well, the thing was done, and both were under her dominion. And who else, she thought suddenly, preening, among the scholars of Osabei Tower, might possess such rare and interesting items? Truly, she came to claim her chair no mere ragged Wanderer, but a woman of property!

"Stand *up*, Jela!" she ordered, experience having taught her the way of dealing with the kobold, whose intelligence was only slightly greater than that of the plant in its care. "Place the pack on your back, pick up the plant, and follow me. *Closely.*"

Brown face expressionless, eyes dull, it pushed to its feet and hefted the pack. It was a powerful creature, and she had seen, during her time at House Chaler, what a single kobold might wreak, under order.

Maelyn touched the bracelet 'round her wrist. She had the means to control Jela, which was, in any case, too dull to be a danger to her.

"Hurry!" she snapped at its broad back, and turned to open the door.

PART FOUR

THIEF

FOUR

Landomist Port

THE ERRANT-SCHOLAR'S tabard was onyx green, Osabei's Theorem embroidered in sable and silver 'round the hems and neckline. Beneath the tabard, she wore a unitard the precise golden shade of her skin. A pair of smart-gloves and a scholar's truth-blade were thrust through the yellow sash that cuddled her slender waist, and the expression on her high-born face was cool enough to freeze a man's blood.

Behind her came a very gnome of a creature, clad all in black leather: squat, thick, and sullen, a pack on its back, and its bulging arms wrapped about a large and ornately enameled pot. From the pot a green plant rose to some distance above the kobold's head, leaves a-flutter in the breeze from the open window.

Scholars were no rare thing on Landomist—and mathematical scholars least rare of all. Angry errant-scholars accompanied by tree-bearing kobolds—that was something rarer, and promised diversion of one sort or another on a slow and sleepy day. So it was that the portmaster himself stepped up to the counter, forestalling the bustling of the lead clerk, and inclined his head.

"Errant-Scholar, how may I be pleased to assist you?"

Her lips tightened and for a heartbeat he thought she would slip the leash on her temper, which would have been—unwise.

Apparently, she was not too angry for considered thought. The tight lips softened a fraction and bent upward at the corners in a fair approximation of pleasant courtesy, as she proffered a scarred and travel-worn document case.

"If you would do what is necessary to clear me, sir, I would be most obliged."

"Of course," he murmured, receiving the case and running it efficiently along the mag-strip.

"One did not quite understand," the errant-scholar continued as he opened the case, popped the data tile from its setting and inserted it into the reader, "that more than simply declaring at the gate was required."

"Of course not," he said soothingly, most of his attention on the hardcopy enclosed in the other half of the case. He rubbed his fingers lightly over the document, feeling the sharp edges of the letters cut deep into the paper, the silky blots of sealing wax with their pendant ribbons.

"Errant-Scholar Maelyn tay'Nordif, native of Vetzu," he said, musingly, and glanced up.

The errant-scholar's eyes were green, he noticed. She inclined her head, her hair soft and silken in the yellow light.

"I am Maelyn tay'Nordif," she answered primly.

"May I know your reason for coming to Landomist, Scholar?" The information would be on the data tile, of course, but it was often useful to hear what else was said—or was not said—in answer to a direct inquiry.

She lifted her chin proudly. "I go to kneel in reverence before the masters of Osabei Tower and petition that my time of wandering be done."

The usual reason, the portmaster conceded, and sent a sharp glance over the lady's shoulder to the silent kobold. The creature had the temerity to meet his eyes, its own black and reflective. The portmaster frowned.

"Landomist has very strict regulations regarding genetic constructs," he said to Errant-Scholar tay'Nordif. "It is not sufficient to merely declare; this office is required to examine, test and certify each and every incoming construct." He looked sternly into her eyes. "A matter of public safety, Scholar. I am certain that you would not wish it otherwise."

It was plain from the scholar's face that she did wish it otherwise, but she was not such a fool as to say so. Instead, she merely inclined her head.

"The safety of the public must of course carry all before it," she murmured. "You will find detailed pedigrees for both the plant and the kobold in the auxiliary index of the tile."

"Of course," he said again, and gestured toward the reader. "This will be a few moments."

The scholar sighed. "I understand," she said.

He bent to the reader, and quickly learned that the vegetative item was a gift from Horticultural Master Panthera vas'Chaler of Shinto to Errant-Scholar tay'Nordif, in token of "the continued growth of our spiritual kinship, which shall forever remain the greatest of my life's pleasures." The Master provided a DNA map for the specimen, and a certification of non-toxicity; the validation programs in his reader reported both genuine, the files extensively cross-referenced to the files of the Shinto Planetary Horticultural Society.

So much, the portmaster thought, for the vegetative portion of the Errant-Scholar's retinue. He bent again to the reader.

The labor class genetic construct "Jela" had also been given by Master vas'Chaler, in order to "transport the token of our kinship and to perform those other services which may avail and comfort the most precious sister of my soul."

The portmaster looked up. "Landomist requires that an inhibitor be installed in all mobile constructs."

The scholar raised a slender hand. "Your pardon," she murmured. Turning her face aside, she snapped at the kobold. "Jela! Place the plant gently on the floor and walk forward to the counter."

This the creature did, moving with a slow-witted deliberation that confirmed its "laborer" class, its footsteps sounding loud and slow against the floor.

"Display your inhibitor," the Scholar instructed.

The big clumsy hands came up and parted the leathern collar, revealing the thick throat and an expanse of wide, hairless brown chest. About the throat and across the chest were intricate lines of what at first glance appeared to be tattoo, but which a second, more sanguine, scrutiny found to be ceramic threads woven into the kobold's skin.

The portmaster leaned forward, extended a hand and rubbed his fingertips across the woven strands. The rough surfaces pulled at his skin. "I see," he said, and leaned back, frowning.

"Is something amiss?" Errant-Scholar tay'Nordif inquired after a moment. "I assure you, sir, that I do not wish in any way to endanger the citizens of Landomist."

That was well-said, the portmaster allowed, yet he felt that she might lose her concern for the public safety were her kobold impounded, or if she should be required to have it refurbished at one of the port shops. Nor would he blame her, either option being more of an expense than it was likely a returning Errant-Scholar could meet. Also, the information provided by her patron made it plain that the kobold and the plant were considered one unit, of which the more valuable portion was the plant. The portmaster looked to the scholar.

"You understand," he said, "that this"— he flicked his fingers at the kobold—"is not the usual device that we employ here on Landomist. I fear that the regulations may require you to have it adjusted at your cost, or to see it impounded."

Her face lost color. "Impound my patron's parting gift?" She exclaimed in horror. "Sir, I—Is there nothing, no sub-regulation which perhaps accommodates persons who are to be on Landomist for only a short time, yet require the services of a kobold or other construct?"

That was a thought. The portmaster frowned, then moved to his screen. "A moment," he said. "It may be that there is something—"

The regs came up; he quickly found his place, perused the language and leaned back.

"The provision is for short-term visits only," he said. "This office is, in the case of visits of less than two Common Months, required to certify that the inhibitor is the *equivalent* of a standardized device, and may be invoked by the Landomist general disciplinary band."

The scholar raised her arm, displaying a slender wrist enclosed by a wide silver cuff, set with three glittering stones.

"This device is the controller tuned to this particular construct," she said. "Alas, it is also tuned to me; should I remove it for your inspection, it will require retuning by an expert of the form."

"I see. However, it will not be necessary to compromise your device, Scholar. What the law requires is proof positive that the standard device in use upon Landomist will be adequate to subdue this creature, should the need arise." The portmaster reached beneath the counter and produced the standard device in question. "You permit?"

The scholar inclined her head. "I do. Indeed, I insist. The law must be honored, sir."

This was so novel a concept the portmaster actually blinked, then smiled into the scholar's face. A pleasant lady, she was, if naive, and accepting of his authority.

"But a moment," he murmured and touched the sequence for mid-level pacification.

Instantly, the kobold moaned, its eyes rolling up as it dropped to its knees, one quivering hand raised in supplication.

"I would prefer," the scholar said, "that it not be rendered unconscious, unless proof calls for a complete demonstration. It does not recover well, I fear, and there is the specimen to be transported—"

The kobold's brown face was growing darker; low, hideous sounds came from its gaping mouth.

"I believe we have established an equivalency," the portmaster said, triggering the end sequence and turning away from the creature with relief. "It is not my intention to cause you inconvenience, Scholar."

Released, the kobold folded forward until its face was against the floor, its leathered sides heaving. The scholar sighed sharply.

"Stand *up*, Jela!" she snapped impatiently. "Resume your work!"

The kobold shifted like a pile of rocks, lumbered to its feet, and stepped back to its original place. Bending, it wrapped its arms about the pot, hefting it and the tree.

"Should your business at the Tower bear fruit," the portmaster said to the scholar, "you will be required to see the creature modified before the end of two months Common."

"I will see to it as soon as my seat is secure," she promised.

"I will prepare the documentation immediately," the portmaster said. "One moment." He slipped the tile into a frame, located the proper permit in the archive, and transmitted it, with the date and his name. That done, he returned the tile to its setting, resealed the document case and extended it to the waiting scholar.

"Welcome to Landomist," he said, smiling.

Errant-Scholar tay'Nordif received the case with a smile and a polite bow. "Thank you, sir," she said, and snapped over her shoulder at the kobold, "Follow me, Jela! Now!" and left the office.

It was only later, when he was processing a stasis box full of genetically altered carnivorous roses, that the portmaster realized that he had forgotten to assess Scholar tay'Nordif her fee.

FIVE

Osabei Tower
Landomist

THE MERCY BELL had rung in the Evening's Peace; truth-blades had been sheathed and proofs lain down until the morrow. In accordance with Tower protocol, the admissions committee had gathered in the public room, ready to entertain the petitions of any and all supplicants. Such was the force of tradition in Osabei Tower that the committee gathered despite a continued and marked lack of supplicants petitioning for admission to the ranks of the Seated. Conditions on the frontier, so they had heard, were unstable, which would doubtless account for the shortage. Indeed, the few Errant-Scholars who had lately arrived at the Tower to sue for a Seat had without exception been those who had chosen to study closer to civilization. No one Wandered the frontier anymore—it was much too unsafe, what with the war which the so-called military did its least to end.

Neither did Osabei Tower, unlike other Towers less devoted to scholarship, conduct outreach in order to draw grudents, Errant-Scholars and light-pupils to them. The Governors held it as an article of faith that the best and brightest would of course come to Osabei, the first, the oldest, and the most prestigious of the Mathematical Towers.

Conditions within the discipline being what they had been over the last few years—quite a number of radical new theories had been proposed and put to proof—a continued lack of eligible Errant-Scholars seeking a seat within the Order would in approximately two-point-three-four-four-eight Common Years become troublesome. But there was as yet no cause for concern.

So unconcerned was the admissions committee—and so certain that this evening would, like a long tale of previous evenings, bring them no supplicants to judge—that Seated Scholar Jenicour tay'Azberg had, as had become her habit, brought along a deck of cards and had enlisted chi'Morin, dea'Bel, and ven'Halsen in a game of Confusion. It was of course, a breach of Tower protocol to engage in any form of the art mathematical—which gambling games most certainly were—after the ringing of the Mercy Bell, but so formidable was Scholar tay'Azberg with a truth-blade that such small liberties were for the most part overlooked.

The fifth member of the committee, Seated Scholar and Committee Head Kel Var tay'Palin, was unabashedly napping, for which the sixth and final member, Seated Scholar Ala Bin tay'Welford, blamed him not at all. tay'Palin had been increasingly called upon of late to provide proofs of his work, and the strain was taking its expectable, regrettable, toll. That the man was tay'Welford's own immediate superior and the head of the Interdimensional Statistics Department only made his decline more poignant. tay'Palin reported to Master Liad dea'Syl himself—a signal honor, though the Master was frail and had not left his rooms to walk even among those of his own discipline for—

The door slid back with a soft sigh, admitting the ostiary, who went down to a knee, head bowed, eyes stringently focused on the ebon floorboards.

"A supplicant comes!" she cried cleverly, thereby granting poor tay'Palin a chance to snort into wakefulness and for cards to vanish discretely into scholarly sleeves. tay'Welford set his logic-rack to one side, smoothed his robe and folded his hands onto his lap.

"Admit the supplicant," tay'Palin said to the ostiary, his voice calm and scholarly.

The guard brought her hand up in the sign of obedience, and leapt to her feet. She straddled the doorway—one foot in the foyer, one foot in the committee room, and called aloud, "The admissions committee will hear the supplicant's prayer!"

There was a moment of stillness as all scholarly eyes turned toward the door. tay'Welford noticed that he was breathing rather quickly, in anticipation, then a shadow moved in the foyer, coalesced into a slender woman in the green tabard and yellow sash of a Errant-Scholar. She walked forward precisely seven paces and dropped to her knees, head bent, arms held away from her body, palms out, fingers wide and pointing toward the floor.

One could feel the air in the room sharpen as the admissions committee took minute stock of the supplicant. She knelt, motionless, pale hair hiding her downturned face. The tabard moved, slight and sweet, over her breast, revealing the unhurried rhythm of her breathing.

Kel Var tay'Palin leaned forward slightly in his chair. "You may show your face," he said, "and give your name into the committee's keeping."

Obediently, neither so quickly that she betrayed eagerness, nor so slowly that she was read as arrogant, the supplicant lifted her head. Her face was an agglomeration of angles, sheathed in supple gold. Her eyes were an indeterminate shade of green, set perhaps a bit too wide beneath the pale wings of her brows. Her mouth in repose was non-committal; the supple skin without wrinkle or flaw. Of Common Years, thought tay'Welford, she might as easily hold as few as twenty or as many as forty.

"Maelyn tay'Nordif," she said, ceding her name to the committee, as she had been instructed. Her voice was high and clear, ringing sharply against the ear, and tay'Welford detected only the very least bit of tremble, which was expectable, and spoke well of her common sense.

"What is your specialty?" ven'Halsen asked, following form.

"Interdimensional mathematics," the supplicant made answer. tay'Welford sighed, and leaned back in his chair.

"Under whom," demanded tay'Azberg, "did you study?"

"Liad dea'Syl."

There was a sharp silence—as well there ought to be, thought tay'Welford. Never, in all his time on the admissions committee, had one of the Master's own students come forth to claim a chair and a place at the Tower. They therefore had before them not merely a supplicant, but a marvel.

"Why," asked dea'Bel in her wistful, cloying voice, "have you come?"

"To beg a place," the supplicant answered, word perfect out of the protocol book, "and that an end be made to my wandering."

"What token," tay'Welford asked pleasantly, lightly, as if it were of no moment, "do you bring us?"

"I have given my coin into the keeping of the guardian of the halls of knowledge." Her voice betrayed no trembling now, nor her face anything but an impersonal, unnuanced respect.

tay'Welford did not remove his gaze from the supplicant's smooth, collected face.

"Ostiary," he said, allowing his voice to reflect the faintest hint of doubt, "pray bring me the supplicant's coin."

The guard straddling the door spun smartly on her heel and marched forward. At the corner of his table, she bowed and opened her hand, offering on the flat of her palm a single tile, shaded green to match the supplicant's tabard—or perhaps, tay'Welford thought whimsically, to match her eyes. He took the tile, his gaze resting yet upon the supplicant's face. The ostiary went back a long step, straightened, turned and marched out of the room. The door whispered shut behind her.

The supplicant's face did not change, the calm rhythm of her breathing was preserved.

Slowly, as though it were foregone that the work preserved on the tile would be second-rate, if not actually shabby, tay'Welford pulled the logic-rack to him, deftly re-arranged the tiles and slid the green into its place within the pattern.

The green tile pulsed. Figures and notations floated to the surface of the reader tiles, framing an argument both elegant and facile. tay'Welford smiled in genuine pleasure as the theory routines accessed the supplicant's data.

"Scholar?" tay'Palin's voice carried an edge of irritated dryness. "Perhaps you might share the joke with your colleagues?"

He bowed his head and answered soft, acutely aware of the rebuke.

"Forgive me, Scholar. The theory cross-check is almost—ah." Very nearly, he smiled again. A *most* elegant piece of work.

"The supplicant," he said, "builds a compelling proof *against* Master dea'Syl's decrystallization equation."

tay'Palin met his eyes, grimly; beleaguered as he was, still the Prime Chair was no one's fool. A supplicant who came offering such a coin for her seat could in no case be allowed to depart.

Therefore did Scholar tay'Palin rise to his feet, and the others of the committee with him. Hands outstretched, he approached the supplicant, who bent her head back on her long, slender neck and watched him. The pulse at the base of her throat, tay'Welford saw, was beating a little too rapidly for perfect calm. It might be that the supplicant was not quite entirely a fool, either.

"Rise, supplicant," said tay'Palin, and she did, swaying slightly as she gained her feet. To the left, tay'Azberg and dea'Bel had risen, as well. They approached the supplicant; tay'Azberg slipped the gloves and the blade free while dea'Bel removed the yellow sash, and stepped to one side.

tay'Welford rose and received the end of the black sash offered by tay'Halsen. They then approached the supplicant and wove the dusky length about her slim waist, tay'Palin stepped forward at the last to tuck in the ends and return blade and gloves to their proper places.

He then opened his arms in the ritual gesture.

"Allow me to be the first to welcome Seated Scholar Maelyn tay'Nordif home after her long wandering," he said.

Seated Scholar tay'Nordif took a deep breath and stepped into the embrace. tay'Palin kissed her on both cheeks, and released her.

"Come," he said. "Allow me to make you known to your family in art."

"Alkia?" The Korak trade master frowned at Tor An, spun on the stool and slapped up her screen, her right hand already on the wheel. Clan names flashed by in a blur, froze, blinked and reformatted as she accessed Alkia's files.

"I'd thought there was something odd," she muttered, whether to him or to herself he was uncertain. "But it's all been odd of late: ships coming in behind-time; ships coming in ahead of time; whole routes collapsing under the weight of the damned war—Wait, wait—" She touched a button, accessing in quick sequence the shipping histories for the last month, two months, three—

And sighed of a sudden, closing the screen with a touch that seemed nearly gentle. She sat with her back to him though there was nothing but the blank screen for her to look at, and then turned on the stool again. Her face was somber, and Tor An felt his stomach clench.

"There is no record of any Alkia Trade Clan ship calling at any port in this sector across the last three months, Common Calendar. We have one report, unsubstantiated, that navigation to the Ringstars has become unstable."

He stared at her, feeling the weight of the datastrip in the protected innermost pocket of his jacket.

"I have," he said tentatively, "not been able to reach the Ringstars. I have data, if it—"

She moved a hand aimlessly, or so it seemed to him.

"I can use the data to substantiate the first report, close the route, file an amendment to the coordinate tables." She reached beneath the counter. "There's paperwork—"

Tor An stared at her.

"Won't you investigate? Try to find what happened? A whole system—"

She looked at him wearily. "Routes have gone bad before, boy. In fact, lots of routes are going bad. It's the damned war." She sighed. "You want to fill out the paperwork so nobody else has to go looking for something that's not there?"

"No," he said sharply. "I want to know what happened."

She sighed. "Then you want to ask the military."

Jela stood in the alcove where he'd been chained, and tried not to worry.

He was unfortunately not having very much success, and the half-humorous observation that this was no time for an M's selected-for insouciance to fail him hadn't derailed his distress. Nor had the tree's cheerful image of a slim, golden-scaled dragon successfully vanquishing some sort of sharp-pinioned flying nasty with an easy wing-flick and a thoughtful application of teeth.

Cantra was, he reminded himself for the sixth time since submitting to the chain, a fully capable woman. She could handle a roomful of soft scholars. Very likely, she could handle the whole population of Osabei Tower with no help from him, which was, if he was destined to spend the greater part of his time on Landomist chained to walls, just as well.

Not that the chain was so much of a problem—just a short length of light-duty links, not even smart—attached to a staple in the wall at the far end and a mag-lock manacle on the near. A long stretch of his arm would snap the chain, if he were feeling unsubtle; or a little judicious pressure with his free hand would spring the cuff, in case subtlety counted.

Trouble was, either play would lose the battle and, if Rool Tiazan and his lady were to be believed, the war. No, he'd agreed to the role of laborer-class Batcher, just about smart enough to pick up a pot and carry it when given detailed instructions by his irascible high-born mistress. His brawn was entirely subservient to her brain, insured by the inhibitor implants, which obviated the need for restraints, even such toys as presently "bound" him. The question then being why they had bothered to bind him at all.

Mostly what we'll be dealing with is culture and the assumptions that go with not ever having been noplace but Inside and knowing deep down where it matters that Inside ways're best, Cantra's voice whispered from memory. *Lot of what you'll be seeing won't make sense, and won't necessarily be keyed to survival. Inside, the important thing is prestige. If a point can be carried by dying elegantly at the exact proper second, that's the choice your well-brought-up Insider's going to make, hands down, no second thoughts.*

Which led him to understand in the here-and-chained that the binding satisfied some deep-seated cultural necessity; that the chain was, in the larger sense, symbolic. What the symbol might say to the core of your general issue Insider, he couldn't hazard, as he was short on context, but it didn't take anybody much smarter than the Batcher he was supposed to be to figure out that the best thing to do—barring emergencies—was allow the restraints to bind him.

How long does it take to show an equation? he thought, cycling back to worry. What if he'd flubbed the proof? The only check he'd had was Cantra, who—make no mistake!—knew her math. But she'd come fresh to the base assumptions of the decrystallization theory, and while she'd proved herself an awesomely quick study, she hadn't lived the last five years with those numbers weaving possibles and might-bes through her sleep.

He was no stranger to subterfuge, misdirection, and papers created solely in support of fabricated reasons for him to be welcomed into places he'd no business knowing existed. In fact, he'd long suspected that Cantra yos'Phelium had a certain way with a Portmaster's Writ herself. But what he'd witnessed from her—he'd never seen the like. What he'd been privileged to see was an art form, he supposed, and in retrospect held something in common with dancing. The intent to deceive was there; the intent to create a whole new fabric of reality which the audience would find not only believable, but preferable to the actual truth.

She forged papers, working with commendable care. She forged data-tiles—trickier, but nothing he hadn't done himself. As she worked, she talked, maybe to herself, maybe to him, maybe to the long-ago teacher who'd given her the skill.

Now, this way here, this isn't the best way to fabricate an upright citizen. Best way is to pull in some genuine papers and tile that've gone astray from their true and proper owner, then alter what's there as least you can. Doing it like that, the paper tests genuine, the tamper-coding and the hey-theres on the tile are what's expected.

Us, we don't got the contacts and the timing's 'gainst us, so we'll build our own as best we can. We're lucky in that we ain't gonna be long, and all my job is to keep 'em from looking at you—

If he'd still had doubts regarding Cantra's status as an *aelantaza*-trained, they died as he watched her build her bogus docs.

But the docs were the least of what she built.

Now, here's something custom-made for treachery, Pilot Jela. House Chaler, what more or less owns planet Shinto. You've heard of 'em?

He hadn't, and said so, watching her pull down data from sources he didn't dare guess at, her face soft and near dreamy in concentration.

Horticulturists, they are. Build you a custom plant to any specs you want and be happy to lease it to you for as long as you like. Catch being that what they build, they own. Being they have extensive gardens, as you might expect, they also breed their own sort of Batcher to work with the plants. The Batchers being 'work units,' for use on Shinto only, they get away with not registering the details of the design. Also doesn't hurt that they're House Chaler, and it's been ugly what's happened to those who was hot-headed enough to try an' push 'em.

She leaned back in her chair then, stretching 'way back, then relaxed and sent a grin into his face.

So, what you'll be, Pilot Jela, is a for-true Shinto kobold, escorting a genuine Chaler custom build. If anybody wants to sample your DNA, won't do 'em any good, on account Chaler don't file, and I'm guessing the military don't exactly publish the particulars regarding M Series soldiers aloud and abroad.

He'd admitted that, not that he'd had to, and she bent again to her task, cutting a wandering scholar from whole cloth, seamlessly working a kobold and a horticultural specimen into her new reality, stitching with a concentration so absolute that he hadn't dared disturb her to suggest anything so mundane as food or sleep. And when she was at long last done, she'd gotten up from her work table, stretched—looked at him where he hunched over his equations, and held out a slim hand.

Him, he'd looked up at her, trying to read her face, but it was fear he thought he was seeing, and that had to be wrong. There'd never been a woman alive less afraid than Cantra yos'Phelium.

Got time for some pleasure, Pilot? I'm thinking it'll be my last in this lifetime, and I'd like to share it with you.

It was maybe the way she'd said it, or maybe again that thing that couldn't be fear in her misty green eyes—but he'd taken her hand, and they'd shared a grand and pleasurable time. At last, sated with delight, they napped, and though he hadn't slept long, or deeply, when he woke she was gone, locked away and a note at his work place, telling him what he had to do next.

He'd followed orders, stowing what was needed in a backpack, and clearing out anything that showed the length of their stay, or the nature of their work. And sometime shortly after he'd begun to consider disobeying his orders, Errant-Scholar Maelyn tay'Nordif, native of Vetzu, one-time student of Master Liad dea'Syl walked into the workroom there at the lodgings, her cold green eyes brushing over him as if he were of less worth than the chair he sat in.

The shadow of a wing passed over his thoughts, and he pulled himself back to the chained present just as the door to his alcove slid open and the guard stepped forward to free him.

"Pick up the specimen, Jela," Scholar tay'Nordif snapped irritably from the hall. "And follow me."

The garrison was at some distance from the port; he hired a cab and sat quietly in the passenger's compartment, one hand in the pocket of his jacket, fingers curled into a fist. He made himself look out onto the port and passing streets, marveling at the busy ordinariness of the day. Surely, if what he feared were so, there would be some sign here, so close to the area of occurrence? Surely, if the Ringstars, with their populations of millions, had vanished, there would be *something* here among the nearest of their neighbors to mark their passing? Business suspended? Banners of formal mourning shrouding the shop windows?

Surely, whole star systems could not simply cease to be, unnoticed and unmourned?

And yet the trade master had behaved as if such disappearances were commonplace, which might be dealt with by filling out paperwork and issuing alerts

His stomach clenched, and he felt ill. Resolutely, he swallowed, and took deep, even breaths.

The cab left the business district and ascended a ramp. There was a slight lurch as the internal navigator ceded control of the vehicle to the slotway overbrain, then a smooth gathering of speed, sufficient to press him out of his tense lean and back into the seat. The window he had been looking out of opaqued, obliterating the outside world. He sighed and closed his eyes. Deliberately, he brought up the image of his garden at home, the last time he had seen it. The piata tree was in bloom, its multitude of tiny flowers casting a pale blue shadow over the dark, waxy leaves. He breathed in, and the imagined scent of the flowers soothed his roiling belly.

The cab slowed, canted, staggered slightly as control shifted back to the internals, and continued on at a sedate pace. Tor An took one more deep breath, the ghost of flower-spice on his tongue, and opened his eyes.

Window transparent once more, the cab stopped before a great cermacrete wall. Before the wall stood two very large individuals wearing maximum duty 'skins, each holding a weapon at the ready.

"Korak Garrison," the cab stated abruptly in its flat, featureless voice. The door to his right lifted. "Disembark."

Stomach upset anew, Tor An climbed out of the vehicle. The two soldiers were watching him with interest, or so it seemed to his over-wrought nerves. They both had some sort of bright decorations on their faces, which obscured their expressions. He did not, however, imagine the intent eyes nor the fact that the nearer soldier moved her weapon a bit so that its discharge slot pointed directly at him.

He swallowed. "Wait," he said to the cab.

"Disallowed," it answered, the door descending so quickly he had to dance back a step in order not to be struck in the head—and another two in order to avoid being run over as it made a tight turn and sped back toward the slotway.

Behind him, he heard the soldiers laugh. He gritted his teeth, took a deep breath in a not entirely successful attempt to settle his stomach and walked toward them, chin resolutely up, lips pressed together in a firm line.

"Change your mind?" the farther guard asked as he approached. "Little one?"

"I merely wished to be certain that I would have transport back to port," he said politely.

"Not a worry," the nearer guard said, and smiled, displaying extremely white and very pointed teeth.

They were surely attempting to unnerve him—and, truth told, succeeding in some measure. However, he had been the youngest amidst an abundance of elder cousins and siblings, and had furthermore survived the hazings which were the lot of the juniormost pilot; thus he possessed some strategies for dealing with bullies.

Accordingly, he bowed—slightly, to demonstrate that he was a man of worth who was not intimidated by mere large persons, no matter how obviously armed—and sent a grave look into the nearer soldier's face.

The artwork—an eight-pointed star and a ship on the right cheek; a vertical series of four blue stripes on the left—was disconcerting, but he concentrated his attention and met her eyes, ignoring her amusement.

"My name is Tor An yos'Galan of Alkia Trade Clan, out of the Ringstars," he said steadily. "Pray announce me to your commander. I bear information of some value."

The soldier was unimpressed. She moved her shoulders, and the discharge slot described a casual arc across his chest. He ignored the weapon and kept his eyes on hers, waiting for his answer.

"What kind of information?" she asked at last, grudgingly.

"I believe it would be best for me to impart it directly to the commander," Tor An said. "Or to the commander's designated aide. If you are that person…" He let the sentence trail off delicately.

The farther guard snorted. The other frowned.

"We don't pass people to the commander just so they can chat," she said sternly. "Tell us what you want. If we think you've got a case, we'll pass you. Otherwise, you can start walking back to port."

He had not wished—And yet, she had a point, this large, rude person with her painted face. Did the doorman at home allow every self-claimed investor access to Alkia's Voice?

He bowed again, even more slightly than previously.

"I have information that the Ringstars are—" his voice cracked. He cleared his throat and began again. "I have information that the Ringstars are—missing. A ship sent to known coordinates within the system falls from transition and reports that the target is unavailable."

The guard's mouth tightened, and she sent a quick over-shoulder glance at her mate.

"Old news," he said, his voice conveying vast boredom.

"Right," the nearer guard answered after a moment. She sighed and turned back to Tor An.

"We are aware of the situation, little one. Get out of here."

For a moment he simply stood, the words not quite scanning—and then her meaning hit and he gasped, spine tingling with outrage.

"You *know* that the Ringstars are missing?" he asked, voice rising out of the tone of calm reason most appropriate for a trader.

The nearer guard frowned. "That's right," she said, and shifted her weapon meaningfully.

He ignored the hint. "What are you doing about it?" he demanded.

The farther guard barked—or perhaps it was laughter.

"Not doing anything about it," the nearer guard said. "What do you expect us to do about it? It's not like the Ringstars are the first system that's gone missing in this war." She raised her weapon this time, and again displayed her sharpened teeth—not at all a smile. "Get out of here, little one. Go back to port, get drunk, get laid. When you wake up sober, hire yourself out and get on with your life."

But Tor An, awash in disbelief, had stopped listening. He stared up into her face. "Other star systems have gone missing?" he repeated. "That's impossible."

"You're the one who came here with information that your precious Ringstars are gone," she snapped. "If it can happen once, it can happen twice. Or don't they teach you civilians stats and probability?"

He took a step forward, hands fisted at his side. "*What are you doing about it?*" he shouted. "You're supposed to protect us! If whole star systems are going away, *where are they going*? And why aren't you stopping—"

"Shut up, you fool!" the nearer guard snarled, but the warning—if it were meant as anything so kindly—was too late.

A section of the wall behind her parted, and a third tall soldier stepped through.

The two guards stiffened, their weapons now definitively trained on Tor An, who was staring at the newcomer.

He, too, displayed various signs and sigils on his face—more than either of the guards, those on the right cheek so numerous that they overlapped each other. Over his maximum duty 'skins he wore a vest hung about with many ribbons, and the belt around his waist supported both a beam pistol and a long ceramic blade.

"Captain," the nearer soldier said respectfully.

"Corporal," the newcomer responded coldly. His face was turned to Tor An, the light brown eyes startling among the riot of color. "What seems to be the problem?"

"No problem, sir," the corporal said. Tor An gasped.

"Very true," he said and was mortified to hear that his voice was shaking. "You have made it quite clear that the fact of entire star systems vanishing is no concern of yours." He took a breath, and inclined his head toward the captain. "This officer, however—"

The officer's cold eyes considered him. If his face bore any expression at all beneath the artwork, it was more than Tor An could do to read it.

"You have information," the captain said, his hard voice free of both inflection and courtesy, "regarding a missing star system."

"Sir, I do." He moved a hand to indicate the two guards. "I had requested admission to the presence of the base commander or an approved aide, and was told that news of the vanishing of the Ringstars preceded me. Furthermore, I am told that the event is of no interest to this garrison. Such events are apparently become quite commonplace."

"More so," said the captain, "here on the frontier. I heard you asking the corporal what the military is doing about these disappearances. The corporal is not empowered to answer that question. I, however, am." He inclined from the waist in a small, ironic bow.

"What we are doing is precisely nothing. We are under orders to withdraw. This garrison will be empty within the next thirty days, Common Calendar, and all the rest of the garrisons in this sector of the frontier."

Tor An stared at him, suddenly very cold.

"Does this," the captain asked, still in that inflectionless, discourteous tone, "answer your question?"

Tor An was abruptly weary, his thoughts spinning. Clearly he would get no satisfaction here. Best to return to the port, to his ship, and work out his next best move.

So thinking, he bowed, low enough to convey respect for the man's rank, and cleared his throat.

"My question is answered," he said, hoarsely. "I thank you."

"Good," the officer said. He turned his head and addressed the two guards.

"Shoot him."

SIX

Osabei Tower
Landomist

THE PLACE WAS a warren, Jela thought as he followed Errant-Scholar—now, he supposed, Seated Scholar—tay'Nordif through twisty halls so narrow that he had to proceed at a sort of half-cant, in order that his shoulders not rub the walls, and with knees slightly bent, so as not to brush the top of the tree against the ceiling. The logistics of trying to secure such an anthill were enough to give a tactician permanent nightmares.

Lucky for them, they didn't have to worry about securing the premises, just lifting some files and making an orderly retreat. He expected to have a line of withdrawal mapped out and secured well before it was needed. But his first order of business was keeping up with the Scholar and her guide, who moved ahead at a rapid walk without ever once looking back.

That guide, now: a soft man of about Can—Scholar tay'Nordif's height, with a plentitude of shiny brown hair rippling down past his shoulders, his skin was the pure true gold by which the citizens Inside judged a man's worth and value. His gaze had passed over Jela as if he were invisible, though the tree took his interest.

"Now, this is something we seldom see!" he'd exclaimed. "Have you brought us a bit of the frontier, Scholar?"

"Not at all! Not at all!" Scholar tay'Nordif extended a reverent hand and touched a leaf. "Yon specimen hails from fair Shinto, a token of regard given me by none other than Horticultural Master Panthera vas'Chaler. A most gracious lady, Scholar; I esteem her greatly. Her many kindnesses—of which the gift of a green plant to cheer me in my scholarly closet is but the most recent—her kindness is without boundary. Truly, I am at her feet."

"She sounds a most gracious and generous lady," the second scholar said seriously. "You are fortunate in her patronage."

"*Most* fortunate in her patronage," Scholar tay'Nordif reiterated worshipfully. "I challenge anyone to produce a patron more thoughtful of one's comfort, or more understanding of the demands of one's work."

"Indeed?" The other scholar turned from his study of the tree, and moved along the hall, walking flat, and with his hands tucked into his sash—the walk of a man used to consistent gravity, and hallways that maintained their orientation. "This way, if you will, Scholar."

"Follow me, Jela," Scholar tay'Nordif had snapped, and that was the last word or attention that either had squandered on him.

They were well ahead of him now, out of sight around a bend in the hall, though he could hear Scholar tay'Nordif's voice clearly enough, extolling the seemingly limitless virtues attached to Master vas'Chaler.

"Will you believe me, Scholar tay'Welford," she was saying, "when I tell you that nothing would do but that my patron give me apartments in her own home, and a servant whose sole duty it was to attend to my comfort and bring in meals so that on those occasions when I became immersed in my work, I should not be obliged to break my concentration in a descent to the mundane…"

It certainly sounded like a soft post, Jela thought, ducking through an arch that was even thinner than the hallway—and damned lucky he was to skin through with the pack on his back, and without breaking any branches off the tree—if it had been in the least part true.

The hall took a jig to the left, to the right, and opened suddenly into a high octagonal shaped lobby. The white light which had been an uncomfortable glare in the tight halls was easier to take here, and Jela breathed a very private sigh of relief as he stepped out onto the dark tile floor. The room extended upward for several stories; a surreptitious glance, under the guise of making sure that the "specimen" could now be held higher without endangering it, found balconies and walkways overhead, but no clear means of attaining them.

From the center of the floor rose a ceramic rectangle as high as Scholar tay'Nordif's shoulder, rich in mosaic-work—

No, thought Jela, looking more closely. Not mosaic. Memory modules, set into the conductive material of the rectangle, creating a single computational device—but to what end?

Scholar tay'Nordif bent in close study of the comp then straightened and stared upward, spinning slowly—and unsteadily—on a boot heel.

"I theorize," she said, yet craning upward, "that yon device is the engine by which the stairways are driven." She described an additional quarter-circle and lowered her gaze to Scholar tay'Welford, who stood yet with his hands tucked in his sash, an expression of interested amusement on his round, pleasant face.

"The question remaining," Scholar tay'Nordif continued, on a rising inflection, "is how the device is induced to call the proper stairway."

Scholar tay'Welford inclined slightly from the waist. "If you will allow me, Scholar, I believe that I may offer you the key to this puzzle."

"By all means, Scholar! Produce this key, I beg you!"

He smiled, and slowly—even, Jela thought, teasingly—withdrew his right hand from its comfortable tuck in his sash, turned his palm up, and opened his fingers.

Across his palm lay a ceramic lozenge, pale violet in color; insubstantial as a shadow.

"Behold," he said, "the key."

"Ah." Scholar tay'Nordif leaned to inspect it, her hands clasped behind her back. She glanced up at the other scholar. "May I?"

"By all means."

She picked the thing up delicately with the very tips of her fingers, and subjected it to close study before folding it into her palm and turning her attention to the comp.

"I fear me," she said after a moment, "that I have been given but half the key."

"Is it so?" The other scholar stepped closer to her side. Jela felt himself stiffen; deliberately relaxed. "Surely, you have seen something like, in your travels along the frontier?"

"Alas, I have not," Scholar tay'Nordif replied, sending a sideways glance into the other's face. "Is this a Test, sir?"

It seemed to Jela as if the other scholar intended to answer in the affirmative, and amended his course at the last instant.

"Certainly not!" he said lightly. "We are not so uncivilized as to present a Test before even one has shared the evening meal with colleagues." He put his hand atop the rectangle, palm down. "Place your key just here, Scholar; the device will read the imbedded data and fetch down the proper stair."

Scholar tay'Nordif stepped forward, and placed the lozenge flat on top the comp. For a moment, nothing happened, then Jela noticed that the conductive material was glowing a soft rose color, and that various of the embedded modules were also beginning to shine. Air moved and he looked up as one of the high walkways swung out from its fellows, canted—and unfolded downward in deliberate sections until the leading edge touched the floor at the base of the wall.

"I am instructed," said Scholar tay'Nordif and bowed.

"A small secret, I assure you," the other said with a smile. He stepped back and swept an arm toward the waiting walkway. "Please, Scholar, mount and ascend! The stair will take you to the correct floor, and the key will guide you to the correct door. I will look for you at the common meal—Ah, and another hint, out of kindness for one who comes into my own Department: It is not done to be late to the common meal."

So saying, he swept around and went on his way, but not before he had sent a measuring look straight into Jela's face. He produced his very best stupid stare, and wasn't especially pleased to see the Scholar smile before passing on.

"Jela, come here!" Scholar tay'Nordif snapped, and he stepped onto the ramp behind her as it began rapidly to rise.

Both of his hands being occupied with holding the tree, he braced his legs wide and sent a look down to the receding lobby, but there was nothing to see other than the shiny floor stretching away like some dark sea to break against eight white walls in which eight identical archways were centered.

The ramp turned, folding back up into the high ceiling. They passed one floor, moving so swiftly that all Jela retained was an impression of a long hallway lined with yellow doors. The ramp turned again, its far end, just behind Jela's boot heels, giving off to empty air and a long fall to the dark floor below. The leading edge—ahead of the scholar's position—snapped into a slot in the floor of the walkway.

She moved forward briskly, setting her feet firmly against the floor, her tabard billowing slightly.

The tree offered an image of the slender golden-scaled dragon, wings full of wind, gliding effortlessly down the sheer side of a cliff.

Jela refrained from answering. He followed her off the bridge and to the left, down a hall lined on both sides with identical orange doors, then again to the left—and abruptly halted to avoid walking on her, the tree's branches snapping over his head.

She slid the shadowy tile into a slot in the surface of the door; there was a loud *snick* as it opened, lights coming up in the room beyond as it did.

The quarters were featureless and functional: smooth white walls, smooth white floor; a basic galley and sanitary facilities to the right, work space, screen and a convertible chair to the left. In the absence of orders, and out of respect for the three spy-eyes that were too easy to spot, Jela stood just inside the door, cradling the tree's pot in arms that were beginning to ache. Scholar tay'Nordif strolled into the room, giving it a casual, bored inspection. Whether she saw the spy-eyes—which the woman she had been would never have missed—he couldn't say. She stepped to the chair and tapped the control on the arm; it shifted, stretching out to form a cot. Another tap, and it returned to its chair configuration.

She walked over to the worktable, and touched the corner of the dark screen. The darkness swirled into gray, the gray into white. Blue words and images floated upward through the whiteness—a timetable, Jela saw, from his vantage near the door, and a map. The scholar raised her head to consult the time displayed on the smooth wall over the screen, and uttered a sharp curse.

"Jela!" she said sharply. "Put the specimen down *gently* and bring me my pack. Quickly!"

Gently, and with considerable relief, he eased the pot to the floor. That done, he skinned the pack off his back, remembering to work slow and stupid for the benefit of those spy-eyes, opened it, and had the scholar's case out. Moving heavily, he went across the room to where his mistress was bent again over the computer—memorizing the map, he hoped—and stood patiently holding the pack out across his two palms, his eyes aimed at the floor.

She spun away from the screen, grabbed the pack and took it to the table, unsealing it hastily and snatching out a tablet, the squat book with scarred covers that she kept always to hand, her extra tabard, a data-case. Muttering under her breath, she reached back into the bag and brought out a second case, but she fumbled in her haste, and it slid from her fingers onto the floor, data-tiles skittering noisily across the smooth floor.

Another curse, this one more pungent than the first, and the scholar was on her knees, scrabbling along the floor, sweeping the tiles in toward her. Body bent protectively over the case, she began to slot them quickly—sent a distracted glance over her shoulder at the clock and abruptly rose.

"Clean up that mess!" she snapped at him. "Then you may rest."

He waited 'til the door had closed and locked behind her before allowing himself a single luxuriously loud sigh, the whine of the jamming device irritating his super-sharp ears. Well, there was one way to put an end to *that* small discomfort, he thought. Rolling his shoulders, he turned his attention to locating the concealed spy-eyes.

Distant yet in time and space, the Iloheen sensed them as they phased. Rool Tiazan plucked the ley lines the way a mortal man might idly pluck at the strings of a lute he was too indolent to truly play. The Iloheen must believe them wary, fearful and furtive, all of their skill bent upon concealment, all of their intelligence focused upon escape. In this they were assisted by the natural order: the Iloheen were fell and awful, fearsome beings from which it were madness to do other than cover oneself and flee.

The Seon Veyestra dominant had known Rool; even as she had dissolved, she had exerted her will to etch his identity into the ether.

It was true that no *dramliza* fell but that the Iloheen saw. Eventually. But that last scream against annihilation, elucidating the tainted genetic code of an escaped slave—that had been heard instantly.

The Iloheen was nearer now to where they huddled, as small and as dim as was prudent, hidden within a dense weaving of ley lines. Did they make themselves as insignificant as they might, the shimmer of energies from the lines would indeed have concealed them. For this game, however—

Static disturbed the placid flowing of the lines, and in that place where there was neither hot nor cold, a chill wind disturbed the soul.

We must not, the lady's thought whispered behind the shields that protected them. *We must seem neither too easy nor too bold.*

If we are then to seem craven, Rool Tiazan's thought replied. *Our moment approaches.*

Have you identified a path? she asked, as the wind grew stronger and the disruptive energies of the Iloheen drew sparks of probability off the lines.

I have.

Remove us, she directed.

Rool teased his chosen line from the sparkling tangle all about them, exerted his will, and took them elsewhere.

In the nexus of probability they had hidden within, the ley lines crackled and spat, sparks freezing against the fabric of time. The wind blew—cold, colder—

And died.

There had been five snoops altogether, which, Jela thought as he sealed the last hack and activated it, seemed excessive for a newly Seated scholar. On the other hand, maybe they were in the high-rent district.

Hacks online, he hunkered down by the quick-built jammer and began, carefully, to dismantle it, making sure as he slotted the tiles into the case that those from which the little device had been created were well-mixed among the others. It would be bad if a couple started associating without supervision, so to speak, and built up a wild interference field.

His best estimation was that the hacks would hold until sometime after he, Cantra, the tree, and Liad dea'Syl's equations were gone from Osabei Tower. It bothered him that they'd likely have to be left in place until whoever had the snoops under their charge figured the game out and came to collect them; he liked to be tidy in his ops. Well, maybe a chance to remove or destroy them would come along.

In the meantime, he was cautiously proud of his handiwork. Since they couldn't know the details of where they'd settle, he had to build the detail in on-site—and quick, before someone noticed the feeds coming from the new scholar's quarters were off. Fortunately, he'd been able to rough in the basics beforehand; adding the detail level had gone quick. Now, whoever was so interested in the doings of a new-arrived scholar would be fed edited versions of real events. Right now, for instance, they should be receiving a nice picture from five different angles of him slumped on the floor next to the "specimen," napping in the absence of orders.

Data tiles slotted all nice and neat, Jela straightened and carried the case over to the worktable. His gear was out and assembled, and he'd be wanting to get to work pretty soon.

He turned his head, considering the convertible chair. It didn't look precisely robust. There'd been a stool shoved under the counter in the galley, he remembered, and he went back across the room to fetch it, moving light and smooth.

As he passed the tree, he was suddenly aware of the minty aroma of a fresh seed pod. He paused, peering into the branches. Sure enough, one of several emerging pods had ripened, the branch on which it grew bending a little under its mature weight. The aroma grew more noticeable. Jela's mouth watered, and the branch bent a little more, inviting him to take the pod.

His fingers twitched, his mouth watered; he hesitated.

"I've been getting a lot of these lately," he said to the tree. "Don't stint yourself for me."

An image formed inside his head: a seed pod sitting on an outcropping of grey rock, its rind broken, black, and useless.

"Better a snack for a soldier than wasted altogether, eh? Well—" He extended a hand, and the pod dropped neatly into his broad palm. "Thank you," he whispered. It smelled so good, he ate it right then, before fetching the stool and carrying it over to the worktable.

Comfortably seated, he cracked his knuckles, loudly, squared his screen off, and took a moment to consider, fingers poised over the keys.

He hadn't exactly discussed this phase of the operations with Cantra. He'd intended to, so they could coordinate. That had been before the conversation that set his hair on end, then and now.

You know how the aelantaza operate, Pilot Jela? Her voice had been light, amused, like she was on the edge of telling some easy joke between comrades.

He'd admitted to ignorance of the topic, which was true enough, conjecture not counting as fact, and she'd smiled a little and settled back in her chair to recount the tale.

What aelantaza do, see, is convince everybody around that the aelantaza is exactly and beyond question who and what they say they are. The way of it's simple to say—they convince other people because they're convinced themselves. The way of doing it—that's not so simple. Drugs're a part of it—drugs the formulae of which the Directors hold more dear than their lives.

The other part of it, that's mind-games—meditation, play acting, symbolism. I'd tell it all out for you, but it'd sound like so much rubbish to the sensible, solid man I know you to be—and besides, we're on a tight schedule. Just let's leave it that those mind-games, they're powerful. Back when I was in school, the teachers were pleased to impress on me that it was the mental preparation, not the drugs, that drew the line between a successful mission and a wipe. That an aelantaza who had prepared mentally but had the drug withheld, that aelantaza had a better—I'm saying, Pilot, a much better—chance of completing her mission successfully than her brother who'd taken the drug without preparing his mind. So you see the odds're in our favor.

She'd given him a nod then, and a straight, hard look, the misty green eyes as serious as the business edge of a battle blade.

What they call it—that mental preparation that's so important to preserving our good numbers—they call it the Little Death, and that's as close to truth as anything you'll ever have out of Tanjalyre Institute or any aelantaza you might meet. Because the point and purpose of all those mind-games is to strip out—as near as can be without losing training—one personality and lay in a different. The prelim drug makes the work easier by softening up the barriers between me and not-me. The finishing drug, that sets new-me a little tighter, so there's less likely to be seepage from what's left of old-me—less opportunity for mistakes on-job, or for a bobble that might crack the belief that the aelantaza is and always has been exactly who she is right now.

He'd opened his mouth then, though he couldn't recall what it was he'd intended to say. Cantra'd held up a slender hand.

Hear me out, she said, and he could've thought that the shine in her eyes was tears. *Just hear me out.*

He'd settled back, fingers moving in the sign for *go on.*

Right. She sat, head bent, then her chin came up and she shook her hair back out of her face.

While the odds favor a prepared mind, she said, her mouth twisting a little in what he thought she might have meant for a smile, *we have to recollect that I'm inexperienced, and plan for to not have any bobbles. So, what I'll ask of you, Pilot Jela, is assistance. You'll know the old-me—what's left—that's beneath the new. Don't, as you wish for us to carry the day and perform the kind lady's bidding—don't for a heartbeat acknowledge that ghost. The one who holds the ghost at her heart—she's the one you'll be dealing with. Call her only by the name she tells you. Don't share out any of your close-held secrets with her. Don't expect her to act or think or feel in any way like the pilot you have here before you would do. Trust—and this is going to be hard, Pilot, I know—trust that, despite all, she'll move you to the goal we've set out and decided between us. Will you give me your word on that, Pilot?*

Well, he'd given his word, fool that he was. Soldier that he was.

She'd smiled then, and stood, stretched her slender hand out to him, and asked him for comfort and ease.

He'd given that, too, and the memory of their sharing was one of his better ones. So much so that he felt a bit wistful that it hadn't happened earlier in his life, so he could have held the memory longer.

When Scholar tay'Nordif had stalked into his life, high-handed and disdainful, he had throttled his horror and kept his word to his pilot. He had, he prided himself, never faltered, acting the part of the laborer, carrying the tree and the scholar's burdens.

And Cantra—or whatever there was left of Cantra in the woman who believed herself to be Maelyn tay'Nordif—she had done her part as well, or better. He doubted—yes, he'd doubted—that she'd be able to manage the jammer, and found himself squeamish about imagining the mental gymnastics involved in getting it done, but she'd done it, as clean and as fumble-free as any could have wanted.

He waggled his fingers over the keyboard, bringing his attention forcefully back to the present and his plan of attack. First, a gentle feeling-out of the security systems protecting the Tower's various brains, and building a map of hierarchies and interconnections.

Enough to keep you busy for an hour or two while the scholar has herself a nice meal with her troop, he told himself and grinned.

After he had snooped out security, he'd be in place to build himself some spies, and after he had his maps, he could start the real job of collecting the equations that would save life as it was from the enemy of everything.

Ala Bin tay'Welford claimed a glass, took up his usual position near the sours table, and surveyed the room. All about, scholars were clustered in their usual knots of allies and associates, avidly engaged in Osabei Tower's favorite pastime: the gaining of advantage over one's colleagues.

He turned his attention to the offerings on the table—a much more interesting prospect—debating with himself the relative merits of the berries vinaigrette and the pickled *greshom* wings. Impossible to be neat with the berries, and one disliked to stain one's robes. The wings, on the other hand—he was most fond of pickled *greshom* wings, which were a delicacy of his home province—the wings were possessed on two days out of four of a certain unappealing graininess. He had constructed an algorithm to predict the instances of substandard wings and, according to those calculations, this evening's would be of the unfortunate variety. He sighed, fingers poised over the plate. He might, he supposed, appease his palate with a sour cookie or—

"So," Leman chi'Farlo's soft, malicious voice fell on his ear, "tay'Azberg will have it that Interdimensional Statistics has Seated a scholar of rare virtue."

He chose a cookie, taking care with it, and straightened. Seeing she had his attention, chi'Farlo inclined her head, the data tiles woven into her numerous yellow braids clicking gently against each other.

"A scholar possessed of an—interesting intellect, I should say," he answered. "To offer Osabei such a coin in trade for a chair."

chi'Farlo raised her glass so that her mouth was hidden. "tay'Azberg allows us to know that the scholar's coin would disprove all the work upon which our department's master bases his eminence," she murmured.

"Aye," he said unconcernedly. "It would seem to do just that." He bit into the cookie, chewed meditatively and sighed. Appalling.

"But this is dreadful!" she insisted. "If the Governors should cut the department's budget—" chi'Farlo was of an excitable temperament. She stood next junior to him in departmental rank, and he needed her calm and focused.

"Peace, peace," he murmured, finishing off the cookie and taking a liberal swallow of wine to cleanse the taste from his mouth.

She laughed sharply. "You may show a calm face to catastrophe, pure scholar that you are, but for those of us who hold hope of seeing the department attain its proper place..."

"The Governors have not cut our budget," he pointed out, "nor even have they called good Scholar tay'Nordif to stand before them and explain herself, her work, or her proofs. It is possible that they will not do so," he continued, though in fact he considered it very likely that the Governors would take a decided interest in Scholar tay'Nordif and her proof. Saying so to chi'Farlo, however, would not serve in the cause of calming her.

He glanced about the room, finding tay'Palin near the door, speaking with dea'San and vel'Anbrek. The time displayed on the wall beyond that small cluster of worthy scholars was perilously close to the moment at which the door would be sealed, and all those left on the wrong side required to report first thing the Truth Bell rang tomorrow to the office of their department head for discipline.

"Our new sister in art is late," chi'Farlo murmured spitefully.

"Not yet," he answered, continuing his scan of the room—but no, Scholar tay'Nordif had not arrived when his attention was elsewhere. Pity, that. He brought his gaze to chi'Farlo's stern, pale face. A taint of Outblood in the line, he'd always thought. Pity, that.

"tay'Palin looks tired, poor fellow," he said, raising his glass and cocking an eyebrow. chi'Farlo glanced over at the small cluster of scholars, and sighed.

"He did not look tired this morning," she said, "when he once again successfully defended his work."

"Indeed he did not," tay'Welford said patiently. "Though I think we can agree that it was a spirited discussion. It is unfortunate that these challenges come so closely of late. If the scholar but had a few days to rest— He is formidable in defense of his work, but greatly wearied by these continual demands to prove himself. And then to have taken a wound—"

"A wound?" chi'Farlo scoffed. "I saw no breach of his defenses this morning."

"Nor did I, during the proving," tay'Welford said. "He is canny, and hid the weakness. I only know of it because I came upon him in his office while he was binding the gash." He met chi'Farlo's eyes squarely. "High on his dominant arm. The sleeve of his casement would have hidden it."

"I see." chi'Farlo sipped her wine, face soft in revery. "Tomorrow perhaps our good department head will find the rest he deserves."

"Perhaps," tay'Welford murmured. "Indeed, it is possible. For surely—"

A movement across the room claimed his attention, which was certainly the door being drawn to—but stay! According to the clock, they were still some seconds short of closure, and, indeed, it was not the door but Scholar tay'Nordif, of course still wearing her Wanderer's garb, the black sash of a Seated Scholar accentuating her slim waist.

"*That* is our new sister?" chi'Farlo's voice was slightly edged, and tay'Welford hid a smile, remembering that his junior cared as much—if not more—for her standing as the department's Beauty as for her scholarship. "She is something bedraggled, is she not?"

"She has just come from the frontier," he said mildly and then, because he could not resist teasing her, just a little—"Doubtless, she will be very well indeed, once she is properly robed, and rested from her travels."

chi'Farlo sniffed, and raised her glass. tay'Welford pressed his lips into a straight line as Scholar tay'Nordif made her way to the group of which tay'Palin stood a member and bowed deeply, fingertips touching forehead, a model of modest courtesy. tay'Palin spoke, and she straightened. tay'Welford understood from the gestures following that she was being made known to dea'San and vel'Anbrek.

Across the room, the door closed, the bar falling with an audible clang. Scholar tay'Nordif was seen to start and turn her head sharply to track the sound, much to vel'Anbrek's delight.

"She will be sitting with tay'Palin at her first meal," chi'Farlo muttered irritably. "Really, she puts herself high!"

"Does she?" tay'Welford smiled, and moved forward, slipping a hand beneath her elbow to bear her along with him. "Then let us also put ourselves high."

"To what end?" she asked, keeping pace nonetheless.

"I think our new sister might have some interesting things to tell us of the frontier," he said.

"Oh, the frontier!" she began pettishly, and had the good sense to swallow the rest of what she might have said as they joined the group around tay'Palin.

"Ah, there you are, tay'Welford!" vel'Anbrek cried. "I began to believe you would miss an opportunity."

Unpleasant old man. It was a wonder, tay'Welford thought, that no one had challenged him simply to rid the community of a source of on-going irritation. But there, the old horror had close ties to the Governors, which was doubtless the secret to his longevity.

"I hope," tay'Welford said evenly, "that I never miss an opportunity to be informed."

"And chi'Farlo had nothing to say to you, eh?" vel'Anbrek laughed loudly at his own small witticism.

"So," said Scholar dea'San to Maelyn tay'Nordif, her hard voice easily heard over her compatriot's noise, "you are Liad's student, are you? I wonder—"

"She is wearing her truth-blade," chi'Farlo interrupted.

"Well, of course she's wearing her truth-blade," returned vel'Anbrek, interrupting in his turn, his voice high and querulous. "She doesn't look a fool to me, does she to you, Scholar?"

"I'm sure that I couldn't—"

"And with all the rest of Liad's students being killed dead as they have—"

"Gor Ton," snapped Scholar dea'San, "you exaggerate. Not all of Liad's—"

vel'Anbrek waved an unsteady hand, missing Scholar tay'Palin's glass by the width of a whisker. "All the important ones," he said airily. "And I recall young tay'Palin here telling us the scholar is new-come from the frontier. I remember sleeping with my truth-blade during the years of *my* wandering. Did you not do the same, Elvred?"

"Certainly not! I hope that I never once allowed the traditions of civilization to be overcast by—"

"Bah!" the old man said decisively.

"The meat of the matter, I believe," said tay'Palin, calmly over-riding both, "is that truth-blades are put aside with the ringing of the Mercy Bell. They are not worn at the common meal, Scholar tay'Nordif."

The scholar abased herself immediately, holding the bow.

"Forgive me, Scholars," she said humbly. "I am ignorant of custom."

"Indeed," Scholar tay'Palin said dryly. "I had trusted that Scholar tay'Welford would hint you toward the accepted mode. It is hardly like him to be so neglectful of one who comes into our own department."

Scholar tay'Nordif straightened slowly, and sent a hard look into tay'Welford's face. He smiled at her and raised his glass, waiting.

"The scholar was kind enough to warn me to be on time for the gather, sir," she said to tay'Palin. "I take him for a man who does not offer advice freely, and I am well-pleased not to stand in his debt."

A certain boldness to that reply, thought tay'Welford approvingly. It did not do for a scholar to be timid.

"You are gracious to impute such noble motives to Scholar tay'Welford," dea'San murmured. "However, the more likely case is that he simply forgot."

"Doubtless, doubtless! Our esteemed tay'Welford can be flutter-witted," Scholar vel'Anbrek said. "Mind on higher things." He laughed, so pleased with his sally that he repeated it. "Higher things! Hah!" He raised his glass, found it empty, and lifted it, still cackling.

A servitor detached itself from an animated knot of scholars some steps deeper into the room and came to the old man's side. It wore an extremely brief tunic, and a half-mask of smart-strands, and stood very straight in order to keep the tray precisely balanced on its sleek head.

vel'Anbrek dropped his empty carelessly on the tray, and selected a full glass. Those others of their group who were in need likewise served themselves, including Scholar tay'Nordif. tay'Welford stood holding his new glass, idly watching as she turned her head deliberately to the right, staring hard down room; thence to the left, then again over each shoulder, and finally returned her gaze to the elder scholar.

"Pardon me, sir," she said courteously, "but I had not heard that all of Master Liad's students had been—killed, did you say? It seems remarkable to me."

"Nonetheless—" It was dea'San who answered. "And allowing for exaggeration, it does appear that the greater portion of Liad's students have met their mortality before the fruits of their work were harvested. *Most* annoying in terms of advancing the discipline."

"It must certainly be vexatious," Scholar tay'Nordif agreed, with no discernible irony. "And yet, ma'am, the words of the great philosopher bin'Arli spring to mind: *Adversity breeds greatness.* Perhaps this trying circumstance will bring forth even greater and more illustrious work from those who are, I believe, the core and the keepers of our discipline."

"How," tay'Welford asked delicately into the unsettled silence that followed this, "do you find things on the frontier, Scholar tay'Nordif? We are so retired here, that—were it not for a certain thinness of scholars come to sue for a chair—we should scarcely have heard that there was a war at all, much less the state of the conflict."

Green eyes considered him with disconcerting straightness.

"Surely you don't think I sought out the war zones, Scholar? I assure you that I studied the alerts closely and kept myself as far as possible from active conflict."

"Certainly what anyone of sense might—" chi'Farlo began, and stopped as Scholar tay'Nordif once again executed her peculiar stare into all corners of the room.

"Pardon me, Scholar, but what do you?" dea'San inquired sharply. "You may be new-come from the frontier, but that hardly gives you license to be rude."

Maelyn tay'Nordif blinked at her, clearly at a loss. "I beg your pardon, Scholar? In what way was I rude?"

dea'San bristled. "Scholar chi'Farlo was speaking to you, and you simply turned your head in that *peculiar* manner and ignored her! I would call that rude, but perhaps on the frontier—"

"On the frontier, we call such things not rude, but survival skills," Scholar tay'Nordif interrupted. "You will excuse me, Scholar, if I suppose that it has been some time since you were last on the frontier. You may not recall the extraordinary and constant vigilance required merely to remain alive. When there is the added imperative of one's work, strategies must be fashioned and practiced without fail. I therefore have trained myself to survey my surroundings thoroughly every three hundredth heartbeat and have practiced the technique so faithfully that I may now perform this function without breaking the concentration necessary for my work."

There was a small silence, before chi'Farlo said, with admirable restraint, "But we are not at the frontier, Scholar tay'Nordif. We are in-hall and safe among our colleagues."

"Doubtless that is true," tay'Nordif replied. "And doubtless in time I shall craft another technique which will accommodate conditions here. Do you not use such techniques to clear your mind so that you may become immersed in your work, Scholar?"

chi'Farlo, whose ambition might in fairness be said to outstrip her art by a factor of twelve, merely murmured, "Of course," and raised her glass. It was well, thought tay'Welford, that Scholar tay'Nordif was newly seated and thus too inconsequential for chi'Farlo to challenge.

"If you will allow one who has been Seated for many years advise you, Scholar tay'Nordif?" dea'San said.

"Indeed, Scholar, I am grateful for any assistance," the other replied, and performed her peculiar stare about the room.

dea'San sighed. "I think you will find, Scholar," she said loudly, "that your best technique here in the heart of our discipline is to simply immerse yourself in your work, trusting to the safeguards of our Tower and the goodwill of your colleagues."

Now here, thought tay'Welford, sipping his wine, was a clear equation for disaster. He wondered whether their new sister would be fool enough to employ it.

The bell rang then, calling them to dinner. He accepted dea'San's arm, chi'Farlo having of course chosen tay'Palin as her meal-mate. That left vel'Anbrek for tay'Nordif, and it must be said that she offered her arm with good grace. So they proceeded to the table in order and took their seats, Scholar tay'Nordif displaying vigilance as they did so.

He finished wrapping the wound, the awkward job made more difficult by the trembling of his icy fingers.

Shot! He'd been shot, well and truly burned, though there was no pain. The lack of pain worried him, distantly. He thought he might be in shock. Certainly, he had cause.

And yet it could have been worse. Much worse. The sound of the soldiers' laughter still echoed in his ears, his skin twitched from the heat of the bolts that had come close—close. He'd run—run until he thought his heart would burst and still he heard them laughing, firing but not pursuing.

He was, he supposed, too inconsequential to pursue. It had been a game to the big soldiers—a diversion, nothing more. And if he had died for their fun—well, and what was one less civilian, who should have vanished, anyway, along with his clan and the entirety of the Ringstars?

He was so cold.

One-handed, he crammed the ruined jacket and shirt into the 'fresher then pawed a blanket from the cupboard and got it 'round his shoulders.

Staggering slightly, he entered the tower, and half-fell into the pilot's chair, squinting against the blare of light from the board. One light in particular caught his attention. He angled the chair so that he might reach the board with his good hand, and touched the access button.

"*Light Wing*," he said, and was pleased to hear that his voice was steady.

"Yard Authority," the response came—a crisp, no-nonsense voice that reminded him of Fraea. "Request for amended departure approved. Stand by to receive clearance."

His fingers moved of themselves, opening the buffer. Somewhere on the board a light flicked from blue to orange, then back to blue as a chime sounded. These things, he knew, were usual and proper and indicated that the ship was functioning as it should.

Screens came on line. He squinted at the detail provided, and again his fingers moved, waking the engines, feeding coordinates to the nav-brain, locking a flight schedule. Distantly, he thought that perhaps a man who had been shot—a man who was so cold—perhaps that man should not be filing a flight plan and preparing to lift ship. It was a very distant thought, however, and he had necessary tasks to accomplish. He must depart Korak now. He must—The thought faded, but no matter—his fingers knew. A pilot trusted his fingers, or he trusted nothing, Uncle Sae Zar had used to say, and if ever there had been a pilot to behold, Sae Zar—

Something beeped, lights flashed, the forward screens displayed orbital trajectories, energy states, timetables. His fingers moved a last time and the ship gathered itself, surging upward, the force of lift pressing him back into the chair. Distantly, he noted that he was not strapped in, but he couldn't reach the engage with his good arm, so he left the straps off, as the pressure built comfortingly. The ship—old *Light Wing* had lifted from more worlds than he had years in his life. She knew what to do, did *Light Wing*. He left her to it, trusting his fingers to notice any failure and make what amendments might be required.

They came to orbit without mishap. The forward screen showed stars; the secondary a star map, route and transition points clearly marked. There was no reason to change them, though he could not at the moment recall why he should be traveling to Landomist. His fingers had a reason. A pilot trusted his fingers and his ship. They were all he had, in the last counting.

He lost consciousness well before transition, but *Light Wing* knew what to do.

SEVEN

Osabei Tower
Landomist

BEING INVISIBLE WAS a marvelous thing, Jela thought. The challenge was to recall that he would immediately and catastrophically become *un*-invisible should he forget his role and act like he possessed slightly more sense than a rock.

Or, in the present instance, a clothes tree. His part was to stand, stoic and unmoving, holding Scholar tay'Nordif's unitard, tabard, sash, knife and gloves while she, garbed only in the so-called "discipline bracelet" stepped onto what the tailor was pleased to call *the fitter*. The tailor then fussed at length about the placement of the scholar's feet, shoulders and hips, until—

"There! Maintain that position, if you will, Scholar!" The tailor scurried from the platform to a small console, and quickly touched several panels. Beams of multi-colored light burst from all directions to enclose the scholar, giving her shape an unsettling luminescence. Jela twitched slightly when her hair began to rise, and settled himself deliberately. Across the room, the tailor made a satisfied sound, and bent to her console as the light slowly faded.

"You may step down from the fitter, now, Scholar. In a moment, your robe and slippers will be here." She hesitated, and sent a furtive glance in his direction, lips pursed in a measuring sort of way.

"Will you be wishing to garb your— servant—more appropriately?" she asked.

Scholar tay'Nordif turned slowly, as he read her, entirely unconcerned by her nakedness, and gave him a long, cold, considering stare.

"It appears to be garbed appropriate to its station," she said to the tailor. "What do you find amiss?"

The tailor ducked her head. "Only that most of the Tower servants are clothed as you would have seen last evening at the common meal, or—well, here!" This as a Small came bustling from the back, a dark bundle of cloth in her arms, and a matching pair of slippers dangling from one hand. The tailor received the bundle and the slippers, snapped a sharp, "Stay," and indicated with a sweep of her arm that the scholar should look her fill.

Jela, who had not been invited to look, did anyway.

The munchkin held frozen by her mistress' command wore only the very briefest blue kilt. A collar set with a stone very like that in Scholar tay'Nordif's bracelet was fastened tightly about her throat, and her eyes—no, Jela thought with crawling horror, her *eye sockets* were wrapped in a mesh of smartstrands.

Scholar tay'Nordif sniffed. "All very well for the size and shape on display," she said, "but I believe that we need not assault the sensibilities of the scholarly community by subjecting them to the sight of Jela clad thus."

"As you say, Scholar," the tailor murmured with a quick, sideways glance at himself. "May I point out that the mask may be of use, as the information uploaded from the slave-brain will confuse any real-time images, and thus preserve the sanctity of your work." She flicked her fingers at the still-frozen munchkin. "Those servants who are bred for the Tower are of course blind, and the mask then serves as a navigational aid."

"Mayhap Osabei Tower requires a degree of intellectual rigor in its servants that is neither required—or desired—in a mere horticultural kobold," Scholar tay'Nordif said with a shrug of her pretty shoulders. "Even had Jela the wit to notice my work, the capacity to understand it is certainly lacking."

"As you say, Scholar," the tailor murmured. She snapped a sharp "Go!" to the munchkin, who departed immediately, walking with utter assurance. "A word in your ear, however. The others may wish—"

"If there is complaint," Scholar tay'Nordif interrupted grandly, "let it be made to me."

"Of course, Scholar." The tailor bowed, then bustled forward, slippers held under one arm, shaking the cloth out as she approached. "Your robe, Scholar, if you would care to dress."

Scholar tay'Nordif held out her arms and the tailor slipped the shimmering sleeves over them.

It was, in Jela's opinion, a cumbersome garment, made of entirely too much cloth in a deep reddish brown. The shimmer was a puzzle, though he was willing to bet—had there been anyone but himself to take the wager—that there were smartstrands woven into the fabric. That was interesting, if not outright alarming. If the Tower slave-brain was also charged with monitoring or controlling the scholars—

The tailor sealed the front of the robe. She offered the slippers one at a time, and the scholar slid her slim feet into them.

"Jela! Come here!"

Summoned, he approached until she ordered him to stop and to hand her sash to the tailor. He did this and watched as that worthy wove it around the scholar's slender waist, carefully tucking up the ends.

Scholar tay'Nordif lowered her arms. The full sleeves fell precisely to her knuckles, the robe broke at the instep of her new, soft slippers. Her golden skin and pale hair somehow took light from the dark color, and seemed to glow.

"Jela! Hand me my knife, hilt first!"

He obeyed, handling the ill-kept blade as if it were no better balanced than a crowbar, and stood dull and stupid while she situated it to her satisfaction. That done, she relieved him of the smart gloves, which she held in her hand as she turned to address the tailor once more. In the absence of further orders, Jela stood where he'd been stopped, the unitard and tabard over his arm.

"I will want more than one robe."

"Certainly, Scholar. You may order as many as you wish. The cost will be charged against your account."

"My account, is it?" Scholar tay'Nordif fixed her in a cool green stare. "From whom would I learn the status of my account?"

"From the Bursar, Scholar," the tailor replied and stepped back, her hands twisting about each other as if they had a life and a purpose of their own.

"Ah. I shall speak with the Bursar, then, before ordering more robes."

"Very good, Scholar." She tipped her head, sending a sidewise glance at the garments Jela held.

"If the scholar would be so kind as to direct her servant to place the Wanderer's costume on the table, here"

Scholar tay'Nordif raised a eyebrow. "Does the Tower purchase my clothing?" she inquired.

The tailor raised her hands, fingers moving in a meaningless ripple.

"It is custom, Scholar. You shed the skin of a Wanderer and are reborn into the plumage of a Seated Scholar."

"I see," said Scholar tay'Nordif. There was a slight pause before she inclined her head. "Surely, there can be no argument with custom. As the great philosopher bin'Arli tells us, *Custom carries all before it.*"

The tailor blinked, but managed a faint, "Just so, Scholar."

"Just so," the scholar repeated. "Jela! Place those pieces of clothing where the tailor directs you."

Slowly, Jela turned toward the tailor. She bit her lip, and drifted back half-a-dozen steps to put her palm flat on the console table. "Put them here," she said, voice quavering.

He stomped forward, the tailor flinching with each heavy step, and dropped the clothing on the spot she had indicated, not without a pang. The tabard was of no consequence, being only wandercloth, but the unitard—The unitard was light-duty armor. So light-duty that any true soldier would call it none at all, but sufficient to turn the point of a weak knife-stroke—or lessen the power of a serious thrust. He didn't like the notion of having nothing between Can—Scholar tay'Nordif and a truth-blade but a layer of smart-wove fabric. Impossible to know what the scholar herself thought of it, of course, though he took hope from that pause before she agreed to the ceding of her garments.

"Is there anything else required of me here?" she asked the tailor.

"No, Scholar," the woman said unsteadily.

"That is well, then. Jela! Follow me." Scholar tay'Nordif swept off the dais, robes billowing, walking light, but nothing so light or so free as Pilot Cantra had done. Obeying orders, he followed her three steps behind—no more, no less—eyes down, giving his ears, his nose, and his peripheral vision as much of a workout as he dared.

"Liad's sole surviving student, is it?" The Bursar's gray eyebrows lifted sardonically, her eyes sharp and blue and giving as ice.

The scholar bowed briskly.

"Maelyn tay'Nordif," she said in her high, sharp voice. "I am come to inquire into the status of my account."

The Bursar pursed her lips. "The status of your account? You have no account, Scholar. You are a drain on the resources of this community until such time as your work attracts a patron willing to pay your expenses, or the artificers find that your work has practical application and market it. In the first case, any funds granted by your patron will of course go first against your accrued expenses. In the latter case, you will receive ten percent of any income generated by the sale or lease of the application incorporating your work, which funds will first be placed against your accrued expenses. At the moment—" She lifted her wand in one hand and fingered the chords absently.

"Yes," she said, flicking a casual glance at the screen. "At the moment, your debt to the Tower stands at eighteen qwint." She smiled. "That sum includes the lease on your quarters and on your office for the remainder of the month; one meal per day for yourself for the remainder of the month; your robe, equipment and storage space; and your share of Tower maintenance."

Scholar tay'Nordif stood silent, her head tipped to one side, her hands tucked meditatively into the sleeves of her robe.

"Is there any other way in which I may be pleased to serve you, Scholar?" the Bursar inquired, her smile now a full-assault grin.

"I would be grateful," the scholar said crisply, "if you would be so kind as to instruct me how I might deposit a flan into my account."

The Bursar's grin dimmed somewhat. "A flan," she repeated.

"It happens to be what I have with me at the moment," Scholar tay'Nordif said. "If it is too small a sum, I will of course be pleased to add another, but in that wise the conclusion of this matter will wait upon the morrow."

The Bursar cleared her throat. "I am able to accept a flan on account, Scholar. You do realize that your current expenses will be deducted—"

"Immediately," the scholar interrupted. "Yes, I quite understand that, thank you. Would it be possible for you to tell me if the six qwint remaining will procure a pass-tile?"

"Pass-tiles are six carolis the pair," the Bursar answered. Jela, standing three steps behind the scholar and one step to her right, thought he heard a bit of irritation there.

"In that wise, I will have two, if you please," Scholar tay'Nordif said composedly.

The Bursar spun her chair, snatched a green folder from one of the many cubbies behind her and spun back, her arm whipping, the packet spinning flat and potentially deadly toward—

Jela gritted his teeth, locking muscles that wanted to leap, crushing instincts that demanded he take the strike and protect his pilot—

Don't, he heard the familiar husky voice whisper from memory. *Don't for a heartbeat acknowledge that ghost.*

Right, he told himself, for the first time taking comfort from his kobold's habitual stolid, stupid stance. *She's not your pilot. Your pilot's—*

He balked at "dead," no matter that she would have said it herself.

Unchecked, the projectile continued along its path. Far too late, and clumsily, the scholar snatched a warding hand out of her sleeve. The packet bounced off of her wrist, hit the wall high and clattered to the floor.

"Jela!" Scholar tay'Nordif snapped. "Pick that—" she pointed "—up and bring it to me."

He moved, stumping deliberately over to the fallen packet, aware of the Bursar's speculative gaze. Bending, he retrieved the folder, then stumped back to place it in his mistress' outstretched, impatient palm.

"Very good," she said peremptorily. She slipped the packet into her sash; extended her hand again. "Jela," she said clearly, "give me my purse."

He counted three of his long, at-rest heartbeats, for the speculation in the Bursar's eyes, then groped in the pockets of his vest, eventually producing a battered coderoy pouch, which he held out uncertainly.

The scholar sighed, snatched it from his fingers, pulled the string and stepped up to the Bursar's desk.

"One flan, as agreed," she said. "Is it the custom to give a receipt for funds received?"

The Bursar's mouth was in a straight line now, facial muscles tight. "You may access your account at any time from any work terminal linked to Osabei Administration, Scholar."

"I am grateful," Scholar tay'Nordif said, bowing just low enough, as Jela read it, to avoid being overtly rude.

The Bursar snorted and spun to face her screen, wand already in hand. "Good-day, Scholar. May your work be fruitful and all your proofs accurate."

The ID plate shone briefly orange beneath Scholar tay'Nordif's palm, a chime sounded and motes of light danced beneath the door's dull surface, joining together until they cohered into glowing script: *Maelyn tay'Nordif*

The scholar made a satisfied sound—something between a chuckle and a sigh—and lifted her hand away from the reader. Immediately, the door opened, lights coming up in the room beyond.

Where the living quarters were sparse and tidy, the office was cluttered and chaotic. It was, Jela thought fair-mindedly, something of an accomplishment to have fit so comprehensive a confusion into so small a space.

Shelves lined three walls, but the scrolls and data-arrays they must once have held were absent, leaving only dust and a scattered handful of unassociated logic tiles.

By contrast, the scarred and chipped ceramic table in the center of the room was over-full with bits of piping, hoses, several canisters marked with the symbol for *poison*, a portable fission chamber, a large wooden box, its lid missing, the interior containing a stained rumple of cloth—and an orange cat, fast asleep.

"Well," Scholar tay'Nordif said, apparently to herself, "I have worked in less favored places." With difficulty, she squeezed past the table and bent over the work desk which had been jammed into the farthest and least-lit corner, as if whoever had occupied the office previously had only wished to be rid of it. The real work, it seemed to Jela, had been done at the table, though what—

Light flickered in the dark corner, which was the work screen coming up. The scholar clattered about a bit in the dimness, located the input wand and straightened, fingers sliding up and down the length, weaving chords at a rapid pace. Jela perforce reprised his impersonation of a rock, his eyes on the jumble of junk on the table, trying to make sense of the disparate bits; to imagine what sort of device might have been built from them—

"Jela," the scholar said in the dreamy, unsnappish way that meant most of her thought processes were engaged with something far more important than him. "Move away from the door."

As kobold-directions went, it was pretty loose, which might mean she really was thinking about something else. Still, he trusted her to give him some clear signal if he was in her line of fire, so he took his time about moving—slow, stolid and heavy—to his right, which cleared access to the door and also put him in a good place to observe both it and the scholar.

For six of his heartbeats, nothing at all happened. The scholar continued to work the wand, her attention fixed on the screen. The cat in the box stretched and sighed without waking.

A chime sounded, followed by a rather breathless, "Grudent tel'Ashon reporting, Scholar tay'Nordif."

The scholar did not look up from her screen. "Enter," she said absently, and the door opened to admit a flustered young woman wearing a unitard and a utility belt hung about with tools and tiles, scrolls and 'scribers—but lacking a truth-blade or any other weapon that Jela could see.

"Scholar tay'Nordif, allow me to say that I am honored—" she began.

The scholar did not so much as glance up from her screen. "Explain," she interrupted, "the condition in which I find my office."

Grudent tel'Ashon swallowed. "Yes, Scholar. This office had previously been tenanted by Scholar ser'Dinther, who failed to adequately prove his work—"

"Does this have a bearing on the condition of my office, Grudent?" the scholar interrupted sharply. She turned from the screen, the wand held quiescent between her palms.

The other bowed hastily. "Scholar, I merely sought to explain the apparatus and the—the—"

"The lack of standard resource works?" Scholar tay'Nordif snapped. "The absence of logic tiles, grids, and storage medium? The fact that the single chair is broken, and this terminal sub-standard?"

Silence.

"I am waiting, Grudent, for an explanation of these lacks and impediments to my work. Am I to understand the deplorable state of this office as a challenge? Perhaps there is another scholar on this hall who believes my work unworthy?" She tipped her head, meditatively. "Perhaps *you*—"

Grudent tel'Ashon raised her hands in what Jela registered as honest horror.

"Scholar, no! Please! There was no intention on my part—The grudent staff has been over—That is, I did not expect a new scholar to arrive so quickly, nor that the Second Chair would place you here, when there are other offices which have been—Had I known he wanted you near to himself and to the Prime—" She stuttered, gasped, and took refuge in a bow so deep she was bent quite in half, a posture she held until Scholar tay'Nordif instructed her, impatiently, to stand up straight.

This the grudent did with noticeable trepidation; squared her shoulders, and folded her hands into a tense knot before her belt buckle.

"That is better. I will expect you to comport yourself as befits a scholar during the time you serve as my grudent," Scholar tay'Nordif said, sharp and no-nonsense. "Scholars do not rely upon excuses; rather, they rest squarely on good work and ample proof. Now." She swept the wand out, indicating the room at large. "I will have this office made seemly. I will have two chairs in addition to my work chair, none of which will be broken. I will have the standard references. I will have both logic and data tiles and several of the larger grids, in addition to the usual kit. I will have *that*—" the wand pointed at the cluttered table—"gone." She lowered the wand. "Am I clear, Grudent?"

"Scholar, you are," the other said, her voice hoarse. "However, I must make you aware of certain budget constraints. Those whose work brings largesse or patrons to the Tower, those scholars receive—"

The wand came up so quickly the grudent flinched.

"My work," Maelyn tay'Nordif said, each word as hard and as cold as a stone, "is paramount, Grudent. I do not allow the dabblings of any other scholar in this department to have precedence. You have heard what I require in order to pursue my work, and you will procure it, by what method I neither know nor care. Steal it, if you must. But you will provide everything I require. Have you understood me, Grudent?"

"Yes, Scholar," the grudent whispered.

"Good. Begin by removing that table."

"Yes, Scholar," the grudent whispered again, then slightly stronger. "I will return in a moment with a cart."

"That is well. I will instruct the door to admit you."

The grudent left; the scholar turned back to her screen, fingers busy on the chording wand. Jela stood and waited.

In the box, the orange cat, which had slept soundly throughout all the preceding ruckus, abruptly sprang up, ears swiveling.

Its wide amber gaze fell on Jela; it sat down and began to groom its shoulder.

Time, not very much of it, passed.

The door chimed and opened simultaneously, admitting the grudent with the promised cart. She paused on the threshold, frowning at the problem, and took note, apparently for the first time, of himself. Her eyes—brown and slightly protuberant—widened but, unlike the cat, she failed to transfer her consternation to a more useful activity.

"Don't," Scholar tay'Nordif said, her eyes on the screen, "mind Jela, Grudent. If you require assistance with heavy lifting, enlist its aid. Jela! Assist the grudent at her request."

The grudent swallowed; her lips parted but no sound emerged. Finally, she just turned her back on him and began to gather up the various odds and ends on the table and move them, all a-jumble, into the cart. She did show what Jela considered to be proper prudence in the matter of the *poison* canisters, and also took the necessary time to be sure that there was nothing in the fission chamber and that the power-source was disconnected. That done, she turned her attention to the box, and the cat inside the box, which had suspended its bath and was watching her with interest.

The grudent extended a hand which was trembling too much to be authoritative. The cat swung a paw negligently, and the grudent jumped back, putting her bloodied finger to her mouth.

The cat yawned.

The grudent set her lips, groped 'round her belt and came forward with a pair of stained work gloves. She pulled one over the wounded hand.

"Leave it," Scholar tay'Nordif said from the back corner.

The grudent blinked. "Scholar?"

"The cat," the scholar snapped, clearly in no mood to tolerate stupidity. "Leave it."

The grudent lifted her eyes to Jela's face. Finding nothing there, she looked back to the cat. "The box, too, Scholar?"

"If you must. Jela! Pick up the box. Pick up the cat—*gently*. Bring the box and the cat—*gently*—here to me now."

He moved deliberately; the grudent dropped back, thoughtfully pulling the cart out of his path. The cat in the box watched his approach with interest, ears cocked forward. As near as

Jela could tell from its body language, it was at rest, unaggressive—exactly as it had appeared in the heartbeat before it mauled the grudent.

The grudent, however, had approached the cat directly. Fortunately for him, he was a kobold, and just about smart enough to follow his orders by the one-two.

He took hold of the box with one hand, catching the cat neatly with the other as it hopped out, and tucking it—gently—between his arm and his side. It stiffened, but if it used its claws, they were neither long enough nor fierce enough to pierce the leather shirt. Jela kept moving, banged the table out of his way with a casual kick, and approached the terminal.

The scholar put the chording wand down on the rickety desk, extended a hand, caught the cat by the loose skin at the back of its neck and transferred it to her opposite arm, keeping a firm grip on the scruff. She jerked her chin at the empty shelf over the terminal.

"Put the box up there, Jela. *Gently.*"

It was an easy one-handed toss, and not too much clatter when it landed. The scholar sighed.

"Grudent tel'Ashon," she snapped, turning to address that worthy, who was busily shoving the last of the bits and bobs from the table onto her cart. At the scholar's hail, she looked up, eyes wide and throat working.

"Scholar?"

"This previous scholar—ser'Dinther? What was the nature of his work? Briefly."

The grudent bit her lip. "As far as a mere grudent may understand a scholar's work, I believe he sought—That is, he had proven the existence of adjacent lines of causality."

"Had he? A pity his proof did not stand rigorous testing." The scholar nodded at the feline on her arm. "What role had the cat in these proofs?"

"I—It was the scholar's intention to provide a practical demonstration. His work led him to believe that a base creature in peril of its life might, certain conditions being met, shift to an—to a situation in which the peril was non-existent." She moved her hand in a shapeless gesture that was perhaps meant to encompass the table and the clutter it had supported. "He had at first worked with the mun—with the Tower servitors. However, experimentation revealed that their nature, though base, was yet too elevated for the state shift to be a matter of instinct. Thus, the cats."

"I see. And the experiment?"

"A cat would be placed into the box, which would then be sealed, excepting the delivery tube for the poison gas. The trigger was a single radioactive nucleus which, in the causality we and the cat co-inhabit, has a fifty percent chance of decaying within a specified time. If it decays, the gas is released."

"Killing the cat," the scholar said dryly. "A singularly one-sided experiment."

"According to Scholar ser'Dinther's proof," the grudent said, leaning forward, real interest showing in her face, "the cat does not die, but escapes to an adjacent line of causality. When we who are continuing along *this* line of causality open the box to learn what has transpired, we see a dead cat, because it is what experience has trained us to see." She gasped, as if suddenly recalling herself, and settled back, her hands twisting together.

"Scholar ser'Dinther was engaged in perfecting an apparatus which would capture and distill the moment of transition. He was— His proof failed before he had completed that aspect of his work."

There was a small pause before the scholar, who had been stroking the cat between its ears, murmured. "I see. And this cat here is the last left alive." She looked up and sent a sharp glance to the grudent. "In this particular causality, of course."

The grudent hesitated, hands twisting 'round themselves with a will.

"That cat," she said—carefully, Jela thought— "That cat, Scholar, was in the box many times. Never once did the nucleus decay."

"A feline of extraordinary luck, I see. Well." She chucked the animal under the chin and moved her shoulders. "I have a kindness for cats. As this one is no longer required for experimental purposes, I shall keep it."

The grudent bowed hastily. "Yes, Scholar. Of course."

"Jela!" the scholar snapped. "Take the chair in the corner behind you to the grudent."

He turned clumsily and located the chair, a rickety item missing a quarter of its back and half of one leg. Hefting it casually, he took it to the grudent as ordered, and stood holding it out in one hand while she blinked at him stupidly.

"It won't fit on the cart like that," she said.

"Jela!" Scholar tay'Nordif ordered from the rear. "Break the chair over your knee and place the pieces on the cart."

No trouble there, he thought, and did as ordered, taking a brief, savage joy in the minor destruction. The grudent shrank back with a gasp, and watched with wide eyes as he dropped the bits into the cart, then gathered her courage and stood tall, taking a grip on the handle.

"I will dispose of this and be back for the table at once, Scholar," she said.

"Jela will carry the table," the scholar snapped. "Perhaps I failed to make plain my necessity that this office be habitable before the Mercy Bell sounds?"

The grudent was seen to choke slightly, but she stiffened her spine once more and sent what was probably meant to be a stern look into Jela's face.

"You. Jela," she said, voice shaking only a little. "Pick up the table and follow me."

The table was much too wide to fit through the doorway. Which was precisely the sort of esoteric detail a kobold would fail to note.

The grudent pushed the cart out the door. Jela stumped forward, hefted the table, and started after, one end striking the shelving with a will and scoring the wa—

"Jela!" Scholar tay'Nordif said sharply. "Stop!"

He stopped, and stood, table in hand, awaiting amended orders.

"Put the table down, Jela," the scholar said, and raised her voice. "Grudent tel'Ashon!"

Immediately, the grudent was in the doorway, eyes and mouth wide. "Scholar? I—"

"Silence! If you are to serve me, you will learn to think logically and to give clear, unambiguous orders. Perhaps the Tower's servitors are more able to reason, but a kobold is only able to follow what directions it is given. Thus, its service is only as good as your instructions. Observe, now.

"Jela! Press the switch on the tabletop. When the table has folded itself, pick it up and follow Grudent tel'Ashon. Obey her instructions until she returns you to me."

Deliberately, he looked over the tabletop, discovering in due time the bright blue button set flush to the surface. He pushed it and stood stoically by as the table folded itself into neat quarters, tucked the resultant rectangle under his arm and headed for the door. Grudent tel'Ashon gave way hastily before him. He followed her, and then followed her some more as she pushed the remains of the late Scholar ser'Dinther's experiments down the hall.

The cart went noiselessly on its cushion of air; the grudent went quietly in her soft-soled slippers. Jela walked as lightly as he dared while maintaining the illusion of clumsy bulk.

Ahead, there were voices, perhaps not yet discernible to the grudent, but clearly audible to Jela's enhanced hearing.

"...gone to the Governors!" The first voice was light—possibly a woman—and clearly agitated.

"So, you have not made your exception to his work known?" The second voice was unmistakably masculine, pleasantly in the midrange, calm—and instantly recognizable as belonging to Scholar tay'Welford, he of the too-knowing smile.

"How could I?" the first voice responded. "But, the Governors! What does it mean?"

"Only that he is gone to report the arrival of our newest sister in scholarship. It has been quite some time, as vel'Anbrek noted last eve, since we have seen one of the Master's students, and the Governors must surely be—"

The cart angled to the right, and a door noisily gave way before it. Jela dutifully marched after the grudent, straining his ears, but the remainder of the scholars' discussion was lost to him.

EIGHT

Osabei Tower
Landomist

JELA PICKED THE chair up and followed Grudent tel'Ashon out into the hallway.

The past few hours had given him a respect for the grudent he had not expected to acquire. She had been tireless in the pursuit of her orders, displaying a subtle creativity that won, if not his heart, certainly his admiration. Realizing early in the endeavor that she would sometimes have need of him elsewhere in the hall, she had *acquired* a pass-tile from an office, the door of which bore the glowing name *Den Vir tel'Elyd.* This she had attached to the collar of his leather shirt, with a small grim smile, and a muttered, "Lackluster research and pedestrian results, was it?" He was then free to roam—on her orders, of course—an arrangement he approved of in the strongest possible terms.

The work had broken down neatly into brain and brawn. It fell to the grudent, as the self-identified brain, to gimmick the doors of offices she considered likely to contain those things required to make Scholar tay'Nordif's life more comfortable. After a quick reconnoiter, she would point out those items she deemed worthy, and direct him to carry them to the scholar's office, while she continued on to the next target. It was a system which had worked admirably in rapidly attaining for Maelyn tay'Nordif all the trappings of a scholar who had by her wit and her intellect captured a seat in Osabei Tower.

In Jela's estimation, the grudent had tarried a bit too long in the selection of the chair which he now carried, but it was hardly his place to criticize—especially as the protracted search had netted what appeared to be a brand new chair of the first order of craftsmanship. There had been no name on the door of the office from which this last item had been pilfered, but the appropriation had seemed to give Grudent tel'Ashon almost as much satisfaction as purloining the pass-tile. In Jela's opinion, she had done well by her scholar. Not that his opinion mattered.

Half-a-dozen steps ahead of him, the grudent abruptly swung close to the wall, sending a sharp look over her shoulder and waving at him to do the same. Not at all a good kobold order, but in light of the man walking toward them, Jela decided it was prudent to obey anyway.

The approaching scholar was, judging by the strands of silver glinting in the dark back-swept hair, in his middle years. His square face was creased, and at some point his nose had been broken. The sleeves of his robe were pushed up, revealing strong forearms, veins like blue wire running tight beneath the skin. In addition to the sheathed truth-blade and smart-gloves, a tile tablet adorned with many fobs and seals hung from his sash. He walked like a man who had recently taken a moderate wound—and who was earnestly trying to conceal that fact.

Grudent tel'Ashon dropped to one knee, head lowered, right hand fisted over her heart. "Prime Chair tay'Palin," she murmured respectfully as he drew level with their position.

The scholar paused, dark eyes sweeping over the grudent, and lingering rather longer than Jela liked on himself.

"Grudent tel'Ashon," he said, his voice smooth and mannerly. "Please, arise, and tell me where you have found this extraordinary—being."

The grudent came to her feet with alacrity, sliding a sideways glance in Jela's direction. He stood, chair held against his chest, eyes focused on a point in space approximately six inches from the end of his nose.

"Prime, that is the kobold Jela, which belongs to Scholar tay'Nordif."

"Is it, indeed?" Scholar tay'Palin took a step forward, his gaze sharp. "And why has Scholar tay'Nordif a Series—"

"tay'Palin!" a woman's voice—precisely the voice of the woman who had been talking to tay'Welford earlier—accompanied by the sound of someone running inefficiently in soft shoes, and an arrhythmic clacking, as if a dozen or more data tiles were striking against each other.

The scholar sighed, closed his eyes briefly, and turned—carefully, to Jela's eye.

"Scholar chi'Farlo," he said distantly. "How may I serve you?"

The woman lowered her robe, which she had held up to her plump knees in order to run, and smiled. Her yellow hair was divided into many braids, each one tied off with a cluster of tiles, which would account for the clacking. Her face was soft and pale; her eyes were round and blue. The smile didn't begin to warm them.

She came close to Scholar tay'Palin, and put a plump, soft hand on his arm. He twitched, so slightly that most observers would scarcely have seen—though Jela did.

And so, he was willing to wager, had Scholar chi'Farlo. Her smile widened, displaying dainty white teeth, and she exerted pressure on the arm, pulling the scholar with her.

"Walk with me, tay'Palin. I have something to say to you."

It seemed to Jela that the Prime Chair's shoulders sagged just a little beneath his robe. He inclined his head to the wide-eyed grudent. "You may go, Grudent tel'Ashon."

She gulped and bowed, hurriedly. Keeping her head down, she snapped, "Follow me, Jela!" and moved away, hugging the right wall.

Jela perforce followed, carrying the chair, and straining his ears. All that exercise gained him was the whisper of slippers against the floor and the gentle clacking of tiles.

Scholar tay'Nordif bent her cool, misty gaze upon the chair. To her left, on the polished and well-kept task table, a brand-new terminal and wand reposed in that space not taken up by the sprawling orange cat, which was watching the proceedings with interest.

The scholar extended a slender hand, pulled the chair to her, sat, and deftly put it through its phases. The grudent held her bow, her tension so marked that Jela's skin began to itch.

"Well done," Scholar tay'Nordif said from her comfortable recline. "I commend you, Grudent tel'Ashon; you have fitted me with honor and—"

A klaxon sounded, shrill and serious. Scholar tay'Nordif gasped, and cringed in her chair, one hand pressed to her breast. Jela could hardly blame her; it was all he could do not to jump for the handholds that weren't there and blink up the command screen in the helmet he wasn't wearing.

The grudent, however, snapped upright out of her bow, a grin on her face and her dull brown eyes sparkling.

"The Truth Bell!" she said excitedly.

"Indeed?" Scholar tay'Nordif said faintly. She fumbled at the chair's control, eventually coming perpendicular to local conditions. She blinked up at the grudent, the pulse at the base of her throat beating rapidly.

"Surely, truth need not be quite so stern?" she whispered. "Indeed, as the great philosopher bin'Arli tell us, *Truth is that silent certainty in one's—*"

The klaxon sounded again, and the rest of bin'Arli's wisdom was lost in a gasp as the scholar staggered to her feet, startling the cat, which leapt to the top of the work screen, tail lashing.

"Come, Scholar!" The grudent was halfway to the door. "The community is called to witness!"

"Witness?" the scholar said faintly.

"Yes, of course!" Grudent tel'Ashon waved an impatient hand. "Quickly, Scholar! We don't want to miss a point!" She was gone.

"I—see," the scholar said. She pushed her sleeves up her arms nervously, took a deep breath and marched resolutely in the grudent's wake.

"Jela," she said, without turning her head. "Follow me."

They sat on risers inside a soaring, airy foyer strongly reminiscent of the octagonal hall of the flying platforms—many dozens of scholars, grudents, and the blind Smalls, all facing a center expanse of creamy floor with what looked for all of space like a training rectangle marked out in rust-colored tile.

Jela stood behind and slightly to the right of Scholar tay'Nordif, which gave him a clear sight of the combat zone, and also of a command room situated about halfway up the wall directly opposite his position. The observation port was opaqued, but Jela felt certain that command of one sort or another was present.

The mass of scholars rippled, murmured, then stilled as a yellow-haired woman marched out onto the floor, the tapping of her tile-braided hair clearly audible in the sudden silence.

Deliberately, she stepped into the rectangle, pulled the blade from its place in her sash and brandished it dramatically over her head.

"I, Leman chi'Farlo, Seated Scholar and Third Chair of the Department of Interdimensional Statistics, challenge Kel Var tay'Palin to defend his Thesis Number Twenty-Seven, in which he avers that the value of Amedeo's Constant as reflected in N-space is a contingent process and is not an ordered process." Her voice echoed weirdly, which Jela took to be an affect of a wide-area amplifier.

"What's this?" a scholar some places to Jela's right whispered to the scholar next to her. "She challenges him on work he published before he was seated?"

"It's allowable," her mate whispered back. "Bad form, but allowable."

The first scholar sighed lightly. "Well, it is chi'Farlo, after all."

"Come forth, Kel Var tay'Palin," a voice boomed across the hall—likely originating, Jela thought, in the shielded command room. "Come forward and defend your work."

And here came the lean figure of the Prime Chair, walking carefully, his knife held business-like. It was, Jela saw, a well-kept weapon, the edge so sharp it shone like an energy blade. He stepped into the rectangle, and bowed slightly to his opponent. She returned the courtesy, lunging out of it low and vicious, going for the belly.

Prime Chair twisted; his opponent's blade sliced robe, and in the moment it was fouled, he chopped down at her exposed neck. Unfortunately, the yellow-haired scholar was more nimble than she looked; she tucked and dove, freeing her knife with a wrist-wrenching twist. There was a clatter of tiles as a severed braid hit the floor.

Scholar tay'Palin spun, a trifle ragged, to face his opponent as she came to her feet and danced forward, knife flashing, pressing him fiercely.

And that tactic, Jela thought, was likely a winner, given that knife fights were never certain. No question tay'Palin was the better fighter, but he was wounded and weary while she was fresh and energized, and that more than balanced her relative lack of skill.

The blonde woman thrust, tay'Palin twisted—and went down to one knee. She pressed her advantage, going for his eyes now, his throat, his face, working close, giving him no opportunity to gain his feet.

Still, he fought on, grimly, blood showing now on his sleeve—which was, Jela thought, the old wound, torn open again—and down the front of his robe from his numerous cuts.

All at once, the woman twisted, feinting. The scholar on his knees realized the deception too late—and, that quickly, it was over, the blonde woman's knife lodged to the hilt in tay'Palin's chest.

Exuberant, she turned, raising her hands above her head. And as she did, the mortally wounded scholar raised his arm, reversed his blade—and threw.

The victor staggered, mouth opening in a silent scream—and fell all at once, blood streaming. Scholar tay'Palin lay on his side, eyes open and empty, his blood pooling and mixing with that of his opponent.

"Scholar tay'Palin," the disembodied voice announced, into the absolute silence of the lobby, "has successfully turned the challenge. Let his grudents amass his work and publish it wherever scholars study. Let his name be recorded on the Scholar's Wall."

There was a murmur of approval from the assembled scholars.

"Scholar chi'Farlo," the voice continued, "is found to have wrongly issued challenge. Let her office be purged, her files wiped and her name struck from our rolls."

"Well deserved," whispered the scholar to the right.

"We have an administrative announcement." the voice said briskly. "Effective immediately, Scholar Ala Bin tay'Welford, formerly Second Chair, will serve the Department of Interdimensional Statistics as Prime Chair."

The Mercy Bell rang.

Lute cast his net wide, watching, as she had asked him to do, while she prepared herself to accept that burden which no dominant had taken up since the first had been born from the need of the Iloheen.

It was Lute's belief that what she proposed to do would alter the bounds of probability more certainly than any mere manipulation of the lines, no matter how bold or subtle. It would be the sum of small things—a truth not said, a law unobserved, a heart engaged—which would, in the final accounting, weigh against the Iloheen.

His lady held otherwise, as did Rool Tiazan and his lady, differing merely on the fine points of process. In the end, process mattered to Lute not at all. That the Iloheen were brought down—he barely dared form the word *destroyed* within the cavern of his secret heart—that had been his only desire, long before his first encounter with Rool Tiazan, long before he listened to what the Iloheen might call treason—and allowed himself to be bound.

He had been mad, of course. Confined, in thrall, compelled against his will to do terrible things. Terrible things. When Rool had proposed a lesser slavery, the acceptance of which might possibly, with luck, on some day long in the future even as they counted, bring the Iloheen defeat—

It was an odd thing, this container in which he had allowed himself to be prisoned. The weight of it dulled his senses, limited his reach. And yet even now, after so long—even now, he sometimes woke, the screams of a dying star ringing in ears unfit to hear them, the pure crystalline agony of Iloheen pleasure stretching his soul to the point of annihilation.

That the new slavery he had agreed to had not been lesser, nor even less horrifying; that the probability of gaining ascendency over the Iloheen was not very much greater than the probability of one of the stars he had destroyed blazing into renewed life—he thought he had suspected as much, even as he agreed to the plan Rool proposed. He thought he might have suspected that Rool, twice a slave and old in treachery, was himself more than a bit mad. And yet, if not they who in their true forms had held dominion over space, time, and probability—if they could not deny the Iloheen the future, who—

The ley lines flared. Lute traced the disturbance, saw a small brilliance, of no more consequence against the blare of all possibility than a spark against a bonfire, dancing hectic before a black wind.

Lute coalesced, wrapped his awareness closely and returned to that place where his lady lay guarded, preparing for her ordeal.

She noticed him at once, and he bowed under the weight of her regard.

"It begins," he said.

Tor An woke with a cry. Before him, the board glowed green; the screens displayed a starfield, perfectly orderly and ordinary. The coordinates of that starfield were displayed at the bottom of the forward screen, with the legend, "Transition complete."

Light Wing maintained position, awaiting orders from her pilot, who struggled upright his chair, gasping once against a flare of pain—and again at finding the belts loose and unfastened. What had he been thinking, to go into transition without engaging the safety web?

He had survived to ask the question, therefore it could be put aside until more immediate concerns were addressed. Such as—what had wakened him?

It must, he thought, examining the board more closely, have been the chime signaling the end of transition. He frowned at the coordinates, which were unfamiliar, and at the starfield, anonymous and soothing. A glance at the elapsed time caused his frown to deepen. He had been asleep for what would have amounted, on the planet of his birth, to two full days while the ship transitioned from—

Memory abruptly returned. His hand rose to the burning shoulder; he felt the dressing, recalled the laughter of the soldiers, his heartbeat pounding in his ears as he ran for his life. Shot. Yes. He remembered.

He swallowed, forcing himself past the memory of terror. He had returned to the ship, dressed his wound as best as he'd been able, sat down in the chair and—

"Landomist," he murmured, reaching to the board and petitioning the nav-brain for an approach, while he struggled to reproduce the reasoning which had led to feeding those particular coordinates into—

A set of syllables rose from the mists of memory, and he gave them shape, his voice a cracked whisper: "Kel Var tay'Palin." A name, certainly—though who the gentleman might be, or where Tor An yos'Galan had acquired—no. Now he recalled what his fingers had never forgot. Kel Var tay'Palin had been an acquaintance of Aunt Jinsu, traveling with her in pursuit of his studies, back when Aunt Jinsu had been a fiery young pilot and the despair of all her elders. It had pleased her that the young man had journeyed at last to Landomist, and taken his chair in Interdimensional Mathematics. He remembered when the letter came. Aunt, home between staid and stable trade rounds, had read it aloud to the youngers, telling them the story of how the young scholar had ridden with her, and perhaps not quite all the truth of how he had paid his way.

And how long ago had it been, he wondered, shifting in the chair to ease his wounded arm, since that letter and those stories? Certainly after he had served his first flight as cabin boy under Great-grandfather Er Thom on *Baistle's* last trip 'round the Short Loop.

Had he done his turn as cargo-rat yet, or had he been awaiting the *Profitable Passage*?

He sighed sharply, out of patience with himself. What did it matter, after all, the exact year? Stipulate that the letter had arrived long ago, and that the truth upon which Aunt Jinsu had based her tales of the bold-hearted and single-minded young scholar had taken place more years before that. Kel Var tay'Palin, if he sat yet safe in the Tower at Landomist, would be an ancient. He might possibly recall the adventures of his youth with kindness—enough, perhaps, to drink tea with Pilot Jinsu herself. Pilot Jinsu's nephew, however, would have no call upon the man.

Now I'll tell you a secret, Aunt Jinsu whispered from memory, eyes glinting mischief as she lowered her voice and looked over her shoulder to be sure that Grandmother wasn't near. *The scholars of the mathematics tower, they'll sometimes hire pilots to fly their theories for them, or to travel to a certain someplace and collect readings. Scholar tay'Palin wasn't one to forget a good turn done him, and more than once he's passed a small flight and a respectful purse my way.*

It seemed that his fingers had listened to Aunt Jinsu more closely than his ears, Tor An thought resignedly. And, truly, what other choice had he? Perhaps the old scholar might direct him to someone who would take his readings and make sense of them—some happier sense, perhaps, than that which he had formed.

The Towers of Learning were powerful, so he had heard. Perhaps the mathematical tower might be powerful enough to command the military to examine the Ringstars' fate, to—to—

To what? he wondered. Unless he truly had gone mad, his readings proved that the Ringstars no longer existed. Did he expect that the learned scholars might force the military to put them back?

He shifted in the chair again, biting his lip as fire shot his arm. Carefully, he angled the chair so that he could reach the board with his good hand.

"Never mind," he told himself softly as his clever fingers chose an approach and gave *Light Wing* the office. "Do your duty, and glory will follow."

It was a thing that his brother Cor Win used to say, most usually with a roguish grin and a wag of the head. How he would have laughed, Tor An thought, locking the course and staggering to his feet, to hear it said in deadly earnest.

The back of Jela's neck stopped itching as soon as the door to Scholar tay'Nordif's quarters locked shut behind him, which just went to show, he thought sourly, that even an old soldier could be a fool. At the same instant, the cat, which had hung quiescent on his arm the whole long way from the offices, began kicking and squirming, claws scoring leather in earnest, demanding to be released. Which just went to show that even extraordinarily lucky cats weren't necessarily immune to foolishness, either.

Unless, he thought suddenly, keeping a firm grip on the cat's ruff, the creature wanted to be put down in order that it might field a credible attack? He'd read somewhere that a single cat could dispatch a wharf rat twice its mass—

The cat made a noise like an airlock with a bad gasket, and executed a complex twist, surprisingly strong for so small a creature. Jela subdued it absently, most of his attention elsewhere.

Super-sharp hearing brought him the uninterrupted humming of the hacks he'd put in place, and a quick visual scan as he crossed to the counter confirmed that everything was as they had left it that morning.

For whatever *that* was worth.

He placed the twisting, hissing cat—*gently*—on its feet on the counter. The animal turned its head this way and that, giving the territory a visual sweep of its own, then stood at attention, ears swiveling. Jela's heart beat three times. The cat shook itself, gave its shoulder a quick half-dozen licks, yawned, sat down, extended one back leg high and began to lick the inside of its thigh.

All clear, then, Jela thought. *Maybe.*

Assuming that the pass-tile fixed to his collar didn't report his every move to the Tower's slave-brain. And even if it did, he—legitimate, honest kobold that he was—couldn't just take it off and crush it.

Scholar tay'Nordif *had* exchanged the tile pilfered from the office of Scholar tel'Elyd by the enterprising grudent for one of the pair she'd had off the Bursar that morning—and had it been Cantra yos'Phelium who had done the deed, he would have had no doubt but what the tile had been rendered as harmless to the mission as it was possible for her to have done. Scholar tay'Nordif, though—the Deeps alone knew what to expect from such a flutter-headed, vain—

Trust, Cantra yos'Phelium's husky, serious voice whispered from memory. *This is going to be hard, Pilot, I know*—

Trust, he repeated to himself now, as he moved into the tiny galley, pulled a bowl from its hook, filled it with water and placed in front of the cat, which didn't bother to raise its head.

A picture formed at the back of his mind: the now-familiar shadow of an enormous wing, gliding over the crowns of monumental trees. Leaves rustled as the dragon dropped close, and closer still, wingtips brushing tree-tops as it approached one particular tree, one particular branch, upon which hung one particular fruit. With no diminishment of speed, the dragon extended its graceful neck. Its mouth opened, teeth as long as Jela flashed, the shadow passed on. The tree stood, unscarred and undisturbed, its branch intact, the seed-pod it had offered gone.

Jela took a breath.

On the counter, the cat paused in its grooming and raised its head, amber eyes meeting his with the look of an equal intelligence which was, at the moment, slightly put out with him.

Trust, Cantra's voice whispered again.

The cat blinked, breaking their shared gaze, and returned to its grooming. Jela went to tend the tree.

A seed pod dropped into his palm. He gave silent thanks, and ate it while mentally reviewing the so-called proving, for the tree's interest. It had been a shocking business, badly done and proving nothing but that the man challenged had been more accomplished with his blade than his challenger. He'd known that the scholars of Osabei Tower rose and fell by such "proofs" of their work; Cantra had insisted that he read the codes and histories of the Towers. But knowing and seeing were two different processes. Which he'd also known.

Not to mention, he thought, opening the hidden door in the tree's pot, that Prime Chair tay'Palin's death had been of benefit to the mission, for the man had recognized a Series soldier and had been, so Jela thought, on the edge of asking difficult questions when he'd been interrupted.

The cat came wandering by, snuffling at the grid. Jela pushed it gently away, and it jumped onto the dirt that surrounded and nourished the tree. He gasped, remembering sharp claws and tender bark—and received a clear sending of a dragon curled 'round the base of a sapling, slitted eyes alert.

For its part, the cat circled the tree, one shoulder companionably rubbing the bark, then jumped down on the opposite side and disappeared into the depth of the quarters.

Jela sighed, lightly, and finished assembling his equipment.

The mood of the common room was frenetic. It was often so, after the passing of a Prime Chair, and all the moreso this evening. tay'Palin had been well-liked, and had held his seat for almost three Common Years. Had his tenure not been cut short, he would have been eligible on his anniversary date to petition the Board of Governors for a place in the Masters' Wing. Whether the Governors would have granted so audacious a request was, tay'Welford acknowledged as he took a glass of wine from a passing tray, entirely up to the whim of the Governors. And, in any case, was no longer an issue.

"Well, there he is!" Regrettably, vel'Anbrek's voice carried easily over the ambient din. It would not do to be seen to snub so venerable a member of the department. No, tay'Welford thought, moving toward the group clustered about the old scholar; there were far more satisfying ways of dealing with vel'Anbrek open to him now.

"Prime." dea'San, never a fool, inclined her head as he joined them.

"Colleagues," he replied, smiling 'round at the three of them. Scholar tay'Nordif gave him his due as well, her beige hair shimmering. When she raised her head, he saw that her face was quite pale. She stood preternaturally still, with none of the overt signs of "vigilance" she had displayed yestereen. Perhaps, tay'Welford thought, today's contest of scholarship had proved a tonic for the department's newest member.

"Today's proving turned out rather well for you, didn't it?" vel'Anbrek said, raising his glass and taking a hearty drink.

tay'Welford frowned slightly. "I am not entirely certain that I understand you, colleague. Are you hinting that I would have wished for anything like today's outcome?"

"You're not such a fool as that, I'd think," the old horror replied. "Certainly, anyone here could have predicted tay'Palin stood on the edge of error. Did so myself, just last night. But who could have imagined he had that last stroke in him—and that he would be moved to save you the trouble of killing chi'Farlo yourself?"

"Gor Tan!" dea'San cried. "What do you say?"

"That chi'Farlo was ambitious," the old man retorted. "Had she won her point, she would have risen from Third Chair to Second, while our good friend and colleague tay'Welford ascended to Prime. And how long, I ask, before she marshaled the tactics that had worked so well against tay'Palin and brought them against our beloved new Prime?"

"Tactics?" Scholar tay'Nordif asked, her voice rather subdued. "What tactics?"

vel'Anbrek shook a finger at her. "It had long been apparent to those of us on the hall that someone had determined to advance by guile rather than by scholarship. An increasing number of challenges were issued against the work of Prime tay'Palin, and by some of the hottest heads in our department, as even cautious Scholar dea'San will admit is true. Though you knew him so short a time, Scholar tay'Nordif, I am certain it will not surprise you to learn that tay'Palin was a solid scholar—a very solid scholar. Over and over he proved himself. But even a solid scholar becomes wearied by constant challenge. It is my belief that Scholar chi'Farlo had today determined that he was worn down enough to err, and thus she called that point—which ought, Prime Chair, to have been disallowed! Are we to permit challenges based on Wander-work which is tangential to the token that gained us our chair? What next, I ask you? Challenges on the 'quations we proved at our tutor's knee?"

"I will," tay'Welford said, keeping his voice serious and soft, "take the matter to the Governors, colleague. It may be that protocol was breached."

"That's very well, then," sniffed vel'Anbrek.

"You would say," Scholar tay'Nordif murmured, "if I understand you, Scholar—that Scholar chi'Farlo felt the Prime—past-Prime! Your pardon, Prime tay'Welford!—would be physically unable to withstand her, and so issued a spurious challenge?"

"A light-minded challenge, let us say," vel'Anbrek answered. "But, yes, you have the essence of it, Scholar. And since it was clearly her wish to rise to Prime—which I do not scruple to tell you she *could not* have done on the strength of her scholarship—plain logic dictates that she would soon have launched the same sort of attack at tay'Welford here, from her position as Second Chair."

"It seems," Maelyn tay'Nordif protested, "a very risky business, Scholar. How if she were found out?"

"But she was found out, was she not?" dea'San said briskly. "The challenge fell to tay'Palin." She fixed vel'Anbrek in a stern eye. "The system works. Though it does occasionally allow for certain untidiness, balance is eventually restored."

"Yes, of course," said tay'Nordif, "but—"

The bell rang, and tay'Welford stepped forward with a smile to offer his arm to dea'San, leaving tay'Nordif to share the meal with vel'Anbrek, much joy she might have of him.

Jela's 'bots and seekers had been busy while he'd been fetching and carrying and seeing bloody murder done. He therefore immersed himself, sitting on the floor next to the tree, absently eating a second seed pod, and a third after it hit his knee a little harder than local gravity could answer for.

The cat had come by again and stuck its nose once between him and his portable array. He pushed it—*gently*—away, and it took itself out of his sight and consciousness.

What he was looking for was the safe-place where Liad dea'Syl stored his equations. He had been forced to make certain broad assumptions in his instructions to his constructs. The quick recon tour he'd taken of the data banks last night had revealed the not-exactly-surprising information that there were many fortified areas within the Osabei Tower architecture. The challenge had then been to build his seekers clever enough to eliminate all but the most likely lockups. He'd at least built them clever enough to move within the Tower brain without lighting any alarms; and they'd also managed to amass a tidy list of six possibles.

The rest of the finicky, risky work was his to do.

He eliminated two of the six before he noticed the timer light blinking insistently at the bottom of the screen. Quickly, he broke the array down, stowed the pieces in the tree's pot, leaned against the wall and became a napping kobold.

No sooner had he closed his eyes than the door chuckled and opened. He heard Scholar tay'Nordif's firm steps, quickly followed by her sharp voice.

"Jela! Open your eyes and rise!"

He did so, in a kobold hurry, which was none too quick, taking care not to crush the Tower servitor who stood just inside the door, a basket held in both of her tiny hands.

"Give the basket to my servant," the Scholar directed the Small, and to him, "Jela! Receive the basket and take it to the kitchen." The exchange made, the scholar waved an imperious hand. "You may go."

The blind servant bowed, turned and exited, silent on tiny, bare feet. Behind her, the door closed, and the scholar stepped forward to seal it while Jela carried the basket into the galley and put it on the counter next to the bowl of water he had drawn for the cat. The animal itself didn't come immediately to sight, and the bowl appeared to be untouched.

Looking into the basket, he saw it full of sealed food packets, not unlike single-rations. Cat food, he surmised, and wondered again where the cat was, which a kobold would not ever wonder, and so he did not look around for it.

"Jela!" Scholar tay'Nordif snapped. "Open a single packet and place it on the counter by the water dish."

He did this while she walked toward the larger room, voicing "*s-s-s-s-s*," and then exclaiming in warm, pleased tones, "*There* you are, clever fellow! I'm pleased to see you making yourself at home. I will be wanting that chair directly, however, and you, I believe, will be wanting your supper."

Jela kept his eyes on the business of unfolding the ration pack into a bowl and spreading the lips wide. He heard the scholar's light-but-not-light-enough steps approach, smelled Cantra's scent over the strong odor of the cat's meal.

"Stand back, Jela," the scholar directed him, and he did what he was told, as she slid the cat smoothly from her arm to the counter, its nose pointed at the food.

The orange tail twitched, the ears flicked—and the cat was at once wholly occupied with its dinner, like any good soldier at mess. Jela dared to look up and observed a smile upon the face of his mistress—a fond and slightly foolish smile, which chilled him to the core, it was so unlike any expression he had ever seen on Cantra yos'Phelium's features.

The eyes moved from the cat to himself, and hardened in an instant. "Jela!" she snapped. "Put the sealed packets—*neatly*—on the lowest shelf of the middle cabinet. When the basket is empty, place it by the door."

Ordered, he obeyed. The scholar watched the cat for a few heartbeats more, then he heard her move back across the room to her workstation.

He finished stocking the cabinet and turned, basket in hand. The ration pack was empty, the cat vanished again. She hadn't told him to clean up the animal's mess, so he passed it by to place the basket, as directed, next to the door.

"What shall I call you?" the scholar inquired, in a high, foolish voice.

Jela turned, slowly, and found her sitting on the chair, cat on her lap, tickling it under its chin. The cat, far from displaying predator-like behavior and having off with her hand, expressed every indication of ecstasy, its eyes slitted and its mouth half-open in pleasure.

"Perhaps," Scholar tay'Nordif said dreamily, "the simple name is best, eh? After all, as the great bin'Arli teaches us, *it is neither name nor house which makes fair fortune*. Therefore, you are now and shall henceforth be—Lucky."

The cat purred loudly, and the scholar chuckled fondly. Jela, his tasks complete, stood next to the door, hoping that she'd notice soon and order him to do something, or else go to sleep so that he could continue with his—

"Ah, what gossip we had at the common gather this evening, Lucky! Truly, you would be horrified to learn how scholars do gossip—but no! You have been employed by a scholar, have you not? You will therefore perhaps not be surprised to hear that Scholar vel'Anbrek believes Prime tay'Welford engineered not only today's proving, but a number of previous challenges made against the work of the previous Prime. Scholar vel'Anbrek believes—ah! not in so many words, you understand; he has not survived so long under walls because he is an idiot, I think—Scholar vel'Anbrek believes that Prime tay'Welford wishes harm to our beloved Master dea'Syl. Is that not diverting, Lucky?"

The cat yawned widely. The scholar laughed, scooped it off her lap and dropped it lightly to the floor as she came to her feet.

"Well, to bed, I believe, so that I am alert for tomorrow's labors!" Without a glance or a glimmer toward the door, where Jela still waited in hope of an order, she stripped off the robe and bundled it untidily onto the shelf that held the half-unpacked travel bag. She kicked off her slippers, pulled a blanket from the storage cabinet and lay down on her cot.

"Jela," she said. "Dim the light and go to sleep."

Bring the lights down, he did, and returned to his place beneath the tree. He waited until the rhythm of her breathing told him that she was asleep before he pulled his equipment from its cache and commenced in again to work.

He roused once, when a seed pod pounced off of his knee, and paused long enough to eat it, sending a silent thanks to the tree. He roused a second time, briefly, when the scholar shifted in her sleep; and a third time, when the cat tried to lay across his array.

And some time just before the end of the scholar's sleep shift, he hid his equipment, settled back against the wall and considered two data points.

One, if Liad dea'Syl's work was locked inside the Osabei data bank, it was well-hidden indeed.

Two, he had the location of Muran's damn' planet-shield that Commander Ro Gayda had ordered him, as his last mission, to procure for the troop.

NINE

Osabei Tower
Landomist

"BUSINESS ON LANDOMIST?" The clerk cast a bored glance over his license, and ran it through the reader.

"I carry data for a scholar seated at Osabei Tower," Tor An said steadily. His shoulder—where he had been shot—hurt in good earnest now, and his thoughts had an alarming tendency to wander. He had dosed himself with antibiotics from the ship's kit, and rewrapped the wound tightly enough that his second-best trading jacket—a hand-me-down from Cor Win and thus a little large—fit over the additional bulk of the dressing.

"Projected length of stay?" the clerk asked.

Until Landomist is consumed by the calamity which has overtaken my—He caught the response before it got off the end of his tongue and substituted, "Much depends upon the scholar. It may be that I will be required for interpretation."

The reader chimed and spat out a datastrip. Bored, the clerk ran it through another reader. This one ejected a pale blue tile with the pictograph for "visitor" 'scribed on its surface. She handed it, with his license, to Tor An.

"You are granted temporary residency for thirty-six local days," she said, her eyes pointed somewhere over his head. "The tile's inclusions degrade at a certain rate. At eighteen local days, its color will phase to red. At the beginning of the thirty-sixth day, it will begin to blink. At the end of the thirty-sixth day, it will phase to black. The mechanism is extremely efficient; however, it is well to arrange to be on your transport before the final hour. If you are required to remain longer than the standard thirty-six day allowance granted by the Portmaster's mercy, Osabei Tower must needs request that this office extend your term."

"I am grateful," Tor An said, slipping his license away into its private pocket with a frisson of relief. The tile he placed in a more public pocket, in case he should need to produce it upon demand.

"Enjoy-your-stay-on-Landomist," the clerk said, and turned away before she had done speaking.

"You wished to see me, Prime Chair?"

tay'Welford looked up from his screen with a smile. "Scholar tay'Nordif. Thank you for coming to me so promptly, and believe that I am deeply grieved that it is become necessary to interrupt you in the pursuit of your work. Please sit down."

She took the chair he indicated, and sat with her hands folded primly in her lap. Her color had not improved over last evening, and overall she seemed a bit rumpled.

"Did you rest well, Scholar?" he asked, noting her condition with concern. "I do hope you find your quarters comfortable."

She blinked and rallied somewhat. "My quarters are more than adequate, I thank you, Prime Chair. As to my rest—on the frontier I was accustomed to sleep in whatever conditions were most safe, which did not—as I am certain you recall!—always equate with 'most comfortable.'"

"I am delighted that the quarters please; we do tend to forget the privations we suffered for our art when we Wandered, working safe here behind walls as we do." He folded his hands atop his desk and considered her. "I do not wish to be forward, Scholar, but I hope you will allow me to say that witnessing one's first proving is a powerful thing. Such a proving as was undertaken yesterday—that is rare, indeed, and more powerful than most. I was unsettled for several days following the first proving I witnessed within these hallowed walls, and it was the veriest street brawl compared to what we were honored to see yesterday."

Scholar tay'Nordif was looking over his right shoulder, her eyes unfocused, and her face slack. Assuming that she was once again relieving Prime tay'Palin's glorious defense, he allowed her a few heartbeats for reverie before clearing his throat.

So intent had she been on the glories of the past, that even that slight noise caused her to start in the chair, her gaze snapping back to his face.

"Your—pardon, Prime," she said rather breathlessly. "My thoughts were elsewhere."

"Surely, surely." He smiled, projecting calmness. The scholar shifted in her chair, smoothing her robe with fingers that were not quite steady.

"But," tay'Welford said, and she jumped again at the sudden syllable, "I had promised not to keep you long from your work! Let us address my topic, if you are willing."

"Certainly," she said again, refolding her hands tightly onto her lap.

"Well, then, I will not conceal that your arrival here—the only one of the Master's own students to reach us—has excited the interest of the Board of Governors. You are called to stand before them two days hence, immediately following the Day Bell. They will wish to ask you certain questions."

He had not thought it possible for Scholar tay'Nordif's face to pale further. Her hands gripped each other so tightly that the knuckles showed white.

"Questions?" she said faintly.

"Indeed." He looked at her with concern. "Are you quite well, Scholar?"

"Yes, of course. It is only—the Board of Governors! What can they possibly wish to ask me?"

"Various things, which seem good to them." He extended a hand and tapped his work screen. "As Prime Chair of our department, I have called you here to put some questions of my own, so that a preliminary report may be sent to the Governors and to the Master. It is the duty of the department to provide the answers to such rudimentary questions." He bent to his screen—and looked up, rueful.

"What am I thinking! There was more—a very great honor for you, Scholar! Master dea'Syl himself will be present during your examination by the Board. Surely, it must be a moment of transcendent joy, to behold once again the face of your master."

"Ah," said Scholar tay'Nordif, in a strangled voice. "Indeed."

This seemed rather subdued for a paroxysm of joy, and tay'Welford waited politely, in case there should be more. However, it appeared that this was the sum total of joyous amazement Scholar tay'Nordif intended to express. tay'Welford cleared his throat, murmured, "Just so," and turned again to his screen.

"Were you acquainted with any other of the Master's students?" he asked, eyes on the screen.

Silence.

He looked up. "Scholar tay'Nordif," he said, sharply. "Pray attend me now. Were you acquainted with any other of Master dea'Syl's students? After all, it is not unusual for Wanderers to form alliances 'mong themselves, to travel and study together for a time."

Scholar tay'Nordif shifted in her chair. "I knew the others but slightly," she murmured. "From the first, I felt that the Master's core assumptions carried a flaw. The others, therefore, did not welcome me among them."

There was a spike of old anger there, which tay'Welford found gratifying.

"How long," he asked, "did you study with Master dea'Syl?"

A short pause, then, "Only—only a short time. Perhaps no longer than three months of the Common Calendar."

tay'Welford frowned. "You studied with him for so short a time—and in addition found his work to be flawed—yet you name yourself his student?"

She glared at him indignantly. "Indeed, I do. How else? Liad dea'Syl's work shaped my own. Were it not necessary to prove those core assumptions false, and to provide truth in their stead, my scholarship would have been broad, yet shapeless."

"I see. So the sum total of your work as a Wanderer was to disprove the work of the scholar you claim as your master?"

Scholar tay'Nordif frowned, stung, perhaps by his disbelieving tone. "You have seen my work, Prime Chair," she said stiffly. "I made no secret regarding the coin I offered the Tower in return for a seat."

"Indeed," tay'Welford said, turning away from his screen to face her more fully. "I have seen your work, Scholar. In fact, I have perused it in some little detail, as my own work has allowed, and it grieves me to state that, while interesting, it is somewhat light of proof. You elucidate the 'reformation' of a single system—but are these results reproducible, Scholar?"

She pressed her lips together and looked down at her folded hands. "I was, perhaps, hasty in approaching the Tower and suing for a seat," she said, muffled. "It seemed to me that the preliminary work was telling. But I should, perhaps, have waited upon the second result."

tay'Welford considered her. "I am to understand that such a result exists?"

"Indeed," her voice took on an eager note. "I had commissioned a pilot to physically access the area and bring me proof—coordinates, spectrograph readings, data."

"And where is this pilot?" tay'Welford interrupted.

Scholar tay'Nordif moved her shoulders slightly. "Late for the rendezvous—you know what pilots are, Prime Chair! I waited at the house of my patron a reasonable time, but then, as I said, I grew restless. I left a message that I might be found at Osabei and came ahead to claim my chair."

He raised an eyebrow at such audacity. "You were certain of yourself, were you not? Do you not consider entry into Osabei Tower a matter of exertion?"

"Indeed, I consider it a matter of the utmost exertion! I had striven greatly, formed and tested a theory which—"

"A theory which," he interrupted, "is a direct attack upon the lifework of one of Osabei Tower's most precious Masters. You knew that such work must gain you entrance, and once entered, you determined to take upon yourself a false mantle of scholarship."

She stared at him, mouth open, plainly and unbecomingly aghast. tay'Welford sighed.

"My work," she managed at last. "My work is revolutionary. It takes our understanding of the nature and function of the natural order a quantum leap ahead of—"

"Your work," tay'Welford snapped, "is trivial and derivative. It proves nothing. Worse, it makes sport of one of the finest mathematical minds to have smiled upon our art since Osabei tay'Bendril gave us the theory of transition."

"How dare—"

He raised his hand, soothing them both. "Peace, peace. My apologies, Scholar. As Prime Chair, it is my duty to facilitate the work of all, and to ease strife, not to create it. Only tell me this—have you reproduced these results?"

"The pilot—" she began, and he sighed.

"Scholar, you had best hope that your pilot arrives with that data before you stand before the Governors, two days hence." He pushed away from his desk and stood.

"That is all, Scholar. Thank you for your assistance."

*

Tor An caught the slideway to the City of Scholars, standing like old bones on the sparsely traveled slow slide, gripping the safety loop grimly and trying to ignore the whirling in his head.

Unlike Korak, with its chaotic streets, and dun colored buildings built tight to the dun colored earth, Landomist soared, the tops of the towers lost in wispy clouds, which filtered the light from the local star to an indeterminate pale yellow. The breeze was damp and cool against his hot face, and fragrant with the odors of the many plants growing in wall niches, in pots, hung from poles and cables, and climbing up the sides of the cloud-topped buildings. Truth told, the air was a little too damp for his taste and he concentrated on breathing in a slow, unhurried rhythm, forcibly ignoring pilot instincts which would have him checking pressure valves and holding tanks in search of a leak…

His stomach was beginning to roil in sympathy with the unsteadiness of his head. He adjusted his grip on the loop and dared to close his eyes for a moment. Alas, that only made matters worse, so he compromised by opening his eyes to the merest slits and ignoring, as best he might, the unpleasant sensations of motion.

Soon, he told himself. Soon, he would be in the City of Scholars, and able to exit the slideway. Soon, he would be in Scholar tay'Palin's office, sitting in a chair, perhaps even sipping some tea, if the scholar were disposed to recall Aunt Jinsu well.

Soon.

"What is it?" the young scholar inquired of the elder, who laughed.

"Kobold," he said, his voice over-loud. Jela, standing slack-jawed and idiot before Scholar tay'Nordif's door, as ordered, did not wince.

"What is a kobold?" the younger scholar persisted, daring to drift closer by a timid step and bending down to peer into his face. "It looks a very brute."

"Some of that," the old scholar allowed. "And truth told, this one seems to be a common laborer. Out of Shinto, if Scholar tay'Nordif's tale of her illustrious patron is to be believed—and there's no reason not to believe it, no matter what dea'San may say. Any new-seated scholar able to place a flan in her account must have got it off a patron—there's no other way for a Wanderer to lay hands on that much money together, mark me! And beside, why would anyone with even as little sense as our good tay'Nordif willingly choose to burden herself with this ugly fellow and that plant, aside they were tokens of that same patron?"

"What's wrong with Shinto?" Greatly daring, the younger scholar leaned in and ran light fingers over the porcelain threads embedded in his chest. Jela knew a brief moment of regret that his role of kobold would not allow him to snarl.

"Eh? Nothing at all wrong with Shinto. Perfectly civilized world. Famous for their horticulture—and those they breed to work in the gardens and greenhouses. Some, like this fellow here, are brute labor; others, I've heard, are something more than that. Mind you, it's worth a life—and an afterlife, too—to speak of them outside of House walls, but there's tales. Oh, yes. There's tales."

The younger scholar sent him a sideways glance. "What sort of tales?"

"You mean to tell me that you've never heard of the mothers of the vine?"

"Oh, certainly!" The younger scholar scoffed, stepping away from Jela to more fully face the elder. "Constructs which are more plant than woman, whose essence is required for a good harvest, and who lie with human men on purpose to drain their vitality and impart it to the grapes!" A derisive snort. "Tales to frighten children and the undereducated."

"And yet they're true enough, those plant-women, and the reason why a trade clan may pay a year's profit for a single half-cask of Rioja wine—and count the purchase fairly made."

"Oh, really, vel'Anbrek! I suppose you've seen one of these fabulous women yourself—in your Wander days, of course!"

"I was never so unfortunate," the old scholar said, his voice serious. "But I did meet a chemist who had once been employed at a Rioja vineyard. She claimed to have seen and spoken with the mothers not once, but many times, and had even what she cared to term a friendship with the elder of them. It's true that she may simply have been telling outlandish tales to a gullible Wanderer. But, in that case, there would have been no need for House Ormendir to buy her silence, which they did, and published the death in the monthly census, as required by law."

The younger scholar waved an airy hand. "The fact that the vineyard bought a Silence in the matter only proves the House of Whispers found the commission to be just. Your chemist more likely stole the formula for the House blend than consorted with creatures out of imagination."

"Have it your own way," the elder scholar said with an expressive ripple of his shoulders. "I only thought to warn that those things which come from the horticultural clans first serve the purpose of the clan. Yon simple kobold might be more than it seems."

"Or—more likely—it might be but a simple kobold, given in order that Scholar tay'Nordif's green token from her patron receive the proper care. For you must agree, vel'Anbrek, even the fondest of patrons could not have thought the good scholar competent to water a plant or, indeed, to pay attention to it at all, should she become *immersed in her work*."

Scholar vel'Anbrek laughed. "An accurate reading of our new colleague, I grant."

"And one thing I notice," the younger scholar continued, slipping his hands into his sleeves, "is that this construct is not properly peace-bonded."

"Aye, it is," said vel'Anbrek, with a nod of his gray head toward Jela. "Those ceramic threads that took your fancy—that's how they peace-bond on Shinto. That I *have* seen, as well as the very clones of the bracelet our good sister wears, to which the implants will respond."

"Ah, will it?" the other said with a snap. "And suppose it requires pacification, and there is only you and me to defend the hall against its sudden imbecile rage?" The right sleeve rippled slightly as the fingers of his left hand tightened—

Jela fell to his knees, choking. He raised a hand; the younger scholar smiled, his eyes bright and cruel as he watched him writhe. He pushed his sleeve up, fingers moving on the slim band around his forearm. Jela tried to stand, fell heavily, froth forming on his lips.

"Here now!" cried the old scholar. "It won't do to place Scholar tay'Nordif's creature at risk. Sport is sport, but much more and it becomes an—"

"It becomes an attack upon my work by base means!" Scholar tay'Nordif's voice came shrilly, and it seemed to Jela that he had never heard a more welcome sound. There was the sound of a sharp slap, a cry of outrage, and the young scholar's armband rang to the floor by his head.

Slowly, his muscles relaxed, and he flopped to his back, chest heaving.

"Now, it will be useless to me all the rest of the day!" Scholar tay'Nordif shouted. "Game with the Tower's constructs, if you have the taste, but do not, at your peril, deprive me of the services of my patron's kobold!"

"You struck me!" the younger scholar shouted in turn. "vel'Anbrek! I call you to witness!"

"I saw it," the elder said, shockingly calm. "Though I warn you I will tell Prime Chair that Scholar tay'Nordif was provoked."

"I will have satisfaction!" The younger scholar snarled, and swooped down to retrieve his armband, his nails coincidentally scoring Jela's cheek as he did. "Come, vel'Anbrek, I require your testimony before the Prime!"

"If you will have it, it is yours," the old scholar said, and the pair of them moved off, noisy in their haste.

Jela lay on the floor, eyes closed, breathing. Above him, he heard Scholar tay'Nordif, her own breathing somewhat ragged. He opened his eyes in time to see her stamp her dainty slippered foot.

"Oh, get *up*, Jela!" she snarled and stomped past him to her door.

Tor An exited the slideway and stood blinking in the thin, misty light, trying to get his bearings. Across the wide green-paved square he saw something that looked very much like a public map. He set course for it, taking care where he put his feet, having just missed taking a bad tumble when it came time to step from the slide to the platform. That had been an unnerving moment. He couldn't remember the last time he'd made a serious misstep; a pilot trusted his balance and his reactions and, even on those few occasions when he'd drunk too much wine, they had never failed him.

Unfortunately for his general state of well being, others with business on the square were not inclined to dawdle. A woman in a billowing beige robe pushed by him, muttering. He caught the word "tourist" and something less complimentary, and tried to quicken his pace.

A hard hand slammed into his wounded shoulder, and he gasped aloud, staggering, spikes of red and orange distorting his view of the square and the map.

"Move along!" a man's voice snapped. "You'll be late for class!"

Tor An shook his head and, through the fading flares of color, he caught an impression of another billowing robe and a long tail of black hair.

He touched his most public pocket, but the few carolis he kept there had not been molested, so at least he had not suffered the further indignity of having his pocket picked. Cor Win would never let him hear the end of the tale, were he found to be such a flat.

The map loomed blessedly closer. He managed the last bit without being either assaulted or cursed, and leaned heavily on the rail as he fumbled the input wand from its holster. His first search, simply on Kel Var tay'Palin, produced a line on the message strip at the base of the map: a room number high in the double dozens at Osabei Tower. Squinting, he glanced 'round at the multitude of towers surrounding the square, and had recourse once more to the wand. A dot of red glittered like a jewel on the map, which he understood to be his current position, from it a red line preceded at an angle to the left, and at last a crimson star burst bright.

Tor An turned his head, sighting along the angle indicated on the map, and located a tower of plain red cermacrete. He double-checked its location against the map and, satisfied that the red tower was indeed his goal, set off. His shoulder was afire and his steps had a distressing tendency to wander to starboard. But, after all, the tower wasn't so far away as that. All that remained was to ring the bell and ask to be shown to Scholar tay'Palin. His mission was nearly at an end.

"Yes, Scholar?" Grudent tel'Ashon arrived breathlessly, bringing with her the odor of disinfectant.

"Yes." Maelyn tay'Nordif leaned back in her chair and smiled. "As my grudent, you will be pleased to hear that I have been asked to speak not only to the Board of Governors, but to Master dea'Syl himself."

The grudent's eyes widened. Jela, sitting at command with his back against the far wall, felt his heart stutter.

"Truly, Scholar," Grudent tel'Ashon breathed. "The Honored dea'Syl himself? Your work must be notable, indeed. Did he say aught in praise or—" She swallowed, apparently deciding that it would not be entirely prudent to ask if Master dea'Syl had found any *fault* with Scholar tay'Nordif's work.

"The invitation came to me through the kind offices of Prime Chair tay'Welford," the scholar said calmly. "It would not, therefore, have been seemly to have spoken more particularly of my work. However, I expect a lively discussion with the master when we meet."

If possible, the grudent's eyes grew rounder. Jela, unnoticed at the front of the room, held his breath. Not his most stringent searching had produced Scholar dea'Syl's data-cache. He had modified his scouts and sent them out again this morning as Scholar tay'Nordif was showering, but he expected tonight's results to be much the same. The master scholar stored his precious notes and working papers elsewhere—he knew it, in one of those illogical leaps of faith your generalist was sometimes taken with. Too bad for him, his intuition was usually right.

But if Can—Maelyn tay'Nordif was going to be meeting with dea'Syl—in his office? in his quarters?—specifically to discuss their work, the notes would have to be stolen from the scholar, and whether Maelyn tay'Nordif could pull the thing off or—

"My discussion with our Prime Chair," she said to the grudent, interrupting these speculations, "brought to mind a matter I failed to mention to you. A pilot is expected, bearing data. It is vital that I have the data—and the pilot—immediately upon arrival. Am I plain?"

Pilot? Jela thought blankly. *What pilot?*

Grudent tel'Ashon was bowing. "Scholar, you are most wonderfully plain. I myself will alert the gatekeepers to expect this pilot, so the data will not be delayed in coming to your hand."

"That is well, then." Scholar tay'Nordif reached for the chording wand, her eyes already on her work screen. "You may go, Grudent."

"Scholar." Another bow and go she did, clever girl.

Jela closed his eyes.

TEN

Osabei Tower
Landomist

TAY'WELFORD SAT WITH his hands folded on the desk before him, and heard Scholar tel'Elyd out. He had vel'Anbrek repeat his testimony twice, then sat in contemplative silence, turning the sprung bracelet over in his hands.

"I will," he said at last into tel'Elyd's angry eyes, "of course need to speak with Scholar tay'Nordif before making a final determination. Before I do so, however, I wonder if I may not persuade you to soften your position, Scholar. Our new sister tay'Nordif is to meet not only with the Governors two days hence, but with no one less than Master dea'Syl, who professes himself most eager to renew their acquaintance."

tel'Elyd paled, and drew himself up. "I will have a complete answer from Scholar tay'Nordif," he said frostily.

tay'Welford sighed. "Very well." He put the bracelet aside and looked from the young scholar to the old. "I will speak to Scholar tay'Nordif immediately. You may expect a resolution before the sounding of the Mercy Bell, so that there will be no discord among colleagues in the Common Room. I trust this is satisfactory?"

"Prime Chair, it is." tel'Elyd rose and bowed. "I will be in my office, working."

vel'Anbrek, however, did not rise. tay'Welford considered him and folded his hands once more.

"Is there something else?"

"Scholar tay'Nordif is Liad's only living student," the old man stated.

tay'Welford waited and, when vel'Anbrek added nothing else to that unadorned statement, sighed and murmured, "She made no secret of the fact that she had knelt at the Master's feet for only a few months before the disparity of their thought drove her away. But, yes, technically, Maelyn tay'Nordif is the last living of the Master's students. Is there a point you particularly wished to make?"

"Only that I have often wondered—have you not?—why it was that Liad's students seemed to die quite so often."

tay'Welford opened his hands, showing empty palms. "It is a perilous thing, to wander the galaxy in pursuit of one's art. The sad fact is that more Wanderers die upon their quests than ever come to us with the price of a chair."

"Yes, yes," vel'Anbrek said impatiently. "We all know that Wanderers exist to die. It only seems odd to me—as a statistician, you understand—that all save one of Liad's students have fulfilled their destinies, when at least a few students of the lowly rest of us have lived long enough to purchase a seat. One wonders if there is something inimical in the fabric of Liad's work, the contemplation of which encourages an untimely demise."

tay'Welford smiled. "This is a jest, of course. You have studied the Master's work—and you are the most long-lived of us all!"

Notably, vel'Anbrek did not smile. "I was a full scholar established in my own sub-field when Liad published his first paper. And though I have, as you say, studied his work, that is a far different matter than being a *student* of his work."

Head tipped to one side, tay'Welford waited politely.

Now vel'Anbrek smiled, and rose creakily. "Well, we old scholars have our crochets. I will be in my office, working. Prime Chair."

"Scholar." tay'Welford responded.

The door closed. tay'Welford counted to one hundred forty-four before he pushed away from his desk and came to his feet. Soonest begun, soonest done, as his own Master had used to say. A speedy determination was in the best interest of the community.

In order to enter Osabei Tower from the public square, one must needs pass through a maze constructed entirely of short, dense green plants that gave off an odor which was perhaps thought to be pleasant, but which all but put Tor An's stomach, already uneasy, into open revolt. Breathing through his mouth, he concentrated on solving the maze, which was ludicrously easy, once he realized it was a Reverse. By taking all the avenues that tended most definitely away from the tower, he speedily arrived at its entrance, and pulled the bell rope, hard.

The door snapped open, and a dark-skinned woman in light duty 'skins thick with smartstrands glared down at him, one hand on the ornate gun holstered at her waist.

"State your business," she snapped, with no if-you-please about it.

Tor An swallowed, and bowed slightly. "My name is Tor An yos'Galan, and I seek an audience with Scholar Kel Var tay'Palin."

The guard's fingers were seen to tighten on the butt of her weapon, and Tor An tensed. He took a deep breath and tried to remember that not all gatekeepers summarily shot those who petitioned them for entrance.

"Prime Chair tay'Palin is not receiving visitors."

Well, the scholar—Prime Chair!—was doubtless a busy man, Tor An conceded. He should perhaps have sent ahead. Indeed, Uncle Kel Ven would certainly have scolded him for such a breach of etiquette—and he wished to be a trader!

The guard was staring at him, her 'skins flickering distractingly in the cloud-filtered light. He bowed again. "Would it be possible to leave a message for the—"

"Prime tay'Palin has achieved immortality in his work," the guard interrupted. Her teeth flashed in a grin so quick he could not really be certain he had seen it. "That means—he's dead."

Dead. Tears rose to his eyes. He blinked them away, took a pair of breaths to settle his stomach, and bowed once again.

"I thank you," he murmured, as he tried to form another plan. Surely there was another scholar who—

"Good-day," the guard said, and took one long step backward, the door closing with a boom.

He stared at it, stupidly. Reached for the bell chord and snatched his hand back. No, not yet. Not while he was tired and ill. He would—he would find the pilots hostel, take a room, sleep, and tomorrow consider how best to go on.

Slowly, not at all eager to again subject his stomach to the odoriferous maze, he turned and began to walk back the way he had come.

"Wait!" a woman's voice called urgently from behind, amid clattering. "Pilot! Wait, I beg you!"

He turned in time to avoid being run over by a woman wearing a unitard and a utility belt. She snatched at his arm—mercifully, not the wounded one—and peered earnestly into his face, her eyes brown and wide.

"You are the pilot," she stammered—"the pilot the scholar is expecting? You have the data?"

Tor An blinked. "Indeed," he said carefully. "I am a pilot and I do carry data which may be of interest to the scholar."

The woman smiled, clearly relieved. "I abase myself. I had just come to inform the ostiary—we had not expected you so soon! Ah, but there's no harm done." She pulled his arm as she turned back toward the entrance, where the dark-skinned guard stood, wide-legged and arms akimbo, watching. "The scholar's orders were that you be brought to her immediately."

"I am more than willing to be escorted to the scholar," Tor An assured the woman, trying without success to extricate himself from her grip.

"Come with me, then," she said. "Quickly."

The problem of communication between himself and Scholar tay'Nordif was a sticky one, Jela allowed, as he sat on the floor where he'd been directed by his highly-annoyed mistress, back against the wall. Cantra had been certain that his ingenuity and the core training she and her—and the person she proposed to become shared would be sufficient to the needs of the mission. He'd agreed with that, being, as he now unhappily realized, under-informed. Not that he could put that fault on the pilot. No, simply put, he'd let his own understanding of how the galaxy operated taint his info. Cantra had told him what she was going to do, and he couldn't fault her for plain-speaking. He did have a suspicion that she'd played her cards with exceptional care, having pegged him as a practical man to whom seeing was believing—and gambling that, by the time he saw, and believed, it would be too late to retreat.

Whether providing him with a thorough-going fool for a partner in the rescue of life-as-they-knew-it was the Rimmer pilot's notion of a joke—no. No, there was good reason to acquit her there, too.

For all her faults, Cantra yos'Phelium was a woman of her word. She'd pledged her help, which she would have never done unless she intended to deliver. Which meant that there was something Maelyn tay'Nordif could accomplish to the benefit of the mission that Cantra couldn't have. It was his own lack of imagination that he couldn't think of anything Cantra yos'Phelium might fail to accomplish, given her word and her intent.

Trust, the Rimmer pilot whispered from memory—and it might truly be, he thought, that the only place that pilot existed anymore was in his memory. He took a hard breath, trying to ease the sudden constriction of his chest. Cantra yos'Phelium deserved to live on in the memories of twelve generations of pilots, not sentenced to unsung oblivion when the M who'd asked—and received—a death of her grew old all at once, and died.

Only weeks, now.

He shook that line of thought away, though not the melancholy, and applied himself once more to making sense of this sudden tale of a pilot expected, bearing—

The door chime sounded. He opened his eyes, and saw the scholar hunched over her screen, apparently oblivious.

The chime sounded a second time, followed by a man's voice.

"Prime Chair tay'Welford requests entrance."

At her desk, the scholar muttered something in a dialect Jela didn't recognize, though he figured he got the drift from her tone. She lifted the wand, and chorded in a brief command—very likely shutting down her work screen so Prime Chair wouldn't be tempted to steal her work.

"Come!" she called, slipping the wand into its holster. She spun her chair and stood, arms down straight and a little before her, fingertips just touching the surface of her desk.

The door opened and tay'Welford stepped within, his sash now bearing those items of office which had previously adorned Prime tay'Palin. Scholar tay'Nordif bowed, briefly, and with neither grace nor art.

"Prime Chair, you honor my humble office."

tay'Welford looked 'round him, measuringly, thought Jela.

"Your office seems quite comfortable, if I may say so, Scholar. Certainly far more so than when ser'Dinther held it."

"It is well enough," she answered, "for a beginning." She lifted a hand, indicating one of the chairs on the far side of the desk. "Please, sit."

"My thanks." He took the chair and spent a moment arranging the fall of his robe. Scholar tay'Nordif sat after he did, and folded her arms on the desk.

"I do not," tay'Welford murmured, "wish to infringe upon your time any more than is needful, Scholar, so I will come immediately to the point of my visit. Scholar tel'Elyd has made a formal grievance against you, and he has stated that he will pursue satisfaction to the fullest—"

"Scholar tel'Elyd," the scholar interrupted hotly, "mounted a dastardly and craven attack against my work, Prime! It is not to be borne, and if either of us should have cause to call for satisfaction, it is myself!"

"Ah." tay'Welford inclined his head, and spoke seriously. "I wonder, Scholar, if you would give me the particulars of this attack upon your work?"

"Certainly! I found him abusing the kobold given for my comfort by my patron, in such a manner as to deprive me of its services since—and likely for the remainder of the day!"

"And the kobold," tay'Welford said cannily. "I understand you to say that it is necessary to your work?"

Sitting at the floor at the rear of the room, back against the wall, Jela wished he could get a good look at tay'Welford's face. Cantra yos'Phelium had been able to read a lie off the twitch of a man's earlobe, but he had no evidence that Maelyn tay'Nordif could do the same. tay'Welford's tone had the feel of a trap being set, but what that trap might be, when the old scholar had said right out he'd give evidence that put the lie to the younger's claim—

"The kobold is my patron's gift to me," Scholar tay'Nordif said stiffly. "It is necessary that I be as comfortable as possible in order to give my best attention to my work."

"But to say that the kobold itself is *necessary* to your work—forgive me, Scholar, but that is quite an extraordinary statement. And to come to blows with a colleague in defense of a base creature—I fear me that demonstrates a lack of judgment we do not like to see within our department."

Scholar tay'Nordif sniffed. "And should I have given this so-called tel'Elyd leave to destroy that which has been placed in my keeping? What else, Prime? Shall I allow him to destroy my reference works? My *notes*?"

"One's reference works and notes are—of course!—necessary to one's continued work. But a kobold, Scholar—" He sighed. "No, I do not believe I can allow it."

Jela's chest tightened.

"I beg your pardon?" snapped Scholar tay'Nordif.

"I believe that tel'Elyd may have the right of it, Scholar. You chose to place the continued functioning of a base creature above the necessities of a colleague—and that is a very grave thing."

"Pray, what necessities had tel'Elyd in the matter? 'Twas a random act of negligent cruelty, sir!"

"Alas, it may not have been. tel'Elyd requires a certain amount of titillation in order to do his best work. Happily, his need is fulfilled in the torment of the base, and as he rarely requires more than torment, his necessity is scarcely a drain on departmental resources."

"I—" began Scholar tay'Nordif, but tay'Welford had already risen.

"The matter is clear," he said definitely. "You will stand to answer tel'Elyd in the hour before the Mercy Bell, today. I shall inform him of my decision." He inclined his head. "I thank you for your time, Scholar. May your work be fruitful."

Slowly, Scholar tay'Nordif came to her feet. She bowed, with even less grace than usual, and held it while Prime tay'Welford turned and strolled leisurely from the room, smiling at Jela as he passed out of the door and into the hallway.

"Oh," said Maelyn tay'Nordif, flopping into her chair into her chair the moment the door closed. "Damn."

The path the apprentice scholar set through the twisting hallways of the lower tower would have made his head spin had it not been doing so already, Tor An thought. As it was, he was most thoroughly lost and in terror lest his guide, whom he had at last convinced to relinquish his arm, should outpace him.

The hall opened abruptly into a wide, high-ceilinged room, six of the eight ceramic walls were cast in graduating rows, like seats in a theater. Here, his guide all but ran, and he forced himself into a trot, narrowing his focus to her figure, fleeing and clanking before him. She vanished into another narrow hall. He pursued perforce—and very nearly ran over her where she stood, just within the narrow walls, facing a man in beige robes, his sash supporting various fobs and tablets, as well as a naked blade and a pair of smart gloves. The scholar was frowning down at the 'prentice, who had abased herself. He looked up at Tor An's arrival, and his brows lifted high.

"Who, may I ask, are you?" The voice was pleasant, though carrying a slight edge—whether of bemusement or outright irritation, Tor An couldn't have said.

However, the attitude of the 'prentice suggested that this was a person whom it would be best not to annoy. Tor An therefore bowed as deeply as he was able and straightened with a care he hoped would be seen as respect.

"My name is Tor An yos'Galan, esteemed sir," he said seriously.

"I see." The scholar paused. "And what might your business be in Osabei Tower, Tor An yos'Galan?"

The scholar had an open, pleasant face. Surely, so exalted a gentleman, who was in any wise apparently someone of rank in these halls, could be trusted with his—

"Prime Chair!" the 'prentice scholar had straightened out of her bow and was wringing her hands in agitation. "This is the pilot whom Scholar tay'Nordif expects, bearing the data necessary for her proof! Her word was that, *immediately* he arrived, he and the data were to be brought to her. Her *word*, Prime Chair, which I, as her grudent, am bound to obey!"

The scholar—Prime Chair—turned his attention to her, his head tipped to a side, long brown hair cascading over one shoulder.

"Ah! Scholar tay'Nordif's pilot!" he said, in tones of broad enlightenment. "I confess I had not expected to see him so soon!" He stepped back, moving a graceful hand in a sweep along the way they had been traveling. "By all means, Grudent tel'Ashon, deliver the pilot and his data to our good scholar!"

"Yes," the 'prentice breathed. She bowed hastily, and Tor An once more had his arm gripped as she hurried him with her.

"Be well, Tor An yos'Galan!" the Prime Chair called as they rushed away. "I look forward to deepening our acquaintance!"

"Quickly!" the 'prentice breathed in his ear.

"Why?" he demanded. "We've been given leave to go."

"Because," she hissed, and without lessening her pace, "scholars are mad. It is the business of scholars to be jealous each of the others' honors and position. You may be assured that the Prime Chair means to get the advantage of Scholar tay'Nordif and punish her for rising in the esteem of the Master as he has not. And if his punishment is to be depriving the scholar of yourself or your data, then he will take you from *her*, and not from *me*."

Rushing along at her side, Tor An thought that perhaps it was not the scholars alone who were mad.

"Why do you serve here, then?" he panted.

"I have one more local year of service, after which I shall have my journeyman's certificate. And you may well believe I shall receive it with joy and forthwith seek a position as a mathematics tutor. Here!" She halted before a door exactly like the others lining the hall, and touched the plate with the fingers of her free hand. A chime sounded, and she said loudly, "It is Grudent tel'Ashon, Scholar! Your pilot has arrived!"

There was small delay before the door whisked open. The grudent all but shoved him into the office beyond, letting go of his arm with a will.

He staggered, barely sorting his feet out in time to prevent a spill and stood, breathing heavily and head a-spin, three long steps into a small office. At his right hand, a man in dark leathers sat on the floor, back against the wall, his brown face lean and inscrutable. Before him, a woman in the now-familiar robe of a scholar frowned from behind a too-clean desk, a data input wand held between her palms, her green eyes cold in a stern golden face.

"Well," she said, her voice high and unpleasant against his ear. "At least you had the grace to make haste from Shinto, sirrah!" She pointed her eyes over his shoulder. "Grudent, you have done well. Leave us now."

"Scholar." The 'prentice's voice carried a unmistakable note of relief. Tor An glanced over his shoulder, but she was already gone, the office door closing behind her.

"So, Pilot," the sharp voice brought his attention back to the scholar, who had put the chording wand down and stood up behind her desk. "Approach. I assume that you *have* brought the data?"

Tor An blinked, feeling the datastrip absurdly heavy in its inner pocket. It came to him that it was—perhaps—not wise to have embarked upon this deception. This stern-faced scholar was expecting, after all, a *particular* pilot bearing *particular* data with *particular* relevance to her work, and if the grudent were to be believed—

"Come, come, Pilot!" the scholar said impatiently. "Have you the data or not?"

"Scholar," he bowed, head swimming, and straightened carefully. "I have data. Also, I have information." He cleared his throat.

"The Ringstars are gone. What I bring are the measurements and the logs describing the section of space which is—missing. This may not be—"

"Yes, yes!" The scholar interrupted, holding out an imperious hand. "That is precisely what you have been paid to provide! Bring it forth, Pilot; I haven't all day to stand here trading pleasantries with you!"

He swallowed, and glanced to one side. The man sitting against the wall was watching him from hooded black eyes.

"For pity's sake, Pilot! Have you never seen a kobold before? Come, the data!"

In fact, he *had* seen kobolds before, and the man on the floor bore a superficial resemblance to those of the laborer class he had encountered. But such a one would never have looked at him so measuringly, nor paid attention so nearly—

"Pilot?" the scholar's voice now carried an edge of sarcasm. "Am I to understand that you do not stand in need of the remainder of your fee?"

Abruptly, he was exhausted. Perhaps after all, he thought, *he* was mad. In any case, this woman, whom he had never seen before, was asking for the very data he carried. How she came to want it or he to have it was immaterial, really. And if a second pilot had been commissioned to gather the same readings, then—surely—that was cause for hope?

He slid the 'strip out, stepped forward and placed it on the desk before the impatient scholar.

She smiled, and peered into his face.

"You are tired, I see," she said, suddenly gentle—"and so you should be, having come so quickly from Shinto! Jela will escort you to my quarters, where you may rest yourself. Only allow me to access the data, and you may go. "

She plucked the 'strip up and slid it into her work unit, fumbling the wand in her haste, but at last she chorded the correct commands, and stood watching as line after line of coordinates marched down the screen.

"Aha!" she said and manipulated the wand quickly before bending to the unit. Eyes on the screen, she pulled the 'strip out of the slot and put it on the desk.

"Jela!" she said, loudly. "Stand up!"

At the back of the room, the leather-clad man slowly and stolidly got his feet under him and rose, Tor An thought, rather like a mountain rising out of an ocean. At least, until he was fully afoot, when it could be seen that his height was more hill-like than mountain.

"Now," said the scholar, "you will—"

From somewhere—from everywhere—an alarm sounded. Tor An spun to the wall, snatching for the grab-bars that weren't there. Face heating, he turned back, to find the scholar pale, her mouth set into a hard, pained line.

"Your pardon, Pilot," she said with punctilious politeness. "I am wanted elsewhere. A matter of honor, you apprehend."

She came 'round the desk, moving stiffly, her hands tucked firmly into her sleeves. "Jela!" she snapped as she passed Tor An. "Escort this pilot to my quarters."

The door opened. "Pilot," she said in a slightly less snappish tone, but without looking at him. "Please follow Jela."

Tor An snatched the datastrip up off the desk, slid it into an inner pocket, and turned to see the man Jela moving purposefully toward the door. He bethought himself of the twistiness of the Tower hallways, and hurried after.

ELEVEN

Osabei Tower
Landomist

THE THIN CORRIDOR was awash with scholars, all talking and laughing, moving with one purpose in the direction, so Tor An believed, of the wide, tiered foyer.

Jela was well ahead of him, apparently invisible to the chattering scholars, who jostled him rather roughly, until at last he flattened himself against the wall, where he waited with a bland, intelligent patience no kobold ever bred could have mustered.

Scarcely less jostled, and tender, besides, of his wounded arm, Tor An came to rest at his guide's shoulder, closed his eyes and took stock. On the debit side of the trade sheet, he was tired, his wound ached, and he was certainly bewildered, while the credit side showed a head more firmly anchored to his shoulders than it had been earlier in the day, and a stomach no longer in open rebellion.

Progress, he thought. Eyes still closed, he put himself to trying to filter some sense from the echoing noise.

It seemed, if he rightly understood the bits and flotsam of conversation that fell into his ear, as if Scholar tay'Nordif were about to fight a duel. What the cause of this might be, he did not quite grasp. He sighed, and settled himself more comfortably against the wall, letting the voices rise and fall about him without trying to net any more sense. He allowed himself to hope that the hallway would soon clear, and that the scholar's quarters were neither far removed, nor Jela disposed to run.

He felt something touch his hand, where it rested against the wall. He blinked out of his doze to see Jela already moving down the hall in the wake of the last straggler scholars, walking slow and heavy. Something about that nagged at Tor An, as he pushed away from the wall and followed, then faded.

At the foyer, Jela paused again, in the shelter of the risers; Tor An did, too. Looking over his guide's sleek head, he could see a wide expanse of empty floor, and the seats rising up the walls across. The noise of voices was not so loud here—not, Tor An thought, because the scholars were talking any less, but because their words were not confined by the hallway.

Carefully, he placed a hand on Jela's shoulder. "Let us go," he murmured, but there was no sign that the other man heard him.

For the third time, the alarm bell sounded, bringing silence in its wake. Tor An leaned against the riser that shielded them, and resigned himself to wait.

The tall, brown-haired scholar Grudent tel'Ashon had addressed as "Prime Chair" strolled out onto the floor, a dueling stick held in each hand. Behind him came Scholar tay'Nordif, head high and shoulders rigid, and a slim, delicate scholar with cropped sandy hair, and a long timonium chain hanging from one ear.

Prime Chair stopped in the center of the rectangular dueling area marked out by rust colored tiles, the two scholars flanking him, and brandished the 'sticks over his head.

"What we have before us today is a personal balancing between Scholars tel'Elyd and tay'Nordif. Scholar tay'Nordif admits to having struck Scholar tel'Elyd for taking certain liberties with the construct Jela, which she maintains is necessary to her work—" There was a murmur from the audience at this. Prime Chair shook one of the dueling sticks toward the offending section of seats.

"This action of Scholar tel'Elyd was witnessed by Scholar vel'Anbrek, nor does tel'Elyd deny it. However, it is the judgement of the Prime Chair that in striking Scholar tel'Elyd in punishment for those liberties taken with the construct, Scholar tay'Nordif has placed a scholar on the same plane as a base creature. This affront to Scholar tel'Elyd's honor must be mended."

With a flourish, he brought the sticks out and down to shoulder level. Each scholar stood forward and armed themselves, then spun to face each other, dueling stick held in the neutral posture.

"These two of our worthy colleagues shall contend as equals. The point goes to whichever counts to six upon a fallen opponent. This duel is not to the death. As it is a personal matter, truth-blades may not be employed." He gave each of the combatants a long, grave look, and dropped back to the outside of the rectangle.

"You may engage upon my count of six," he said. "One…"

Scholar tel'Elyd spun his stick, getting the feel of it, Tor An suspected, that having been the route advised by those who had sought to instruct him in self-defense: *Always test the weight and balance of an unfamiliar weapon, conditions permitting.*

In contrast, Scholar tay'Nordif stood gripping the stick tightly in the neutral position, her stance stiff and awkward. He wondered if the scholar had ever received self-defense instruction, and hoped for her sake that the Osabei Tower weapons-master kept the charges on the dueling sticks toward the low end of match range.

"Three…"

Scholar tel'Elyd took up the stance: legs slightly apart, knees flexed, right foot pointed at the opponent, left foot at a right angle, primary hand at the bottom of the handle, off-hand above, spine relaxed and slightly curved. Tor An was slightly heartened to see Scholar tay'Nordif arrange herself in a similar configuration, though she stood too tall and too stiffly, her feet were placed awkwardly, and her hands were too close together.

"Six," said Prime Chair.

Scholar tel'Elyd snapped his 'stick sharply, releasing a heavy blue bolt in the direction of the hapless Scholar tay'Nordif. To Tor An's mingled surprise and relief, she managed a credible parry, the sizzle of mingling energies loud in the sudden silence, finishing her move with a neat little twist that sent a glob of red speeding toward her opponent—who destroyed it with a sneer and shook another heavy bolt from his 'stick, and a second more quickly than Tor An would have believed possible, had he not seen it for himself. Scholar tel'Elyd must have a supple wrist, indeed.

Scholar tay'Nordif deflected the first of the pair, but at the expense of her precarious stance. The second bolt got through her wavering defense, and scored a solid hit on the her hip.

She flinched, her hand dropping instinctively—and disastrously—to the wound. Scholar tel'Elyd followed up his advantage immediately, sending a line of short bursts one after the other in a really remarkable display of skill.

Scholar tay'Nordif parried, one-handed, off-balance and, as Tor An knew from his training, hurting, but it was plain who was the master of the duel. Scholar tel'Elyd could put up his 'stick at any time and no one among the silent spectators would challenge his win.

But Scholar tel'Elyd was not disposed to be merciful. Whatever dispute stood between him and Scholar tay'Nordif, it quickly became clear that he considered a telling demonstration of superiority at arms to be inadequate balance.

Scholar tay'Nordif swayed under the pain of repeated strikes, and flung an arm up to shield her eyes. Her dueling stick fell from her hand and lay, sparking fitfully on the surface of the dueling court. Tor An waited for Prime Chair to rule the match ended and tel'Elyd the victor, but the man stood mute at the sidelines, calmly watching the punishment continue.

This was no longer a duel, Tor An thought angrily. He started forward, meaning to end the thing himself—and found a hard, broad shoulder blocking his way.

"He goes too far!" he said, loudly, in Jela's ear.

There was no sign that his escort heard him, but someone on the benches above them did.

"He goes too far!" A woman's voice called out. "Honor has been rescued. Brute punishment only tarnishes it anew!"

The cry was taken up by others around the room, and very shortly Tor An had the satisfaction of seeing the scholar's hand falter. He straightened out of the dueling crouch and pointed his 'stick at the floor.

Then only did Prime Chair step forward, placing himself between the victorious scholar and the beaten.

"Honor has been rescued!" he announced. "The matter between Scholars tel'Elyd and tay'Nordif has been balanced and shall be spoken of no more."

There was general, sparse applause, and a bell rang.

"Colleagues!" Prime Chair called. "It is time to lay down our labors and meet in the common room!"

Warm fingers touched his hand. Tor An looked down to see Jela moving across the floor, angling for one of several doors. He stretched his legs to catch up.

All of Rool Tiazan's sincerity regarding "luck" and its fondness for him, the tree, and especially Cantra hadn't prepared Jela for the moment when the yellow-haired pilot staggered into the office, helped along by a kindly shove from Grudent tel'Ashon.

It was enough to turn an old soldier to religion, and no use, he decided, trying to work out if the luck had whispered the pilot's nearness to the scholar or simply shoved the pilot into the scholar's path. What mattered was that he had arrived—and that the mission had need of him.

He put the key in its niche atop the controller and waited while their home stair lowered itself. It had taken all his discipline to thrust the memory of the duel between Maelyn tay'Nordif and Den Vir tel'Elyd into the back of his mind. Those strikes—he'd felt each one as if the energy had lashed his own nerves. And if ever proof were called for that Cantra yos'Phelium had died in creating Maelyn tay'Nordif, that duel was everything that was needed.

The end of the stair touched the floor. He retrieved the key and walked into the very middle of the ramp so the pilot, who had followed silent and uncomplaining from the dueling hall, would not feel exposed. Or, he amended as the stair began to rise, not much exposed.

The stairway seated itself at the proper floor, and he led the way to the door of the scholar's quarters. Again he used the key, stepped inside and did a rapid scan.

The cat was crouching on the galley counter, tail wrapped around its toes, amber eyes hooded. The tree sat in its pot by the door; Jela received a flutter of interested curiosity as Tor An yos'Galan stepped into the room. The hacks were in place and emitting on the proper frequency. He sighed and turned.

"*Brrrrrt?*" The pilot said, his soft voice shocking against the high hum of the hacks. He approached the cat, who watched him with interest, and gave the finger he extended careful study before daintily touching it with its nose. The pilot smiled, which made him look ridiculously young, and very tired.

"What's his name?" he asked, sliding a sideways glance at Jela from beneath heavy golden lashes.

"The scholar calls it Lucky," he answered, and the sound of his own voice startled him. It seemed years since he had last spoken.

The pilot inclined his head gravely, and rubbed the cat under the chin. "Lucky, I am very pleased to make your acquaintance," he murmured. "I have been missing cats." He straightened, carefully, sending another of his sideways glances at the tree. "And plants. At my—" His voice broke. He took a hard breath, and began again, resolutely. "At my home, there is a back garden and a certain piata tree of which I am most fond."

Inside Jela's head a picture formed: a half-grown dragon staggering across a grey sky, wings trembling, rock-toothed cliffs too near below.

Right.

"I couldn't help but notice that you've been wounded," he said to Tor An yos'Galan. "I have a kit, if there's need."

This time the look came straight from amethyst-colored eyes. "There may be need, I thank you. The wound is in an awkward place. I've done my best, but—"

Jela waved him to a stool. "Take your jacket off, then, lad, and let's see what you have." He crossed the room to get the kit from Scholar tay'Nordif's travel bag.

"Well," Jela said a few minutes later, keeping his voice light for his patient's peace of mind. "That's as pretty a burn as I've seen in some time." It would leave a black, ridged scar on the boy's soft golden skin, but that was minor. The important news was that it was healing well, with no sign of infection or any ancillary damage. "I've got something here that'll leach the last of the heat," he said easily. "It'll feel cold." He broke the ampule and rubbed the lotion into the burn site. His patient hissed, shoulders tensing, but otherwise made no complaint.

"Give that a count of twelve to set, then we'll get a dermal-bond on it."

"Thank you," the boy murmured, the starch already leaching out of his shoulders, which would be the topical anaesthesia starting its work.

"How did you come by that particular wound?" Jela asked, sorting through the supplies and pulling out a sealed bond pack. "If it can be told."

Tor An sighed and moved his shoulder experimentally.

"The captain of the garrison on Korak ordered me shot," he said in a tone Jela thought was meant to be expressionless, but which carried a payload of anger and terror.

If that were the case, the boy was lucky in his own right. Jela began to repack the kit.

"Why?" he asked, though he thought he knew.

"I went to them—to the garrison. I thought the military commander might investigate the fact of the Ringstars vanishing. The trade office would only—" hard breath "—would only list the route closed and the ports unavailable."

Jela cracked the seal on the dressing and stretched it wide between his fingers, eyeing the burn site.

"The soldier—on guard," Tor An continued, and despite his best efforts his voice was sounding a trifle ragged. "The guard said that the Ringstars were far from the first to go missing, and that in anywise it was none of Korak Garrison's affair, as they'd been called back—called back to the Inner Arm."

"Well, the guard was right that the military's being moved back," Jela said judiciously. "You'll feel some pressure now, and it might nip you a bit, which I know you won't regard, Pilot."

He moved quick, and as sure as he was able. Despite the topical, it must've hurt, but Tor An yos'Galan sat a quiet board.

"Good lad," Jela murmured approvingly. "You'll do fine, now."

The boy sighed, and simply sat for a moment, then slid off the stool and reached for his shirt, which the cat was sitting on, all four feet poised beneath it. Tor An smiled.

"I believe my need is greater," he said politely and extended one slim hand, scooping the cat up beneath its belly, cool as you please, while liberating his clothing with the other.

"Thank you," he said, replacing the cat in its spot. "Your understanding during this difficult time is appreciated."

The cat, which had endured both handling and nonsense with nary a spit nor a glare, settled itself flat onto its belly and curled its front feet against its chest. Tor An shook out his shirt—good quality, Jela saw, but plain. Respectful and quiet. Much like the boy himself.

Jela finished his own tidying up, and carried the kit back across the room, replacing it in the scholar's baggage.

A chime sounded.

Jela spun, pleased to see that the boy had done so as well, fingers gone quiet on the fastenings of his shirt.

The chime sounded again.

Tor An sent a questioning glance in his direction; Jela replied with a quick flicker of pilot hand-talk: *Answer.*

The lad blinked. "Who is it?" he called, finishing up with the shirt.

"Please," called a stilted, childlike voice. "Food arrives for Scholar tay'Nordif's pilot."

"Ah. Just a moment." He moved, while Jela stayed where he was—out of the immediate line of sight, with his kobold mask in place, on the principle of taking as few chances as possible.

Came the sound of the door opening

"Food arrives for Scholar tay'Nordif's pilot," the high voice repeated, clearer now without the filtering of the announcement system. "It is hoped that the meal pleases. Also given are tickets for future meals in the grudents' cafeteria, after the pilot is rested. The pilot is not permitted to dine with the scholars in the common room. If the pilot has other needs, he may petition Scholar tay'Nordif. Has the pilot questions?"

"None whatsoever, I thank you," the boy said gravely. He bent; there was a small clamor of cutlery as he received a tray.

"Scholar tay'Nordif sends that she will be a little delayed this evening," the Small chirped, "and prays that in her absence the pilot will regard her quarters as his own, stinting his comfort in no wise. Scholar tay'Nordif very much regrets the delay."

"I thank you," Tor An said again, "for bearing this message. I am made quite comfortable here, and anticipate the Scholar's arrival so that I may express to her my gratitude for her care."

"The scholar also asks," the Small continued, "that the pilot honor her by feeding the cat, and seeing that he has fresh water."

Jela closed his eyes.

"I will do so, gladly. He is a fine cat and has made me very welcome."

"Message ends. Responses on file," the high voice announced, and Jela caught the sound of bare feet on tile before Tor An closed the door.

He bore the covered tray to the counter and put it down, giving Jela a troubled look.

"She sends no meal for you?"

"Kobolds don't each much," he answered lightly. Tor An frowned.

"You, my friend, are no kobold. And I am ashamed that I failed to see you as a pilot until you bespoke me just now."

"I have," Jela said, leaning a companionable elbow on the counter, "been doing my best not to seem pilot-like."

"And doing rather well," Tor An allowed, making a brave attempt not to look famished. "However, you do not seem quite kobold-like, either, if you will forgive my saying so."

Jela sighed and nodded at the tray. "Eat your dinner, Pilot."

But it appeared the lad was stubborn as well as mannerly, which, Jela allowed wryly, was only what could be expected from a pilot.

"Why," asked Tor An, "are you pretending to be a kobold?" He hesitated before adding politely, "If it can be told."

Not a bad question, though it meant Jela had to make an immediate decision regarding how much truth it was going to be necessary to tell Tor An yos'Galan.

"Well," he said, giving the boy a straight, earnest look, "for one thing, Scholar tay'Nordif believes I'm a kobold, and I don't like to disappoint a lady."

That earned him an unamused glare from those dark purple eyes before the pilot moved 'round the counter.

"Why," he asked, "are you deceiving the scholar in this manner?" He opened the cabinet door and extracted a ration pack of cat food. Jela sighed to himself.

"That's a bit complicated," he said, watching the cat dance back and forth along the counter ahead of the boy, doing its all to impede any progress that might be made in opening its rations.

"The Ringstars vanishing is also a bit complicated," Tor An said tartly, his gaze on the task in hand. "I am not a child, Jela—" He looked up. "What is your name? Pilot."

"As it happens, my name's Jela," he said easily and offered a comfortable grin. The other pilot looked away and put the open ration pack down on the counter. The cat, tail straight up and quivering, fell to. Tor An picked up the water bowl and turned to the sink.

"My full name," Jela said, having decided on his course in the heartbeat between his last sentence and this, "is M. Jela Granthor's Guard. My rank is captain and wingleader, and I'm on detached duty to acquire that which may, just possibly, keep the rest of the Arm from following the Ringstars into Enemy territory."

The slim shoulders tensed. "You are a soldier, then," Tor An said, a little too breathless to be as uncaring as he obviously wished to appear.

"I am," Jela said. "But I'm not the sort of soldier who shoots civilians for sport. At a guess, those guards and their captain at Korak were X Strain soldiers—tall, eh? With maybe tattoo work on their faces?"

"Yes," the boy whispered.

"Right," Jela said, voice deliberately companionable. "They're the new design. I'm the old design. M Strain. If there were more Ms and less Xs, it might be that the military wouldn't be quite so easy with those orders to pull back and cede the Rim and the mid-Arm to the *sheriekas*."

Tor An carried the refreshed water bowl to the counter and put it down beside the cat. He looked up, eyes troubled.

"There is something—here?—that will prevent any more disappearances like—*do you know what happened to the Ringstars*?" It burst out of him like a war cry, and for a moment Jela thought he might put his head down on the counter and weep—but Tor An yos'Galan was tougher than he looked. He mastered himself, took a deep breath and waited, hands folded tightly on the counter.

"I do," Jela said, warming to the lad. "And I can show you the math. The short of it is that the *sheriekas*—the Enemy—have perfected a way to decrystalize portions of space. Like the guard at Korak told you, the Ringstars are only the latest in a list that's getting long fast, and will pretty soon encompass the whole galaxy, unless we liberate the equations that describe the counter-crystallization process from where they're hidden inside this very Tower."

Tor An yos'Galan closed his eyes.

"Pilot Jela—" he began.

"I know," Jela said soothingly. "I know it sounds lunatic, but I do have those equations for you. I'll set them up on a tile array while you eat your dinner."

Tor An opened his eyes. "What will you eat for dinner?" he asked, and Jela gave him a comfortable smile.

"I'll just have a ration bar while I work," he said easily. "It's what I'm used to."

Exhaustion, youth, and hunger were Jela's allies, but for a long moment, he thought they wouldn't be enough. Then the boy inclined his head, moved down counter and lifted the lid off of the tray.

Tor An looked up from the grid, purple eyes bleak.

"These equations are rather dense, are they not?"

Jela looked at him with sympathy. "The process for folding up bits of the galaxy and putting them away in some other alternity takes some describing," he said. "I've been studying those numbers for a good long while, now. I'm almost sure I've got the major points mastered."

"Ah." The boy touched the frame. "May I have the use of this?"

Jela waved a hand. "It's yours," he said—and waited. He was in his usual place by the tree; Tor An was cross-legged atop the counter, cat on one knee, grid balanced precariously on the other.

"I think," he said, "that you had better tell me what place Scholar tay'Nordif has in your mission. Is it she who has formulated these equations you seek?"

The boy knew how to ask a question, Jela thought, and took a moment to resettle himself against the wall and breathe in a good, deep breath of tree-filtered air.

"Scholar tay'Nordif," he said then, because he had to make some start or risk losing whatever small trust he'd managed to instill in the lad, "Scholar tay'Nordif is part of the effort to recover the equations. Without her, I wouldn't have been able to gain access to the Tower. She provides misdirection and cover. This operation depends on her abilities. She—" He closed his eyes, considering the tangle of it all—and what well-mannered and respectful boy from out of a well-mannered and respectful trading family would believe in *aelantaza*, or line edits, or the Uncle, or—

"Why," Tor An asked, "does the scholar believe you to be a kobold?"

Jela sighed and produced the most believable part-truth he had to hand.

"There are certain protocols available, which help certain people to believe things other than what they usually know to be true," he said slowly. "The lady you see here as Scholar tay'Nordif is in fact my pilot and my partner. She volunteered to subscribe to those protocols, in order that the mission have the best chance of success."

Tor An gave that grave consideration as he stroked the cat on his knee.

"Is she a soldier, then?" he asked finally.

"We're all soldiers," Jela said, "in the last effort to defeat the *sheriekas*. But, no—if by 'soldier' you mean to ask if she's enrolled in the military. She's a volunteer, like I said. The best damn' pilot I've ever seen." His eyes stung, and the room wavered a little before he blinked them clear.

"A pilot," he said again, "and a true, courageous friend. The safety of the galaxy rests on her, Pilot, and I'll tell you straight out that I would rather it was her than anyone else I can name."

Tor An was in his garden. That bothered him momentarily—but then he remembered that Melni, who had the tutoring of him and Cor Win in the afternoons, had been called to a Family Meeting. He was supposed to be reading trade protocol, and it would go badly for him if he failed of being the master of the assigned chapter by dinner—but the breeze wafting in the open window had tempted him to step outside for just a *little* while, and walk down to garden's end to visit his tree.

The zang flowers were blooming, their tiny blue and green blossoms like so many stars against the pale yellow grass. He was conscious of a feeling of deep approval as he skipped down the path, pleased that the plants had been given leave to grow as they would, not tamed and confined, as were the showier, costlier plants the gardeners tended in the public gardens at the front of the house. The back garden was for children, and for elders, a comfort—and an occasional temptation for shirking one's lessons.

The grass flowed like water beneath the subtle wind, and he could hear the bell he'd hung in the piata tree's branches. A deep breath brought the taste of leaf and bloom onto his tongue—and there before him was the piata, its branches heavy with fruit. As he approached, one of the high branches dipped down toward him. He raised cupped hands, and a fruit dropped into his palms.

"Thank you," he murmured, and climbed up onto the boulder, settling his back against the warm silver bark as he leisurely ate his fruit. Eventually, he closed his eyes, and dozed, knowing himself safe, cherished, and—

A chime sounded. Tor An stirred, and settled more comfortably, for surely it was only the bell high up in the piata's limbs—

The chime sounded again, and he gasped into wakefulness, the dream shattering around him, and a great weight upon his chest—which was only the orange cat, Lucky. Half-laughing, Tor An set the animal aside, ignoring the glare of betrayal, untangled himself from the blanket, and gained his feet as the chime sounded a third time.

"A moment!" he called and stepped forward, careful in the dimness of the strange room. Jela was snoring against the wall beneath the scholar's plant, and Tor An spared a moment's wonder for a pilot who could sleep through such a din, then forgot about him as he opened the door.

Scholar tay'Nordif pitched into his arms.

He caught her, though they were nearly of a height, and bore her clumsily to the chair, kicking the borrowed blanket out of his path. He got her seated, snatched the blanket up, shook it out, and draped it over her shoulders before dropping to one knee by her side, peering into her shadowed face.

"Scholar?"

She put a slim hand against his shoulder, fingers light and trembling.

"A moment, of your goodness, Pilot," she murmured. "I—I had hoped the effects of the—of the duel would have dissipated by now."

"Did they not care for you?" he demanded, outraged. Dueling stick injuries were not trivial and the punishment she had taken—

"Nay, nay. Mine colleagues were everything that is kind and accommodating. Surely, vel'Anbrek fetched me a chair and with his own hands dea'San brought me a glass of wine—and another, as well, insisting that I must rebuild my reserves. Truly, they would allow me to do nothing, but must needs serve and cosset me. Many came to the chair in which I rested, and spoke for a moment, showing such concern—'Twas my own folly that I thought myself sufficiently recovered that I declined Prime Chair's kind offer of escort to my room."

She lifted her head, and gave him a brave smile, the misty green eyes awash with tears. Her face was too pale, and showed two livid marks upon her right cheek.

"He never struck you in the face!" Tor An cried, outraged over again.

"Peace, Pilot. Scholar tel'Elyd felt himself very ill-used. Indeed, he believed that I had not only dismissed him as a colleague, but held him at less value than a kobold." She laughed breathily. "Who would not be outraged at such?"

"Scholar—"

"A moment, I beg you." With an effort, she straightened on the chair, and took her hand from his shoulder, a loss he felt keenly. He sat back on his heels as the silence grew, and he began to wonder if perhaps she had taken lasting harm from—

"I know that you owe me nothing, Pilot," she said finally. "Indeed, it is I who owe you the remainder of your fee. But, I wonder if you would be willing to accept another commission from me."

Tor An opened his mouth to tell her that he had never taken any commission from her, but before he could frame the words, she had pushed on.

"I hold no secrets from you, Pilot," she said, her hands fisted on her lap. "I have enemies—powerful enemies—among those who are said to be my colleagues. Even now, there are those who seek to devalue what credit I hold with our department's master, whose own student I had been, and whose work set me on the path to finding my own. The Prime Chair—you would not believe such infamy! Indeed, I scarce believe it myself, and I have studied the principles of scholarship as nearly as I have studied within my own discipline, for I *will* succeed! My work is too important to be buried as the result of some ill-considered proving! I—my work can save lives, Pilot! Countless lives! Whole star systems might be snatched from the jaws of entropy!"

Tor An's head was spinning. He was fairly certain that the scholar was raving, yet he wanted nothing else but to aid her in whatever way she asked. Which, considering his early evening conversation with Jela, whose own story had contained certain thinly covered gaps of logic—

He sent a quick glance aside but, to all appearances, Captain Jela slumbered still beneath the tree.

"Will you aid me, Pilot?" Scholar tay'Nordif asked, breathlessly.

As if there could be a question! So fragile and vulnerable a lady, who further held the key that would preserve others from the Ringstars' fate. Except, he remembered suddenly, that didn't entirely align with Jela's insistence that the scholar was no scholar at all, but a pretender who had volunteered to run interference while the soldier undertook the real labor of locating the—

"Pilot?"

Tor An sighed. "Jela—" he began, fighting the impulse to pledge his life to her purpose.

The scholar stared at him blankly. "Jela? Pay no attention to Jela, Pilot. He's less aware than—than the cat!"

As if on cue, the very cat leapt into her lap, burbling. The scholar put her arms around it and buried her poor, abused face in his fur.

Tor An took a careful breath. "What is it," he asked carefully, "you would have me do for you?"

The scholar lifted her face and smiled at him, and his heart lifted.

"A small thing, Pilot, I assure you! It is necessary that I undo the harm that mine enemies have done. I must assure my master that I am true and hold him in no less esteem now than when I sat at his feet and snatched the pearls of wisdom as they fell from his lips. The best way to do this, of course, is to send a gift." She looked at him expectantly.

Tor An blinked. "A gift," he repeated.

"Indeed! And here we may marvel anew at my patron's wisdom and foresight! For I will tell you that I did say to her, when she would press upon me the specimen she had engineered with her own hands and its keeper-kobold—When I did protest and ask what a poor scholar might do with such trappings of wealth and plenty, do you know what she said to me, Pilot? Why she said, 'I have faith, Maelyn, that you will find a good use for both.'" She smiled at him again, her chin resting on the cat's head.

"A good use for both," she repeated. "And so I have found an *excellent* use for both! They shall be my gift to Master dea'Syl, which will assure him of my constancy and my unflagging respect."

"You mean to make your master a gift of Jela and—and the tree?" Tor An said slowly.

"Certainly!" The scholar said. "The tree is a worthy gift. Indeed, I have its pedigree, which you will of course bear with you and place into the master's own hands."

"And—Jela?" Tor An inquired.

"Jela tends the tree," the scholar said patiently. "It is the role for which it was designed. Surely, you don't expect that *Master dea'Syl* will wish to get dirt under his fingernails from tending a plant? Of course not," she answered her own question. "So it is quite settled. Tomorrow, when I betake myself to my office and my work, you shall bear the tree—Jela, of course, will carry it—with its pedigree and the letter I shall write for you, in secrecy, to Master dea'Syl. Will you do this for me, Pilot? I swear you will be well-rewarded."

"I wonder," he said, somewhat breathlessly, "how I will find my way, secretly, to Master dea'Syl."

"Ah, that is the fortunate circumstance! Scholar vel'Anbrek will serve as your guide. You will meet him at the proving grounds tomorrow morning as the Day Bell sounds. He will take you by the quiet ways to the master's rooms."

"I—see," he said, though he was moderately certain that he did not. He shot another look at the slumbering soldier, though how anyone could sleep through—And there, a broad hand was outlined against the shadow, fingers spelling out *say yes.*

Tor An cleared his throat and brought his gaze back to the scholar. The color had returned to her face, though the shock-marks still showed livid.

"I will be happy to perform this service for you, Scholar," he said, softly.

TWELVE

Elsewhen and Otherwhere

THEY RAN, ROOL sifting the ley lines so quickly they blurred into a single strand of event, all possibility melded to one purpose. He trusted *her* to keep them viable as they phased from plane to plane, and concentrated upon the pattern of the lines, choosing this one, rejecting that one, sorting consequences at white-hot speed.

There! He snatched a line, whipping them into the seventh plane, snatched another, phased to the third, glissaded to the fifth. The lines sang about them as small probabilities shifted, the sick were healed, the dead were raised, water was turned into wine.

And still the Shadow pursued them. Suns froze where it fell; planets trembled in their orbits. The fabric of space stretched thin, the ley lines themselves beginning to attenuate.

Rool chose a slender line describing a pocket possibility, rode it to the end, dropped to the fourth plane and doubled back, directly through the tattered skirts of Shadow.

It was a bold move—very nearly too bold. Cold touched him, burning his essence as a kiss of frost will blacken a flower. At the core of his being, he heard *her* scream.

Blindly, he chose a line, another, a third—phased, and fell to his knees onto silken silt, her slender body cradled in his arms.

"Love?"

Her eyes fluttered, amber and dazed.

"You must not risk yourself," she breathed.

He laughed, short and bitter, and lowered her onto the soft silt.

"I risk myself and wound my heart," he said. "Quickly, do what you must to replenish your essence. We dare not—"

She extended a thin hand, placed cool fingers against his lips.

"Hush. What place is this?"

He lifted his head, blinking in the glare of the local star—and again as the breeze flung grit into his face. All around was desolation—rock, wind, sand. Three paces to the right of their resting place lay a huge, bleached trunk, the stubs of what had once been mighty branches half-buried in the silt.

"The homeworld of the *ssussdriad*, or I am a natural man," he murmured, and looked into her dear eyes. "Art ready, love? The Iloheen will not be long behind us."

"I am ready, yes," she said softly, and took his hand, weaving her fingers between his.

He bent his head and kissed her small hand. "We phase, then," he said, and gathered himself, noting as he did that the Shadow's kiss had done more damage than he had—

"No." Her will rang across his, anchoring him to the physical. "Here. This place. This time. This plane."

He looked at her, dread filling him; raised his head and looked out over the desert once more. Sterile, dust-shrouded, devoid of any tiniest flicker of life.

"I cannot prevail here," he whispered.

She laughed, high and gay and sweet. "Of course you cannot," she said. "And neither can I."

"Love—" he reached for her even as he extended his awareness, searching for the shape of a likely line—

Static filled his senses. He snapped back wholly to the dead world, the dying sun, the gritty breeze.

"We are found," he said, and his lady smiled.

"The great Iloheen comes to us," she murmured. "Help me to rise."

He lifted her to her feet, and braced her while she gained her balance.

"Behind me now," she said, "and cede yourself to me."

He stepped back, took one deep breath of sand-filled air, closed his physical eyes, and centered. Before him, glowing gold within the ether, was the channel. He threw open the doors of his heart, and sent his essence to her in a tide of living green.

Static distorted the galaxy. The dying sun flared through a quick rainbow of color, growing large and orange. The gritty breeze gusted and died.

A Shadow fell over the land.

Foolish halfling, the Iloheen sent. *Didst think to elude ME?*

The cold grew more bitter still, until the very light froze in its path, and Rool Tiazan tasted the tang of oblivion. His lady, bold and courageous, held them aloof, his energy pooled and secret behind her shields.

Have you no answer for the one who gave you life? The Iloheen's thought struck her shields like a storm of comets—yet they held. They held. And still she kept their true seeming hidden, showing them obdurate and dull, waiting.

Be unmade, then, flawed and treacherous child!

Darkness fell. The stars froze, screaming, in their courses. The ley lines shriveled, sublimating into the blackness. Rool Tiazan felt his body begin to unravel, the golden channel that linked him, essence-to-essence with she whom defined the universe and all that was good among the planes of existence—the golden link decayed, frayed, un—

In the darkness of unmaking, his lady dropped her shields.

A lance of pure light opposed the darkness. The stars sang hosanna; the fog dissipated; and the ley lines reformed, binding the universe and all that lived into the net of possibility. Rool Tiazan felt his heart stutter into rhythm, and drew a breath of warm, sweet air.

Darkness thrust, light countered—fire rained in frozen flames at the congruence of their fields.

Again, darkness struck. The light feinted, twisted—and struck! The Iloheen howled, and withdrew, winding its dark energies into one thick skein of oblivion.

His lady, a cool and slender blade of light, closed the channel that linked them.

Rool Tiazan screamed as the Iloheen's blow gathered and fell; saw the brave blade rise to meet it—

—and shatter, into nightmare and ice.

He screamed again as his essence unraveled, and his consciousness splintered into dark teardrops.

THIRTEEN

Osabei Tower
Landomist

"SHE'S MAD," TOR AN said to Jela's broad back.

The soldier grunted as he shifted tree and pot out of the corner, preparatory, Tor An supposed, to delivering it to Master dea'Syl, whoever and wherever he might be. How they were to transport the tree was another question, for if there was a cargo pallet or luggage sled within the confines of the scholar's quarters, it was masquerading as a desk, or a chair, or a cat.

"*Mad*," he repeated, with emphasis.

Jela, the tree apparently situated to his satisfaction, straightened and turned 'round to face him. "You say that like there's something wrong with being mad," he commented.

Tor An glared at him, and the soldier laughed, softly, soothing the air between them with his big hand.

"I'm not the one to complain to about the scholar's state of mind," he said. "Think about it: I'm here to steal a set of equations that might save the galaxy from an enemy we can't possibly overcome."

Tor An caught his breath. "Is that certain? I thought—the soldiers were being pulled back to a more defensible—"

Jela sighed. "The soldiers are being pulled back to defend the Inner Worlds because the Inner Worlds bought the High Command," he said, with a sincerity that was impossible to doubt. "The Inner Worlds think to buy themselves free of the fate that overtook the Ringstars, but what they've bought—at the price of countless lives and numberless planets—is a few years, at most. The decrystallization process is going faster, according to my information. It's as if whatever technique they're using, it's cumulative, so the more space the Enemy decrystalizes, the more they *can* decrystalize."

Tor An glanced aside. The cat was sitting on the counter; he extended a finger, received a polite nose-touch. "So, are we all mad, then?" he murmured, skritching the cat's ear.

Jela laughed, a low, comfortable rumble deep in his chest. "Well, let's see. We're in a fight to destroy an enemy that can't be defeated." A pause, as if he were seriously weighing the merit of this statement, then, "Yes, Pilot. We're all mad."

Tor An sighed. "What shall we do?" he asked, the cat purring against his fingers.

"Unless you have an idea that seems more likely to move us along the road to victory than the one the scholar gave us, I suggest we follow our orders."

Tor An thought briefly of the back garden at home. He wanted nothing more in that moment but to sit under his piata tree, nibble on a fruit, perhaps nap, and awaken some while later blanketed in fallen leaves, safe, cherished and protected.

Gone forever, he thought. And if there were a chance—even a vanishingly small chance—that he might preserve someone else's tree and garden, was that chance not worth taking?

And it wasn't as if he had anything else to do.

Reluctantly, he stopped skritching the cat and picked up the sealed packet the scholar had left on the counter. He weighed it in his hand before slipping it away into an inner pocket, and turned again to face Jela.

The soldier gave him a critical look, for all the worlds like Melni making certain that he hadn't done his shirt up crooked, back when he was still in the schoolroom, and held up a blunt finger.

"You're missing a very important accessory, Pilot. A moment, if you please."

He moved across the room, absurdly light for so bulky a man, rummaged in the scholar's rucksack and was back, holding in his big hand a discipline bracelet the twin of that which Scholar tay'Nordif wore. Tor An frowned.

"Problem?" Jela asked.

Not quite able to mask his distaste, Tor An took the bracelet and turned it over in his hands, looking for the hair-thin wires that would pierce his skin and bond him to—

He looked up and met the soldier's bland black eyes.

"Two problems, in fact," he answered crisply. "One, you are not a kobold. Two, this bracelet lacks the coding wires. It won't work."

"Well," Jela said, untroubled, "that makes it a match for Scholar tay'Nordif's, now doesn't it? And as for me, I'm a kobold, sure enough." He rubbed the ball of his thumb over the ceramic threads woven into his chest. "If it falls that way, discipline me, Pilot. I'll trust your judgment."

Tor An sighed, and used his chin to point at the tree. "How are we to transport that?"

"I'll carry it," said Jela.

"*Carry* it? It must weigh—"

"I'm strong, Pilot, never fear. I've carried that tree since it was shorter than I am."

"But—"

"And we'd best be going," Jela continued, moving over to the subject of the discussion and flexing his arms. "It wouldn't be polite to keep Scholar vel'Anbrek waiting."

He went down on a knee, wrapped his arms around the pot, heaved—and came to his feet, tree cradled in his arms. "After you, Pilot," he said, under no apparent strain.

Tor An took one last, reflexive look around the room. Not a very tidy room, truth told, and Lucky nowhere in sight. The first irritated him—he was a meticulous lad—and the second saddened him—he would have liked to have stroked the cat one more time, for luck.

Well. He pushed the unaccustomed annoyance of the bracelet up over his arm until it stuck, and smoothed the sleeve of his jacket over it. Jela stood, face slack and stupid, holding the tree as if it weighed slightly less than nothing. Tor An sighed, went forward, opened the door and led the way down the hall.

"True pilot timing," Scholar vel'Anbrek snapped, "cut to the last fraction of a second." He moved off hurriedly, robe flapping around his legs. "Come along, we must needs be away from the arena before it begins."

"Before what begins?" asked Tor An, moving determinedly to the scholar's side. A quick glance over his shoulder reassured him that Jela was keeping up, even at his stolid "kobold" walk.

"Ah, she didn't tell you the whole of it, did she? Just as well. This way, now, and be quick!"

They rushed single-file down a hall so thin Tor An's shoulders each brushed a wall. A single ceramic track down the center of the floor—a supply tunnel, Tor An thought. Another quick glance showed Jela proceeding sideways, somewhat the slower for the tight quarters. Ahead, the scholar darted right into another tunnel.

An alarm sounded, frighteningly loud.

Tor An stumbled, but the walls were too close to allow of a fall. At least this time he did not mistake it for a ship's system in ultimate distress. This time, he knew what it was—and his blood grew cold.

"Scholar tay'Nordif," he gasped and the old man turned his head, with no decrease in speed.

"Come along, Pilot! This is more important than a single scholar—or even a whole Tower full of scholars too blind to see aught but their own comfort and petty quarrels. This way!"

He dodged into a left-tending hallway as the second alarm sounded, opened a door and waved them inside. "Keep a good hold on the strap! This lift is calibrated for cargo."

It was a nasty trip up, and how Jela bore it, with no hand free to steady himself, Tor An could not imagine. The alarm sounded for the third time during the short, brutal lift, and then they were following Scholar vel'Anbrek down a tunnel the twin to those below-deck, the track set into the floor shiny with wear.

"In here!" the scholar snapped, and pushed through another door.

The hall beyond was dim, the air slightly sour, the track dusty with disuse. Their passage disturbed moths and cobwebs—and then the scholar halted, put his hand against a section of blank wall like all the rest of the blank wall up and down the tunnel—and waited. Tor An came up beside him and a moment later Jela arrived at his shoulder. Still the scholar stood with his hand against the wall—which suddenly showed a moire pattern of golden motes—and disappeared altogether.

Scholar vel'Anbrek stepped through the opening. Tor An hesitated, then bethought himself of Scholar tay'Nordif, risking her life in order that this opportunity be made available, and followed the old scholar into the unknown.

The seats filled quickly, many of the scholars with breakfast cups and pastry sticks in hand. There was a murmur, a rising wave of voices exclaiming over a third challenge coming so close upon the heels of the others—and then rising again, as those who had already downed their first cup or two of morning tea recalled that the challenge which had deprived the Tower of Prime tay'Palin had been but the last of many.

Maelyn tay'Nordif stood inside the proving court, head bowed, hands tucked inside the sleeves of her robe, and wondered if she was going mad. Almost, she would have thought that the wine dea'San had pressed upon her so solicitously last evening had been poisoned, only she could think of no poison which would act in this manner—There! What did she know of poisons or their action? She was a scholar of Interdimensional Mathematics, lately Seated within Osabei Tower, as she had long ago determined that she would be. None of the other, lesser, Towers would assuage her pride—it *would be* Osabei, the First—or a lifetime of wandering.

And so she had fulfilled the task her pride had set her, disproven the master's own lifework, gained the coveted Chair in the only Mathematical Tower that mattered—only to find that her mind, far from being that honed instrument she had always felt it to be, was rather a weak blade which had speedily shattered upon the rock of Tower life.

These random thoughts which afflicted her, now, at the moment of her trial—Surely, the port police had not required her to look upon a certain broken and battered corpse which she then claimed for her mother? Not only did she remember her mother very well, she thought, taking deep, calming breaths as the noise of the seats filling continued around her, but she was still alive, and serving in the Distaff House of Nordif, which was charged with keeping the 'counts and inventories of the mercantile branch. Her mother was a senior receivables manager—a respected and respectable woman of a respected and respectable House. It had been her mother's support and encouragement which had given her the courage to pursue her scholarly studies, and to stand in defiance before Aunt Tilfrath, who had wished her to remain and serve the House as had her mother, and her mother, and—

And *surely*, she thought in cold horror, as the sounds of the gathering observers began to settle into some semblance of quiet, *surely* she had never—never allowed a—a *kobold*—

She took a shuddering breath, hoping to still the roiling of her stomach, and thrust the thought away. Such things were the stuff of nightmares; and, like nightmares, were mere disorders of the imagination. She was neither mad nor depraved. She would meet what was to come with sure mind and sure blade, and rightly overcome this challenge. Her work was elegant; pure. She would not be found in error.

"Silence, Scholars!" Prime Chair tay'Welford's voice sounded near at hand. She raised her head, and forced her eyes open. Across from her in the proving court stood a scholar not immediately familiar. She mentally reviewed her acquaintance of the common room—Ah, of course! Scholar ven'Orlud, whose speciality was pretransitional spatial coordinates, was it not? What could such a person find to prove or disprove in her own work?

"Scholar ven'Orlud," Prime Chair said loudly enough to be heard in the back seats, "challenges Scholar tay'Nordif to defend the point made in her Wander-thesis Number Three that intermittent vectorization within the universal metacrystal could prevent accurate energy-field summation."

Scholar tay'Nordif felt a jolt go up her spine.

But I later refuted those findings myself! How can I be called to prove an error which I later corrected?

"This is a true proving, not merely a point of personal honor," Prime Chair continued. "Blades will be engaged, and scholarship rests upon the outcome. Scholars, prepare to defend the Truth."

"This is a fraudulent proving!" The voice rang against the high ceiling, struck the walls and rebounded—by which time, Maelyn tay'Nordif had recognized it as her own.

They were in what once had been a cold storage room. Here and there vacuum cells and yellowed foam could be seen through the scored laminate walls. Looking about them, Tor An felt a certain sense of dismay.

"Forgive me, Scholar," he said politely when some time had passed without their guide continuing. "This scarcely seems an apartment suited to the honor of one of your Tower's great masters."

Scholar vel'Anbrek smiled humorlessly. "Quick off the mark," he said obscurely. "Good."

Tor An frowned. "Scholar, I must insist that you bring me to Master dea'Syl, so that I may present Scholar tay'Nordif's gift, as she bade me to do."

"Patience, Pilot. You will be with Master dea'Syl—ah!—very soon now, I hear."

Were *all* the scholars here mad? Tor An wondered, and gathered his patience, for, mad or no, that had been well-advised.

"Sir," he began again—and stopped as the wall directly opposite vanished in a cloud of golden vapor, and a carry-chair bore through, silent on its supportive pad of air.

The man in the chair had an abundance of white hair plaited into a single thick braid and tied off with a plain red cord. He was bent forward, his shoulders bowed beneath the weight of the robe, and his thin hands rested one atop the other on the control stick.

Halfway across the room, he made a minute adjustment, and the chair's forward progress halted, though it did not settle to the floor.

Slowly, as if the braid hanging across his shoulder was nearly too heavy a burden, the old scholar raised his head.

His brow was high, his eyes deep, his nose noble, and time had writ its passage boldly upon his features. Tor An bowed, reflexively, and straightened into the scholar's thoughtful regard.

"Now, here's a pretty behaved lad," he said, his voice thin and clear. "By which sign I know him to be something other than a scholar of Osabei Tower."

vel'Anbrek stepped forward and placed his hand on the chair's tumble guard.

"This is the pilot, Liad. The one of whom I spoke."

"Pilot?" The thin lips bent in a smile. "He scarcely seems old enough." A hand lifted, trembling slightly, showing Tor An an empty palm. "I mean no offense, Pilot. When one reaches a certain age, the galaxy itself seems a child."

"I have not been insulted," Tor An assured him, and felt his cheeks heat as the scholar's smile grew momentarily more pronounced.

"I am pleased to hear it, for I do not hide from you, Pilot, that it would go badly for me, were we to meet on the field of honor."

"Liad—" Scholar vel'Anbrek said urgently.

"Yes, yes, my friend. Time is precious. Allow me a dozen heartbeats more, that I might beg you to reconsider your position."

"I never had a taste for adventuring," the other scholar said, taking his hand from the guard and going two deliberate steps back. "I will remain, and do what might be done here."

The old man sighed. "So it shall be, then. Keep well, old friend, as long as that state is possible."

vel'Anbrek bowed. "Go forth and do great deeds, Master." He turned on his heel and strode away; the wall misted before him, and reformed behind, as solid-seeming as Jela, standing patiently to the rear, tree cradled in his arms.

Tor An blinked. It had seemed for a moment as if the bark had grown ears, but—

With a burble of joy, Lucky the cat leapt out of the tree's pot and galloped, tail high in ecstacy, toward the carry chair. Without hesitation he bounded over the tumble bar and into Master dea'Syl's lap.

"Well." The old man presented a finger, and received an enthusiastic bump. "You must tell me who this fine fellow is, Pilot."

"That is Scholar tay'Nordif's cat, sir," Tor An said politely, unaccountably relieved to see the animal again. "She calls him Lucky."

"Does she so? May she be correct in her estimation."

Tor An took a breath, reached into his jacket and pulled out the documents the scholar had entrusted to his care.

"If you please, sir," he said. The master's dark, sapient gaze lifted courteously to his face. "If you please," Tor An repeated, stepping forward. "Scholar tay'Nordif sends you these tidings."

"Ah." The master considered the packets gravely and at last held out a hand. Greatly relieved, Tor An surrendered them and then turned, gesturing toward the immobile Jela and his burden.

"Scholar tay'Nordif also makes you a gift, sir."

There was a small silence; the master absently skritching the cat's chin with one hand, the documents on his knee, unopened and apparently unregarded, while he looked past Tor An to Scholar tay'Nordif's offering.

"A gift of an M Series soldier is generous indeed," Master dea'Syl said at last. "I believe I have not seen the like since my Wander days. Introduce me, pray, Pilot."

Tor An stared at Jela, stricken. The soldier smiled slightly and inclined his sleek head.

"My name's Jela, sir," he said in his easy voice. "Am I right in thinking you intended to hire Pilot yos'Galan to lift you out of here?"

"Indeed you are. Am I correct in thinking that the military has at last come to its senses and will act upon my findings?"

"Unfortunately, no," Jela said seriously. "I'm working with an independent corps of specialists. Our mission is to liberate your work and use it to aid as much of the galaxy as possible in escaping the *sheriekas*."

"A worthy mission, and one with which I find myself in harmony. I willingly align myself with your corps of specialists. Pray put down your camouflage and let us depart."

"No camouflage," Jela said, "but a member of the team."

"Ah? Fascinating. Please, M. Jela, place your associate on the cargo rack at the rear of this chair. I shall be honored to bear it with me."

Jela hesitated, then stepped 'round and slid the tree into the rack, using the straps to fasten it securely.

"Excellent!" Master dea'Syl said, giving the cat one last chuck under the chin and placing both hands on the control stick. "Allow me to show you the back way out."

He spun the chair on its pad of air and moved toward the wall through which he'd entered, Jela right behind. Tor An stood where he was, hands fisted at his sides.

"Scholar tay'Nordif—" he protested. Jela sent him a look over one broad shoulder, his face expressionless.

"Our first objective," he said patiently, "is to secure the equations. No one of us is more important than that."

Tor An glared. "*Your* first objective!" He snapped. "I claim no membership in your team of specialists, and I will not abandon Scholar tay'Nordif to—"

Jela held his hands up, showing two wide, empty palms. "How," he asked quietly, "are you going to get her out of the arena, assuming she's managed to survive this long?"

Tor An opened his mouth, closed it.

"Right," the soldier said, sounding weary. "Come along, Pilot. You're needed at your board."

FOURTEEN

Osabei Tower
Landomist

ABSOLUTE SILENCE FILLED the arena, the scholars on their benches shocked wordless by her outburst. As who, Maelyn tay'Nordif thought bleakly, would not be? She should abase herself before Prime Chair, beg pardon of her challenger and let the match proceed. To whinge or to argue—it was unseemly, unworthy of one who had attained her long-coveted Seat.

"In what way," Prime Chair inquired, dangerously soft, "do you find this challenge to be fraudulent, Scholar? Do you deny having authored the work under challenge?"

"I do not," she answered hastily, before that *other* took the initiative—to what new disaster, who could predict? She cleared her throat. "I do, however, object to your continued manipulation of the scholars of this Tower, Prime Chair, and I call upon you to explain yourself!"

Horrified, she brought her hand to her lips, but the terrible words had already been uttered, and hung, vibrating, in the charged air.

"*You* call upon *me*—" tay'Welford breathed, and smiled. "Scholar, you misunderstand. It is you who are called to explain certain assertions incorporated in the work referenced in a properly submitted Petition to Prove, which has been filed by one of your colleagues. I have reviewed this petition as well as its supporting documentation, and find that the challenge has merit. You are therefore called to defend your work, here and now, before the full gathering of your colleagues."

"The blades need not enter into it," she said reasonably. "Prime, I myself located the error and subsequently repaired it. If you will allow me—"

He turned away from her, raising his voice so those in the most distant seats could hear, "Scholar tay'Nordif pleads a stay of challenge. It appears that she lacks the courage to defend her own work! How say you, colleagues? This Tower is built upon the integrity of its scholarship! Are we to allow this—"

"If this Tower is built upon the integrity of its scholars," Maelyn heard her traitor voice ring out, "then the walls crumble around us where we stand!" She spun, raising her hand to point at each section of seats in turn. "I call upon the scholars gathered here to do the math!" she shouted. "How many of your colleagues have fallen in proof during the last dozen semesters? How many of them stood between Ala Bin tay'Welford and his ultimate goal—the Prime Chair?"

There was murmuring in the stands now, and consternation. Some scholars rose to their feet, others brought out math-sticks and personal diaries.

"Do the math!" she cried again as she fought the strange, false conviction that she knew tay'Welford in some other guise, and that she perfectly understood his purpose, which was neither the glory of the Tower nor the preservation of its scholars and their work. "Tally the loss to the field since this man came among you! Consider his purpose!"

"What can we know of his purpose?" someone called down from the stands. "He is a scholar, as are we all; his purpose must be the peaceful pursuit of his work!"

"It is not!" she returned, and knew it for truth. She turned and faced tay'Welford, who stood as a man quick-frozen, as sometimes were the laborers at home, if night caught them outside the dome. His smile was rigid, and his eyes full with dire warning. Behind him, Scholar ven'Orlud frankly gaped.

Fascinated, Maelyn watched her hand rise, the wedge of her fingers pointing directly at Ala Bin tay'Welford.

"This man is no scholar," she shouted. "He is a liar and a thief. His whole purpose in being here is to lay this Tower to waste in the name of his masters, and to steal away our most precious treasure!"

"You fool!" tay'Welford hissed, and snatched the blade from his sash.

Master dea'Syl set a brisk pace, leading them through a maze of dusty tunnels, up yet another cargo lift, and thence into another tunnel, this one bearing all the markings of being in current use.

"This way," Tor An panted, "is not so secret as some."

"That is correct, Pilot," the master said, unperturbed. "There is a measurable risk of discovery in this section of our journey. I do assure you, however, that the risk is acceptable—and in any case, it must be run. There is no other path from where we were to the place we must come to. Quickly, now. We are almost—"

Abruptly, the chair braked, skewing sideways on its cushion of air. The pot in the cargo bay slammed against its restraints; the tree's limbs trembled. Jela flung out an arm, stopping Tor An in his tracks, then crept forward alone, stealthy and silent, to peer 'round the next corner.

Tor An gripped the side of the carry-chair, watching as Jela raised a hand, palm out, fingers waggling briefly in something that might have been hand-talk for *wait*.

Moments dragged by. Tor An's whole attention was focused upon that broad, steady palm—when a spot of damp coolness touched the fingers that gripped the sled's tumble bar so tightly, he jumped and bit his tongue in his endeavor not to gasp. Glancing down, he saw Lucky the cat looking earnestly up into his face, amber eyes depthless and clear. Carefully, one eye still on Jela, he moved his free hand and rubbed the cat's ear. His attention was rewarded with a purr so soft he scarcely heard it where he stood—and then Jela's hand swept out and up—*come on*.

The blade came in low, impossibly fast. She knew a heartbeat of utter terror before she sidestepped, spinning out of the path of danger in a swirl of robes.

"Murderer!" she shouted. "Thief! Take him! Hold him for the Governors!"

For a instant, it seemed as if every scholar present had been quick-frozen, then a few found their feet and surged forward, shouting. Their movement thawed the others, who swarmed down the stands, some with blades drawn, others with math-sticks still in hand. Crying aloud, they closed on Ala Bin tay'Welford. Scholar ven'Orlud, who yet stood by, abruptly came to life, snatching at tay'Welford's sleeve, her hand going to the knife in her sash. tay'Welford spun, blade flashing—

Maelyn tay'Nordif did not stay to see more. The onrushing wave of scholars was no longer interested in her, and by dint of dodging, ducking, and simple pushing, she quickly reached clear floor. She paused a moment to take her bearings, thoughts a-whirl with half-grasped questions and calculations—what matter to her where the spaceport lay?—while she pulled the hem of her robe up through the sash, freeing her legs for quick movement. She had the clear sense that a decision had been made, though what it might be, she could not have said. Her feet, however, were better informed. She spun, spied a hallway that matched some parameter of that unknown decision, and began to run.

Once again, they were in an ancient and long-undisturbed supply tunnel. They went more slowly now, Master dea'Syl setting a pace that showed some respect for the tricky footing his carry-chair floated above.

"How time does render us all obsolete," the old man remarked. "Would you believe, gentles, that this was the main supply line for Osabei when I was a child? Many hours did I labor at the receiving dock, absorbing the principles of practical mathematics. Far too often, I was called to right a supply train which had jumped the track, or to carry out some measure from a barge which had foundered from overload."

Tor An blinked. "You were a child within these walls, Master?"

"Indeed, I was once a child, Pilot, though I grant one might find it difficult to credit. In those days, you see, it was possible for Houses of a certain status to pledge a child to the Tower from which the House elders wished to receive notice. I am not able to tell you what it was my own House sought, as of course this was never disclosed to me. However, when I ascended to grudent, I was shown the contract of pledge, on which the signatures of all six elders appeared."

"It seems a hard price," Tor An observed, blinking away a sudden rising of tears, as he thought of the bustling and busy house that was no more—

"Perhaps. Certainly others have thought so. I cannot fault the arrangement, myself, as in it I found my lifework and perhaps—as M. Jela may have imparted to you—the means to preserve humankind from oblivion."

The tunnel, Tor An thought, was widening gradually and tending somewhat to the right. He shot a glance to Jela, walking in his chosen position at the rear, and saw that the walls no longer crowded those wide shoulders quite so nearly.

"We are in fact, approaching the very thing which first struck fire from my mathematical curiosity," Master dea'Syl said, and raised his voice somewhat. "M. Jela, you will find this interesting, I think."

The tunnel continued steadfast in its rightward tending, the walls widening even more, into a neglected receiving bay. Carts and barges lined the left wall, awaiting cargos; on the right, empty twine spindles were set into the walls, a hose dangled untidily from a cobweb-covered canister, the graphic denoting spray sealant barely visible through the dust. A shelf still held a set of dust-shrouded tools, neatly laid out by function; a hand-cart and a cargo-sled leaned against the wall beneath. Three tracks described a tricksy dance through the dust: in-going, out-going, and in-process, Tor An thought, oddly soothed by the simple ordinariness of the arrangements. It was plain that the bay had been abandoned for some time, and yet, with only a little bit of cleaning and stocking, it could be made as functional as it had been during Liad dea'Syl's long-ago boyhood.

At the far end of the hall, where the bay doors would normally be, was a curved blank wall of made of some unfamiliar milky orange material. It gave back no reflection; seemed, indeed, to absorb what feeble light came from the panels set into the ceiling. There appeared to be *things* moving within and beneath the milkiness. Tor An walked forward, eyes squinted against the vaguely unsettling color, trying to get a clear sight of those things. As he approached, he felt his skin prickle, as if a charge leaked from the whatever it—

"Where," Jela said, in a voice that Tor An registered as too quiet, "did Osabei Tower acquire this thing?"

"M. Jela, you delight me!" the master exclaimed, as Tor An turned to face the two of them. "Am I really to believe that you know what this is?"

"I'm a generalist, sir," Jela said, still in that too-quiet voice, "with a special interest over the last few years in *sheriekas* technology." He nodded toward the milky orange wall. "Based on my studies, I'd guess that was a shortcut, left over from the First Phase."

"Your guess is admirably on-target," Master dea'Syl said, stroking the cat absently. "As to where Osabei Tower acquired it, I cannot say. When I had status enough to gain access to the documents regarding the device, I only found that it had been purchased from a company called Oracle Odd Lots, and that Osabei Tower had—and has—a standing order to purchase objects related to its area of scholarship."

There was a small silence before Jela spoke again. "In the deep files of Osabei Tower there is mention of a world-shield, which is based—or was based—on Vanehald. I'm interested in that device, also, and would appreciate anything you can tell me about it."

"Ah. I regret, M. Jela. I know very little of that device, merely its location and the fact that no patron was found to fund a study of it. It has languished for some very long number of years, as you will have seen from the file. Very likely, it is no longer in place, or no longer functions."

"I understand," Jela said quietly. "Thank you, sir."

"You are quite welcome. Well! Time, as my dear vel'Anbrek would no doubt remind us if he were here, runs quickly. If you gentles are quite prepared, let us proceed to the port."

Jela held up a hand. "Consider, sir, that this device—fully as ancient as the world-shield, and by the state of the bay, many years unused—may no longer function."

Master dea'Syl inclined his head. "You are a soldier, and it is your nature to be cautious. Allow me to put your fears to rest, M. Jela; I have over the last few years been seeing to the maintenance and upkeep of the device, as I was taught to do as a boy. Its functionality—while I daresay not optimal—is adequate. You observe it in its ready state, which I initiated as soon as vel'Anbrek brought me news that chance had at last placed an unaffiliated pilot-owner within my grasp."

It seemed to Tor An that Jela stiffened. Certainly the face he turned toward the unsettling hatchway was devoid of any expression, lips tight, black eyes bleak.

"My pilot, who has some experience of the Enemy's devices, and who sat co-pilot for yet another pilot who had even more practical knowledge of such things, holds as truth that the devices of the Enemy never forget who made them, and that they call out to their makers," Jela said slowly. "What they say, not the elder pilot, or my pilot, or I can hazard—though I believe we agree it holds nothing that we'd call good."

The master sighed. "You would caution me that I put a world at risk by employing this device. I would remind you, sir, that the *galaxy* is at risk, and this is the only door which will open to its possible rescue. Created by the Enemy, it certainly was, and no doubt treacherous beyond our ability to understand. Yet, in this instance it is our ally, and we must grasp the means that come to hand."

"Soldier's logic," Jela said, "which ought to sway a soldier." He was quiet for a moment, and it seemed to Tor An that he stood less straight, as if the weight of what they were about to do was heavier even than a strong man could bear.

"Go," he said.

Maelyn tay'Nordif ran as she had never run before, down the hallway that mad, secret portion of her mind had chosen. Past empty labs and lecture rooms, she ran, the shouts and noise from the proving court fading behind her. Surely, she thought, she was now beyond any immediate danger. Best to utilize one of the vacant rooms for a period of rest and meditation.

She slowed to a jog, her soft slippers raising faint chuffing sounds from the smooth floor, and then to a walk, passing three sealed doors, status lights glowing red—reserved rooms, and keyed to the palms of particular scholars and their disciples. Maelyn passed on.

The sixth door showed a green light—general use. She placed her palm against the plate and stepped inside a modest lecture hall; sixty work chairs arranged in six curving rows of ten, the scholar's station front and centered, with only the most minimal expanse of floor to separate her from the students. The air was frigid, the lighting dim.

Sighing, Maelyn tay'Nordif ordered herself; unkilting her robe and brushing it smooth with hands that trembled rather a lot; making certain that her sash was tidy, the truth-blade in its place. Her stomach cramped at the recollection of her unscholarly behavior. She could not, in fact, imagine what might face her in the scholar's common room this evening. To call down a mad crowd upon the department's Prime Chair—on causes that could scarcely be thought to contain a grain of fact, fabricated as they must have been on the edge of the moment—

It was true, she admitted, folding her arms tightly beneath her breasts and hugging herself in an attempt to ease the trembling, that she was not very skilled in the art of the blade. Indeed, if she were to be honest with herself, she would own that the survival of her Wander years was due not so much to her vigilance and ability to protect herself, but to her habit of affiliating herself with a succession of "patrons," some of whom had been no better than bandits. She had been gently raised, she thought, beginning to pace, and her talents lay elsewhere than in brute physical—

The door opened.

She spun, feet tangling in her robe, and scrambled for balance as Ala Bin tay'Welford stepped into the room.

The old scholar went first, his chair moving with deliberation toward the pass-portal. As Jela watched, the energies within the portal began to swirl, forming an unsettling vortex into which chair, man, cat and tree receded until they were indistinguishable from the dancing milky motes.

The process was eerily silent, though Jela noticed a slight breeze brushing his cheeks as the vortex sucked air into it.

At the side of the bay, Tor An yos'Galan hesitated, for which Jela blamed him not at all. The thought of surrendering himself to the action of the vortex was unnerving at best, and if the whole business was enough to twitch nerves spun out of data-wire—or so they had assured each other in creche, when they were learning the basic skills of soldiering—

"Pilot," he said, keeping his voice matter-of-fact, like stepping off into infinity was an everyday affair. "I'll take rear guard."

The boy threw him one wide glance out of those improbable flower-colored eyes, took a breath, faced about like a good troop, and walked determinedly into the swirling doom, hands loose at his sides. The energies swirled, shrouded—and Tor An yos'Galan was gone, swallowed by the vortex.

Jela considered the energies before him, his feet planted flat on the floor, as if he intended to take root in the considerable dust. Duty lay before him—the old scholar, with his equations locked safe and secret in his head; the tree; the pilot he'd appropriated.

And behind him—his partner, or the person his partner had died to become—not from some vague sense of obligation to the galaxy or life-as-it-was, or to honor the oath she had never, in truth, taken—but *for him*.

Duty required him to move forward. Duty required him to leave her to die.

She took rear-guard, he told himself. *She knew the risks.*

And maybe that was so—and maybe it wasn't. She'd known there were risks. She'd known, if he were to trust her, like she'd asked him, that there were good odds that neither one of them would finish this campaign alive. Rear-guard, though—Cantra yos'Phelium had never been a soldier.

He closed his eyes.

A co-pilot's first care was for his pilot, which left the pilot to care for the ship and the passengers, if any. *That* was a protocol Cantra had known well.

Trust, her voice whispered, faint and husky.

He threw away all she had done—for him alone—if he turned his back on duty now.

"Advance, Soldier," he told himself. And again, "Advance."

His feet at least knew an order when it was said, and he was enough of a soldier—yet and still—to not wish to bear the shame of having been ordered thrice.

So, he marched, shoulders square and hands ready, across the dusty floor, and into the maw of energy.

tay'Welford had fared roughly at the hands of the crowd; a bruise darkened one cheek and there was blood on his robe. How much of the blood may have been his, Maelyn thought, was unclear. Certainly, he was not impeded in the speed with which he spun and locked the door, nor in the certainty with which he raised his blade and touched its pommel to his heart in ironic salute.

"You made a dangerous gamble, did you not?" He inquired, advancing upon her slowly. "Did you think to find me so easily unseated? I am no green boy, maddened by his first dissolving. You, however—the last of a flawed line, and encapsulating all of them. Rash, heedless, vicious. *Stupid.* So stupid to have come here—"

She gave a step—and another—before him, and that was wrong. He was trying to get her against the chairs. Biting her lip, she did *not* yield a third step, belatedly reaching to her sash and pulling the truth-blade free.

tay'Welford inclined his head. "So you will fight now, will you?"

He moved, blade flashing. She countered, clumsy and ineffectual, felt the pain on the right side of her face, and stumbled back a third step and a fourth, gasping. Her free hand went to her cheek, came away smeared with blood.

Her opponent laughed. "Such an *interesting* choice. Meek, ineffectual, and ludicrous. It fetters you, does it not? In a moment, you'll find that it has killed you."

"I don't understand you!" she shouted at him, feeling the chairs against her back. She would have to attack, move him out of the way, get to the door—

She lunged.

Surprise drove him back a step, his blade weaving a bright dance, countering her attack, breaching her defense, slicing through cloth and into her arm.

Screaming, she lunged again. His blade was fouled for a moment in her sleeve and she scored a strike of her own—red blood blooming on the side of his robe. He grunted, staggered, and she was past him, running for the door.

She pressed her hand against the plate, but the blood on her palm fouled the reader and the lock remained engaged. Sobbing, she turned, back against the door, blade up, hilt slick with blood from the slash on her arm.

tay'Welford smiled, crouched, one hand out, ready to grab her if she tried to dart past him, knife held almost casually in the other.

"What shall I do to sweeten your passage?" he murmured, eyes bright and utterly devoid of pity. "Ah, I know. Listen closely. I want the sense of this to strike deep, before I complete the lesson." His smile widened. "'Twas I killed Garen. She died as she had lived—a fool, and begging me not to harm you."

Trembling, she stared at him, seeing a curious waiting in those bright, pitiless eyes, unable to think of anything but that she was about to die at the hand of a madman—

Pay your debts, baby, a woman's voice seemed to whisper in her very ear. *There ain't no living with yourself, if you don't.*

Her eyes stung. She blinked, and tears ran down her face, mingling with the blood.

tay'Welford laughed, softly. "Yes, very good. Savor that a moment. I want you to die blighted." The knife moved, leisurely.

She ducked, taking the strike on her shoulder, coming in under his guard and setting her blade in his throat.

"*Veralt*," she hissed, though what the sense of the word was, she could not have said.

His eyes widened, hand rising—and falling as he slumped to the floor, bright eyes fixed and dulling.

She stood there for a moment, swaying and bloody, then haltingly turned to deal with the door.

FIFTEEN

Landomist

THERE WAS A moment of extreme unpleasantness, as if he were being dismantled molecule by molecule, followed by an instant of agony as he was abruptly jammed back together.

Jela's boots hit solid 'crete. Inside his head, he saw a wall of fog rolling in from the ocean, obscuring cliffs and treetops. Then, in the fog—a shape, small and indistinct, rapidly growing into a black dragon, flying strongly, breaking all at once out into the light.

"Over here, M. Jela," Master dea'Syl called softly.

Shaking the memory of his transit away, he took quick stock. They were in a cargo shed, dim and in none-too-good repair, the light sources being the holes in the crumbling metal roof, and the pale, flickering orange light from the shortcut. The carry-chair hovered some two dozen steps to his right and ahead. He could see the outline of the tree, and the old man's silhouette.

"Where is Pilot yos'Galan?" he asked, moving forward quickly.

"Here," said a faint voice, and the boy stepped out of the deeper shadows beyond the chair.

"The pilot had a difficult passage," Master dea'Syl said smoothly. "And no shame to him. Many strong stomachs have been humbled by that walk, short as it is." He raised a frail hand. "We are within the port, M. Jela. It is now yours to lead and mine to follow. The door is fifteen paces to the left of your position, and may require persuasion which I believe you are qualified to apply. While you are about that, I will deactivate the portal."

"Right." He moved forward, located the door, tested the ancient opening mechanism and found it as the old man had suggested.

"Stand back," he said to Tor An, who had followed him, perhaps to offer aid. "I'm going to give it a push."

As it happened, three pushes were necessary to open it to a width the carry-chair could negotiate, and as the luck would have it, the roof didn't come down on them as a result. Jela went through first, then waved his companions out.

Before them spread the glittering expanse of Landomist Port. Jela looked to Tor An.

"Where's your ship, Pilot?"

"Near, I'd think," the boy said, standing forward briskly enough despite his pale face. "Ship's fund was scarcely able to bear the cost of a berth in the private yards." Eyes squinted against the light, he surveyed the situation then raised a hand, pointing.

"There! The Dejon Forty-Four in the third six-row. You can see the star-drake—"

Jela looked. The ship was old, but in good repair. Sharpening his eyesight somewhat, he made out the words *Light Wing*, painted in bold bright letters along her side, and beneath, *Alkia Trade Clan, Ringstars*. The sigil, up near the nose, was a sinuous, winged reptile, a bright, stylized star held in each fore-claw.

"Let's go," he said, and took a breath, trying to ease the dull ache in his breast. She deserved better of him, he thought, and another image formed inside his head: the slim, lethal golden dragon the tree had settled on as a description for Cantra, riding the high currents, questing and calling. He closed his eyes—sent a thought of Rool Tiazan receiving the linked pods which had sealed their alliance.

Again, the golden dragon, alone and calling for her absent comrades.

She took rear-guard, he thought, and carefully built another picture: Wellik as they'd last seen him, dour and tall, a single brown star very nearly the color of his skin tatooed high on his left cheek. The tree projected interest. Encouraged, Jela continued with his picture, building the rest of Wellik's office, star map and briefing table—and there, right next to the captain's own desk, the tree, sitting honored and safe—

The office dissolved; Wellik shifted form and became Jela himself, covered in sweat and sand, battle-blade to hand, cutting a trench 'round the tree's scrawny trunk. He bent down, got his hands under the bulb, heaved—and felt the strength of those roots, gripping the planet tight; no effort of his could possibly move it.

"Captain Jela?" Tor An yos'Galan's voice was tentative—as well, Jela thought wryly, it should be.

He opened his eyes and manufactured a smile. "Sorry, Pilot. Truth told, my passage was a little rough, too."

The boy's tight face eased a little. "I understand," he said.

"Right. Let's go."

She had done the best she could to bind her wounds, cutting strips from tay'Welford's robe for bandages. Still, she was none too steady on her feet as she made her way down the quiet hallway, until she found a service door.

It opened to her palm and, as luck would have it, the corridor beyond was empty. Not that it was likely to remain that way. Painfully, she pushed onward, breathing shallowly and ignoring the ragged blackness at the edge of her vision.

Past the recycling room she went without encountering anyone, though she heard voices as she approached a branching of the hall. She proceeded slowly and peered 'round the corner, spying a group of the Tower's tiny servitors pushing trays and serving carts away from her down the right-hand hall. Leaning against the wall, she closed her eyes and concentrated on breathing until she could no longer hear them, then straightened and went on at a jog, bearing left, following the gleam of track set into the floor.

Can't be far, she thought. *Can't be far.* Her undamaged hand moved, groping in her sash for—for...But Jela would have it, she thought, as her feet tangled and she fell hard against the wall. She got herself sorted and her feet moving in synch again—walking, now, just that—and all but unconscious until a bit of cool breeze against her slashed cheek woke her, and she smiled.

The hall curved gently, widening into a work area. Empty delivery carts lined one side of the room; a cargo pallet, half unloaded, was in the center, attended by several of the Tower's busy servitors. Another pallet, empty, was poised on the track by the sealed hatch, waiting to take the ride back to port for more goods.

She staggered forward, ignoring the high-pitched shouts and the scurrying of the servitors. One got between her and the pallet, and she pushed him out of the way, feeling a distant pang as he fell and cried out.

More shouts; she ignored them, even when voices not so high nor so childlike joined in. She extended a hand and hit the manual trigger a good one before she collapsed onto the pallet, bruising her slashed face, and wrapping her hands around the lifting bars as the hatch opened and the powerful suction grabbed the pallet and threw it at the port.

*

"Your contact," Jela said to Tor An yos'Galan, "is Captain Wellik, at the garrison on Solcintra." He put a gentle hand on the boy's arm. "I know you have no love of soldiers, especially the X Strains, but I personally vouch for Wellik. He'll see and hear you."

"If," the pilot said, voice taut, "I am allowed to see him, rather than being summarily shot."

"He'll see you," Jela said, as if there were no doubt of it, "because you'll have the tree with you. Wellik will recognize it, and—"

A series of pictures flared inside his head, hard enough to hurt, strong enough to obscure the sight of the ships and the port around him: the golden dragon, voice faint, calling against the fall of night. From the darkening sky, the black dragon swooped, behind and beneath her, bearing her up, moving them both toward a distant cliff-edge and the tree growing there, the scent of seed-pods clear and enticing on the wind.

"M. Jela, are you well?" the old scholar asked sharply.

He shook the pictures out of his head, and blinked the port back into existence.

"Disagreement among the troop," he muttered, and took a hard breath. "Pardon, sir. It's been a long campaign."

"Longer for some than for others," the old man said tartly. "If you are wounded, sir, you endanger the mission by concealing it."

Wounded? Almost, Jela laughed. In his head, the golden dragon drooped, wings dangerously close to the uneasy surface of the sea.

He took another breath, trying to ease the tightness in his chest, and looked again to Tor An yos'Galan, who was watching him with a startlingly sapient gaze.

"Perhaps," the boy said softly, "I will not have the tree with me?"

Jela sighed. "You'll have a token, instead. And Wellik will see you, Pilot. My word on it."

"Ah." There was a small pause, then. "Very well. Let us have it that Captain Wellik will accept the token and consent to see me. I am to tell him—?"

"You are to tell him that Jela sends him the master of the equations, who is sworn to aid us in our project. You will say that Jela asks him to turn over to you the full amount Wellik owes from the last card game he played with Jela. You will then do as he instructs in regard to the master, after which, having been paid—which you will be!—you're free to pursue your own life."

They were at the base of old *Light Wing's* ramp. Jela held up a hand to stop the carry-chair and fixed Tor An with a stern eye. "Do you agree to this commission, Pilot?"

The boy sighed, looked to the old master, and sighed again. "I agree," he said, tiredly. "But what of you—and the tree?"

"I—" Jela stopped. *Duty*, he thought—and shook his head. "I'm going back to the tower."

Tor An's lips parted, eyes taking fire. "To bring away Scholar tay'Nordif?"

"If I can," he said reluctantly, and looked to the old man, expecting ridicule, perhaps, or censure.

Liad dea'Syl inclined his white head. "We all must do as our heart compels us," he said, softly. "Allow me to lend you this chair, M. Jela. It can move much faster than a man afoot, even an M Series soldier at a run."

"Thank you," Jela whispered, and stepped 'round to the back of the chair. For the tree, he formed an image of Wellik as they had last seen him, holding in his wide palm a leaf from the tree. He raised a hand; two leaves detached themselves as his fingers touched them.

"Thank you," he whispered again, and carried the tokens to Tor An yos'Galan.

"Now, M. Jela," Master dea'Syl said, as Jela carried him up the ramp to *Light Wing's* hatch, "pray attend me. The shortcut, as you style it, has been deactivated. However, there is still a quicker way to the tower than the slideways. Speed you to the market section, yonder—" he pointed out the long line of gleaming warehouses, bristling supply tubes and conveyers "—and follow the signs for the tradesmen entrances. Each tower has its own entrance, and you will be quickly brought to the Osabei dock by this means. After—you will contrive, I am certain."

"Thank you, sir."

Ahead, Tor An yos'Galan, the cat draped like a stole 'round his neck, triggered the hatch and proceeded them into his ship—Captain's Privilege. Jela carried the scholar within, through the lock and down the short hall to the piloting room.

"Here," Tor An said, folding out the jumpseat. "I regret there's nothing better, Master, but—"

"But a singleship is meant to be guided by one pilot's hand," the old man finished. "My piloting days were long ago, child. The jumpseat is well enough for me; I will enjoy observing you at your art."

Jela placed the old man carefully, stood back, saluted—

"Go, M. Jela!" Master dea'Syl snapped.

"I'm gone!" Jela responded—and he was.

The smaly tube spat her pallet out; it lofted and slammed onto the feeder-tracker, the mags locking solid. Groaning, she raised her head, saw the stacker up ahead, opened her hands, slid off the pallet and dropped through the gap in the mags. She heard shouts, distantly. Then her head smacked 'crete, and she didn't hear anything else.

Eyes narrowed against the wind of their passage, Jela raced the carry-chair toward the gleaming line of warehouses. The tree, lashed to the cargo-plate, bent and danced, leaves fluttering like scarves. He caught the edge of an image of storm, boiling clouds and driving rain, and an echo of jubilation.

Speeding, he reviewed his plan, such as he had. First, to the trade transport then to Osabei Tower. After he was in Osabei Tower—there were too many unknowns to usefully plan. The main objective: to recover Cantra yos'Phelium or, as he couldn't quite bring himself to believe, though it was the most probable—her body. And if he had to take Osabei Tower down stone by stone to do it—well, he'd been ripe for a fight for days.

He was among the warehouses now, pushing the carry-chair for all it could give him—and more. His eye snagged on the pointer to the tradesmen walks, and he whipped the little craft around, dodging between a robofreighter and a port ambulance, while the tree cheered rain-lash and lightning.

Inside, the path went along a catwalk—to keep casual strollers out of the line of work, Jela thought, and sent the chair up the ramp at a brisk clip.

From the tree, a urgent sending: the golden dragon, one wing folded beneath her, blood bright against gleaming scales—

Jela braked and looked down, sharpening his vision on the figures in medic 'skins bent over a woman—blood on her hair, blood on her face, blood soaking her tattered robe.

"Cantra!" he yelled, and threw the chair into reverse.

"What're they thinking of up there?" The shift boss yelled at Jela. "She came *through the smaly*! Damn lucky she didn't get crushed, or knocked loosc or—"

Jela pushed past the man, as gently as he could, "Hazing," he said shortly. "The scholars are having a party."

"Some party," the lead medic muttered. She glanced up at him, eyes widening, then quickly down again.

He looked at Cantra's bruised and bloody face. Still breathing, and the medics had quick-patched the cuts. What other damage there might be—

"Took a pretty bad knock when she fell off the stacker," the lead medic muttered, not looking at him. "Her good luck she did, too, before she got crushed. Got some funny readings on the scan." A pause before she raised her head and looked at him again. "You have an interest in this case?" she asked. "Sir."

He looked at her, seeing the signs now. This one had served, and knew all too well what an M Series soldier looked like.

"I'm prepared to relieve you," he said, meeting her eyes.

"Right then." She motioned to her mate, who began to pack up the kit, his head also studiously bent. The lead stood and faced him, keeping her eyes pointed at a spot just beyond his shoulder.

"There's paperwork, and a fee for port services," she said, stiff-faced. "You settle up at the portmaster's office."

"I'll do that," he said insincerely, and turned to make the necessary adjustments to the carry-chair, reformatting the seat into a stretcher that he could steer by standing on the folded out booster step.

"Let's get her on the stretcher—"

"Hold on, here!" shouted the shift boss. "You just can't send her—Suppose she dies? Or this person—Did you even ask for ID?" he demanded of the lead medic.

She sighed, jerking a chin at her partner to carry the kit out to the ambulance, while Jela webbed Cantra into the stretcher.

"As it happens, I was on-call two nights ago when this trader got into a little discussion with the wrong people on the old port," she said tiredly. "I've got his particulars on file." She pulled a portable unit from her belt and held it up, one hand on her hip and a frown on her face. "Want to see?"

The shift boss considered her, and—wisely, in Jela's opinion—decided not to pursue the matter.

"Nothing to me," he said. "I just don't need any trouble, is all."

"Right," the lead medic said, snapping the portable back onto her belt. "None of us needs trouble." She sent a quick, speaking glance to Jela.

"None of us," he agreed. "Thank you, medic." He stepped onto the carry chair platform, reached for the stick, and got them gone.

They were at the weaving—delicate work requiring concentration, a light touch and strong protections. It was not enough to be merely invisible, of course; the Iloheen would suspect so simple a gambit. No, it was necessary to seem to be part of the fabric of space itself and, in order to make such a disguise convincing, it was also necessary to partake of the surrounding space and integrate it into their essences.

It had been his lady who devised the way of it, meaning only to grant them protection from the Iloheen. For his part, he had merely noted that sharing their essences thus created them less like the poor limited creatures of flesh whose form they mimicked, and more like unto that which he had been before his capture and enslavement.

So it was that the Great Weaving arose from the simple necessity to hide. There were but thirteen *dramliza* at the work, for it required not only skill, and daring, and a desire above all else to see the Iloheen annihilated, but the willingness to accept a total melding of subordinate and dominant, and a phase-state which would be like no other—

The ley lines flared and spat. Lute extended his will, seeking to soothe the disturbance, but the lines writhed, stretched to the breaking point of probability, mixing what was with what could be, shuffling the meanings of life and death. And across the limitless tracks of space, at the very edge of his poor diminished perception, a Shadow was seen, and the awful flare of dark energies.

The Iloheen! he sent, and threw himself back from the weaving, seeking his lady.

Here. Her thought was a lodestone, guiding him. He manifested beside her within the pitted rock that was their base, and spread his defenses, shielding her behind the rippling rainbow of his essence, as the Shadow spread, sending the lines into frenzy. The asteroid phased wildly, becoming in rapid succession a spaceship, a hippogriff, a snail. Lute rode the storm of probability, felt his Lady take up the burden of maintaining their defense, and reached out, daring to snatch the lines that passed most nearly and smooth them into calmness. A small circle only he produced—enough to draw upon, not so much as to elicit the Shadow's notice.

Behind their defenses, he felt his lady busy at some working of her own then pause, waiting—the last link only unjoined, or he knew her not—awaiting clarity.

Out *there*, across the seething chaos of probability, the Shadow coalesced, shrank—and was gone.

Lute waited. The ley lines slowly relinquished their frenzy, spreading out from the small oasis of peace he had created. Nowhere showed a hint of Shadow.

He felt his Lady unmake her working, dared to somewhat relax his shields—waited—and, when the levels remained clear and untroubled, brought them down entirely.

"The others?" his lady asked.

"I do not believe the Shadow located aught," he replied, and paused, recalling that storm of dark energy, the untoward disturbance of the lines.

"I shall inquire," he said, extending his will—

A spinning mass of darkness exploded out of probability, blazing through the levels like a meteor, haloed in silvery green.

Lute threw his shields up. Impossibly dense, the darkness tore through, plummeting to the physical level. He grabbed for the ley lines—and felt his lady's thought.

Wait.

Shackled by her will, though by no means accepting of it, he waited. Waited while the dense darkness ricocheted around them, spilling wild energy—a danger to his lady, to himself, to the destruction of the Iloheen!

And still his lady held him impotent, as if the uncontrolled and dangerous object that had invaded them was the most trivial of inconveniences.

He coiled himself, making what preparation he could, should she loose him before—

The invader exploded. Streamers of ebon, gold, silver, and green washed across probability, inspiring the lines once again to frenzy—and at once, all was still, and as it had been.

Excepting the figure kneeling on the rough rock floor, back bowed until his head near touched his heels, red hair crackling, up-lifted face streaked with tears.

Lute leaned forward. His lady held up a hand to stop him, but did not compel his obedience. He considered the aspects of the ley lines, and acquiesced. Strange energies were at play here, and if this were in truth—

"Rool Tiazan," his lady said coolly. "We bid you welcome."

Slowly, he straightened; slowly bowed his head, and raised his hands to hide his face. "Lady Moonhawk," he whispered. "It is done."

"I see that some portion of it is indeed done," she agreed. "Yet I wonder after my sister, your dominant."

A moment he knelt silent, then dropped his hands and looked to her. "Gone," he said somberly. "Unmade. As was foretold. She stood as a goddess against the Iloheen, Lady Moonhawk. Never could I have struck so true and straight a blow—nay, even in my youth and true form!"

"Stand," Moonhawk said then, and Lute felt her will, compelling obedience.

Rool Tiazan laughed as a predator laughs, with a gleam of teeth and less mirth than menace.

"I am beyond you, Lady."

"As was also foretold," she acknowledged calmly. "You are an anomaly, Rool Tiazan. As dangerous, perhaps, as the Iloheen. Shall I destroy you, to protect our plans of survival?"

"You swore to my lady, your sister, that you would not do so," he returned, rising to his feet of his own will. "Her death does not free you from that oath. And I am come, as she swore I would, to show myself to you and to ask if now you will not join your forces to ours. Since last we spoke upon the subject, we have attached allies of great potency. The lines have been cast for a victory, Lady Moonhawk. We might all yet escape the Iloheen."

"A victory?" She turned away. "Lute?"

Rool likewise looked at him, a slight smile on his face, the fires of his true form very bright, as if the prison of his body was too frail to contain him. Lute shivered.

"Show me," he whispered, "what you have done."

"Of course. Walk with me, brother."

Rool phased, rising through the levels, and Lute with him until, side by side, they contemplated the ever-changing eternity of probability. Slowly, a particular cluster of ley lines became defined. Lute studied them closely, casting the outcomes and influences.

"A narrow hope," he judged at last. "The enterprise we are embarked upon has as much chance of success—perhaps more. Even if we are engulfed in the Iloheen's disaster, yet we will be a part of the warp and woof and may thus be free to act—whereas you and yours will be annihilated, and your energies used to annihilate even more—and more quickly."

"There is much," Rool admitted, "in what you say. Yet it was my lady's wish that I return and put the question to the lady who has accepted a Name."

"All those who weave have done so," Lute said. "It is believed the Names so accepted are artifacts which will resist assimilation, through which action may be channeled, even against and within the will of the Iloheen."

"It may be so," Rool conceded. "However, we shall not forsake our champions."

"We?" Lute inquired, but Rool had already returned to the rock base. Troubled in his heart, Lute followed him.

Moonhawk heard his description in silence then turned her regard once again upon Rool Tiazan.

"We shall persevere," she stated. "It comes to me that this movement to neutralize the Iloheen future is a jewel of many facets. Perhaps *all* of our actions are necessary."

"Lady, it may well be so," Rool Tiazan said. "We venture where none save the Iloheen have gone before. How may we, the Iloheen's very children, predict which action will bring success?"

"Or, at the least, less failure," Lady Moonhawk said drily, and bowed. "I believe our business is done, Rool Tiazan. Pray remove yourself, before the Iloheen realizes its error and seeks to correct itself."

"Lady." Rool Tiazan bowed in return, straightened and swept Lute in his regard. "Brother. May we all fare well. To the confoundment of our enemy."

With the faintest twitch of ley lines, he was gone, leaving Lute and his lady to consider each across the empty cavern.

SIXTEEN

Spiral Dance

HE'D CARRIED CANTRA to her quarters, performed a rough-and-ready exam, finding the damage to be mostly cuts and bruises, all ably dressed by the port medics. She was still unconscious—which was the knock on the head, or the blood-loss, or both—but not shocky or feverish. Tough woman, Cantra yos'Phelium, he thought—none tougher. Having assured himself that his pilot was in no immediate need or danger, he webbed her into her bunk, in case they had to lift in a hurry, and went to tend her ship.

Some time later, *Dancer* was in queue with a scheduled departure of just under six hours, ship-time. Keeping in mind the way his pilot preferred things to be done on her ship, Jela had given the nav brain leave to suggest alternative lifts, real-time. That done, he'd perused the public charts, finding *Light Wing* well ahead of *Dancer* on the schedule, with Dimaj the filed destination, courier run the reason.

Jela smiled, though on consideration that minor subterfuge had probably sprung from the mind of Liad dea'Syl rather than the boy pilot.

From the tree, lashed in its spot at the end of the board, came a quick image of a young dragon, wings still wet, eyes alert.

"That's right," Jela said, coming out of the co-pilot's chair with a sigh. "A likely lad, just needs a little season."

He did some quick stretches, and a mental exercise to raise his attention. He'd lashed the old man's carry-chair into the maintenance cubby just inside the lock, where it ought to ride safe enough. Which left the decision he'd been putting off making. He shot a glance at the panel concealing the secret room and the *sheriekas* healing unit. If it was only cuts and bruises, there was no reason to open that door. The problem was the "funny" readings the medic had reported on her scans. If Cantra'd done herself real damage, which a fall from a height with a whack on the head at the end of it might produce—

There was a sound at his back.

Retching, she convulsed against the webbing. Someone had shattered the light. There were shards and slivers of it everywhere, piercing her eyes, her brain, her nerves. Elsewhere, hidden behind the broken blare of the light, were people; she could hear them talking, talking, talking. She wanted to tell them about the light, warn them that the edges were sharp, but she couldn't seem to find a language that fit the shape of her mouth. She tried every language she had, but they were all too big or too small or too hard or too soft, and besides the inside of her mouth was bleeding, multiply punctured by tiny daggers of light, and even if she found the right language, it would hurt unbearably to speak.

Inside the light, sharing the pain, were flashes of image, odor and sound: her mother, sitting at the 'counts table, her hood folded back onto her shoulders; a whiff of mint; the glitter of dust against starless Deeps; a scream, cut off short by the sharp snap of breaking bone; the taste of strong, sweet tea; a line of equation; a hand on her hair; hot 'crete and cold metal—The sharp fragments of light flared and she screamed, or tried to; she twisted against the straps that held her, fingers fumbling the seals, and all at once, she was free, falling face-down onto the deck.

They were doing this to her. She caught the thought and pinned it against the shattered light. They were doing this to her.

Staggering, retching, she pushed herself across the floor until she ran into the wall then used it to claw herself upright. She could only see bits and flashes of color around all the broken light in her eyes, so she put her shoulder against the wall and followed it.

"Cantra!"

She was upright, just, listing hard against the wall, her breathing ragged. Her eyes were wide, pupils dilated, and whatever she was seeing, Jela hoped it wasn't him.

"Cantra?" He walked toward her, easy and light, face forcibly pleasant, hands out and showing empty.

From the tree came a sending, laced with urgency: the golden dragon, staggering in flight, landing clumsily in the crown of a monstrous tree. A branch rose, offering a seedpod, which she greedily consumed. Jela shook the image away. "Not now," he breathed.

"Cantra!" she shouted suddenly, her body writhing, and it was Maelyn tay'Nordif's voice, hoarse with horror. "You swore—you swore not to call her!"

"Yes, I did swear," Jela agreed. He took a deep breath, deliberately calming, and another, knowing that most people would unconsciously mimic what he was doing, and calm themselves.

Not that Cantra yos'Phelium had ever been most people.

"I swore, for the length of the mission," he said, taking another step, not wanting to crowd her, but needing to be within catching distance when the agitation left her and she buckled. "Mission's accomplished, Cantra. You can stand down."

"You will murder me for your own gain!" Maelyn tay'Nordif shouted at him, and threw herself forward.

He caught her, but it was like trying to hold a wind-twist. She kicked, clawed and punched without any regard for defense, leaving herself open a dozen times for the blow he wouldn't strike.

A knee hit his stomach, hard enough to hurt, and a flying fist got him solid in the eye. He caught her wrist, spun her 'round, got a leg behind her knee, twisted, and took her with him to the deck. He broke her fall as best as he could, and tucked her tight against his chest, legs pinned between his thighs, one hand holding both wrists, the other cradling her forehead.

She twisted, shouting at him in a cargo-can load of languages, most of them unfamiliar—which, judging from those he did understand, was probably a good thing.

"Cantra, Cantra," he murmured, though it was doubtful she could hear him with all the ruckus she was making. From the tree came the image once more, this time with more than a taste of urgency: the golden dragon, staggering. A safe but risky landing in the tree. The branch, the pod, the thanks.

"Not *now*," Jela said again, just as she twisted hard in his arms and got a leg free.

He could have held her, but he would have had to break something to do it. Instead, he rolled, and she got in a couple good kicks before he had her solidly pinned, face against the deck.

Now what? he asked himself, as she struggled to be free. If she kept up at this rate, he thought worriedly, she'd do herself an injury.

"You cannot kill me," she ranted. "I refuse to die. My family will intervene. A scholar Seated at Osabei! My mother—"

Something hit Jela's knee. He looked down and saw a seedpod. As he watched, it split into neat sections. For a third time, the tree sent the saga of the weary golden dragon, this time augmenting the image with blares of lightning and rocks the size of *Dancer* tumbling down the sides of sea cliffs.

Well, it was a better idea than any he'd had so far.

Carefully, he lifted one section and brought it to Cantra's lips, fully expecting to be bit for his trouble. She stilled, as if the pod's fragrance had reached her—he expected that the pod was fragrant, though, strangely, he couldn't smell it—then daintily ate the thing from between his fingers. He offered the rest in quick succession and she ate every one, after which she lay quiet until all at once her muscles released their tension and she slumped bonelessly to the deck.

Heart in his mouth, Jela turned her, found a pulse—strong and sweet—brushed the hair out of her eyes and gently peeled back a lid. From the tree, another sending: the golden dragon drowsing on her branch, her mate the black dragon at her side, rubbing his head against her and singing.

"*What?*" It wasn't that he didn't know any songs, but most were bawdy, or camp songs, or bits of soldier lore—and what use or need of them, when she was quiet now and on the mend?

Again, and no mistaking the impatience: the black dragon singing and cuddling the golden.

Jela looked down at his pilot, bonelessly asleep on the deck, then across to the tree.

"I don't understand."

For a moment nothing came through, and he thought the tree had given up on him. Then, slowly, deliberately, a picture began to form behind his eyes: a tea mug, that was all—perfectly ordinary, plain white, and completely empty. The image solidified until he felt he might reach inside his head and wrap his fingers around the handle.

"All right," he said, when nothing else manifested. "An empty tea mug."

A whiff of mint was his reward. Inside his head, icy cold water poured down, filling the mug, which altered, darkening from bright white to cream, to gold, shifting and stretching until it was a tiny, perfect golden dragon.

Jela shivered, heart caught in his throat, and heard her husky voice again, saw her hand outstretched. *Got time for some pleasure, Pilot? I'm thinking it'll be my last in this lifetime.*

"I don't know enough," he whispered, but all that got him was the black dragon and the gold again, her sheltering beneath the curve of his wings.

The co-pilot's first care is his pilot. And who else did she have, he thought, except himself?

"Well." He rose, picked her up in his arms and carried her to the co-pilot's chair, where he settled in and folded her long self onto his lap, her undamaged cheek against his shoulder. Reclining them slightly, he settled one arm around her waist and rested his chin against her hair.

"Your name," he said, as easy and calm as he could, refusing to think about what might be riding on his getting the story right. "Your name is Cantra yos'Phelium, heir to Garen. You're owner of the ship *Spiral Dance*, and the best pilot I've ever seen or heard tell of in all my years of soldiering…"

SEVENTEEN

Spiral Dance

CANTRA DRIFTED TOWARD wakefulness, the usual and ordinary sounds of her ship a comfort in her ears. Except, she thought, as sleep receded, she shouldn't be on *Dancer*, should she? Shouldn't she be on Landomist, getting the last of the documents doctored up and doing the pretty ceramic stitching that would remake Jela into a kobold?

Her throat tightened, and she shifted in her bunk, waking an astonishing chorus of aches and pains.

It went bad, she thought, which notched the concern into panic as she scrambled to recall just how bad it had gone, and when, and *what the date was*. If she'd lost Jela—

She took a hard breath, forcibly shoved the panic aside, and tried to remember what had happened, to no avail. There was a gaping, tender hole in her memory, like a tooth fresh knocked out, but many times worse. Her throat tightened. Deeps, if she'd drunk herself or doped herself to the point of losing memory—It had been bad when Garen'd died. She could suppose it would be worse, when Jela—

She took another breath, and another, imposing calm by nothing more than brute force. Well, she thought, if she couldn't remember what went wrong, what *could* she remember?

Clear as clear, she remembered setting down at Landomist Yard and filing the proper with the Portmaster's office.

She remembered engaging the lodgings, paying the landlord a local half-year on account.

She remembered coming back to the ship and coaxing Jela into the space between the floor and the not-floor in the small cargo wagon, and going through the checkpoint. She particularly remembered how the guard had to handle every item, and twice go through the documentation she'd gimmicked to explain away the tree, before calling over somebody higher on the brain chain to go over it a third time and clear her through. And how she'd expected Jela to be some peeved by the time she'd got them all safe-so-to-speak at the lodgings and peeled back the floor to let him out. Which he wasn't —not that he hadn't seemed grateful to be able to move about.

What else?

She remembered him trying to snoop Osabei Tower from wayaway and finally allowing as how the thing couldn't be done.

She remembered building docs and certs out of vapor and stardust.

She remembered sharing considerable pleasure with Jela and rising while he was still asleep.

She remembered trembling like a newbie before what had to be done, taking the tree's gift, and sinking down into the trance.

She remembered waking up in her cabin on *Dancer*, bruised, contused and about to be scared all over again.

Wait—No. She remembered Veralt, from noplace other than Tanjalyre Institute of fond memory, weaving a knife at the end of her nose and telling her how he'd murdered Garen.

Which made so little sense she figured it for a fever dream, and *damn*' if she was going to stay webbed in her bunk like a kidlet, waiting for somebody to bring her tea and news of the day.

She opened her eyes to the easy familiarity of her cabin, retracted the webbing, pushed back the blanket, and got to her feet with due caution. A quick inspection discovered dermal-bond over a number of cuts in silly places.

Fell into a bowl of razors, did you? she asked herself as she snatched open the locker door. She sighed at her reflection—another bonded cut on her cheek—and reached for her ship togs.

Jela was in the co-pilot's chair, his big hands calm on the board. He tipped his head slightly as she stepped into the pilots' room, tracking her reflection in his screen. Cantra blinked, her eyes unaccountably having teared up, and nodded at him.

"Pilot," he said, nice and respectful, which, knowing Jela, meant nothing but trouble.

She walked to the pilot's chair, sat, grabbed a look at the screens and the status lights before spinning 'round to face him.

"You in good repair?" she asked. "Pilot?"

A quick sideways glance out of unreadable black eyes.

"Tolerable repair," he said, not giving anything away with his voice, either.

"Excepting the odd shiner or two," she said, tapping the corner of her left eye with a light fingertip. She looked down-board to where the tree sat in its usual place, leaves dancing gently in a breeze that wasn't there, and back to her uncommunicative co-pilot.

"We're out of Landomist," she said, like maybe he hadn't noticed. "Like to tell me where we're bound?"

"Vanehald," Jela said. "If the pilot will indulge me."

She sighed. "Before I decide whether to indulge you or space you, tell me what befell us on Landomist?" She tipped her head. "Start with who gave you a black eye and what you did with the body."

Jela sent her another quick, Deeps black look, made a couple of unnecessary adjustments to his board, and spun his chair 'round to face her.

"You gave me the black eye," he said softly, and there was something tentative and—who would believe it?—uncertain behind the forcible blandness of his face. He took a visible breath. "Cantra?" he asked, and not at all like he was sure he'd care for the answer.

Well, that was a question, wasn't it? she thought, with her mind on the gaping hole in her memory. She looked down at her hands, idly wondering what she'd done to skin them up so thorough. It came to her, like a hard punch to the gut, that Jela considered the Rimmer pilot was a real, true person—like he was, and not some fabrication born of survival and a crazy woman's need. She sighed, and raised her eyes to his, letting him see her uncertainty.

"Mostly Cantra, I'm thinking," she said, telling as much truth as she knew how. "For your part in that, I'm grateful—and believe me most sincerely sorry, Pilot, for having done you a hurt. You deserve better from me."

"You were out of your mind," he said, and abruptly closed his eyes, head dropping back against the rest.

"Jela?" Did a soldier have warning of his decommission, she thought wildly, or did he just—stop? She came up out of her chair, saw he was breathing—saw a thin trail of moisture sliding down each brown cheek.

"Hey," she said, soft, and put her hand on his shoulder. "Jela."

His hand rose and covered hers, strong fingers exerting the least and most delicate pressure. Scarcely breathing, she looked down at him. His face seemed to her to be thinner, and she thought she saw—yes. Silver marred the perfect blackness of his hair.

"Old soldier," he whispered, his voice not steady at all. He opened his eyes and smiled an odd smile, mixing happy and sad, and with no artifice about it at all. "Good to have you back."

"I'd say it's good to be back, but I don't remember anything of having been gone," she answered, making her voice light with an effort. She looked away with something more of an effort and swept the board and screens again.

"Coming up on transition," she noted, and didn't quite meet his eyes when she turned back, though she was aware of her hand still on his shoulder, and his fingers covering hers.

"What's to want on Vanehald, Pilot Jela?"

The smile this time was small and tending toward twisty, with a hint of self-mockery.

"A world-shield left over from the First Phase," he said, and tipped his head, so that she was looking straight into his eyes again. "The last assignment my commander gave me was to hunt down the rumors until I located the device or certain proof that it no longer existed—or never had. If I found the device, I was to secure it for the troop."

She frowned down at him.

"This would be the same troop that let itself be persuaded to pull back Inside so the Enemy could eat all the Rim it wants?"

"No," Jela said patiently. "The troop I'm talking about is the double-secret unit personally sworn to Commander Ro Gayda, garrisoned at Solcintra. There's those couple dozen twilight ships you might remember I mentioned in close orbit. That's where I sent Liad dea'Syl and the boy. It's the only place left."

"What's the date?" Cantra asked, her voice harsh in her own ears.

Jela sighed and lifted his hand away from hers. Reluctantly, she released his shoulder and took a step back, keeping her eyes on his.

"I'm twenty-one Common Days short of decommission," he said quietly.

And what he wanted to do, which Cantra saw plain in his eyes, was to finish out his last mission, and die a good soldier. She wanted to shout, break things—whatever she had to do to get him *angry* at those who'd done this to him—which would've been less than useless—Jela was going to die in twenty-one days, angry or patient, and whatever his private choice in the matter might be. The choice left to him was how he'd be using those days. He'd decided to do something maybe useful, and who was she to call him a fool?

"There's also," Jela said, still in that quiet voice, "a full-staffed garrison at Vanehald. I'll be able to file my final papers and report to the medic there in good order."

Cantra breathed. Nodded.

"Right," she said, and swept a hand out toward the board. "You take us through transition. I'll get a meal together and then you'll tell me the whole tale of Landomist, hear it?"

Jela grinned, and damn if it didn't look real. "Yes, Pilot."

The universe was dark, without form or meaning.

All about, the ley lines sang and shimmered, thrumming with power and with promise. He could change the course of fate, make or unmake worlds, simply by reaching forth his will and desiring that it be so. There was none to thwart him, nothing between him and the full measure of his potential. He was finally, and again, complete unto himself; the plan that he had formed so long ago was come to fruition. He was whole. He was alone.

He was free.

"Beloved?" His thought was tentative, full of hope and fear.

No answering thought leapt to meet his own. No presence shadowed the austere symmetry of his isolation. No voice murmured the hated syllables which had for so long defined his prison.

They had failed.

The ley lines dazzled possibility, mocking his despair.

Failed. It was scarcely conceivable. She had been so careful. Infinitely careful, his lady; infinitely subtle, and above all clever. Once, she had told him that what cleverness she possessed she had learnt from him, but he did not credit it then—and did not credit it now. She knew her instrument—himself—too well to have failed in what she—in what they—had wrought.

"Beloved?" This time, he cast his thought wide, actively seeking her, desperate, as a wounded man seeks water, air or some other force necessary to life itself.

His seeking remained unanswered.

He forced himself to consider the possibility that they had *not* failed—that she had intended this—that he be returned to his natural state, unfettered, governed only by his own instinct and desire, to do what he alone judged to be needful, here in the galaxy's last hour.

Free, he thought. Whole and free. It was everything he had wanted. He had subverted himself to another intelligence, formed an equal partnership with a being whose only thought had been to enslave him—and worse. Much worse. All toward this moment, when he hung on dark wings within the dark universe, and knew himself master of everything he surveyed.

And yet—he could not have named the moment when it changed, when his jailor became dear to him and the jail itself the form he preferred, when the possibilities were without limit.

Far, far and away, though nearer than it had been, he could sense the cold encroachment of oblivion. The Iloheen went forth with their plans, as well.

And what matter, he thought, that the Iloheen should have the galaxy and all that was precious within it, when he had lost that which was infinitely more precious?

Lady Moonhawk had the right of it: he should be destroyed. Mayhap he would seek her out and ask the boon.

He considered the thought and the far, growing glare of perfection, weighing both against the near and feeble vortex of chance and mischief which was the galaxy's best hope of survival. Those lines which passed nearest the vortex twisted in weird complexity, so dense and layered with possibility that even he could not read them with surety. Terror shook him; terror and despair. For wherever the Iloheen's future took form, there the lines did shrivel and die. The volatile marriage of possibility and luck they had nurtured—which they had sacrificed so much to protect—there was no way to predict what such a thing might shape, or to know if it were less inimical than the Iloheen's future.

Carefully, he extended his will toward the vortex, probing, seeking a path by which it might be understood, or perhaps, now that he was alone, influenced—

Be still, her thought suffused him. *Be still and know that I am with you.*

INTERLUDE

She walked to the gate of the garrison with him, which wasn't maybe the smartest thing she'd ever done, and stood to one side while he showed his papers and was passed through, walking away across the yard, shoulders level, limping off his right leg so plain it set a lump into her throat—which was nothing more than senseless.

'bout halfway across the yard, he turned and saw her standing there like an idiot. He lifted one broad hand high, fingers signing the pilot's well-wish—*good lift.*

Her own hand came up without her thinking to do it, fingers shaping the usual in reply—*safe journey.*

He caught it—she saw him smile—then he turned away again. She watched until a marching squad obscured her sight of him—and when they were gone, Jela was, too.

EIGHTEEN

Vanehald

"INSPECTION?" COMMANDER GORRITI laughed. "What use an inspection, Captain? We're pulling back. Tomorrow, I will be gone."

Jela considered the officer thoughtfully. A natural human, with a foolish face and a uniform far too fancy for his post. A show-soldier, he expected, which was poor judgment on *some*one's part. He supposed that no one of this man's commanders had taken the time to research Vanehald, and so learn that this wasteball, as Cantra had aptly termed it from orbit, occupied a pivotal place in the history of the First Phase. One of the last battles of the First Phase had been fought at Vanehald. The planet, once populous, was now very nearly deserted, largely due to the damage done to it during that battle. A few mining bases, Jela thought, a lower tier spaceport, a First Phase fort. What here could possibly be worth protecting? And so they had assigned this popinjay to command the garrison, never thinking that perhaps what had been strategic once might well come into play again.

"You're pulling out tomorrow?" he asked Gorriti, who inclined his head and touched the front pocket of his shirt.

"Indeed, Captain," he said with barely concealed delight. "I am pulling out tomorrow. My orders are quite plain."

"What about transport for your troops?"

"I ordered transport," the officer said with a shrug of one elegantly clad shoulder. "That it hasn't arrived is beyond my control. *My* orders are clear." Again, he touched his pocket.

Jela frowned. "You'd abandon your troops?" he asked, unwilling to believe that even a fool and a thorough-going incompetent would do such a thing.

Another shrug. "When the transport arrives, my troops will follow." He reached into his pocket and pulled out an orders case, which he unfolded, showing Jela the authenticity of it, with its seals and ribbons straight from High Command.

"I am to report to Daelmere, departing tomorrow with as many of my troop as I am able to bring."

And how many would that be, Jela wondered, having seen the commander's craft on the apron when they came in. Perhaps a half-dozen M Series soldiers might be crammed into that tiny craft with their commander, or three of the X Strain. Not enough to matter, even if he bothered to take such a guard with him.

"What about the civilians?" Jela asked. "It's our duty—"

"Vanehald never had many civilians, and those that were here have mostly fled, saving a few miners and eccentrics," the man said unconcernedly.

"The strategic placement—" Jela began, and was cut off by laughter.

"Strategic placement! Well." Gorriti wiped his eyes. "Even supposing it had any, my orders remain unequivocal, and I will tell you, Captain, that *I* am not one of those who feel we must hold the Arm at any cost!"

Jela took a hard breath and kept a firm grip on his temper. "I'll still need to inspect your defenses," he said evenly, that being the reason for his visit, according to the papers Cantra had produced for him. Commander Gorriti waved an unconcerned hand.

"Go, inspect! Orders are orders, after all. Allow me to provide you an escort." He raised his voice. "Sergeant Lorit!"

The door in the right-hand wall popped open and an M Series soldier stepped briskly into the room with a sharp salute for her commander.

"Sir?"

"Sergeant, the captain here is under orders to inspect our defenses. Take him on a tour, won't you?"

"Yes, sir," she said and transferred her attention to Jela. "This way, Captain."

"Thank you, Sergeant," he said. He hesitated, trying to form something useful to say to Commander Gorriti, something that would bring him to a sense of a soldier's duty—but the man was engrossed in reading his orders, fondling the appended ribbons. Sighing, Jela crossed to the patiently waiting M, and followed her out of the room.

The fort, to which Cantra turned her attention after Jela disappeared for his-forever behind the guarded inner gate, was something interesting. She set herself to walking about, getting a feel for the layout.

It was a substantial edifice, formed out of cermacrete. The first gate, and all behind it to the inner, was public and looked a deal like any spaceport, only much smaller than even the smallest she'd seen. There were three eateries, a bar, two sleepovers, some sorry looking shops selling necessaries, and a sagging trade hall where the choices on offer were "antiques" and ore.

Despite there being nothing much there, really, the public gate area of the fort was buzzing. Cantra hadn't supposed there were any law-abiding citizens left, but as it happened, her supposition was wrong. Granted, those left looked to be miners, which it was likely a charity to give them "law-abiding," and most still working claims, which explained the ore on offer, but not necessarily the type or grade.

A pilot is only as good as her curiosity bump, or so Garen'd maintained. Besides, there might be something here that was wanted elsewhere. *No sense lifting empty*, she told herself, trying hard not to think just how empty *Dancer* was going to be.

It ain't you that's dying, she snarled, aghast to find her vision swimming with sudden tears. She took a hard breath, and looked around her.

Live pilots need food, she told herself carefully, *and their ships need fuel. That means cargo, Pilot Cantra. Focus.*

Focus. Right. A sign advertising eats caught her eye, which seemed propitious. She crossed the street and sauntered in, looking for info.

That she shortly had, by way of one Morsh, who was agreeable to paying for her tea and rations with amiable chat about her homeworld.

The mines, according to Morsh were nicely full of timonium.

"Not like the oldays, mindee," Morsh cautioned her. "Back de before, all dem shafts fill wit stuff? Back de before, dose shafts still bean work. Yeah, it was timonium, then, too, and ollie made money hand over hand. Miners, they made considerable less, but still not too bad. Now, timonium he hide harder, so ollie pull out, de money bean less easy. Us, dough, we know where timonium hide, so we do. Not in mine-outs er garbage pits. Timonium, he hide in little pocket an sharp corner. We fine him, yeah, an we sell true de tradehall, freelance. Do bout as good as when ollie run it, and no olliecop stickin his nose where don it belong."

"Stuff in the shafts?" Cantra murmured. "Ollie leave his boots?"

Morsh snorted a dry laugh, and had her a swallow of tea. "Ollie take him boots, missy. Dat stuff, it here before ollie. M'gran, she said de Vane been mine longtime. Story was, de Vane solid timonium, clear true." She shook her head. "Ain't, dough."

"The antiques on offer at the tradehall, they're out from the mines?" Cantra persisted, thinking about Jela's world-shield, and, truth told, feeling just a little uneasy about a major cache of oddments dating back to the First Phase.

"Dey are," Morsh agreed. "Tecky like dat ol stuff."

Cantra sipped her tea. "Old stuff still work?"

"Ah, who know," Morsh said, with great unconcern. "Tecky don care. Wanna peek at de possibles, er maybe takem souvenir." She grinned. "Soften up tecky bed-bounce."

Cantra laughed. "Maybe so." She picked up the pot and refreshed the tea mugs. "Supposing," she said. "Supposing I was interested in hunting some old stuff down in the mine-outs. How'd I go about that?"

Morsh laughed, and shook her head. "You ain no treasure-tecky, missy."

"'deed I am not," Cantra agreed. "But a woman sometimes needs a bit of extra something to keep her warm 'tween paying jobs, if you understand me."

"Timonium pay better. I sign you partner."

"'preciate," she said. "But I'm thinking I know somebody might have an interest in the old tech."

Morsh shrugged. "Get you a paydown wit pit boss," she said. "You risk, you take. You fail, nobody care. You don fail, nobody care, too."

She nodded. "Fair."

"Soldier, he take a piece on de port. You don wanna pay, you come see Morsh, she show you freedancer."

I'll bet you will, Cantra thought, keeping her face thoughtful as she sipped her tea. "Don't know 'bout the dark market."

"Nothing dark," Morsh said firmly. "Ain soldier port, ain soldier ore. Soldier ain sweated and toiled. Wherefore dey get a piece?"

"I guess," Cantra said dubiously and finished off her tea. "It was an idea, is all. I'll jig around and see what else might turn up."

"Do dat," Morsh said with a chuckle. "Maybe jig down Inside. Fortunes waitin for to be made Inside, I hear."

"Yeah," said Cantra rising and dropping a few coins onto the table. "I hear that, too."

The defenses, duly inspected, were in better shape than Jela had feared, given Commander Gorriti; though it was likely the M soldiers who had made sure the old fort was defensible. There were a good many refurbs of older, not to say obsolete, equipment in evidence, and a couple outright fabrications. Lorit stood by with a blank, soldierly face while he inspected it all, not offering him much more than, "Yes, sir," "No, sir," and "Couldn't say, sir," which was how he himself would treat an unknown officer appearing on the eve of evacuation with orders to inspect the defenses.

"That's the lot, then?" he asked.

"Yes, sir," she answered stolidly.

Jela eyed her, made his decision. "I'm going to level with you, Sergeant. Your defenses are in top shape, considering what you had to work with—but you know that. The reason I'm here so close on the heels of the pull-back order is because somebody at Command realized they'd been ignoring something pertinent. There's a record from the First Phase that indicates this fort was equipped with a world-shield capable of turning away a *sheriekas* attack. That it was partly the use of this device that stopped the *sheriekas* here, and disheartened them so much that they pulled back." He gave her a straight look, which she met expressionlessly. "I'd appreciate being taken to that device, Sergeant."

She didn't say anything, and he didn't rush her. Just met her eyes straight on and let her make her own determination, trusting to her M nature—

"To the best of my knowledge, and the knowledge of the troop," she said, carefully, "there is no such device here. Sir."

"But," he prompted, and damn' if she didn't smile.

"But," she acknowledged, "this planet has so many mines through it, it's a wonder the surface doesn't collapse. And somebody, somewhen, stockpiled a shitload of First Phase tech down in the shafts. Could be your armor's down there. But I wouldn't know how to start to look for it. Sir."

Jela blinked. "How much tech," he asked, but Lorit only shrugged her broad shoulders.

"A lot," was all she said, then, "Are you done here, sir? I can escort you back to the gate."

"I'm done," he said, "but where I'd like you to escort me, if you would, is to the M services medic."

She gave him a hard stare. "Problem, sir?"

"Not necessarily," he said, keeping his voice even. "To the best of my knowledge, I'm approaching decommission."

Her stare softened, and she turned, leading him back the way they'd come. "This way, sir," she said.

Cantra headed back to the tradehall for one more tour, though it was beginning to look like lifting empty was her option. She had a commission, should she choose to accept it—deliver a leather log-book to Solcintra, which was a fair trip from Vanehald, though not so far as Vanehald from Landomist—and nothing to trade for there, either, she thought, trying to work up some annoyance. Nobody went to Solcintra, which Solcintra liked just fine, the founders of same having explicitly wished to divorce themselves from the so-called "dissipated lifestyle" embraced by the citizens of the Inner Worlds.

There'd been some little discussion of whether she would or wouldn't also be delivering the tree to Solcintra; the tree being of one opinion on the subject and Jela another. In the end, what he'd done was asked for her promise to keep it safe, which seemed to satisfy both.

Whether it satisfied her—Well. There was a reason why they said, "Crazy as a Rimmer."

She sighed and shook herself back to the here-and-now. Maybe she could try at the pilot's hall, should there be one. Might be some courier work to be had or—

"Pilot Cantra!"

She almost stumbled, it surprised her that much, but she caught the boggle and turned, smooth and easy, pasting a smile on her face, and showing her hands empty.

"Dulsey," she said, flicking a quick glance over the crew clustered 'round the ex-Batcher and finding nothing overtly life-threatening among them. "You're looking well."

The medic was a natural human, a woman with the burdens of years he would never see etched into her face. He would have preferred, Jela thought, in case his preferences had to do with anything, another M, but he also owned to a feeling of relief, that the medic wasn't an X.

"Imminent decommission, hmm?" The medic's nametag said 'Analee', and there was a lieutenant's chop on her sleeve. "ID number?"

"M-nine-seven-three-nine-nine-seven…" He recited the long string of digits that described his particular self to the military. Beside his personal name, it was the first thing he'd ever learned, but it felt odd in his mouth, as if the shape or the weight of it had somehow changed over the years he'd been on detached duty.

"Hmph," said Analee. "Well, you're in the range. Lie down on the table there and let's have a look at you."

Obediently, he put his back against the table, feeling the sensors pierce him in a thousand places.

"Hood coming down," Analee said, stepping to her control board.

Above him, the hood flared, light gleaming on a thousand more sensors, bristling like teeth, and began to descend. Jela closed his eyes.

There was the usual space of hum-filled disorientation, then the sensors withdrew, the hood rose, and Jela opened his eyes. Analee the medic was frowning at her readouts, having apparently forgotten about him for the moment. In the absence of further orders, he swung his legs over the side of the table and stood.

"Now, that's odd," the medic murmured, maybe to herself; then, clearly to him, "You're certain of your date, Captain?"

Jela sighed. "I thought I was," he said wryly, "but I'm told the mind is the first to go."

Analee raised her eyes, spearing him with a look. "They say that," she acknowledged seriously, "but it's hardly ever so, with Ms." She frowned down at her screen, touched a series on her pad. "I'm calling up your complete medical file," she said, "to see if there's some clerical error which would account for this."

"This?" Jela asked.

"This," she jerked her head at her screen. "You'll be relieved to know that, according to records, your calculations are correct, and sometime within the next two days, local, you should be undergoing decommission. Visually, I've got clear signs of aging—hair going gray, some loss of mass and muscle tone—which are consistent with the early phases of decommission." She raised her eyes to his again, hers pale and tired. "We have drugs, to ease the last of it," she said, gently.

"Thank you," Jela said quietly, and considered her. "But?" he suggested.

Her lips bent slightly. "But, what I have on the scan is the portrait of an M Series soldier who is several months short of decommission. Which is why we're going to check—Here we are." She bent to her screen, manipulating keys, her concentration palpable.

Perforce, Jela waited. For no reason other than his tricksy generalist mind, he thought of the tree, and the taste of its pods. It came to him that he'd been eating quite a number of pods, lately—it had gotten so he'd scarcely noticed. And it also came to him that the tree had demonstrated some versatility in its production of pods—the one it had insisted he feed Maelyn tay'Nordif in order to ease her passing had been specially grown for her, and for that sole purpose, he thought. It could even have been, he thought suddenly, that the very first pod he'd ever had from the tree, in the desert with both of them at risk—which he'd eaten and straightaway fallen into an energy-conserving sleep that might just have saved his life—and the tree's life, too.

He wished, suddenly and sharply, that he could talk to the tree about this new insight. But the tree was gone by now, lifting out on *Dancer*, with Cantra at the board. His heart twisted painfully in his chest, he could see her sitting there, just as clear.

"Oh-ho," Analee said from her computer. She looked over to him. "You were the one survived the attack on the lab at Finthir."

He blinked. "And that explains—"

"Nothing—and everything," she said briskly. "You're an anomaly, is what you are—the only one of your cohort. Nothing else in the birth lab survived that attack. The *sheriekas* poured raw energy down on the facility—and I'm not telling you anything you likely don't know when I say that they should have aborted everything in the nursery wing. The *sheriekas* were pressing, though, and every soldier was needed. So you were reassigned, allowed to mature, and to serve out your time."

He knew this, of course; the tale of the quartermaster's mercy was at the bedrock of his existence. The few personnel remaining after the *sheriekas* attack had been repelled had needed a mascot; a reason to hope—so the quartermaster reasoned. And who was M. Jela, standing now at the end of his life, to say he'd been wrong?

"But," he said yet again, and this time Analee didn't smile.

"But that means you're not a standard M Series soldier. The anamoly hasn't shown up in any important way until now, and what it looks like is that you've got a while longer to serve, Captain." She nodded at her screen. "I'm going to enter into your file that the high dosages of radiation you absorbed during a vulnerable developmental stage has lengthened your life expectancy. Short of a battle, or a nasty fall down the stairs, you're going to see tomorrow, and a good few tomorrows after that."

At Dulsey's insistence, they'd staked out a table at what passed for a bar hereabouts, Cantra keeping an uneasy peace with the ex-Batcher's comrades, haphazardly introduced as Arin, Jakoby and Fern. Arin, who Cantra had pegged as the leader of the expedition, was tall and lean and tough, with gray eyes set deep under strong black brows, and a perpetual frown on his face. Jakoby was fair and small and showed a business-like gun on her belt; she sat slumped in a chair at Arin's right hand, her arm around Fern's waist.

"Have you been in the mines, Pilot Cantra?" Dulsey was the only one of them having a good time, Cantra thought, though it didn't seem exactly like her to be blind of her companions' moods.

"Can't say as I have," she answered, watching Fern wave a hand at the 'tender. "Just hit dirt a couple hours ago, figure to be gone before local dawn."

"So soon? I had hoped you would be willing to accept a commission."

Jakoby sat up straight at that, and Arin's frown got frownier, but neither one said a word.

"Always willing to listen to a paying proposition," Cantra said carefully. "But I have to tell you straight, Dulsey—I'm not looking at jumping off the Rim any time soon."

"Certainly not," she said primly, as if such an idea would never occur to her. "What I wondered is if you would be able to take several canloads of artifact to—"

"Dulsey!" That was Arin, goaded at last to speak. "She's not in."

"Not *in*?" Dulsey rounded on him. "Do you know who this is? The *Uncle himself* has spoken highly of this pilot! Why, he had even offered Pilot Jela a place among—" She stopped and turned back to Cantra.

"Where is Pilot Jela?"

Well now, Cantra thought, that was a question, wasn't it? She moved her eyes, taking her time about scanning the street outside the bar, thinking how best to put the thing. Dulsey'd been fond of Jela—maybe more than fond. It wouldn't do to—she blinked as a familiar pair of shoulders hove into view among the thin crowd, moving quick and purposeful. Cantra looked back to Dulsey.

"Jela?" she repeated, around the sudden lump in her throat. She nodded toward the window and the street beyond. "Here he comes now."

He'd drawn a room in the officers' barracks and a meal card. There was, said the assistant quartermaster—a scarred and sardonic Y Strain—plenty of room, and plenty of food, too, stipulating base rations were food. His kit he'd left on-ship, thinking there might be something in it that Cantra could use, and nothing he needed for his last couple days.

And if he'd known those "last couple days" were in actuality *months*, he could have—he could have been on *Dancer*, sitting co-pilot and content. As it was, *Dancer* was no doubt long lifted, maybe even heading for Solcintra. He thought she'd take the book to Wellik, like he'd asked her to. Just like he thought she'd do her best to keep the tree safe. He had to trust to that.

He shook his head, ran through a focusing exercise—and sighed. Months. If he'd known—

No use thinking about that. And truth told, he could put months to use here, same as he'd intended to use his days. He had the info he'd lifted out of Osabei Tower's brain, and all his generalist's intuition to bring to bear on the problem. If he could locate that world-shield, he could send that info along to Wellik, who he trusted would use the weapons that fell into his hand. Had to trust, in fact. Wellik was the only one left.

Being as he had months, it might have been best to put himself into his bunk for a nap, but he was an M, and an M hates to be idle.

So he drew a local map from stores, and headed out for a stroll through the port—whether for distraction, to gather information, or to walk off a mood hardly mattered.

"Pilot Jela!" a familiar voice shouted. He spun, spied Dulsey at the front of what the map told him was Watt's Bar, waving at him energetically, her grin so wide it was like to split her face.

He felt his mood lighten somewhat, and changed his course.

"Dulsey," he said, giving her a smile. "You're the next-to-last person I'd expected to see. How are you?"

"I am exceptionally well," she assured him, her grin dimming somewhat as she got a good look at him.

"Something wrong?" he asked.

"I—Have you lost weight, Pilot Jela?"

In fact, he had, as the medic had also mentioned. No sense involving Dulsey in all that, though, so he gave her another smile and moved his shoulders in a dismissive shrug. "Had some short rations for a while," he said easily.

"Of course." She hesitated then rallied. "You must come in and meet the others!"

NINETEEN

Vanehald

THERE WERE OTHER people in the bar, but he could only see one, elbow on the chipped table, next to a beer she hadn't touched, chin resting on her palm.

"Cantra." He had the impression he'd been about to say something else, though he couldn't have guessed what, and in the end it was no matter. His throat had closed and squeezed off all the words.

For her part, she gave him a wide, too-bright smile, which was nothing less than he deserved. "That didn't take long," she said, falsely cheerful.

He cleared his throat. "The commander's a fool," he told her, which piece of nonsense earned him a wise look from foggy green eyes and a knowing, "Ah."

"Here," Dulsey broke in, intent on introducing him to her troop. She touched his arm lightly, and nodded toward a tall glowering fellow with a strong jaw. "This is Arin, our librarian and linguistic specialist."

Jela gave him a polite nod, which Arin, despite his glower, returned.

"And this," Dulsey continued, indicating a pale port-rat of a woman wearing her only weapon out in the open on her belt, "is Jakoby, our weapons expert—and Fern, our archeologist and pilot." She smiled 'round at the three of them, seeming not to notice that none of the three smiled back, and told them, "This is Pilot Jela, who the Uncle offered a place among us."

"The soldier," Jakoby spoke up, her voice a dry whisper, "who killed fourteen of us?"

Jela gave her a grin, feeling rather than seeing Cantra get her balance adjusted for a quick move, if it came to that—which it shouldn't. He hoped.

"The soldier," he said to Jakoby, "who was attacked on a dock where he and his pilot had been guaranteed safe crossing. That's right."

There was a sharp pause. When next anyone spoke, it was Arin, remarkably civil.

"Uncle has spoken to me often of these pilots and their role in bringing the *Fratellanzia* to his attention," he said, and inclined his head once more, this time like he meant it.

"Pilot Jela and Pilot Cantra, I know Uncle would wish me to convey to you his gratitude as well as his feeling of obligation. If there is anything I, as Uncle's representative, might do to serve you, please do not hesitate to ask my assistance."

"That's said pretty," Cantra allowed. "Don't exactly compensate for the loss of custom 'skins nor Pilot Jela's peace of mind, but I 'preciate the sentiment. I can't off-hand think of anything that might bring us more into alignment, but I'll be sure to let you know if something occurs."

Arin inclined his head yet a third time. "I am at your service, Pilot."

"No you ain't," she said agreeably, "and neither Pilot Jela nor I is fool enough to believe you are. Though it might be we'll be taking you up on that offer of balance, like I said."

"Dulsey," Jela said, before Arin could get his tongue around an answer to that, "what brings you here? If it can be told."

"There are certain items of antiquity in which the Uncle has an interest," the silent pilot—Fern—said. "Our team was sent to collect them, if they are here, as well as those other objects we deem to be useful."

"If what I'm told about the mine-outs being full of First Phase artifacts is true," Jela said, "I'd say you had your work cut out for you."

"It is," Dulsey said eagerly, "a most exhilarating and involving task, Pilot. But the mines are not *all* filled with antiquities, you know. Some of them—a great many of them—are still being worked."

Jela frowned. Lorit hadn't mentioned that. "Worked? What are they bringing out of the ground here?"

"Timonium," Cantra said laconically, and Jela felt ice down his spine.

Something must have leaked out onto his face, judging by the frown Cantra gave him. Dulsey, though, had noticed nothing amiss and was continuing to talk about the Uncle's project, as animated and energetic as he had ever seen her. Freedom, he thought, agreed with her.

"So rich is the area," she was saying, "that we have already extracted more artifacts than we can ship ourselves. Only today, we had been talking of perhaps sending the ship on with two of us to pilot while the second pair remained to continue the work. Such a solution would be less than ideal, for Arin is our back-up pilot, and his skill with the old records is crucial to the success of the project. However, if you and Pilot Cantra would take our few cansloads to the stockpile, then we might all remain at Vanehald."

"Sounds like it might could be worked out," Cantra said, rising and stretching to her full, long height. "Pilot Jela and me'll talk about it, Dulsey, and let you know."

"When?" asked Dulsey. "For I do not hide from you, Pilots, that time is not plentiful."

"I'll come talk to you tomorrow morning," Jela said, rising in his turn and smiling impartially all around. "Where will I find you?"

"Anytime after dawn, at Shaft Four-Four-Eight on the north end. There is a comm-box by the entrance. Call down when you arrive and I will come up to you."

"Suits," Jela said, and dared to look Cantra directly in the eyes, much good it did him. "Pilot?"

She moved her shoulders. "Your call," she said, like she didn't really care and likely, Jela thought, she didn't. She gave the gathered Batchers a cordial, insincere smile. "Good to see you, again, Dulsey. Arin, we'll be talking about that balance." She nodded at the other two, added a "Pilot," and moved off toward the street, Jela right behind.

"Tomorrow?" Cantra murmured as they walked through the port, by silent agreement heading toward the outer gate, the shipyard and *Dancer*.

"Tomorrow," he asserted, and shot her a sideways glance. "Seems my date was off by a bit."

They walked a few steps in silence while she digested this, then, "I never knew you to have a slack memory, though I guess the stress of the last whiles might've addled your brain."

"Might have," he agreed, "but the medic confirms my recollection—I should be decommissioned over the next couple days."

"But you're not—because?"

"Well, now, the medic seems inclined to blame the peculiar circumstances of my birth for introducing an anomaly which is only just now showing up. But I don't think we need to look any further than the tree."

Cantra sent him a look.

"The tree's keeping you alive?"

"The tree's been feeding me seedpods as fast as it can grow them," he said, talking it out to see if still made sense. "In fact, it could be that it had to produce those pods *too* fast, so there's less virtue in them, and that's why I've got a few extra months instead of the second half of a natural human life." He shot her a sidewise glance. "It's not much of a tree, after all."

Cantra didn't say anything.

"I think the tree's practicing biochemistry," he continued, figuring he might as well finish his reasoning out. "Life-extending drugs for me; a psychotropic conditioner for you."

"Two for me," she corrected quietly. "Right before I let Maelyn tay'Nordif have her life, the tree gave me a pod to eat. I thought it was a going-away present, something to maybe comfort me, but if what you're thinking is true, it produced a good approximation of the trance-drug. All the time telling me as how it and you wouldn't let me fall—you'd bring me on home and everything would be happy-fine."

"I saw the antidote to the scholar work," Jela said. "You went from berserk to calm sleep inside six heartbeats, and then the tree insisted that I tell you stories." He sent her another glance, and found her watching him seriously. "The only story I could think to tell you was the story of who you were. I was afraid I didn't know enough to bring you back."

They were at the base of *Dancer's* ramp. Cantra gripped his arm. "You knew enough," she said huskily, then let him go and ran lightly up to the hatch.

Exuberant images hit him as he came into the tower: A thousand dragons dancing against a brilliant sky, trees swaying in a warm wind, branches spread to receive nourishment from the local star.

Cantra walked over and leaned on the back of the pilot's chair, arms crossed, pose non-committal. Jela went to the tree, saw the branch bent under the weight of a pod, the aroma promising all measure of good things, and reminding him of that first pod, given so long ago, that had sealed the promise between them.

His mouth watered; he wanted the pod, and what harm, he thought, would it do?

A dark shadow passed over the dragons dancing in his head, gliding lazily toward the sun-sated trees. A branch rose, and it settled—the black dragon, its scales iridescent in the downpour of light. Jela caught the impression of age—vast age—and a breadth of wisdom entirely unlike that of an elder tree.

"No," he said softly. "I appreciate the effort, but it's a bad solution. You'll use yourself up trying to keep me alive past design. A good soldier knows when a battle's not winnable, when he needs to cut his losses and rebuild his resources, so he can win a greater battle later. You're a good soldier, from a long line of good soldiers, and I'm not telling you anything you don't know."

Silence from the tree; the dancing dragons, the sunny, joyous day vanished from his consciousness, replaced by that mental tenseness which meant the tree was paying attenion. Hard.

"Right," he said. "Remember, you held a whole planet against everything the *sheriekas* had—held it when you were too young to leave the nursery. But you were the last soldier the world had, and duty called you up. That duty still holds you, like it holds me. And my duty doesn't allow me to steal from a comrade—and never from a brother-in-arms."

Slowly, an image: the old black dragon perched on one side of a gargantuan nest, the slim golden dragon on the other. Inside, a small creature slept curled, while the sun gently dried its wings.

"Is that true?" Cantra's voice was quiet.

The image repeated, which might have been taken for yes. Jela sighed and looked across to her.

"I don't know how it could be," he said. "It said something similar to me, once. I took it to be more general: it'll stand its duty to the next generation."

"Though it seems prone to working in particular rather than general," Cantra pointed out, and straightened out of her lean, face neutral. "Well, it'll sort itself out." She nodded at the pod-heavy branch. "You going to have that?"

It was, he told himself, already made—made especially and only for him. It would be a waste, and a bad use of a comrade's care.

"All right," he said, standing forward and holding out his hand. "This is the last." The pod hit his palm and he sighed as much in anticipation as regret. "Thank you," he said. "For everything."

He ate while Cantra did a quick check of the security systems. When she was done, she spun the chair and looked full at him, foggy green eyes wide and guileless.

"Are you wanted elsewhere this evening, Pilot?" she asked.

He thought of the narrow cot in the officers' barracks, and of duty. He smiled at her, letting her see all his admiration of her, and his care—another true comrade. And more.

And more.

"As it happens," he answered, holding his hands out to her; "I'm at liberty."

TWENTY

Vanehald

BEING ON THE port early in the morning seemed contraindicated after their comfortable untwining and the easy companionship of a meal. After, Cantra made a pot of garden-tea, its soft, tangy taste everything that was different from the usual ship-board brew. He savored it no less than the quiet ease between him and his comrades, and put the cup down with a pang when the tea was too soon gone.

"Business on the port?" Cantra asked, reading him sharp and accurate.

"I told Dulsey I'd come by, and I do want to talk to her," he pointed out.

She leaned back, long legs thrust out before her and crossed at the ankles. "You're thinking the Uncle is looking for that same bit of Old War tech you're after yourself," she said, "and that the rest of the treasure hunt's a shadow-play?"

"I wouldn't go that far. The rest of the artifacts are probably of interest, if the Uncle's as keen a collector as you've said. And it could be that they're the only reason the team's here."

"And it could be that Dulsey won't be telling you the truth, either side. If she knows it, which she might not. Young Arin struck me as being a thought tight on the need-to-knows."

"A man who keeps his orders to himself," Jela agreed. "I thought so, too." He hesitated, suddenly and forcibly remembering that, comfortable and comforting as he was here, he'd signed off of *Dancer's* crew.

Cantra raised her eyebrows. "Problem, Pilot?"

"I wonder," he said, slow and careful, "if you'd be willing to do me a favor."

"A favor, is it? And for a change you're asking first?" She gave him an edged grin and lifted a shoulder. "What's needed?"

"Here." He pulled the map he'd drawn from stores out of his pocket and smoothed it down on the table between them.

"Sergeant Lorit tells me that the world-shield's not in the garrison proper—and I think she was telling the truth. She suggested that it might be stashed in the mines, which is possible."

"But you think it's nearer to hand," Cantra finished, coming out of her lean to frown consideringly down at the map. One long finger tapped the outer fort. "In here, is where I'd put it." She looked up at him. "Let me do some soundings and a bit of a wander-round. Meet you at that bar where we saw Dulsey last e'en?"

He nodded. "Mid-day," he said, standing. He looked down, but Cantra was studying the map.

"Mid-day it is," she answered absently. "Give my best regards to Dulsey, Pilot."

There was a sense of anticipation in the dusty air as Jela strode off across the port, angling toward the civilian mines. It made sense, he supposed; business at the port today would be featuring Commander Gorriti's leave-taking, which Jela hoped was being done with circumspection and not a marching band. If he hadn't thought it might cause a riot or a ruckus he could have shot Gorriti for desertion and been well within his standing orders.

It was about the time he was considering that option again that the distant sound of a lift-klaxon sounded, hard on the heels of the familiar vibration of tarmac. *That* would be the commander's shuttle departing, no doubt.

Into his mind came one of the tree's more unsubtle images: a large rodent, and another, rushing about.

Yes, exactly, he agreed, *a rat hurrying to safety among other such. Much good it will do him!*

The image, however, became more insistent: the number of rodents and their energy increasing as they nibbled on tender roots. It would seem that the tree had some concerns regarding the commander's influence at his next station.

No, there you're wrong, my friend, he thought, meaning it for comfort. *That tree is rotten already!*

But still the tree wanted to push the image of rodents at him, while Gorriti's ship dwindled and was lost in the tan sky.

Enough! Jela answered. *We agree. Agreeing won't change the facts!*

He strode on, the tree's images of a gnawing horde all too firmly in his mind.

*

"Pilot Jela." Dulsey was in full thermal 'skins, the scanplate pushed up off her face reflecting the weak light from the local star. Below it, she was smiling and animated.

"Dulsey," he answered, giving her a smile of his own, though he feared it was a good bit less heartfelt than hers. "I meant to tell you last night—this new life of yours seems to be treating you well."

"Very well," she acknowledged, and swept a hand toward the comm-shack. "Come, let us be out of the wind." She hesitated. "Will Pilot Cantra be coming?"

"Not this time," he said easily. "There's something I asked her to take a look at for me down in the port."

"Ah," she said, and pushed the door to the shed open.

"Also," Jela said, following her in and closing the door behind him. "I wonder if you've found that specific item the Uncle sent you to collect."

Dulsey's smile faded. "Pilot Jela—" He held up a hand and she stopped, face wary now.

"I'm going to try not to make you chose between loyalties," he said slowly. "But it seems to me that the Uncle is a resourceful man, who also happens, as Pilot Cantra tells me, to collect *sheriekas* tech. He's got Arin and I'm betting a dozen more like him, doing research, deciphering old records, maybe even old military and captured *sheriekas* documents from the First Phase. The Uncle also knows that the end of the war is coming fast, and there's no way we can win—"

Dulsey shifted and he raised his hand again. "Humor an old soldier," he said. "This won't take long. The Uncle knows, like I know, that we can't win this war. But he knows his military history, so he knows that an important First Phase battle took place around Vanehald. The Enemy wasn't able to land and occupy the planet; and the Frontier Fleet, despite being outnumbered and pretty much out-gunned, pushed them back.

"Now, what wasn't written down anyplace was *why* those Enemy forces couldn't land here. The device was secret—barely more than a whisper of a rumor, which I spent the last six years of my life, between other things, looking for.

"My information is that it's still here—and I'm betting the Uncle has access to information as good or better than mine.

And I'm betting he sent his best engineer to bring that device back to Rockhaven."

Silence, while Dulsey thought it through. He waited, not rushing her, prepared to take silence as his final answer, or a lie, if she felt she had to. Dulsey had never been good at lying, but the Uncle might have taught her the way of it.

"I believe," she said slowly, "that I am able to share this information with you, as it will benefit you precisely as much as it has us." She sighed.

"If I understand you correctly, the device you seek is that which the Uncle terms a '*sheriekas* repellor.' The literature is not clear, but it gives the impression that this is indeed a device similar to the many others stored here. In fact, it is not stored here at all. It is installed here."

Jela stared at her. "I'm hearing you say that the device exists, but can't be moved."

"That is correct."

He thought about that, considering his next question carefully. "Dulsey, have you seen this device?"

"I have seen plans of the installation in the outer fort," Dulsey said after some consideration of her own. "Understand, when I say 'installed', I mean to convey that it is hardwired into this planet, especially tuned to its composition. It may well be that such a device could be duplicated on another planet, indeed, the project has a certain appeal. However, with current technology, it would take on the order of eighteen hundred years, Common, to produce and mount it."

Jela considered her. "Eighteen hundred years," he repeated slowly. "I'm afraid I wouldn't be able to see it through to completion." The tree, now, he thought, with its dizzingly long life—

"Nor would I," Dulsey said. She hesitated, then blurted, "Pilot Jela, are you well?"

"Well?" he repeated, genuinely startled by the change of subject. "Why wouldn't I be well?"

She frowned, outright irritable. "I observe that you have lost weight," she said, ticking the points off on her fingers, "more than 'short rations' might account for—especially as Pilot Cantra, who I believe would share such rations as there were equally, has not suffered a similar reduction. I observe that your hair is turning grey, and that you are favoring your right leg. Last evening, I observed Pilot Cantra, who was—startled—to see you." She drew a deep breath. "So, I wonder if you are ill, Pilot. Forgive me if the question intrudes. I ask as one who holds you in esteem and bears you nothing but good will."

Who would have known, he thought, that he had so many comrades? He sighed. There were, after all, certain courtesies owed to comrades, such as a clear answer when information was requested.

"I'm functioning according to design," he said to Dulsey's serious eyes. "More or less."

She blinked, once. Waited. Jela sighed again.

"Pilot Cantra didn't expect to see me because I'd told her goodbye and gone to the garrison to report to the medic, and do the necessary paperwork before being decommissioned. As it happens, I misremembered my date, but the signs you see—those are in line with the design. I'm old, Dulsey. Typically, what happens with an M is we have all our old age in one short burst, and then—we stop."

Another blink; a hard breath. "Such design characteristics may sometimes be circumvented," she said, in a voice of calm reason. "Come with us to the Uncle, Pilot Jela, and—"

He shook his head. "I doubt there's a work-around. The military does a tight job on its soldiers, and there's been a good bit of time to work all the design bugs out of the Ms." He gave her a smile, trying to ease the sadness in her eyes. "Don't think I'm ungrateful, Dulsey, but I've got my duty, and my life isn't really my own."

She bowed then, full low. "I understand."

"Yes," he said slowly. "Of all the people I've met in the last half-dozen years, you're probably the only one who does understand." He cleared his throat. "Now," he said, returning to the matter at hand, "about those artifacts."

Dulsey straightened with a startled look.

"The artifacts are many and varied," she said. "Truly, Pilot Jela, this planet is a treasure house! There are grids, data tiles, and maps enough to keep Arin for thirty years and more! There are devices—"

"Dulsey," he interrupted, "did you hear Pilot Cantra say yesterday that what's in these mines besides your treasure is timonium? Raw timonium?"

"Yes, but—"

He interrupted again, ruthlessly. "The *sheriekas* have an affinity for timonium. Think about it—all the captured *sheriekas* tech—all the old battle tech left over from the First Phase—what's the power source?"

She paled. "Timonium."

"Timonium. Which is why Vanehald was so hotly contested in the First Phase—for the timonium. That's my hunch, anyhow, based on research. Tell me now, has your team activated any of those devices?"

"Of course," she began—and stopped, horror filling her eyes. "They are operating in various energy states," she said rapidly, "within a certain limited range of frequencies and harmonics. Only last evening, Jakoby said that it seemed they were building a network."

"Building a network," he finished, "and getting ready to send a beacon to the *sheriekas*."

"If they have not already done so," Dulsey said grimly. "If we have called the Enemy down upon this world—"

"The *sheriekas* have a long memory," he said. "They know what's here and why they were defeated. I'm wondering whose idea it was to stockpile First Phase equipment here." He paused, made his decision.

"Dulsey, listen to me. I know the Uncle sent you here for treasure, but I urge you—I *strongly* urge you—to lift out of here on a heading for Solcintra. Send a bounce to the Uncle telling him that I said that the only chance for his people to survive the upcoming chaos is to immediately raise Solcintra and put himself and his at the service of a man named Liad dea'Syl."

She bowed, stiffly. "I will bring this to Arin immediately. And, Pilot Jela, if I do not see you again—go with my very best good wishes."

"Thank you, Dulsey," he said, warmed. "You do the same."

With an assist from *Dancer* and Jela's local detail map, it wasn't hard to pinpoint a couple likely spots to look. The first and most likely from the scans and map—wasn't, viewed up close. The second possible, though—that was everything a fond smuggler could want.

The stairs hadn't even been guarded. Oh, there'd been an old spy-eye on the door at the top of the flight, which it had taken her half-a-heartbeat to disable before she turned her affectionate attention to the lock. That had been a bit more of a challenge, being older than the tools in her kit were used to dealing with. She'd finally resorted to her thinnest zipper and a ceramic pick, which did the trick neat, and she was through, the door closed and locked behind her, and down the stairs.

The door at the bottom of the flight was slightly newer, and bore a sign warning her that only authorized personnel of Osabei Tower had the right to open it. The standard tool made short work of that lock and she was in.

What she was in—that was a question worth asking. She'd expected a control room, and she supposed that's what she had, though it wasn't like any control room she'd ever seen. There weren't any screens; there weren't any chairs, just an old steel stool in the corner. The walls were cast out of cermacrete, like the rest of the fort, and there were niches and handholds formed into them, though what they were for, or how they were to be manipulated was a matter, she thought with a sinking feeling in her gut, for study.

At the center of the room, a tangle of burnt looking wire was crumpled into a shallow depression, lined with—Cantra squinted, eased closer and went down on a knee, feeling the fine hairs on the back of her neck tremble and try to rise.

"Don't go jumping to must-bes," she told herself, her voice coming back weird and mushy off the cermacrete. "Could be any old rocks that happened to come to hand." She opened her kit, pulled out the scan, and punched it up. Sighed.

Timonium.

Well. The man'd only asked her to find the thing and get a good look at it. She'd done both. There was also the question of was it working, which she supposed Jela might have a passing interest in knowing, and to which her uninformed answer was no. Whether it could be made to work, she had no idea, lacking the manual. Whether it could be extracted from this room—Deeps, the thing *was* the room, and the room was an integral part of the ancient pour that was the fort. It wasn't coming loose for anything short of a pretty persuasive explosion—and maybe not then. Cermacrete was *tough*, which was why there was still so much of it in use and being occupied all this time after the Old War'd been fought and barely won.

She slipped the scan back into the kit and pulled out the ambicorder. Might as well get as much as she could. Judging by the layer of dust on the pile of burnt wires and the old stool in the corner, the place wasn't exactly a popular meeting spot; she should have plenty of time to record conditions.

Jela hurried back toward the fort, thinking, his quick steps startling the rare casual passersby. The *sheriekas* tech was a present danger. He'd have to alert whoever was in command at the garrison now that Gorriti was gone, which could call into question how he knew these things, and might entail a trip to the psychs—though there his M nature would stand him in good stead. Ms almost never went delusional, and he was prepared to stand his brain in front of the doctor for a second time if need be—if the mission demanded it.

Between one step and another, he became aware of someone walking beside him, matching step for step down the dusty, near-deserted path, and turned his head.

His companion smiled, red curls disordered by the breeze. "M. Jela," he murmured. "I hope I find you well?"

"Rool Tiazan. What brings you to this garden spot?"

"The ardent desire to renew your acquaintance, dear sir! What else might I be doing?"

"I'd hate to have to try to imagine," Jela said honestly.

Rool Tiazan laughed with every evidence of delight. "My apologies, sir. We did not mean to disconcert you at our last meeting. But, here! I bring news that I am certain you will be eager to have!"

Jela eyed him. "News," he repeated.

"Indeed." The little man smiled. "I was only just now visiting my associates who ready themselves to battle the *sheriekas* upon their own terms. While there, I was made privy to certain of their intelligence, which I feel must be of very close interest to yourself. Therefore, I made all haste to your side."

"Intelligence?" Jela asked. "*Military* intelligence?"

"Just so!" Rool Tiazan paused and looked around him, at what passed for day on Vanehald, with the chill breeze carrying dust and the light a weak and unappealing tan. "What a delightful planet!"

"I've seen better," Jela said, pausing as well, his weight distributed so as to put less strain on his right leg.

"Ah, but I have policies, M. Jela. And one of them is to find any planet which has successfully stood against the *sheriekas* to be delightful."

"There's that," Jela agreed. "But you said you had news. Of Master dea'Syl?"

"I have news of Master dea'Syl, if you would like to hear it," the *dramliza* said agreeably. "He and the cat and the young pilot have arrived at Solcintra and been made welcome by your good friend Wellik. All should go forward as desired, to the hopeful ascendence of our cause." He turned his hands up as if he had heard Jela's impatience.

"Forgive me, M. Jela, I chatter while you pine for intelligence. You wish to know what it is that my associates have discovered. It is this: the *sheriekas*, whose memories are long, are determined to have Vanehald, and to that end they have dispatched a great many of your kindred on purpose to take the planet, the mines, and the shield."

"My—kindred?" Jela frowned. "I don't—" He stopped, skin prickling, and looked into Rool Tiazan's depthless blue eyes. "The prototypes," he breathed. "The *sheriekas* Ms."

"Exactly so." He looked over Jela's head, as if judging the progress of something discernible only to himself. "Yes," he said as if to himself, "the energy level is almost sufficient to sustain a transition point."

"They're coming in through the mines," Jela said, abruptly seeing it all. "The devices, and the timonium—It's not a comm network they're building, it's a shortcut. The shield—"

"Activate the shield, and it will only be one more source of energy to sustain the gate, this far into the proceedings."

Rool Tiazan's eyes sharpened. "It were best that the *ssussdriad*, Lady Cantra, and your son be on their way—soon. And all of the lines in which I am the one to suggest this to her directly, those lines return diminishing rates of success."

Jela stared at him. *Son?* he thought, then shook it aside. There was no time to discuss the realities of M Series genetics with this oddest of his allies—not with battle soon to be joined.

"I need to warn the garrison," he said, giving his attention to those things which were a soldier's proper concern.

The *dramliza* moved his shoulders. "I am hardly one to tell a man what he must or must not, yet surely it is imperative that you move your comrades—" He paused, then murmured distantly, "Yes. Your pardon, M. Jela, I do see." Another pause, and Rool Tiazan appeared to *fade*, into or beyond the dust-filled air. "In fact you are correct. Every moment that the Iloheen are denied surety here adds to the percentages for our ultimate success."

Jela blinked. If his eyesight was going—The thought was interrupted once more by images of ravening rodents, and now he understood too well what the tree had been telling him this while.

"I'll warn the garrison," he said, briskly, "and see to Cantra. The tree's aware of the danger, as it happens—" He looked to the other man, who was solid enough now, and considering him quizzically.

"You get Dulsey and her team out of here."

The thin eyebrows twitched. "I?"

"I thought we were allies?"

"Ah. Indeed. We are allies." Rool Tiazan bowed his head. "I will arrange it, M. Jela. Allow me, also, to hurry you on your way."

A sudden downburst of wind raised dust in a swirl. Jela threw an arm over his eyes; the wind struck again, lifting him off his feet as if he were no more substantial than a leaf, then set him smartly down again.

He staggered, recovered his footing, lifted the shielding arm away from his eyes—and looked directly into startled face of M Sergeant Lorit.

"I need to talk to command," he gasped. "Immediately."

TWENTY-ONE

Vanehald

"WE ARE NOT," Arin said sternly, "aborting this project and going off to Solcintra on the say-so of the old M soldier. We do not take orders from M soldiers; we take orders from Uncle, who—"

"Arin," Dulsey broke in. "The devices are calling the Enemy *here*. Whether or not we take Pilot Jela's advice regarding our destination, it might well be prudent to load what we can now and lift out."

"How close d'you think the Enemy is?" Jakoby asked in her ragged whisper. "Even if the devices have networked and put out a call for aid, it's going to take some time to transition from the raw end of never—"

"We don't know," Fern said quietly, not looking up from her work, "where the Enemy *is*, Jakoby. I remember hearing tales of crews put to sleep with their ships, parked off the traveled routes, waiting. When the Enemy needs them, up they wake, with their destination already coded into the nav-brain."

"Baby-stories," Jakoby scoffed. "The Enemy is no more or less—"

"Arin," Dulsey said urgently. "We should go. I think that Pilot Jela has the right of it. We do not wish to be caught in a battle for this planet."

"No," Arin said sharply. He looked at each of them in turn. "I am the team leader, Uncle's representative on this project. We will complete our assignment. I checked the ship-boards last night. There's a freighter due in within the next two local days. When it's on-port, I'll negotiate for space with the captain."

"Arin—" Dulsey began, and he rounded on her, eyes snapping. "That is my final word!"

Dulsey's mouth tightened and her shoulders sagged.

"Yes, Arin," she said softly.

At which point, the workroom went away.

*

Cantra eased open the door at the top of the stair, wincing as the noise hit her: klaxons, people yelling, and the unintelligible drone of an automated voice. Carefully, she looked both ways, then slipped out into the hall and relocked the door. The ruckus was coming from the street and—she hoped—had nothing to do with her or her little look-see. Straightening her jacket and adjusting the kit over her shoulder, she ambled down the hall to have a closer look.

The noise was both better and worse outside. Worse, because there was more of it. Better because she could finally make out what the autoshout was saying.

"We are on attack standby! Repeat: Attack standby! All citizens are urged to evacuate. Those who choose not to evacuate and who have weapons are advised to arm themselves now and report to the garrison. This is not a drill. This is not a drill. Situation Level Two: Imminent Enemy Action. Message repeats…"

Imminent Enemy action? Loitering in her doorway, Cantra saw some people run, some laugh. Most just shrugged their shoulders and kept on about their business like announcements of imminent Enemy action were an everyday affair. She watched a woman with a old-style blunderbuss over her shoulder walking purposefully toward the garrison. A couple others followed, including a boykid with an energy pistol strapped to his leg. All in all, not much help to the garrison, if an Enemy attack really was imminent.

At least, Cantra thought with a sigh, she knew exactly where to find Jela.

She eased herself out into a lull in traffic, thinking to check the needle-gun riding in its inside pocket. She'd left her heavy weaponry on the ship, not having expected to need it on a snoop job, and set out toward the garrison at a light jog.

Fern was webbed into the pilot's chair; Arin sitting co-pilot. Dulsey and Jakoby were strapped into the jumpseats behind each pilot.

"How—" Jakoby began, but her broken whisper was overridden by Fern's crisp, "Co-pilot, report!"

"My screens are clear, Pilot," Arin replied, his voice shaking only a little. "We are in transition."

"We are," Fern agreed, her fingers busy on her board. "*How* and *why* can wait until we are certain that the ship is hale and functioning as it should. Systems check, if you please. All remain strapped in until the pilots give the aye."

There was silence while the pilots worked. Then—

"The ship is secure," Fern announced. "Unstrap at will." It was, Dulsey thought, notable that she herself did not unstrap.

"If the pilot pleases," she said softly. "May we know our condition and course?"

Fern sighed. "We're on course for Solcintra, Dulsey. Your M seems to have the means to enforce his suggestions."

"No mere soldier could have instantly transported us from the workroom to our ship, already in transition, with a destination coded in!" Arin protested. Fern shrugged.

"Can or can't, that's what we have."

"We need to change course," Arin said firmly. "There's no need for us to raise Solcintra."

"Yes, there is," said Fern, at last unstrapping and rising in a single, fluid dancer's motion. She met each of their eyes in turn. "The course is *locked*. Pilot's override is non-functional."

Soldiers were coming out of the inner gate in pairs, moving with that same ground-eating quick-walk that was so frustrating in Jela. Wide-shouldered and solid, clad in military 'skins; heavy, dual-energy rifles held at ready; helmets on, face-screens down, they were disconcertingly alike, and not a little frightening. Cantra faltered, staring. *Jela's mates*, she thought. Those calm and faceless forces of destruction moving out quick and light to face the incoming Enemy—*This is what Jela was bred to love.*

Which meant, she reminded herself forcefully, that the man was likely in the garrison, getting 'skinned up, and in need of a sharp talking to on the subject of getting to his ship and off-planet before jolly hell broke loose. She only hoped the garrison folks would count her friend rather than foe at the gate.

She moved into the jog again, pushing past the crowd that had gathered to watch the soldiers march out, like it was some kind of play-parade, instead of an earnest deployment against a fast-approaching doom.

"Cantra!" His shout was 'way too loud in her ear, his fingers too hard 'round her arm as he dragged her back out of the crowd.

Concentrating on keeping her feet, she let him pull her clear then dug her heels in, thinking it was going to hurt something bad if he dislocated her arm.

Fortunately, he was paying more attention than that, though he did scowl at her, and if she didn't have bruises on her arm the size and shape of Jela's fingers for this day's work, it would be through no fault of his.

"You've got to get to *Dancer*!" He yelled at her. "Now!"

Jela wasn't quite in full battle dress, she saw with relief. He'd thrown on a flak vest and grabbed himself up a rifle, which was only prudent, given the circumstances, and he wore a light helmet with an embedded com-set. There were marks on the helmet that looked like some of that silly new-soldier script, and some bright silver bars on the shoulders of the vest.

"I was coming for you!" She yelled back at him. "Let's go!"

He nodded and started off at his quick not-run, she jogging after—and six full-'skinned soldiers fell in behind and at the sides, weapons up, status lights glowing ready.

Might be the escort was heading to occupy the port, she thought, as the substantial wing of them sliced through the crowd. That would make sense. The port could need defending.

It comforted Cantra some little bit that their party grew as they rushed on—it seemed that one in every ten or twelve of the soldiers was getting direction from somewhere, or saw Jela's helmet or vest and knew that they were heading toward the proper duty station.

She hadn't run so far in a long time; and it was a good thing she'd had time to heal up from the strain of being a scholar. Their group moved with a quiet clatter; and now over all came new sounds, the sound of firing somewhere, out toward the mines Dulsey and her team were working—and of an attempt to bring order. The port gate was half-shut as they approached, a single forlorn police-type with a handgun nervously eyeing them as they ran toward her.

"Attention! Attention!" The autoshout gave out. "Enemy soldiers on the ground in Druidill Park. Enemy ground action to east and south of Wister. Enemy forces emerging from the Southard mines. Repeat! Enemy soldiers at the mines. The planet is under attack! All soldiers to stations! All civilians to cover!"

Their group was through the gate, the policewoman giving way gladly to the soldiers, and flat-out running across the near-empty yard, *Dancer* before them. From the left, another, smaller, squad was approaching, their battle dress slightly different from—

"Enemy in sight!" Jela shouted. "Intercept!"

Three of their escort peeled off in the direction of the interlopers.

The rest of them ran for the ship, and there were more soldiers in those subtly different battle 'skins coming in, Cantra saw. Hundreds of them.

"Perimeter three!" Jela ordered, without breaking stride. "Expanding circle!"

Half their little troop responded instantly, deploying toward the advancing enemy.

"Go!" Jela roared, and the rest of their escort was gone, running and firing, and it was only the two of them and *Dancer's* ramp right there!

Around them the sounds of firing intensified, and in the distance the chatter of heavier weapons sounded. There were sounds of ricochets, likely off the space-hard hull of *Dancer* herself.

"Up!" Jela shouted, a solid presence behind her; his weapon up and firing as they advanced. She jumped the "Captain's Out" barrier, landed light on her feet and ran the rest of the way, never faster, knowing he was behind her, triggered the hatch, ducked in, turned—

He halfway to the unstoppable wave of the enemy, dodging and firing, and there was no way—

"Jela!" She screamed, but he didn't hear her. Couldn't possibly hear her.

"GO!" His voice came back to her over the terrific noise of the fighting. "Damn you, Cantra, *GO*!"

She took one more look out over the port and the plain beyond, at the steady stream of soldiers in the wrong color 'skins—and she went.

"...GO!"

The plan, in so far as there was a plan, was working. He'd brought troops to the port, intercepted a rash attempt to take the field, gotten Cantra to her ship. Now to clear launch room—

"Expanding perimeter!" he ordered. "Charge fifty paces!"

He was among them now, his troops, and they were doing well. They were advancing, they were pushing the stunned enemy back against their own on-rushing troops, creating consternation.

Into his head stormed the largest dragon the tree had ever shown him, wings black and terrible, scattering dozens of the less mighty with roar, tooth and talon—

Before him, he saw the enemy scuttle, retreat, fall.

He picked a target, fired; fired again, a head shot, then the next.

The cermacrete trembled as the mass of *Spiral Dance* lifted on maneuvering jets behind him.

"Down all!" he shouted.

Following his own order, he fell forward, let the steam and gas wash over him, and rush out toward the enemy, obscuring everything. He laughed and the dragon in his head echoed him.

There was a glow within the steam, the pulse of low carrier power booming, and he knew the plan could work. The ship's rising would give them time to gather their strength.

And now the steam was thinning. Time to move.

"Ahead fire four count, charge ten paces!"

He came up with his troops, never doubting that they'd drive the enemy back to the perimeter. The dragon in his head screamed defiance, and he echoed it at full volume into the mic and across the field.

"Back to their holes! Chase them back! No prisoners, no surrender!"

He jumped a downed comrade, and another, fired ahead, felt the presence of someone too close, had time to swing the butt of his gun into a yielding face, fell, got up—numbness was growing in his left leg, but he refused to notice it, shot again, but now the noise wasn't right, he couldn't separate his own yelling from the sounds of the weapons.

A quick glance behind showed three of his own and an X with a bloody grinning face, firing his weapon one-handed, screaming along with him. His right arm went numb, and the gun slid away—but no matter. His knife came to his left hand and he brought it about, his leg not quite giving him the distance he wanted and not working at all, really, but there was the enemy within reach—

Black wings roared in his ears, or it was it *Dancer* lighting up full thrust? Hah! The ship was lifting! His knife was gone, wrenched out his hand as the enemy fell. He snatched at his belt, freed the wicked ceramic whip with a snap that took the arm off an approaching soldier. Another snap, but his leg gave out and the whip flew out of his fingers—

It was silent on the field; in his head, he could hear the black dragon singing.

Jela sighed a last sigh, and the black dragon lay down beside him. Above them, wings flashing against the brilliant sky, a golden dragon danced.

She hit the chair hard, called up systems and screens. She found him almost at once, surrounded, firing, each shot taking its target, but there were too many, too—

They were charging the enemy like a bunch of madmen, giving her room for lift off. She had her eyes on him, and watched his back in the screen as the maneuvering jets puffed their first lift.

"Override, dammit," she spat as the warning bells screamed. "I need some room!"

The ship started a lazy drift, and she lost sight of him, hit the jets harder, setting an auto-orbit switch, saw his back again. Far away, he looked, and so small, leading a knot of soldiers into a sea of Enemy. They'd gained ground somehow, but the tide was turning and—

Down.

No, he was—There. No—

No.

The fighting stilled. The Enemy had the field.

The tree screamed. Or she did, or all the tiny dragons in her head.

Her fingers moved on the board. *Dancer* leapt, spun on its axis and flared, flames incinerating soldiers where they stood. Her fingers moved again, and she flew as low as she dared over the field, sweeping with flame and jets, sweeping again, and when all was obscured by streaming fire she savagely slapped the lift to orbit button, and relished opening the armament switches. Firing Jela's precious cannon, she launched the Jayfours still on board across the seething mine shafts, dropped flares and test rounds—whatever there was—until the magazines were empty.

It wasn't until *Dancer* was safely up and out that she realized she was crying, silently and steadily.

TWENTY-TWO

Long Savannahs of the Blue

THE SCREENS SHOWED black; the only sounds in the tower the soft mutter of machinery, the whisper of the ventilating system—and the ragged breathing of the woman in the pilot's chair.

She sat with shock webs engaged. It had come to her that it might not be safe to let those straps loose just yet. No telling what she might do—She'd thought that without stipulating what it might mean. She was cold to the point of shivering, and her chest ached, like she'd been working too hard in thin air—*Hyperventilating, that's what*, she told herself, raising a hand to brush at her face. Her fingers came away wet. *Deeps.*

Behind her closed eyes, an image formed, tentatively: the shadowy outline of a too-familiar black dragon.

"Don't," she snarled, or tried to, her voice thin and unsteady in her own ears. "I'll break you into toothpicks if you try me now."

The dragon-image faded, and she was alone in her head. Alone on her ship. Alone—

"Shift changes, Pilot," Jela said, his voice easy and warm. "Time to get some—"

"*Stop it!*" she screamed, surging upward. The straps grabbed her, pressed her into the chair, and she fell back, eyes shut but seeing it again: Jela falling, rising, shooting, losing the gun, cutting someone, down—

Dead.

No harm in grieving a good friend lost, Garen whispered from memory.

"No harm," Cantra whispered, ragged. "I think—" She cleared her throat. "Garen. Listen to me, now, I've got something in my mind. I know you done it for the best, and we gave it a good run—but I'm thinking what you did there at Tanjalyre—I'm thinking you skimped on the planning. What was the use of flying under the Director's scans when Veralt found you anyhow? What's the use my carrying on, all alone and not fit for it? *Dammit,* Garen." Her voice choked out, and she wilted sideways against the straps, like she had ribs stove, or maybe'd taken a bad cut. The tower faded—maybe she passed out, or maybe she just fell asleep, exhausted, adrenaline-lagged as she was—no matter, really, other than to say that when she blinked back to consciousness, she wasn't crying any more.

She straightened and released the webbing, though she didn't try to stand up. Her muscles were like water, and she felt unconnected to the reality around her.

Saving one.

"You," she whispered.

Call it a change in the air inside the tower—whatever. She knew it was listening to her. Jela's tree, that she'd promised to take to safety. Whatever that meant.

"You," she said again. "You tell me straight. I'm figuring Jela was bred sterile—military wouldn't want those special tailored genes crossing out to the general population, now would they?"

Silence, saving ship noise; no pictures took shape behind her eyes. Cantra sighed.

"Right. I'm also figuring you didn't find that little fix too much of a challenge, considering all else you put yourself to—and accomplished. I'll just mention the tiny inconvenience of my own deliberately non-fertile state."

More silence, the air in the tower fair a-quiver with attention.

Cantra levered herself onto her feet and walked unsteadily to the end of the board. One hand braced against the wall, she stared at the tree, noting more than a few leaves drooping and showing some brown along the edge, and a couple undergrown pods turning yellow on the limb.

"You tell me the truth, now," she whispered. "Am I carrying Jela's true and biologic child? Yes or no'll be fine, stipulating I don't want to hear his voice."

The air in the tower shifted in some indefinable way, and the top branch of the little tree snapped, as if in salute.

"*Yes,*" her own voice whispered raggedly back at her from the walls. "*Jela's true and biologic child.*"

She closed her eyes. Took one breath, then another—and another, concentrating on keeping them uniformly deep and unhurried.

"I see," she said at last, opening her eyes. "I'm grateful to have the information." She pushed away from the wall.

"I'll be in my quarters," she said.

Energies moved in slow, scintillant waves, melding and separating; nothing more than a turgid eddy among the exuberant forces that defined the leading edge of the galaxy.

A star fell into the eddy and was instantly absorbed, cleverly woven ley lines confining its renegade brilliance.

"Again?" The lady lounged on her velvet chaise, a dope stick in a long, gem-sprinkled holder in one indolent hand; the other tucked beneath her head. She considered him out of half-closed emerald eyes, her hair a honey swirl against the tasseled pillow, her long limbs sheathed in light. Beside the chaise, her submissive knelt on the thick rugs, his back crisscrossed with old scars and new stripes, his will concentrated on the form and the substance of the cage.

"Lady." Rool Tiazan said respectfully. "I come to you once more at the behest of my dominant."

"Who perished foolishly, which might have been the greatest folly of her existence, had she not first performed a greater." The lady paused to draw on her dope-stick; illusion, of course, as was everything in this place, saving the cage formed of ley lines. "It astonishes one, the choice to insure the survival of the lesser part. Surely, she might have more easily preserved herself, and absorbed your energies at the instant of your destruction."

"Such a course would have served my purpose not at all," his lady said tartly, moving to the fore within their shared essence. "Sister."

The lady on the chaise blew a smoke ring, and watched it waft, blue and fragrant, toward the cage. Rool gave it attention, but it was merely a diversion, and not a threat.

"Rool Tiazan's dominant retains existence," the lady on the chaise said, thus informing the invisible and ever-present corps of her sisters. She shifted, her hair moving seductively on the pillow. "What errand brings you here, then? Sister."

"I would ask," his lady said, "that you coordinate your action with mine, and with that of Lady Moonhawk."

"Why would I wish to do this?"

"Because it becomes increasingly plain that the Iloheen cannot be halted by any one of our actions. Only by acting in concert do we hold a chance of gaining our goals."

"And yet we each of us hold goals which are fundamentally different," the other lady pointed out.

"In outcome, perhaps," his lady agreed. "However, we are united at base: the Iloheen must not go forward with their destiny. On this we agree."

"Indeed. And yet I say again—our desired outcomes diverge greatly. Lady Moonhawk wishes to steal a mite of the Iloheen future and seal it away for all life to share equally. You—you wish to run away. And I—" she smiled slowly, showing small, pointed teeth. "I wish to depose the Iloheen, and take up dominion of this galaxy."

"Sister, these goals are not incompatible. Allow me to explain. Rool."

Carefully, and masking his distaste, he made contact with the submissive, and downloaded the relevant data into the dull, half-crazed mind. He withdrew and the dominant on the chaise blew a smoke ring. It settled about her submissive's head like a misty crown. She drew again on the dope stick and the ring thickened, tightening until the submissive moaned.

She smiled, eyes half-closed. "I see," she said after a moment. "The calculations of energy are very fine, are they not? Are you able to produce your share? Sister."

"Of course. Sister."

"Ah." Another smoke ring, this one *not* a simple diversion. Rool extended his thought and nullified it before it intersected with the lines forming the cage. On the chaise, the lady smiled, languidly amused.

"The word of a sister to a sister," she observed lazily, "is of course inviolate. However, your situation, if you will allow me, sister, is so odd that I fear me I will require something more." She sat up, suddenly neither languid nor lazy; the ley lines spat and hissed as power amassed in a thunderhead of possibility.

The cage contracted, poison rising in the heat from the lines. Rool exerted his will, knowing that she would see the effort it cost him; leached the poison and stilled the contraction.

His lady's sister laughed.

"Rool Tiazan!" She commanded him, and he shuddered to hear her.

"Lady," he answered, forcefully projecting calm.

"You will bind yourself to this promise: At the Moment, you will wholly support my action."

"There is another yet to convince," his lady spoke briskly; "who will also wish to seal our bond with power. It is mete and fitting that guarantees be made. Therefore at the Moment of the Question, you shall have one-third of what you measure here and now of our worth, in support of your Answer."

Power rolled and clashed. The lady's thought enclosed him, violating him on every level; and he would certainly have screamed, had she left him any means to do so.

An eternity of torment passed—and he was released. He collapsed within the poisoned walls of their prison, bleeding energy from a thousand wounds.

His lady's sister relaxed into the chaise, her eyes bright and cruel, crimson smoke wreathing her head.

"We are in accord," she said. "Have your submissive weave a strand to mine, so that I may draw my portion, when it is due."

"Indeed. Rool."

Unsteadily, he did what was needful, spinning out a thread of his essence to weave into that of the scarred, mad submissive. "It is done," his lady said. "Look for contact—soon, I think, sister. The process accelerates."

"So I have noted, as well. Simbu, relax the energies."

The cage wavered, lines loosening. Rool collected himself and snatched them out of that place, a star blazing thinly against the flickering purple of the Rim, and then gone.

TWENTY-THREE

Solcintra

TOR AN YOS'GALAN moved down the hallway at a pace just slightly less than a run, passing many soldiers—Ms and Xs, Ys and natural human. Most ignored him, some acknowledged him with a casual salute or tip of the head. None molested him, for which he believed Captain Wellik was to thank, though that large, brusque individual swore otherwise.

"Don't judge all soldiers by a bunch of rowdies with a withdrawal order on their belts. Troops here are disciplined, and we know our duty—to hold this world against attack, and to guard the civilians, should attack become imminent."

Though he could hardly credit it himself, Tor An had developed a liking for Captain Wellik, who remembered Jela fondly, and received Scholar dea'Syl with reverence. He had immediately installed the scholar in spacious apartments within the garrison, gathering each and any small thing the old man could think to want. Captain Wellik had even taken the third member of their party in his long stride, merely observing that Lucky was an exemplary name for a cat.

The hallway opened into the garrison commons, and Tor An allowed himself to stretch into a real run.

That he had stayed on as man of all work for Scholar dea'Syl was reasonable. The old man was comfortable with him; he had young legs and a willingness to be of use. And it wasn't as if he were needed elsewhere.

Today's errand necessitated a trip down into the town, to the wine-shop of one Tilthi bar'Onig, there to pick up the Scholar's mid-week order. Of course, there was no real reason for Tor An to go himself—the errand could have been accomplished by any one of the soldiers attached to the garrison quartermaster's office. However, it was a tonic—so said Master dea'Syl, and Tor An found himself in agreement—to be able to leave the garrison and walk among civilians.

"Mark me, I have been a prisoner," the old man had said to him, as he sat in the window of his apartments and looked out over the evening commons. "You might say that everyone is bound by duty, and thus each stands a prisoner in his own jail—and you would be correct. To a point. Do you know what that point is, young trader?"

This examination was familiar enough. Tor An had looked up from the newsfeed, and considered the old man's silhouette.

"Choice, sir?"

For a moment, there had been no response. Then Scholar dea'Syl sighed.

"Choice," he repeated, as if it were some rare and precious gem laid out on the trade cloth for his consideration. "You've been well-schooled, I see." He'd held out his glass then, not looking away from the window.

"Be a good lad and fetch me some more of the same."

Tor An slowed to a brisk walk, and waved his pass at Corporal Hanth on the gate, as his partner Jarn was engaged with a—

Tor An spun on his heel.

"Scholar tay'Nordif!"

The woman in trade leathers did not turn her head, and Tor An hesitated. Perhaps he was mistaken, he thought. It had taken him some days not to see Jela in every M Series soldier he passed; perhaps this lady—tall and slim, with pretty tan hair and strong profile—perhaps this lady merely had the seeming of—

"I'll explain myself to Captain Wellik, and none other," she was saying, her husky, laconic voice bearing a Rim accent—and that was certainly wrong. Maelyn tay'Nordif had spoken with a scholar's finicking care, her voice high and clear.

"You can call him here or I can go to him there," she told Jarn. "Either way, your job's to clear me, and what you need for that is this: *Jela sent me.* Send it on. My name's—"

He was *not* mistaken!

"Scholar tay'Nordif!" Tor An moved toward her, aware that Hanth had shifted, and that Jarn was looking stubborn. The scholar herself—she turned to face him, pilot smooth, the line of frown between her brows.

"You're talking to me, Pilot?" There was no glimmer of recognition in her face. Yet, if Jela had sent her—Surely there could not be two such! Tor An took a deep breath and bowed.

"Scholar, perhaps you will recall me. It is Tor An yos'Galan. I had not expected—has Captain Jela come with you? Just yesterday, the master was wishful of speaking to him, in regard to—"

He stopped. The lady was no longer frowning; indeed, there was a complete and frightening absence of expression on her face.

"Jela's dead," she said flatly. "And my name, if you'll do me the favor of recalling it, Pilot, is Cantra yos'Phelium." She moved a hand, showing him Hanth and Jarn. "Might be you're able to talk sense to the gate guard? I'm bearing a message from Jela to Captain Wellik, and I'll not hide from you, Pilot, that my temper's on a thin tether at this day and hour."

Dead. Yet another loss. Tears rose. He blinked them away and inclined his head.

"How?" he asked, his voice cracking. He cleared his throat, and raised his head to meet her eyes. "If it can be told. Pilot."

Something moved in the foggy green eyes, and the lady's mouth tightened.

"He took rear guard," she said softly. "I see you honor him, Pilot. Get me to Captain Wellik, and we're both in the way of following last orders."

"Certainly." He turned to Jarn, who was still looking stubborn, and then to Hanth, who was looking wary.

"This pilot," he said to both, "is known to me. I vouch for her."

"She's so known to you," Jarn answered, "that she had to tell you what name she's using today."

"I knew her as Maelyn tay'Nordif," Tor An admitted. "However, Captain Jela—who I know you honor, Hanth—told me that this lady is vital to the profitable outcome of the scholar's work. Captain Wellik will wish to see her. If you will not pass her, then call him to the gate."

Hanth exchanged a glance with Jarn; she hitched a shoulder and jerked her head, using her chin to hit the comm switch set inside her collar.

"Captain," she murmured. "Pilot at the gate asking for you by name. Says she carries a message from Captain Jela. The boy claims to know her, but calls her by a different name than the one she gives to us." Silence, then "—Cantra yos'Phelium," she murmured. "The boy says Maelyn tay'Nordif." A shorter silence. "Yes, sir."

A sigh and another jerk of the chin, then Jarn looked up at the tall pilot.

"Captain's sending an escort," she said.

Cantra yos'Phelium inclined her head and moved to a side, leaning an indolent hip against the wall and crossing her arms across her breast. Tor An hesitated, his mind half on Scholar dea'Syl's errand, and yet loath to let the scho—Pilot yos'Phelium—go.

"How," he began, moving toward her. She looked up, face neutral in a way that he recognized. He paused, and showed her empty hands. She inclined her head.

"How did you escape?" he asked, letting his hands fall slowly his sides. "We—the captain would have the duel a diversion engineered to allow us to win free with Master dea'Syl. When we had raised *Light Wing*, and the scholar was safe inside, then he—he and the tree—left us. They were going back to Osabei Tower, he said. For you."

She sighed and closed her eyes briefly. "Stupid damn' thing," she muttered then opened her eyes and gave him a hard look.

"I came out through the smaly tube, since the topic's stupidity. Jela scraped me up off the floor and took me back to our ship."

Tor An stared at her. "The smaly tube?" he breathed. "You might have been—"

"Killed," she finished. "That's right."

She seemed to find the matter of no particular interest, nor the fact of her survival astonishing. And yet—this was the pilot Jela had claimed as partner, who had accepted self-delusion in order that Scholar dea'Syl might be brought out of his prison, and his work placed at the disposal of—

A tall shadow moved inside the gate, resolving into Corporal Kwinz, her tattoos blue and vivid in the sunlight. Her gaze passed over Tor An and settled on Cantra yos'Phelium.

"You're the one with a message from Captain Jela?" she asked.

"That's right," the pilot answered, straightening out of her lean to stand tall and ready on the balls of her feet.

"Come on, then," Kwinz said. "You're late for the party."

The pilot fell in behind the soldier, and the two of them marched away across the commons. Tor An tarried, in case she should have need—but she never looked back. For all he was able to tell, she had forgotten his existence entirely.

"You'll want to move smart," Hanth said, "if you expect to be back from town by curfew."

Tor An blinked. He should have asked her, he thought, if she wanted her cat.

"The pilot—" he said to Hanth, but that soldier jerked a shoulder.

"The pilot has business with the captain," he said. "You have business outside. And if you're not back by curfew, *you'll* have business with the captain, which I think you'd rather avoid, eh?"

Well—Yes.

Sighing, Tor An took up his errand, moving into a jog and finally into a run, keeping his thoughts determinedly on the scholar's mid-week order.

The soldier with the blue tattoos didn't waste any time marching them through the garrison's center and into the dim quiet of inside. Cantra followed, keeping her hand away from her gun and projecting calm good citizenship. She tried not to think about the yellow-haired pilot at the gate, who'd been a breath away from crying true tears on hearing of Jela's demise—and who'd looked so happy to see her that on-lookers might've supposed them kin. Clearly, she'd made an impression on the kid, though she couldn't say the same for him. If she put her mind to it, she could probably dredge some tenuous recollection of him out the mists that served as Maelyn tay'Nordif's memory. Memories she shouldn't have, come right down to it, and best left alone. Might be they'd fade full away, over time.

She could hope.

"Down here," her guide said, triggering a door and standing aside to let her pass, then closing up behind her as they moved down a narrower, more private hall.

"First door on the left," the soldier said, and Cantra squared her shoulders and marched on.

She sighed, feeling the weight of Jela's book in the inside pocket. Now it came to turning it in to its rightful owner, she felt a certain reluctance to let it go, which was nothing more than plain and fancy nonsense. She'd read it, o'course—as much of it as she could read. A firm, precise, strong hand, that was what Jela wrote—who would expect different?—and most of what he'd set down had been in cipher. Even stipulating she could crack it—which she likely could, given time and *Dancer's* brain—the information would only be of interest to Captain Wellik and his kind, now that Jela's commander was gone.

The passages not in cipher were descriptions of people he'd seen, cogitations on this or that thing that had caught his fancy. At the back, he'd kept an informal ship's log, detailing *Dancer's* ports o'call, cargo movement, and interaction of ship's personnel. Reading those firm, precise words, it seemed he'd found the time pleasant and easeful—comforting in some way that defied belief, yet was no less true for being incomprehensible.

"Right here," said the soldier, and Cantra stopped, turning to face the door.

The soldier leaned over her shoulder and hit the button set in the frame.

"Corporal Kwinz escorting Pilot Cantra yos'Phelium," she said, nice and smart.

The door hesitated, as if weighing the likelihood of such an assertion, then slid silently up and out of the way.

Captain Wellik was a big man, which she'd expected, his only concession to the X Strain fashion of facial decoration a tan star tattooed high up on his tan cheek.

What she hadn't expected was to find him standing three steps inside the room, dwarfing the chairs along the side walls, his arms crossed over his not-inconsiderable chest, legs braced wide, and an ice-blue glare aimed at the center of her forehead.

Cantra stopped, there being no place to go save through him, which course of action she thought she'd reserve until later, and craned her head back.

"I ain't," she said tiredly, "in any mood for games. Jela said you were a true man and stood his friend. If that's so, then cut the pose and we can deal."

The glare didn't abate, nor even did Captain Wellik uncross his arms.

"And if it's not?" he thundered.

She sighed. "If it's not, then I'm gone."

The glare stayed steady, but the eyebrows were seen to twitch.

"There's a soldier behind you," he said, slightly less thunderous, "armed and ready."

"Right. I'd hate to have to hurt her, being as I hear there's a war on and every soldier's needed. But it's your call."

Wellik threw back his massive head and roared. It took a heartbeat for abused ears to process the racket as laughter, by which time he'd recovered himself enough to send an amused glance over her shoulder.

"Afraid, Kwinz?" he asked.

"If Captain Jela trained her," the reply came, "I'm afraid. Sir."

"If Jela trained her, *I'm* afraid," Wellik said, unfolding his arms at last and bringing his attention back to herself. "So, little pilot, did Jela train you?"

"He did not," Cantra answered. "And my mood's not getting any better, with regard to games."

"I apologize, Pilot," he said, surprisingly. "You're the latest in a string of people arriving at this garrison of late, all bearing a token or a message from Jela. It's getting to be something more than a joke—soldier's humor, you understand."

That she did, soldier's humor being not unlike Rimmer humor in hue and edge. Cantra inclined her head. "I'm just through a bad campaign," she told him, almost hearing Jela murmuring the words into her ear. "Took some damage, lost—" her voice broke; she cleared her throat. "I'm on a thin edge, Captain. Take the message and let's part easy."

The pale blue eyes considered her seriously now. "When's the last time you saw Jela, Pilot?" He held up a hand. "Need to know."

Cantra took a hard breath. "I last saw Jela on Vanehald, about eleven Common Days ago. You'll also have a need to know that the last I saw Vanehald, it looked to be overrun by the Enemy."

Wellik nodded. "I have intelligence from Vanehald, thank you, Pilot. But you last saw Jela on Vanehald. You left him alive?"

"He was leading a defensive squad, rear guard at the port," she said, keeping her voice steady. "I saw him fall."

"Eleven Common Days ago," the big man repeated thoughtfully. "And he was hale enough to lead that squad."

Cantra sighed. "The medic at Vanehald Garrison gave him a couple months more. Reason was the fact he'd absorbed some *sheriekas* energy off the event that destroyed the birth lab he was in at the time."

Wellik frowned. "Stupid—" He caught himself and glanced aside. "Eh, well. The medics have their own arts. What's important to me is that date." Another quick blue glance over her shoulder. "Dismissed to the door, Corporal."

"Yes, sir," Kwinz answered, sharp as you like. There came the sounds of her departure, which Cantra didn't turn to see, preferring to keep both eyes on Captain Wellik.

The door shut with a hiss and a bump, and the captain's thoughtful blue gaze was back on her face.

"Your message, Pilot?"

Right. She took a breath and raised her hand. "It's inside my jacket," she told Wellik, in case he had a nervous disposition. He nodded, and she used that same hand to reach, slow and careful, into the jacket, fetched Jela's book out of the inner pocket, and held it out.

"Well, now." He received it with respect, and Cantra dropped her hand to her side, fingers curling to preserve the feel of the worn leather against her skin.

Wellik opened the book, riffled the pages with rapid gentleness, then closed it and slipped it into his right leg pocket. Cantra saw it disappear with a pain that was like a knife thrust through the gut. She ground her teeth, met Wellik's eyes and gave a sharp nod of the head.

"That's done, then," she said, briskly. "I'll be on my way."

"Actually, you won't," Wellik said, stepping aside and jerking his head at the door his bulk had concealed. "Step into my office, please, Pilot."

"Why?" she demanded, giving him as good a glare as she had in her.

"Something you can help me with," he said. "It'll take but a moment of your time."

She considered turning around and walking out, but there was Kwinz on the outside, not to mention a good many other soldiers between her and the gate, and she'd gone and promised Jela to see his damn' tree safe, which she couldn't likely do as a dead body.

Not that she had much chance as a live body, either.

So, she gave Wellik a shrug and moved forward. The door opened ahead of her and she stepped into what was properly the captain's office, blinking at the crowd of folk around the table—

"Pilot Cantra!" One of the crowd leapt to her feet, and rushed forward. She paused just a few steps away, her face suddenly Batcher bland.

"Dulsey," Cantra said, keeping her voice slow and easy with an effort. "Nice to see you again."

"It is good to see you again, too, Pilot," Dulsey said softly. Slowly, she extended her hand, keeping it in sight. Cantra brought her own hand up in reaction.

"Careful, Dulsey."

"Indeed," she said, voice breaking, as sudden tears spilled down her cheek. "Indeed, Pilot. As careful as may be." Her hand moved slowly, slowly, and Cantra stood frozen, aware of Captain Wellik at her back, and the stares of the other Batchers from 'round the table.

Dulsey's hand touched hers, warm fingers slipping between her cold ones.

"He's gone," Dulsey whispered. "I can see it in your face."

Cantra stared at her. "Not exactly comforting, Dulsey," she said, and for the second time in an hour heard her voice break. She swallowed. "He died in battle, like he wanted to." The room was going a bit fuzzy at the edges. She took a hard breath and focused herself, suddenly realizing that she was gripping Dulsey's hand hard—hard enough to hurt, it must've been.

"Sorry," she said, and tried to unlace their fingers, but Dulsey wasn't having any.

"And his tree?" she asked. "He guarded it with his life."

"He did. Tree's on *Dancer*, hale and well."

"Good," said Dulsey. "That is good, Pilot." She tugged on Cantra's hand, pulling her toward the table.

"Come," she said softly. "Sit down and rest."

Wasn't any use trying to talk her out of it, Cantra thought, especially not with Wellik at her back like a mountain to be gone through, if she tried to leave now. She sighed, and dredged up a smile.

"A sit-down would be welcome, as it happens," she said. "Thank you, Dulsey."

TWENTY-FOUR

Solcintra

JELA'S FRIEND WELLIK was ace, all right, Cantra thought as she poured herself a cup of tea. Another man might've put an obvious Rimmer claiming to be his old friend's partner in an actual lock-up, with smooth cermacrete walls, a constant, unwavering light source, and nothing to do but chew over regrets. Wellik, though—friendship counted with him. He'd had her escorted to a nice little apartment up inside the garrison, with a foldout bed, a kitchenette, and a blast-glass window overlooking the courtyard where a plentitude of soldiers went about their lawful business. There were only two minor inconveniences: the door was locked, and there was a guard standing on the hall-side of it.

She sipped her tea, watching the soldiers move to and fro in the growing dusk. Dulsey and her crew had been escorted elsewhere, and were doubtless enjoying their own comfortable imprisonment. She did own to a small amount of gratitude that she hadn't been confined with the Batchers, though that happenstance likely had more to do with Captain Wellik not wishing them to come up with a consistent story to beguile him than any kind consideration for her feelings.

The story that the Batchers had told on their own—it was enough to give a Rimmer religion, if that Rimmer hadn't made the acquaintance of Rool Tiazan and his gentle lady. The sudden transition from mineshaft to ship, the route locked and untouchable, that had the warm, homey feel of *dramliza* interference. Not that she'd managed to say so, there being no reason to frighten the children.

Jela's notion that the Batchers might serve Liad dea'Syl—that was interesting, too. They hadn't said, precisely, but she had received the definite impression that the Uncle wasn't ignorant of the whereabouts of his treasure team. And if Jela had deliberately called in the Uncle, what did that say about his belief that his good friend Wellik would do the needful with regard to the old scholar's equations?

Sighing, she leaned her forehead against the cool glass. She'd studied the math Jela'd given her as hard and as deep as she'd been able, given time constraints, and there was no way she had them cold, nor even understood a half of what those 'quations were trying to tell her. Jela. Jela'd lived with those numbers for—Well, she didn't know how long, really, but she had a qwint that said it'd been years. There was a damn-on-to-certain chance that he *had* got them cold, not to say able to make them stand up and do tricks.

There was a slight sound at the door. Cantra turned, poised, the half-full mug held innocently between her palms.

The sound came again and the door opened to admit none other than the boy pilot—Tor An yos'Galan. Without his jacket, dressed in plain shirt and pants, he looked even younger than he had earlier in the day, his yellow hair crisp, his eyes wide open and the color of amethysts.

Two steps into the room, he stopped and bowed to her honor, just like she was respectable—which, come to scrutinize it, she might well be, to a boy who'd only known her as a true-and-for-sure Osabei scholar.

That being so, she returned the bow, as serious and respectful as she was able. "Pilot," she murmured, "what can I do for you?"

"I bear a request from Scholar dea'Syl, that you share a cup of wine with him," he said in his soft, mannerly voice.

Cantra blinked, and sent him a hard look. He met her eyes with calm patience, clearly waiting for her response.

Funny—he didn't look like a half-wit.

She inclined her head. "I am honored," she said, "by the scholar's notice. Alas, I am not at liberty, and so must decline the invitation."

The boy frowned slightly, and glanced over his shoulder at the open door, beyond which the guard's shadow could be seen.

"Not at liberty?" he asked. "In what way?"

Cantra sighed. "Why do you think there's a guard on the door, if it's not to prevent my leaving this room?" she snapped.

The frown vanished. "Ah! It is true that Captain Wellik wishes to hold you secure," he said. "However, you are certainly free to accept the scholar's invitation. That has been cleared."

"Oh," Cantra said. "Has it." She bowed. "In that case, I am very pleased to accept the scholar's invitation. Lead on, Pilot."

Liad dea'Syl was sitting in a power-chair by the window, an orange cat on his lap. He inclined his head in answer to Cantra's bow.

"Forgive me, that I do not rise," he said. "I ceded Age my legs that I might keep my reason. It seemed a well-enough trade at the time, but lately, I wonder. I wonder." He moved a frail hand, showing her the chair opposite him, and she sat, hearing the small sounds the boy made over in the galley area.

"I hear from Tor An that the estimable M. Jela has departed this coil of intrigue and treachery. Please accept my condolences on your loss."

She swallowed, and inclined her head. "I thank you, sir."

"Not at all, not at all. I knew him only a short time, and feel his absence keenly. Quite remarkable, the pair of you."

"The pair of us, sir?"

"Certainly. Tor An has shared with me the information which M. Jela felt it safe for him to have. While I understand that such information was of necessity edited and simplified, yet I feel confident that the pair of you are remarkable, indeed. Ah." This as the kid approached with a tray, bearing a pair of wine cups.

"Serve our guest first, child," the old man directed. "She will wish to choose her own."

If Tor An found anything odd in that, he kept it to himself, merely stepping to her side and offering the tray.

"Pilot?"

"Thank you," she murmured and took a cup at random. What, she wondered, had Jela told the boy, which was then passed on to the old scholar? The possibilities were limitless, knowing Jela.

"Master," Tor An handed the scholar the remaining cup and faded back to the kitchenette, tray in hand.

"He is a good lad," Liad dea'Syl said, "and has been a great help to me in my work here. I commend him to you as an excellent pilot." He raised his cup.

"Let us drink to absent friends," he murmured.

Cantra raised her cup in turn. "Absent friends," she whispered, and sipped.

"Excellent," the old man sighed, which, if he happened to be talking about the wine, it was. Cantra had another sip, eyes half-slitted in pleasure.

"My friend vel'Anbrek, who was for many years my eyes and ears in Osabei Tower, fretted that I would fall into the hands of one whom he had determined to be an agent of the Tanjalyre Institute," Scholar dea'Syl said softly. "It was therefore with a good deal of amusement that I heard him propose to put me into the hands of a second such agent." He sipped his wine. "He said 'twas the presence of the M Series soldier which had convinced him that submitting to you, Pilot, was the lesser of a triad of evils, and so he conspired to place me in your way." He had another sip of wine, and Cantra did the same, keeping her face and her body language carefully neutral.

"I see," Liad dea'Syl murmured, smiling slightly. "But surely you have a client, my dear."

"I did," she said shortly. "M. Jela Granthor's Guard was my client. Our arrangement was that I'd run interference while he liberated your updated work from Osabei Tower's brain. When he found that he was being offered you, presumably with your work in your own brain, he varied." She sipped her wine. "He sent you here, and I'm thinking there's an end to my involvement."

"Ah. And yet you are here."

"I am," she said, and sighed. "Jela'd asked me to bring some things of his to Captain Wellik. That errand's been discharged as well. At the moment, I'm being held against my will, and I'm none too pleased by the circumstance."

"And your plans?" the old scholar murmured. "Forgive me if I pry. You will return to Tanjalyre Institute?"

"My line was edited years ago, sir. I've spent my life since avoiding the notice of the Directors. That's what I'll go back to, as soon as Captain Wellik lets himself understand that there's nothing more he wants from me."

A small silence, then, as the scholar sipped wine. The orange cat, which had been sitting quiet on his lap, suddenly stretched tall, jumped to the floor and strolled over, giving her knee a friendly bump before leaping onto her lap.

"My apologies for not returning him immediately," said Liad dea'Syl. "Your cat has been a comfort to us, Pilot."

She looked up from rubbing the square orange head. "My cat?"

"So M. Jela had it. In the case that it has slipped your mind, his name is Lucky."

The cat was purring. Loudly. *Lucky*, she thought. Now there was a sterling name for a cat.

"Tor An?" the scholar called. "Pray attend us."

A rustle and the movement of shadows heralded the boy's arrival from the kitchenette. "Master?"

"I wonder if you might recount for the pilot those things regarding his mission that M. Jela thought it wise to share with you."

"Certainly." He turned to Cantra. "I had asked Jela why he was pretending—not very well—to be a kobold. He said that you and he were after certain updated and expanded equations, which were necessary to winning the war. He said that you were a volunteer, who had undergone protocols which made it possible for you to accept as truth those things you would ordinarily reject as falsehood. He gave me a copy of the equations, so far as he had them, with annotations—" he glanced at the old scholar sitting still and attentive in his chair "—which I have given to the master." He paused, waiting for some sign from her, or so it seemed. She inclined her head.

"Yes," he murmured, and cleared his throat. "He then said that—that the safety of the galaxy rested on you alone, and that he would have no other, save his true and courageous friend, bear the burden."

"*Jela* said that?" She stared at him, fingers arrested over the cat's head. "He was having some fun with you, Pilot. Be sure of it."

"With all respect, I believe not. It seemed—It seemed to me that his duty pressed him hard, and he wished to ally me to his cause. Time was short, and I do not begin to believe that I was told everything of which he—or you—were aware. But I do believe that what little I was told was truth."

The scholar cleared his throat, drawing her attention back to his face. "I have, as Tor An tells you, the annotated equations that M. Jela provided as earnest of his good intentions," he said. "The annotations, if I may say so, are remarkable. They show a depth of understanding and intuition that astonishes as well as delights. May I know if these insights are your own?"

"Not mine," she said as the cat bumped her fingers forcefully with his head. "Jela had studied your work for years, Scholar. Those are his notes." She rubbed an orange ear, waking a storm of deep purrs.

The old man sat back into his power-chair. "Then I feel his loss even more keenly." He sighed, and drank off the last of his wine. Tor An slipped forward and received the empty cup.

"More, Master?"

"Nay, lad, I thank you."

"Pilot?"

"Thank you, Pilot, but no." Cantra handed off her cup, and sighed as the cat curled onto her knees, purrs unabated.

"There are several matters which I would like to discuss with you, Pilot," the scholar said, and continued without giving her a chance to say that she didn't feel like talking.

"Firstly, the fact that the intelligence which grasped my work so fully has informed us that you are the determiner of the fate of the galaxy. The fate of the galaxy is, as our good Captain Wellik believes, soon to be decided. What he does not say, but which I think must be in his mind, is that fate will not favor us, but rather the Enemy. I would, in such circumstances, allow M. Jela's assertion to bear a great deal of weight."

Cantra sat, the cat warm on her lap, and did her best to radiate patient, weary, politeness.

Scholar dea'Syl smiled once more. "You must tell me someday why your line was edited, Pilot." The smile faded.

"My second topic is one which I had hoped to be able to lay before the intellect behind those remarkable annotations. As this is no longer possible, I will, with your permission, put them to you, his partner and the person to whom he remanded the fate of the galaxy.

"I find that I cannot complete the necessary equations with the necessary precision. I wonder if you might—"

A bell sounded, and the old scholar held up a hand as Tor An walked to the door and opened it. There was a moment's subdued discussion, and then the kid was back, bowing apologetically, but Cantra had already risen, putting the cat on the chair she'd vacated.

"Captain Wellik sends an escort for you, Pilot," Tor An said.

"Thank you, Pilot," she answered, holding to polite and civilized for all she was worth. She bowed to the old scholar. "I am sorry not to be able to help you, sir."

"Perhaps later," the old man said. "Will you take your cat?"

She glanced down at the cat in question. Amber eyes squinted up at her.

"Keep him for me," she said, and turned toward the door and the soldier waiting for her.

"Just some paperwork, Pilot," Captain Wellik said, looking up from his screen. "I won't keep you long."

"Paperwork," she repeated, keeping it lightly inquisitive, and neglecting to ask if she'd be freed to her own devices afterward.

"Take a seat," he advised, eyes back on the screen. Cantra sighed lightly and sat in one of the shorter chairs, her feet gratifyingly on the floor. Wellik tapped a few more chords then spun, throwing something at her, hard and fast.

She caught it reflexively, only then seeing that it was Jela's book. Her fingers closed hard around it, even as she sent a glare into his face.

Wellik grinned.

"He said you were damn-all fast and that nothing caught you by surprise," he said, like he'd just been given a present.

Cantra sighed, and put the book on her lap, forcing her hand flat atop it.

"This is my paperwork?"

"Part of it," he answered, pulling a file toward him across his cluttered desk. "This is the rest of it." He flipped the file open. "It happens that Jela named you his next of kin." He looked up and met her eye, though she hadn't said anything. "You're right that Series soldiers don't have next-of-kin in the ordinary sense of things, but the protocols exist and I'm the one to make the decision, so I've decided to honor his request." He glanced back at the folder. "As next-of-kin, there's a certain amount of money due you—hazard prizes, battle pay, that sort of thing."

"I don't—" Cantra began, but Wellik kept on talking like she hadn't said a thing.

"Next, there's this—" Something else shot out of his hand.

Cantra snatched it out of the air, fingered it, and held it up in disbelief.

"A ship's key? I have a ship, Captain."

"Now you've got two," he told her, flipping the file closed and pushing it across the desk. "That's yours, too."

She eyed it. "What is it?"

"Personnel records. Gene map. Letters of reprimand. Couple odds and ends from his various commands."

"Why do I want that?"

Wellik rolled his shoulders. "Don't know that you do want it, and frankly, Pilot, that's not my concern. Jela wanted you to have it, and that *is* my concern. What you do with it is up to you." He rummaged on his desk, pulled out an envelope and put it on top of the file. "That, too."

Cantra sighed. "And that is?"

"Copy of a letter with your name on it. Don't know what he was thinking, writing it all out in cipher like he did." He gave her a fleeting, unreadable look. "Your copy's decrypted; I'd hate to tempt with challenge to break the code."

"I—"

"The money's been transferred to your ship's account. About that ship: it's been in twilight for the last few years and some. There's a crew bringing it back up. Should be ready for a tour day after tomorrow."

"I—"

"Dismissed to quarters," he said, spinning back to his screen. "Kwinz!"

The door opened and the corporal was there.

"Escort Pilot yos'Phelium to her quarters, Kwinz," he said without looking up. "Same protocol as before."

"Yes, sir." Kwinz looked to her. "Let's go, Pilot."

Cantra took a hard breath, deliberately riding her temper down. She stood, picked up the envelope and the file, and turned, giving Kwinz a curt nod as she stalked past.

The Great Weaving was all but accomplished. They waited now upon the Sign, the moment of which not even the best of the prognosticators among the Thirteen could foretell, save that it would be soon. Soon.

Hovering above their base, Lute considered the order and turn of space and time. Soon, all would be different, excepting perhaps the ley lines. Though, if the Iloheen prevailed, they too would fail, shriveling in the outpouring of inimical—

The lines flashed and flared. Lute threw out a query, caught the response, and opened the way, following the visitor into the asteroid.

They manifested at once, the lady haloed in cruel energies, her submissive crouched, trembling, at her feet. Moonhawk looked up from her work, set the loom aside and rose. Lute, who knew their visitor of old, kept to the shadows and thought it wise not to manifest entirely.

"Sister," Moonhawk said calmly. "This is an unexpected visit."

The other lady swept out a glittering hand, dispensing with courtesy. "Have you bargained with the Rool Tiazan dominant?"

"Indeed, the Thirteen have made a pact of mutual support with Rool Tiazan. His dominant, however, is destroyed."

"Oh no, she is not—but leave that! Have you yet discovered, Little Sister, how we have been played? Have you Seen the event of massive proportion which is bearing down upon this probability?"

Moonhawk tipped her head. "Certainly. The work of the Iloheen goes forth, and the more quickly as it progresses. The Day is nigh. We all of us know this."

"Did you also know," the other hissed, "that we are *locked* into this probability? That the ley lines have been rendered fixed and unmoveable by some art beyond imagining, while the luck swirls as it may, obscuring all and everything on the far side of the event?"

"Ah." Lady Moonhawk smiled. "Yes, we had discovered that."

"And yet Rool Tiazan and his dominant have not been unmade." The lady shifted, and a ice-fanged wind cut through the asteroid, freezing rock, loom, and—Moonhawk lifted a hand and smoothed it into a warm, gentle breeze.

"Whether or not we have been played," she said softly, "is moot. What remains is our agreement and that Moment which so concerns us all—which would just have certainly overtaken us, were the lines fluid and malleable. The maelstrom of the luck—you are correct to be concerned. However, as you are aware, the luck is beyond the beck of even the Iloheen. What weakens our enemy must strengthen us."

"An ill-considered sentiment," the other lady snapped. "To invoke the luck in such measure, to lock the lines and deny us the possibility of escape to a more fortunate probability-"

"We are committed," Lady Moonhawk interrupted serenely. "That is correct. Was there something else you wished to discuss? Sister."

Their visitor flared and melted. Lute threw open the way and made himself as small as possible—and still her energies burned him as she passed. He sealed the shields and fell into the asteroid, manifesting with a stifled scream—and then sighed as his lady cooled the pain and repaired the injuries.

"Will she," he asked, "abide by the agreement?"

"She has no choice," Moonhawk replied, moving back to her niche and pulling the loom to her.

"It is within her scope," he insisted, "to unmake Rool."

"It is," she agreed placidly. "But to do so she will have to hunt him through the luck. That the luck will deny her, I have no doubt."

Cantra closed the folder with a sigh and leaned back in her chair, rubbing at the crick in her neck. Deeps, but the man hadn't been in trouble for a day of his life, had he? The reprimands stacked as thick as her thumb—and the citations did, too. He'd been a Hero, once; held rank a dozen times, and always managed to get himself busted back to a comfortable level. His last promotion—to Wingleader/Captain—had stuck for more than a half-dozen years only, so Cantra thought, because he'd been free to carry out his orders as seemed best to him.

The citations and the reprimands, the write-ups for the offenses that earned him detention wove a kind of narrative, as if the Jela in the file was a character in a story who touched some points with the man she'd known, but was otherwise wholly imaginary. Not that she couldn't perfectly well imagine Jela taking on an entire squad of soldiers—and winning the fight!—but the smile and the sheer joy coming off him while he courted and committed mayhem—that didn't come through the reports. For Jela, she thought, had been bred, born, and trained to fight and destroy—and he'd been happy in his work. He'd been bred for that, too.

The gene map. Deeps. A military secret; it had to be. Here she had the formula for producing her very own army of M Series soldiers—which Jela had wanted her to have. That bore thinking on, since Jela had reasons for what he did. Why Wellik would have released such sensitive info to her—that was another puzzle. Though she supposed he could've thought there wasn't any harm done, Ms being the past and X Strains the up and coming kiddies on the street.

She pushed the folder away, eyeing the envelope. A letter, so said Wellik, written to her in a cipher she could be expected—pretty much—not to try to crack. And this from Jela, who always had reasons for what he did.

Her hand hovered over the envelope, fingers trembling. In the one case, she wanted—Gods of the Deeps, she wanted!—to read what he had to say to her, direct and intentional. On the other case—

Ship's necessity, Pilot, Jela's voice murmured in her ear. She took a breath that sounded like a sob in her own ears, caught up the envelope and pulled out the single sheet of machine-copy.

> *Private Correspondence To: Pilot Cantra yos'Phelium*
>
> *About now, if I've got my timing right, you'll be wondering what I'm thinking, increasing ship's mass by a quarter-tonne of hardcopy. Call it an old soldier's fancy. I am a soldier, and so never gave much thought to what might go on after I fell. But I'm asking you, if you'll humor me, Pilot—I'm asking you to carry me in that long, deep memory of yours, like you carry Garen. Maybe the files will help; maybe not. I can only give you what I've got, and hope.*
>
> *It comes to me that I owe you an apology—more apologies than I've got time left to say. A soldier does his duty, and mine pushed me to alter the course of your life, which I never should have done. Asking you to die for my mission—that was wrong, and no excuses.*
>
> *It's come to the point, now. You'll be carrying the war on from here. I know you'll be as strong and as brave and as tough as you need to be. I know you'll prevail. The Enemy—they don't have a chance.*
>
> *I'll shut it down now, before you get irritable.*
>
> *Remember me for as long as you can, Cantra.*
>
> *I'll do the same for you.*
>
> *Jela*

TWENTY-FIVE

Solcintra

SOLCINTRA PORT DIDN'T precisely tantalize a trader with promises of wealth and treasure, be that trader Light, Grey or Dark. Point of fact, Cantra was near to calling it the sorriest port she'd ever had the misfortune to find herself on—excepting there'd been worse. Vanehald, for an instance.

It was something funny, too. There were plenty of ships in—that was not counting the slowly waking fleet under Wellik's care. Far more ships, indeed, than she would've thought likely—given Solcintra—including a cruise liner that had been sitting in close orbit when she'd brought *Dancer* in. She'd've thought the liner'd been long departed, maybe having stopped for repair, but she'd seen more than a few luxury class uniforms on port during the course of her ramble.

The reason she was on-port, with a pass all signed and legal in her pocket, instead of cooling her heels behind locked-and-guarded doors—well, there was a tale worth repeating.

Deeps preserve me from gently-brought-up kiddies, she thought. For it would be the boy who had talked Wellik into unlocking her door and vouching for her good behavior like he was even younger than he looked.

"Didn't your grandma teach you not to speak for strangers chance-met on the port?" she'd snapped when he came to put the pass in her hand.

He'd frowned, absurd purple eyes clouding. "Surely, she did," he answered in a clipped, too-formal tone that he might've thought hid his spurt of temper. "She had also taught me that pilots aid pilots, and that a co-pilot's first duty is to his pilot. So I put the case to Captain Wellik, who appears to have received the same lessons from his grandmother, and thus you are free to tend business on the port." He stopped there, though she could tell he had more to say, his lips set into a straight, firm line.

She grappled with her own temper, concentrating on breathing even and deep until she was sure she could answer him mild.

"One. I'm obliged to you for your trouble, Pilot, but the fact of the matter is you ain't my co-pilot.

"Two. All honor to your grandma, but there's some pilots you don't want to be laying down your good word to aid. I'm the sort of pilot who'd like to've curled her hair, and *ought* to curl yours. You got no way of knowing if I'm going to ever walk back in that gate once I'm on the outside of it."

That should've ended the discussion, but the kid was tougher than his soft face gave a pilot to think.

"Jela vouched for you," he said, his voice still clipped and cool. "He said you were the best damn' pilot he'd ever seen."

"*Jela* was the best damn' pilot he'd ever—"

"And he sat co-pilot to *you*!" The boy interrupted in his turn. He took a hard breath and produced crisp, angry little bow. "Pilot. Duty calls me elsewhere."

And who would've considered, she thought now, that so soft-looking a boy had so firm a temper?

She paused at a table to inspect a display of hand-thrown pots. Indigenous handwork was usually a good sell; even lopsided pots had their admirers. These, though, were not only lopsided, but dull, the glaze unevenly applied and the finish rough. It could, she supposed, be a School, but the smart money said it was just bad pots.

Well. She turned away, moving quiet and alert down the ragged rows.

Cool reflection established that the boy hadn't taken as much risk in his vouching as it first seemed. There was, after all, Jela's ship to be dealt with, though what she was likely to be able to do with a troop transport wasn't at the moment clear to her. She supposed she might sell it to her profit—though not on Solcintra. Nor was it any such vessel as could be flown by a single pilot. Two might manage, if the voyage wasn't long and the pilots fresh. Four were best, running shifts and rotations 'tween them. She'd studied the specs during her happy time confined to quarters, and allowed herself to be in awe of such a ship. The keepings of a small planet could be packed into the outer ring of pods, if the balancing was done fine, and more soldiers than she felt comfortable thinking about could ride at slow-sleep in the second.

The third ring was quarters and mess for wide-awake crew, while deep inside, at the very heart and soul of the cluster—that was the pilots tower. Each section had its own set of engines; the tower could be broke entirely away from its pods and run as its own ship. And even stripped right down to the tower, *Salkithin* was twice again as big as *Dancer* entire.

Not exactly the best kind of vessel for a pilot whose fondest desire in life was to fly low and unobserved. She wondered—not for the dozenth time—what Jela'd been thinking, leaving her such a monstrosity to deal with—or Wellik, for approving the transfer.

Now she was out of lock-up, she could give over wonder and turn her back on the whole mess, get to her ship and lift out, never mind she was empty. Jela's death-and-bonus money would keep her 'til she could raise a port that had some profit to offer. That would be the sensible thing to do—and teach the boy a needed lesson, too.

She considered that course of action, trying to visualize the sequence of events, and found herself instead hearing the echo of the boy's voice: "Jela vouched for you."

Dammit.

She bent over a jeweler's table, not so much because the cloudy gems called to her, but to give herself time to recover from a certain shortness of breath.

Wasn't no harm, she thought, to send word up that she'd like to inspect her new toy. She owned to a certain curiosity to see the sort of vessel Jela was accustomed to—

"Ah, there you are, my dear!" The voice was too close, unfamiliar—No. She knew whose voice it was. Sighing to herself, Cantra straightened and turned.

"Uncle," she said, non-committal and easy. He was, she noted with approval, standing at a respectful distance and slightly to one side, his hands empty and in plain view. He was wearing a layer of Solcintra port dust over a dark cloak, and his hair was in a simple, unadorned braid. No tile showing, no strands, neither. Even his rings were gone.

"Pilot Cantra." He bowed slightly. "How fortunate I am to find you. I wonder if you may be thirsty."

She considered him. "That depends on if you're buying," she pointed out. "And where."

"Naturally." He smiled, which expression of goodwill didn't reach his eyes, and moved a hand, gracefully. "Please, choose a direction; I trust that you will be able to locate a suitable establishment. As the one who has extended the invitation, I will, of course, be buying."

It fair warmed a pilot's heart to find a man in so cooperative and expansive a mood. Not to say that she wasn't a bit thirsty, now she put her mind to it. And—who knew?—Uncle might have a lucrative suggestion to make.

So she smiled, no more real than he had, and inclined her head, moving off to the left. He fell in beside her with barely a rustle.

"Passed something a couple streets over this way," she said. "Looked like a quiet place for a chat."

"Excellent," the Uncle murmured. "I am in your hands, Pilot."

"Tell me," he said some little while later as they settled into a back table, "how fares the excellent M. Jela?"

"He's dead," she said shortly, giving the room another look-around. It was dim, which was good, and the few patrons within eye-shot were mindful of their own bidness after subjecting them to the obligatory distrustful stare. The 'tender hadn't looked especially pleased to seem them stroll in the door, but he hadn't thrown them out, either. She'd drunk in less hospitable places.

"Dead," the Uncle repeated. "That is unfortunate. A sudden affliction, I apprehend?"

Cantra didn't sigh, and she made sure her hands were nice and relaxed. Jela wasn't on the short list of those things she cared to talk with the Uncle about, though she could hardly ignore a direct question. She could, however, demonstrate displeasure.

So she gave him a frown with her answer, granting him leave to take the hint. "You could call an enemy invasion sudden, I'd guess."

"Ah. An affliction we all of us hold in common," he responded with a look of bogus sympathy, and glanced up as the bartender approached, glower in place.

"Drinks, *kenake*?" he asked, like he was hoping they'd admit to having made a mistake, gather themselves up and go. And with *kenake* being the local impolite for not-one-of-us, he'd probably thank them for leaving.

Cantra flicked a glance to the Uncle, meeting an expression of well-bred patience.

"Please, Pilot," he murmured. "Choose what you like."

Right, then. She leaned back in her chair, sighting around the bartender to the rows of drinkables on display behind the bar. Not a very tempting display, and she was about to call for beer when her eye caught on a distinctive shape high on the backest, darkest shelf. She looked to the Uncle.

"I'll have a glass of Kalfer Shimni, if you please."

His eyebrows went up but, "Excellent," was all he said to her before addressing the 'tender. "We will have the Kalfer Shimni. Bring the bottle—and two glasses."

The man's attitude of warm welcome got even chillier. "Coin up front, *kenake*," he said, as ugly as you like and then some.

The Uncle sniffed, and raised a hand, displaying nothing more nor less than a qwint. The 'tender reached for it—only to see the coin disappear inside the Uncle's fist.

"When you bring the bottle and be certain those two glasses ring."

There was a quiet few moments while the 'tender worked it out then he turned and left them.

"Do you wonder, Pilot, how such a bottle would have found its way here?"

She moved her shoulders. "There was a luxury liner up top when I came in. Might be the crew likes to have something drinkable when they're here."

The Uncle pursed his lips. "My information regarding the liner is that it was engaged by the High Families." He glanced about them, meaningfully. "This is hardly the usual sort of port for such a vessel."

"There's that," she agreed and was about to pursue the High Family tangent when the 'tender approached again, with a bottle and two glasses on a tray.

He placed the tray on the table, and stood by sullenly while the Uncle picked up each glass in turn and struck them with a delicate fingernail. Both sang, high and sweet.

Cantra took it upon herself to inspect the bottle, finding the seal in place, the special glass and the label authentic—or very, very good forgeries.

"Looks to be what we want," she said to the Uncle's raised eyebrows. He smiled slightly, and held out the coin.

The bartender took it in a snatch, turned, and left them. The Uncle sighed lightly, shrugged beneath his cloak, and inclined his head.

"Will you do the honors, Pilot?"

She did, with dispatch, and they both sat silent until the first sip had been savored, the Uncle with his head to one side, and a true smile on his lips.

"Excellent," he said for a third time, putting the glass down gentle on the table. He looked at it meditatively then transferred his glance to Cantra.

"This sudden affliction to which M. Jela regrettably succumbed," he murmured, for her ears only. "May one know the location?"

She sighed. "Vanehald."

"Ah, yes. Vanehald." He loosened the brooch at his throat and shrugged the dusty cloak back over the chair. Beneath, he was wearing dark shirt and pale vest, looking like any respectable person of reasonable wealth and consequence, excepting the smartstrands woven into the shirt, shimmering just a little in the dimness.

"Tell me," the Uncle said. "How was that accomplished?"

She blinked at him. "The enemy invasion? Buncha old tech in the tunnels started talking to each other and opened up a trans-spatial gate, is what I heard."

"Indeed; I have also heard this. But what I had meant to say was—how were my children instantaneously transported from deep inside their claim to their ship, which was already in transition, with the course set and locked away from even the pilot's codes?"

"Oh, that." Cantra had another sip of brandy. Deeps, but that was good.

"Jela had some interesting allies," she said to the Uncle's bland, patient eyes.

Silence. She let it stretch while she enjoyed another sip of brandy.

"I see," the Uncle said softly, conceding momentary defeat with a slight tip of his head. "On a related subject—I wonder, Pilot, if you have news of my children."

"Oh, aye," she said easily. "They're safe under lock and key inside the garrison. Captain Wellik, you understand, not being wishful of having anything ill befall them."

"The captain's care humbles me." His voice was too quiet to hold an edge of irony. "I am to understand from the message sent me that M. Jela believed catastrophe was imminent, and that the best hope of survival for myself and my children was to hie ourselves to this unfortunate planet and place ourselves at the service of a certain scholar."

"Right. He's at the garrison, too," she said, and smiled to show she was being helpful.

The Uncle sighed. "I believe it may be pointless to bait me at this present, Pilot," he said softly. "Though you must of course please yourself." He raised his glass, and the 'strands gleamed along his sleeve. "I must assume M. Jela realized that we do not place ourselves *at the service* of anyone. Nor am I best pleased to find my children held against their wills."

"I don't know it's exactly 'gainst their wills," Cantra said judiciously. "There's books and 'quations and agreeable work to be had inside, nor Wellik isn't shy of sharing. Last time I saw your brother, for an instance, he had six scrolls open and a notepad to hand. Can't remember when I saw a man look so content."

"I can scarcely," the Uncle said, letting the reference to Arin pass with no more than a hard look, "knock on the gate of that garrison and offer myself up for arrest."

"'Course not," she said soothingly, and looked up as a shadow moved in the side of her eye, expecting to see the bartender.

What she did see was less welcome.

One of the patrons who had been so politely tending their own business at the center table was staring hard and ugly at the Uncle—or say, Cantra amended, putting her glass down and pushing slightly away from the table—at his shirt.

"Smartstrands," she growled, in just that tone of revulsion an honest trader reserves for the announcement of pirates on the for'ard screens. She snatched, the Uncle twisted, shoving his chair back and away, surprisingly quick—and a good move it would've been, too, if the chair hadn't got snarled up in his cloak.

Over he went with a clatter and a bang while Cantra was up and spinning, figuring that now looked like a good time to leave, except there was the offended woman's mate planting himself in front of her, and the shout going up behind—

"Smartstrands! *Kenake* spies are among us!"

You did well, she murmured at the core of their shared being, *to bind the lines.*

Ah, no, credit me not, he answered with a ripple of green-and-ebon laughter. *Merely, I aligned conditions. The lines bound themselves.*

A quibble, but you may have the point. Now the question: is it enough?

He opened their awareness, allowing them to fully experience the galaxy: the luminescence of the ley lines; the singing of the spheres; the warmth of life; the encroaching, echoless perfection of the Iloheen's desire.

We will know the answer, he whispered. *Soon.*

"Cantra yos'Phelium?" The lawkeeper behind the fines desk spared him a single disinterested glance before looking back to his screen.

"Ah, yes." he murmured after a moment, and there was slightly more interest in his eyes when he honored Tor An with a second glance. "Bail is set at two flan."

Great gods. With an effort, Tor An kept his horror from reaching his face. He inclined his head, buying time, congratulating himself that he had thought to bring the pouch containing the astonishing amount of money Captain Wellik had assured him was the sum of the gambling debts he had owed to Jela.

"The amount," he said with perfect truth, "is significant. With what crime is the pilot charged?"

The lawkeeper grinned, and tapped his screen with a fingertip, as if it held a most excellent joke.

"Brawling in a public place," he read, with relish. "Damage to public goods. Damage to private goods. Damage to the person of one Kellebi sig'Ralis. Swearing in a public place. Resisting detention. And," he concluded, "creating a nuisance."

"I see." He sighed to himself, slipped the required coins from their pocket and placed them on the counter in front of the lawkeeper. The man glanced down, then up, holding Tor An's eye with an insolence that set his teeth on edge.

"Of course," he murmured, and added a qwint to the sum. The lawkeeper grunted, perhaps not best pleased, but the qwint disappeared, and the two flan were deposited into a slot in the counter.

"The claim against Cantra yos'Phelium has been retired," he said into the air. "Pray escort her to the bail room." He gave Tor An a squint. "She'll be up directly," he said, and turned back to his screen.

Tor An looked about for a chair, then spun as a door in the wall to the left of the counter opened to admit a guard leading a woman in damp and rumpled trade clothes, a cut across her left cheek, her right eye swollen shut. Her hands were bound together before her, her knuckles raw. The guard stopped, blinked, and spoke over her shoulder to her captive.

"*This* is your co-pilot?"

"That's right," Cantra yos'Phelium said, her as voice easy and warm as if she were in the best of health and surrounded by friends.

The guard frowned. "He doesn't look old enough to hold a license," she objected. Cantra considered her, one-eyed and bland.

"Looks deceive." She raised her bound hands suggestively. "Bail's paid, is what I heard. That means I'm no longer your bidness. Unlatch 'em."

The guard looked to the lawkeeper behind the counter, who shrugged.

"He paid two flan for her, so he must want her." He sent a slow, insolent gaze up and down the pilot's slim, bedraggled shape, and shrugged again. "No accounting for taste."

The guard muttered, touched the control on the restraints, and whipped them off the pilot's wrists. It must have hurt her, Tor An thought, but her battered face revealed nothing.

"Let's go," she said to him, and walked toward the door, limping slightly off her left leg. Perforce, he followed, nose wrinkling as he caught the odor—the near overpowering odor—of liquor.

The pilot walked briskly, despite her limp, and acknowledging his presence at her side by neither word or glance. Tor An kept pace, taking deep breaths to calm his temper—a strategy doomed to failure, as every breath brought him the stench of liquor, which reminder of her lapse only made him angrier.

He told himself it was his place to hold his tongue; that she was his elder in years and in skill; that her reasons and necessities were her own—and hold his tongue he did, until they were at last well away from the lawkeeper's station, and she turned suddenly aside to enter a public grotto, bending to sip from the elaborate stone-faced cat gracing one of a multitude of fountains.

The grottoes had bemused Tor An in his first days on the planet. Who could imagine a place with so much snow and clean water that it could be shared freely—even extravagantly—with casual passersby? Who would have spent the money to build such things?

Curiosity being a pilot's curse, he'd pursued the question through the amazingly self-centered Solcintra Heritage Library, where events of galactic importance lay near-forgot in favor of High Family histories and genealogies, which was, after all, where the answer was found: the grottoes and fountains were the result of a bitter rivalry between the Families, each bent on showing how much they could do for the public good.

And here, of all things, a *kenake* pilot was using a beautifully hand-carved grotto to wash off the stench of a stay in the jail, which had also been funded in that orgy of building.

Cantra straightened slowly and looked about her, as if she did not understand where she was or how she had arrived there.

"You are most welcome, Pilot," he heard himself say, in a voice as cool and formal as anything Aunt Pel might muster to scold an errant younger. "I wonder, though, that you thought to call me to stand your bail."

Pilot Cantra spared him a one-eyed glance over her shoulder. "I thought you had it that you sat my co-pilot." She eased herself carefully down to sit on the ledge of the wishing pool.

"And I thought you had it," he snapped, "that I was not!" He glared at her; she raised an eyebrow, and sighed lightly.

"Boy—"

"I am not a boy! And, indeed, Pilot, I believe you have the right of it: I have no ambition to sit as co-pilot to a heedless, drunken, brawling—"

"That's enough!"

"—who cares so little for those who wish her well that she does not bother to thank them for their care of her!" he finished, ignoring her shout, and more than a little appalled at the words he heard tumbling out of his mouth.

Silence.

Pilot Cantra turned and put her hands into the pool up to the elbow, heedless of her sleeves, and held them there for the count of twelve. That done, she raised water in her cupped hands and splashed her face, sucking breath noisily through her teeth. The worst of the blood and grime rinsed away, she finger-combed her tangled, reeking hair. She did these things with great concentration, as if each task were of the utmost importance. Tor An bit his lip and watched her, ashamed of his outburst, and yet—

She sighed, folded her hands into her lap, and sent a serious one-eyed look into his face.

"Forgive me, Pilot. Manners tend to slide on the Rim, and mine never were shiny. I do appreciate your timely arrival and the payment of the fine on my behalf. I'll be reimbursing you when we get back to the garrison. I'd make it right between us now, excepting the law on the spot thought to relieve me of my ready-cash before she took me in to the station."

Tor An drew a breath. She raised her hand, and he bit his lip.

"Now, that list of yours. Heedless, drunken, and brawling, was it?"

"Pilot, I—"

She speared him with a glance. "I'm talking, Pilot."

He inclined his head. "Forgive me."

"Right," she said after a small pause. "Now, it happens I'll admit I was heedless in this case, and—with stipulations—I'll even allow that I indulged in some brawling, as you'll see I did throw a punch or two—" she half-lifted her raw-knuckled hands off her lap "—but drunken I will not have." She looked down at herself then back at him, her nose wrinkled slightly. "Despite the evidence. For I'll not have you believing, Pilot, that I'm so lost to everything civilized as to use Kalfer Shimni in such a wise."

He cleared his throat. "What happened?" he asked, which is what he should, he told himself bitterly, have said at the first. "If it can be told."

"I met the Uncle on the port, and I thought he might divert me from an unhappy line of thought," she said. "Happens he was wearing smartstrands, and a local spied them, whereupon the bar rose up, and the peacekeepers were called to quell the riot." She grinned, one-sided. "By which time, the Uncle had got himself gone, which I might've known he would. And I only got but three sips of my drink."

"Your uncle left you to—"

She raised a hand. "Not *my* uncle," she said. "*The* Uncle. Which is more than a pretty, mannered boy from a nice legit family has any need or desire to know about the underside of the galaxy." Putting her palms flat against the ledge, she pushed herself to her feet, and took a deep breath.

"Let's go home," she said. "Pilot."

TWENTY-SIX

Solcintra

HER APARTMENT WITHIN the garrison included a steam-cleaner, which fabulous luxury she was happy to avail herself of, once she'd shaken the kid off her arm, and failed to notice the open amusement on the hall guard's broad face.

It took three cycles to steam the booze and the sweat and the mad out of her pores, and a fourth to melt the worst of the sting from the various scrapes and bruises. Wasn't any reason beyond sheer hedonism to trigger the fifth cycle, and she stood there with her eyes closed, picturing the steam easing in through her ears and unkinking what passed for her brain.

Were you bored, Pilot? Jela asked from too near and too far. She sighed.

"Wasn't bad enough when I only had one ghost," she said, trying for cranky and failing notably.

And truth told, he had a point. She knew better than to drink with the Uncle, and she *damn well* knew better than to be doing him any favors. Viewed from that angle, it was a rare blessing the local'd took exception to the 'strands and cried pirate before she'd taken coin whereby to sneak Dulsey and team out from under Wellik's nose.

The whole of which seemed pointless and worse, with the Enemy's works increasing exponentially, and nothing mere humans—be they Batch-grown, Series, or natural—might do to say them nay. The sheer numbers of them—

She shivered despite the steam, seeing them again, coming up out of the mines in an unending line of black, exultant death; for all their might, the most human—and by their counting, the least—of what the Enemy might field.

She'd seen a world-eater, up close and more personal than anyone'd sane ever want to; she knew the sick feeling in the gut when the ship fell out of transition, light-years short of a port that would never be raised again.

Jela insisted that the Enemy'd been human once, but even if so, they were something other now. Something powerful and all-encompassing.

Something unbeatable.

Even Jela'd admitted that—and she'd seen plain on his face what it cost him to say so.

Come right down to it, she thought, as the cycle clicked over and the steam began to thin—what was it made humankind particularly worth preserving and continuing? If the Enemy manufactured biologics and smartworks to do their heavy lifting, how was that different, or worse, than those same things performed by the so-called natural humans of the Spiral Arm? If the Enemy dealt harsh with its creations—Well, examine the life of your typical Batcher. And if the Enemy was cruel, measure the cruelty that bred a man alert, sharp, and able, with a taste for life as wide as the Deeps themselves, while making sure and certain he'd die before he could reason his way into damaging his makers in the style they most deserved.

She shivered. The steam was gone, the tiles cooling. She had the robe out of the cabinet and shrugged into it, relishing the feel of plush against her skin.

Tying the sash 'round her waist, she moved from the bath to the great room—and stopped, the hair raising along her arms, breath-caught and heart-clutched—all and any of which was nothing more than missishness.

"You," she said, and slipped her hands into the robe's pockets, feeling the ache in her abused knuckles as the fingers curled into fists.

Rool Tiazan turned from the window and bowed, deep and respectful.

"Lady."

He straightened, lissome and sweet, the red ringlets tumbling across his shoulder, his face ageless and smooth.

"*You*," she said again, voice harsh in her own ears. She took one deliberate, foolish step forward. "You let him die."

The dark blue eyes met hers, and she saw there honest sorrow. His voice when he made answer was soft. "He chose, Lady. You heard him."

"He chose between two choices offered—but who held back the third? You could've given him a good, long life—"

"No." He held up a hand, a ruby luminescence haloing the black ring on his first finger. "Forgive me, Lady, if what I say wounds you further. However, the only one who seems likely to have had a good, long life at the end of this day's work is—you."

She closed her eyes, suddenly nearer to tears than mayhem.

"I don't want it," she whispered.

"I know," he said, voice gentle. "The luck swirls where it may, and not even the great Iloheen—whom you call the *sheriekas*—can force it to their will, or see through it to what will be."

"Which makes it a risky weapon, wouldn't you say?" she snapped, opening her eyes again to give him a glare.

He bowed slightly, accepting the challenge, and in no way discommoded. "Indeed. The very riskiest of weapons. If there were another so likely—" He moved his hands in that peculiar gesture of his, as if he were soothing the air itself. "It is futile now to discuss might-haves. The course is set. The *sheriekas* advance ever more quickly; and we are very soon come to the point of proof."

"Which is why you're here," she said, and sighed, and sent a searching glance 'round the room.

"Speaking of proofs and points—where stands your own kind lady?"

"Ah." He inclined his head. "She fell in our flight from the Iloheen, yet not before striking a blow which will be recalled."

Another to add to the tally of too many gone. Despite she had neither liked nor trusted the lady, Cantra bowed, and gave her full measure honor.

"My sympathy," she said formally, "on your loss."

"There is no loss," he answered, "for she is with me."

Like Jela was with her, and Garen, too, Cantra thought, and moved a shoulder. "Chill comfort, as my foster-mother would have it."

"Yet comfort still, and nothing I would spurn."

"Well." Carefully, she slid her hands from the robe's pockets, flexed her aching fingers. "You'll be pleased to know that the task you set us is accomplished, and the scholar himself, with all his thought and work to hand and to head, lies in a room further along this hall. I'll tell you that Jela felt his oath bound him but, as he's in no case to finish it out, I'm sure you'll find some way to use both the man and his work to your own ends."

Silence, then yet another bow.

"Forgive me, that I did not inquire after the *ssussdriad* immediately. I trust good health and virtue attend it."

"It seems spry enough," she said shortly.

"I am delighted to hear so," Rool Tiazan answered seriously. "May I speak with it?"

"Can't stop you." She twitched a shoulder. "It's on *Dancer*."

"On *Dancer*," he repeated and tipped his head, dark eyes slightly narrowed. "Lady, surely you are aware that your actions upon departing Vanehald have engaged the attention of the Iloheen. They have seen you and your ship."

The aches and pains which were her take-home prizes from the bar fight were beginning to complain again. What she wanted, she thought, was to find her bed and sleep off the over-rush of adrenaline and anger, not stand arguing points of precedence and ownership with a tricksy, self-serving—

"The *ssussdriad*," Rool Tiazan said softly, "is needed here. It holds some part of the answers which yet elude the revered scholar's grasp."

She glared at him. "Jela asked me to make sure that damn' tree was taken someplace safe. Whether or not I happen to think that it's his last and best joke—or that only an addlepate would've promised so daft a thing—I *did* promise, and I intend to stand by it. Solcintra's not looking like 'safe' to me, though I'll allow a certain unfamiliarity with the parameters. That being the case—"

"Lady, hear me! The Iloheen have your ship in their eye! They know it for one of their own, and if they have not yet bespoken it, they will soon do so. Such safety and shelter as it has offered you is about to be withdrawn. If you wish to honor your promise to M. Jela, you will remove yourself, the *ssussdriad*, and all that is valuable from that vessel and send it away from here!"

She stared at him, reading honest alarm in the set of his shoulders.

You be careful of them toys, baby, Garen counseled from memory, *and you be careful of our ship. While some pilots might have a safe haven in their ship, we got what you'd call a paradox. Our ship's good for us; she's top o'line and quality all the way. But she's carrying those things that're Enemy-issue. And it's true, baby—as true as I'm sitting here telling you this—that those things, they never forget who made 'em.*

"Don't you *know*," she asked, not meaning to taunt him, "if they've called *Dancer* to heel?"

His mouth tightened. "The more nearly the event from which we wish to emerge ascendent approaches, the less I know—anything."

She sighed. "Welcome to bidness as usual."

His lips twitched. "I fear I may require some time to become accustomed." He lifted a hand, sparks dripping like blood from his ring. "Nonetheless, I am as certain as may be that the *ssussdriad* is in a position to greatly assist the scholar and, by extension, all life." He sent a quick, sideways look into her face. "Mayhap the *ssussdriad* also feels bound by its oath."

"It might," Cantra said wearily. "Ain't something I've discussed with it."

"The *ssussdriad* is needed," Rool Tiazan persisted, "here."

"I heard you the first time. Seems to me, you being the one who wants it here, that you can bring it here."

He raised his eyebrows. "Oh, indeed?"

"Indeed. Jela might've been able to carry that damn' tree around like it didn't weigh no more than a data tile, but it's more'n I can do to get it up onto a cargo sled. Besides which, as you've no doubt noticed, I'm a bit hard-used lately and not feeling quite the thing. It being your necessity that wants the tree here, 'stead o'there, I'm thinking you can shift it, or it can stay where it is."

Silence, his face a study in blandness.

With a *fwuummp*! of displaced air, the tree in its pot arrived overlooking the charming vista provided by the window, leaves fluttering wildly. Around it, manifesting with smaller, overlapping *fwuummps* of their own came Jela's kit, the ceramic blade he'd taken off the X Strain a million years ago, a neat pile of her own clothes, and the bank-box.

She inclined her head. "That's thorough. I'll ask you *not* to take *Dancer* in hand."

"Lady—"

"My ship," she growled. "I'll do what's needful, when it's needful."

He bowed.

"Right." Her knees were beginning to wobble, by which sign she knew she needed sleep. She pulled up the sternest look she had on file and gave it to Rool Tiazan.

"You have bidness with the scholar, now's the time to tend to it."

"Ah." He raised his hands, fingers wide. "My lady wishes to give you a gift," he murmured. "Will you accept it?"

She eyed him. "Her being dead—"

"Nay, did I not say that she is with me?" He smiled. "You will take no harm from accepting; so I do swear."

Unless madness was contagious, which, according to everything she'd ever seen on the Rim, it was.

"Fine," she said. "A gift. And then you move on to haunt Ser dea'Syl. Do we have an accord?"

Rool Tiazan smiled.

"Pilot, we do." He stepped forward, hands extended, palm up.

"Your hands on mine," he murmured, and it seemed to her that his voice was higher, sweeter, sterner.

She put her palms against his, felt warmth spread, swift and soothing, through her veins.

"The seed is not well-rooted," Rool Tiazan whispered. "Is it your will to carry the child to term?"

Yes, she said, or thought, or both.

"Let it be so," the other answered, and stepped back, breaking the connection between them.

Cantra looked down at her hands, the knuckles healed and whole, and then to Rool Tiazan, who was bowing yet again.

"Lady," he murmured. "Until soon."

He blurred at the edges, his body melting into light—and she was alone, saving the tree, in her room.

Slightly unsteady, she looked at the tree and the tumble of her belongings 'round its base. It came to her that her face didn't ache anymore. She applied her fingertips, lightly, to her right eye, found it open and unbruised, the opposite cheek smooth and unmarred.

"Well," she said to the air and the aether, and closed her eyes. "Thank you."

"Impossible, Master?" Tor An went to one knee by the scholar's chair, the better to see into the downturned face.

The old man did not look up; he watched his own hand stroking the orange cat as if the action and the animal were the most important things in the galaxy.

"Allow me to know," he said softly, "when my own work has described a impasse. It is impossible to continue. I have been in error."

Tor An blinked, aghast. "But—your life's work, an error? Surely not!"

The scholar smiled and looked up. "Simply because one has spent one's life at a work does not mean that the work must be correct, or of use." He raised a hand and cupped Tor An's cheek, as if he were one of Alkia's grandfathers soothing a distraught younger.

"What," Tor An asked carefully, in case, like a true Alkia grandfather, this mood of sudden gentleness should evaporate even more suddenly, leaving the younger's ears ringing from a sound boxing. "What of the Enemy, Master? Captain Jela had thought your work the best means of their defeat."

The old man patted Tor An's cheek—lightly, even fondly—and tucked his hand 'round Lucky's back.

"Captain Jela was a wise and perceptive man," he told the cat. "Yet even wise and perceptive men can sometimes be mistaken. Certainly, he wished, as I do and you do, to discover some way in which we might outwit the Enemy and snatch liberty from defeat. That was, as near as I am able to know his mind from his annotations, the breadth and depth of his hope for us all. It was not an unreasonable hope, and indeed it seems to me that he was correct in believing my work represented the best potential of realizing it. It is no dishonor to his memory that his best hope was not good enough."

Tor An considered. It was, he thought, very possible that the scholar was merely exhausted. He had stinted himself on sleep and on food, the hours of his days spent with his notes and his tiles, his work screen a riot of nested calculation.

"My Aunt Jinsu had used to tell us youngers," he began slowly, "that a pilot's best friend was—"

Lucky the cat jerked to attention on the scholar's lap, ears pricked forward. A moment only he stared past Tor An into the great room, then leapt to the floor and ran, tail high. Tor An twisted 'round, peering into the dimness, then came all at once to his feet, situating himself between the scholar and a red-haired man in formal black tunic and pants. The man paused, eyebrows up, Lucky weaving complex, ecstatic figures around his ankles, tail high and whiskers a-quiver.

"Did the guard admit you, sir?" Tor An asked sharply. "I did not hear the door."

"Nay, Housefather, I admitted myself," the man said in soft and cultured accents. He bowed, low and respectful. "My name is Rool Tiazan. I was allied with M. Jela and seek to continue his purpose. I am come to offer assistance to the master, if he will have me, and it."

"Stand aside, child," Master dea'Syl said to Tor An, "you obscure my view of our guest."

Reluctantly, Tor An stepped to the right, keeping his eye upon Rool Tiazan.

"Well," the master said after a long scrutiny. "Certainly one who was allied with the estimable M. Jela is welcome on that count alone. What sort of assistance do you offer, Ser Tiazan?"

The man moved a graceful hand, encompassing the abandoned desk, notes, and screen. "I believe your work founders on the particulars of an energy state transformation under special, near-ideal, and probably unique circumstances. It happens that I am something of an expert in energies and their states, and have also some insight into the nature of the approaching, probably unique, event. Also, I bring with me another ally, who has seen the Enemy falter."

"Hah." The scholar leaned forward in his chair, eyes gleaming. Tor An took a careful breath. "If you can show me the error in my work, I shall be most obliged to you." He raised a hand, beckoning. "Come here, young man. Seat yourself. Tor An—a glass of wine for our guest, if you please."

"Certainly." He inclined his head and moved to the kitchenette as Rool Tiazan walked forward and took the chair by the scholar's table.

By the time he returned with the tray, the two gentlemen were deep in conversation, and the cat was asleep on Rool Tiazan's elegant lap.

TWENTY-SEVEN

Solcintra

CANTRA WOKE UNEXPECTEDLY refreshed, more filled with energy than she had been since Jela died, and with the clear sense of having taken a decision while she slept.

She dressed quickly from the store of clothes Rool Tiazan had so kindly delivered to her, watered the tree, which offered her neither comment nor salute, and was on her way down the hall, headed for the gate.

It was early yet. The overnight dusting of snow still glittered in the abundant shadows. Sitting in a pool of sun on the low wall near the gate was the odd couple of Tor An yos'Galan and Arin the librarian, dark head and light bent over a shared scroll. Cantra hesitated, then changed course.

"'morning, Pilots," she said cheerily, and gave them a grin to go with it when they looked up, startled.

Arin recovered his wits first, inclining his head respectfully. "Pilot Cantra. Good morning."

The boy echoed the sentiment a heartbeat later, his voice a bit strained, and dark smudges showing under those improbable eyes. The scroll was an old star-map, its edges tattered and the three-dee grainy; she couldn't tell which sector from a casual glance, and she wasn't there to discuss maps, anyway.

"Arin," she said, holding his eye. "Some happy news for you. Saw your brother on-port yesterday."

The dark eyes sparkled. "I thank you, Pilot. This is, as you say, welcome news. Did he mention when he might come to us?"

"Got the impression he thought you'd rather to go him," she said. "Seemed to be having a couple lines of trade going—you know how he is."

"I do indeed," Arin said, with irony, "know exactly how he is." He fingered the scroll, and sent a sideways glance at the other pilot's face. "Your thoughts on my small difficulty were very welcome, Pilot. However, filial duty calls, and—"

"I understand," Tor An assured him, voice soft and sad. He extended a hand and touched a portion of the map lightly. "It would be my pleasure to assist you further, if you have need, after duty is answered."

"In the meanwhile," Cantra put in, "if you're at liberty, Pilot Tor An, I wonder if you'd bear me company."

He looked up, brows pulled into a frown. "I, Pilot?"

"Exactly you," she assured him, as Arin adroitly rolled the scroll. "I'd like your opinion on a certain vessel." She tipped her head. "You've had training on the big ships—I mean real ring and pod-carrying transports, multi-mounts, that kind of thing?"

Interest dawned behind the frown. "I have, of course, but—"

"But I ain't had that luck," she interrupted, watching out of the corner of one eye as Arin stood and moved off toward the interior, walking like a man with a pressing errand in mind. "My life's been small ships. I don't know how to take the measure of anything more than a six-crew shuttle or a four place courier." She paused. "If you'll honor me, Pilot."

It might've been the polite that won him, but she thought it was rather the basic human desire to be useful and busy. A good boy was Pilot Tor An, she thought, as he came to his feet and inclined his head. So much the worse for him.

"I will be glad to assist you, Pilot," he said formally.

"Good," she said, and jerked her head toward the gate. "Let's go."

"All of your equations are correct, as far as they go." Rool Tiazan leaned over the scholar's shoulder, Lucky the cat weaving 'round the base of the work screen they studied so intently. He tapped the screen with a light forefinger, feeling the attentive presence of the *sussdriad* within the sphere of his being.

"So here," he murmured, "this term is correct, but makes an incomplete assumption."

"Of course it does!" Liad dea'Syl answered. "There are several values that might be added, all derived properly from the rest of my work." His fingers moved on the coding wand. "Add this one—and behold! We attain an equation which is quite beautiful, though it must be impossible to achieve. At this point in our adventure, surely practical mathematics outweighs mere elegance."

Rool allowed the old gentleman's irony to pass unremarked, taking a moment to skritch Lucky carefully under the chin. The chin being properly taken care of, he turned back to the discussion with a polite smile.

"Grandfather, of course it is practical mathematics which will carry the day. And as you have seen, I am far easier with the practical than the theoretical."

The mathematician snorted, drawing the cat's attention.

"The boy is elsewhere, sir; you may dispense with the fiction that I am your elder, as we both realize that I am not. I suspect that your age is some centuries beyond mine."

Rool paused, then inclined his head, sincerely respectful. The old one's mind was both agile and facile. Of course he would have formed the proposition that a being which was not bound by possibility would not be bound by time.

"Well," he murmured. "I am here because you are no fool, and I am no mathematician."

"It is possible that you err on both points," the scholar murmured. "But let us not quibble. Pray elucidate this incomplete assumption, and tell me if you have a proof which ties this together so that young Jela's excellent work does not go to waste."

"The value here," Rool tapped the screen again. "This assumes that when the final decrystallization event begins, it will propagate across space. It will not. The event will, as your initial numbers demonstrate, occur across the affected dimensions and energies simultaneously."

The old man seemed to wilt in his chair, though the glow of his life energies were as bright as ever.

"There, my friend," he murmured, "lies the paradox. If the event occurs simultaneously, there will be no wave."

"The triggering event, however," Rool continued. "The trigger event propagates at the highest possible velocity of transition. When the energy state is sufficient, a coherent decrystallization is the result. Now, note that this is not a reversion to what was, as implied by our limited vocabulary; this is a new state. In this event prior conditions cannot be recalled, they cannot be calculated. Within the new state there is no information exchange or reversibility with the preceding state in any manner that affords sense." He paused, frowning at the screen, and leaned forward to tap another phrase.

"But here, sir," he murmured, "I fear I misapply language again. Let us consider *this*, which implies that what shall occur is that the act of transitioning *will* inform the new location. That is, it will contain the ships, their contents, and whatever else might be accelerated to transitional velocity—and it will contain that impetus and energy—"

"Yes!" Liad dea'Syl said, abruptly enthusiastic. "Of course the transition will inform the new location, just as the new location will inform that which arrives. And observe! It furthermore implies that the arrival of the ships, the end of the transition, will in effect not be contingent on their relationships before the transition. It *also* implies a transformational energy change, one that will exclude any further energy or information exchange. The universe we arrive at will not be the one we left."

"And here," he sighed after a moment. "Here is where I falter. It would appear that, no matter the prior conditions, we shall arrive in a universe where certain spins will be—let us say *preferred*, and where the energy excess we bring with us will mean that space will expand infinitely over time. There will be no steady state, though there may be the practical illusion of it for billions of years."

Rool considered that in all its fullness before meeting the old scholar's eyes.

"I propose," he said seriously, "that an infinitely expandable universe is much preferable to one which is about to become largely uninhabitable."

"Yes, of course. Well said." The mathematician rubbed a tired hand over his eyes. "Yet, should we continue down that path, we soon discover that we lack vital information. We have near proof that this escape we posit is possible. However, if we may not know the time of the spontaneous great event—within fractions—we shall be lost. We must have more information than M. Jela's prognostication and death brings us." He paused, his eyes wandering from the screen to the window, and the bright day without.

"If I might but look upon the works of our Enemy, and understand what it is that they accomplish, perhaps—"

Abruptly, the room, the screen, the cat were gone, replaced by a vision of sand, and the vast, fallen corpses of trees; the wind swirled dust into a funnel—and the room returned.

Rool Tiazan folded his hands and waited what the scholar might make of such communication.

"Our other ally speaks, I apprehend." The old man raised a hand and sighed. "That is a mighty work," he said sadly, "and an irredeemable loss. Yet how was it accomplished?"

The room flickered, there was impression of baleful energies, greatly confused yet more accurate than Rool would have expected from a form-bound intelligence—and then nothing more.

"Ah." The scholar turned looked to him, his eyes deep with wisdom. "You, my master of energy states. *You* know how it was accomplished, do you not?"

Rool bowed his head. "Grandfather, I do. The Iloheen caused probability to be altered so that increasing amounts of inimical energies were aimed at the world which had been inhabited by the *ssussdriad*."

Liad dea'Syl laughed. "So I am told, and having been told, understand nothing."

Rool smiled, and swept out a hand. "Forgive me, Scholar. I am as a bird in the air—"

"Indeed. Indeed. And yet, you have the means, as I understand from our discussions in the night hours, to change state, and to observe the workings and progress of the Enemy. Is that so?"

"Stipulating that I dare not show myself, nor come too close," Rool said slowly, "yes, that is so." He paused. "Shall I go, observe what I might, and return to tell you?"

"Will the bird bring news of aerodynamics, lift, and thrust?" The scholar smiled, and reached out to rub Lucky's ear. "Perhaps you might bear me to a point of observation."

It had been within the possibility described by the current configuration of the lines that this boon would be asked. Rool closed his eyes and took counsel of his lady.

"It is," he said slowly, "possible." He opened his eyes. "Whether it is desirable—-" He sighed. "There is a price."

"There is," the old scholar interrupted tartly, "*always* a price, Ser Tiazan. I am not a child."

"Indeed. Indeed, you are not a child, Grandfather. But I must be selfish in this; you may not die before those equations are set."

Liad dea'Syl smiled. "Guard me, then," he said. "And snatch me away to safety when you judge it best. But I would see this work of the Enemy."

Rool bowed. "I am at your command. When shall we proceed?"

"At once."

The port was more crowded than ever he recalled, with a great many high-caste persons about. Nor was he the only one to notice it.

"That's a lot of expensive citizens I'm seeing," Cantra yos'Phelium commented at his side. "Streets weren't near so full, yesterday."

"The High Families are not usually so well represented on-port," he agreed, and touched his tongue to his dry lips.

"Forgive me, Pilot," he murmured, and felt himself flush when she glanced at him.

"What's on your mind?" she asked easily, giving no sign of noticing his discomfort.

"I wonder—your face, and—your hands. How is that they are healed?"

"One of Jela's friends stopped by last night and did me the favor," she answered, and gave him another casual glance from green eyes. "Last I saw him, he was set to call on the scholar and yourself."

"You will mean Rool Tiazan," he said around a feeling of relief. "He represented himself as an ally to Captain Jela." He bit his lip. "Are you easy with this person, Pilot?"

"Not to say easy," she answered after a moment. "'Takes some getting used to, does Rool Tiazan. Don't care for doors"—another quick green glance—"which may be what's bothered you, Pilot?" She used her chin to point to the left. "That's our road, I think."

"There were," he pursued, turning his steps to match hers, and dodging 'round a floater piled high with expensive luggage, "several things which were worrisome. The first was, as you say, the matter of not entering by the door. He—You will think I refine too much on it, perhaps, but he seemed to know me on sight, Pilot, though he addressed me as 'housefather.'"

"Right. Calls me 'lady,' in case you've taste for irony, Pilot. Doubtless it amuses him, and it does me—nor you—no harm. How'd the old gentleman take him?"

"Well," he answered, and sighed to hear how bitter voice was. "Very well," he said again, trying for a more moderate tone. "They were at work together through the night, and still in deep converse when I rose to keep my appointment with Arin. Lucky also seems favorably impressed," he added after a moment, recalling again, and with a pang, the sight of the cat curled tight on Rool Tiazan's knees.

"Sounds like all's in hand, then. Wink an eye at his oddity, is what I advise, Pilot."

Yes, well. "But"—he said, as the military shuttle hove into view—"*what* is he? Rool Tiazan?"

Pilot Cantra didn't answer immediately, and when she did, it was slow, as if she was feeling her way toward an answer.

"Calls himself a *dramliza*. What that means in practical terms—which is what you an' me need to think in, Pilot—is that he was a soldier for the Enemy. Him and some of his, though, they deserted, for reasons that seemed good to them. Rool Tiazan and his-lady-that-was, they offered themselves as allies to Jela, who thought it would be of benefit." She sent him another quick glance, and sighed. "It was by way of serving the interests of that alliance that Scholar dea'Syl was brought out of Osabei and given to Wellik for safekeeping."

"He offered the scholar aid. He said that he was an expert on energy states."

"That he may well be," Pilot Cantra said judiciously, and gave the guard at the shuttle door a friendly nod. "I'm Cantra yos'Phelium, heir to M. Jela Granthor's Guard. I'd like to go up and inspect my ship, if there's a shuttle to be had."

The guard frowned down at her, his facial tattoos gaudy in the pale morning light. "What ship?" he rumbled, deep in his chest.

"That'd be *Salkithin*," she said composedly.

"Would it. And who's with you?"

"Tor An yos'Galan," she answered, and if her heart quailed under the X Strain's stare, as his did, no hint of it was apparent on her face. "My co-pilot."

The guard jerked his chin, toggling the comm, muttered, hit the toggle again, and stepped back.

From inside the ship came another X Strain, this one with lieutenant's chops on her sleeve. She crossed her arms over her chest and stared down the ramp at Pilot Cantra and himself.

"Jela's heir, is it?"

Pilot Cantra bowed, brief and ironic; the lieutenant grinned, broadly.

"Ilneri's going to be real happy with you," she said in a voice that Tor An thought did not bode well for the coming ship's inspection, and stood aside, sweeping an exaggerated bow. "Please, pilots, enter my humble shuttle. I hope you're in a hurry."

The lines lay thick about them, red-gold and vital, spilling energy enough to conceal one wary, weary *dramliza,* and the essence of an ancient human. The *ssussdriad* was also with them, its regard lying so gently amongst the lines that Rool could scarcely discern it.

The *ssussdriad* was the best husband of itself, as it had proven, many times. That which was on the physical plane Liad dea'Syl burned with a hunger for knowledge so bright that lesser urges—such as survival—paled beside it. The scholar was a danger to himself in this place, and a danger thereby to all that was.

Rool held the scholar's precious essence furled in green-and-ebon wings, both shielding it and directing its attention out to that far yet too near space where the Iloheen worked their changes.

The process approaches critical mass, he sent gently. *Observe.*

It was a small thing to observe, even from this level: a Shadow fell across lines, stars and lives, replacing all with—nothing.

The lines stretched then parted with a sob; the stars screamed as they were extinguished, the lives they had engendered gone before they realized the danger. The anguish of unmaking struck Rool at the core, and from the one he protected came a gasp, a wail—and an ominous wavering among his energies.

You have seen enough, he sent, and received no protest. The *ssussdriad* had already departed. Rool folded his wings and followed.

As it happened, Sergeant Ilneri *had* been happy to see them, after a period of attitude adjustment which hadn't maybe been all that good on the boy's nerves. Test passed, though, the rest of the crew had been pleased to see them, too, and nothing would do except they show off every cranny and cubby of proud *Salkithin*, talking twelve qwint to a flan about Jela.

Happened this particular crew'd been Jela's own from when *Salkithin* had been put to sleep, six Common Years ago and a bit. It were a mixed crew—three X Strains, two Ms, a Y and Ilneri, who was, as far as Cantra could make it, a natural human—and they all had something to tell about the "little Captain."

There was the time Jela and two others had come down late from the work, and were set on by a gang of what passed for toughs on Solcintra. And the time that Stile—one of the Xs—the time that Captain Jela had talked Wellik out of slamming Stile into detention for—well, it didn't exactly matter for what—saying he needed her on the roster or the work would fall behind. And the next day, didn't the captain put her up against the wall hard and let her know he didn't tolerate stupidity in his crew, and if there was *any* additional slippage, detention was going to look damn' soft.

"There were some of the troop," Vachik, the second and most talkative of the X Strains, told them, "some of them thought to taunt us with our captain, and called us 'Jela's Troop,' like it was less than soldier's honor to take his orders."

"They learned better," Ilneri said with a wide, wolfish grin. "And we're still Jela's Troop."

And so, what with one thing and a tale, it was deep into Solcintra night-time when the shuttle settled back into its cradle at the port, and her and the boy and Ilneri and Stile strolled down the ramp.

"Missed the party," the night guard told them, jovially. "Damn' near had us a genuine riot to quell."

Ilneri frowned and looked around, and Cantra did, too, seeing only a peaceful backwater port about its lawful evening bidness, saving a broken window or six, and some extra trash on the street.

"What happened?" the good sergeant asked, in a tone that conveyed it would go bad if the guard was indulging himself with a short round of leg pulling.

"Service Families finally figured it out," the guard answered, clearly disinterested in the why. "Wellik's got the speakers-for with him now. Got the word from the gate there's a crowd waiting for them to come out, but everybody's staying peaceful. So far."

"All right, then." Ilneri looked over his shoulder. "Stay close, Pilots."

"Right you are," Cantra assured him with a grin. Ilneri laughed.

"B'gods, I can see why Jela liked you, Pilot. But—mind me, now: *stay close.*" He turned a stern eye on the boy. "You're her co-pilot; make it so."

"I am certain that the pilot will not put herself in danger," Tor An said, straight-faced and earnest, and for all Cantra could tell, believing it as he spoke it.

Ilneri nodded, directed Stile to bring up the rear, and the four of them moved on, the sergeant a bit ahead and concentrating on shadows. Cantra kept pace with the boy, and a watchful eye out.

"What," Tor An asked, for her ear only, "did the Service Families figure out, Pilot?"

She sighed. "The man I was drinking with yesterday, before things went and got interesting, had it that the High Families were vacating the premises, which was what all the extra shipping—including that liner—was up to."

He turned wide, shocked eyes on her, like this was the first story he'd ever heard when them what had took advantage over them what didn't.

"They removed to safety and left the Service—but no!" He frowned. "That cannot be possible. The High Families—You understand, Pilot, that they govern. The Service Families—They do everything that is needful. They—They cannot have—"

"Thought it through, sounds like," Cantra agreed. She put a soft hand on the boy's sleeve. "Listen. You hear that crowd breathing?"

He tipped his head, holding his own breath, until— "Yes."

"Good. Let's close it up with Ilneri, Pilot. We want to pass through this quick as we can."

He didn't argue, nor did Stile object to coming up tighter, as they rounded the corner and saw the crowd before the gate.

Hundreds—maybe thousands, Cantra thought, standing still and watchful in the searchlights from the garrison. There were soldiers deployed, long arms on display and combat shields down over their faces, keeping the road to the gate clear. The tension rising up off the crowd was enough to make a pilot's ears ring and the heart squeeze a little in her chest, despite everything being peaceful.

For now.

Ilneri set them a business-like, unalarming pace down that long row of watchful faces. When they finally passed through the gate and were inside the garrison proper, Cantra let out the breath she hadn't known she'd been holding.

"Ah!" Tor An gasped and would have stopped, excepting Stile reached out and gently pushed him onward.

"There's the lieutenant up ahead, Pilot," she said to him, in a large whisper. "We'll need to get cleared."

Twelve paces out from the officer's position, Ilneri stopped, smacked his heels together smart, and whipped off a salute so sharp it was like to cut somebody.

"Sergeant Ilneri and Specialist Stile escorting Pilots yos'Phelium and yos'Galan," he rapped out. "Sir."

"Troops report to Technical Services," the lieutenant said. "Pilot yos'Phelium. You and your co-pilot are to report to Captain Wellik, soonest."

TWENTY-EIGHT

Solcintra

"THERE'S NO COMPROMISE on Captain's Justice," Cantra said for the third or eighty-fourth time. Her voice was barely more than a cracked whisper after all these hours of negotiation, and at that she wasn't the most worn of those at the table. The boy—Tor An—he was running on guts and honor; and Vel Ter jo'Bern—second on the Service Families side—was actually trembling. The first on the Families' side of the table, and Cantra's opposite, was one Nalli Olanek, who looked as fresh and as perky as a new coin, damn her timonium-wrapped nerves.

"Pilot," Nalli said again, "surely you must see that we cannot submit to the decision of a single individual in matters of life and death—"

Cantra pushed back her chair and stood. Tor An blinked, and came to his feet within the next heartbeat—a proper co-pilot, backing his pilot's judgment. Vel Ter jo'Bern gaped. Nalli Olanek waited, her hands folded neatly on the table.

"We been through this," Cantra told her; "and I'm only going to say it one time more, after which we'll be leaving you gentles to decide just how much you want a ride out of here. I will take leave to remind you it's the Service Families seeking this contract, not the pilots. The pilots have a vessel and are free to depart as they will. Their need for passengers is—" She bent forward slightly, staring hard into Nalli Olanek's gray eyes. "Let's just say our need for passengers isn't *acute*. That read out clear to you, Speaker?"

The other woman inclined her head, face bland.

"Good. Now—Captain's Justice. Despite whatever might work on the ground here in terms of councils and consensus, on a ship there can only be one voice that's law, one person who decides for the ship, and therefore the common good. The difference between a ship's life and death is sometimes only heartbeats. There's no time to consult a committee and have the matter discussed and re-discussed until a compromise can be had. If it comes down to it—which, Deeps willing, it won't—and the choice is whether to jettison half the outer ring in order to preserve the other half and the pilots—then that decision of ship's survival rightly falls to the captain. Not to the passengers, and not to the co-pilot, neither, saving if the captain's incapacitated. The hierarchy of a ship, Speaker—as I've said, and as Pilot yos'Galan has likewise said—is this: the co-pilot cares for the pilot. The pilot cares for the ship and for the passengers. In that order." She took a hard breath and traded long stares with Nalli Olanek.

"If you and yours can't abide by that hierarchy, then you and yours can find some other way off this world."

Nalli Olanek inclined her head. "Your insistence that the captain be the final arbiter of any disputes between the passengers is—"

"Is non-negotiable," Cantra interrupted. "Part and parcel of the captain's duty to the greater good. If the integrity of most of the passengers can be insured by spacing one person, you can be sure that's what will happen. Now." She bent forward, putting her hands flat on the table, and looked from Olanek to jo'Bern.

"If you object to the captain having final judgement over your folk, then all you have to do is solve your own problems and never let them reach the captain's ear. Once the captain's aware of a problem, it *will be* solved. Am I clear here, Speaker? I don't want to leave you any doubts."

Stares again, and for a wonder Nalli Olanek looked away first.

"Pilot, you are clear. We should perhaps, as you suggest, adjourn, and meet here again in six hours to finalize the contract."

"Suits." Cantra pushed herself upright and caught the boy's eye. "Pilot."

He bowed to the two Grounders. "Speaker," he murmured. "Elder Hedrede." Cantra let his courtesy count for both of them and strode to the door, knocked, and strode out when it opened, the boy at her heels.

Kwinz was waiting at the end of the hall, looking neither rested nor tired.

"Pilots," she said with a respectful nod. "Captain Wellik requests a word."

Cantra stopped and frowned. "There was something I meant to settle with Wellik," she said, her voice cracked and wandering. "You recall what that might've been, Pilot yos'Galan?"

The boy cleared his throat. "I am not perfectly certain, Pilot," he answered, his pretty voice scarcely more than a thread, "but I believe you intended to tear off his arm and use it to beat him to death."

"That was it." She grinned up at Kwinz. "It'll be my pleasure to have a word with the captain, Corporal. Lead on."

If Kwinz thought about grinning, she didn't share the moment. Blank-faced, she spun sharp on a heel and marched straight-backed down the hall.

The aether was thick with ice, the ley lines shriveled and thin. Tentatively, Lute extended his will, touched a line—felt it tremble, stagger, and sob. It lost luster even as he enclosed it within his regard, all bright promises of hope shredding away into darkness.

He released the line with a pang, while the icy wind brought him the taint of a separate poison—his lady's sister, bringing her troops and her weapons to bear.

Slowly, he slipped toward the physical plane, tarrying at the fourth level where the Spiral Arm displayed itself in a simple dance of light—and all but cried out.

He *knew*—at the very core of his being, he knew—what it was that the Iloheen intended, and yet to see it thus—the dance blighted, the light blotted—and the Shadow growing so quickly—

Wailing, he fell into his body, and lifted a tear-streaked face to his lady.

"What is it?" She asked, looking up from her loom with a frown.

"The stars," he began, as if he were a child—and could go no further. He bent his head, covered his face—and looked up with a gasp when his lady's hand came warm upon his shoulder.

"Nay," she said softly, and there were tears on her face, as well. "Weep for the dying of the light. Who has more right?"

Who, indeed? he thought, but made an effort to master himself, nonetheless.

"Your sister," he whispered. "Her lance is poised."

"Ah." Lady Moonhawk inclined her head. "We shall seek Rool Tiazan, then. When you have finished dispensing your grace."

Wellik was standing over the tank-map behind his desk, staring into the starry depths. He glanced up as they entered, delivered himself of a brief, "Thank you, Kwinz. Dismissed," and returned to his stare.

Kwinz took her orders to heart, the door closing emphatically behind her.

"You'll want to know, Pilot Cantra," Wellik said, his attention still on the tank, "that the archeology crew vacated this afternoon. Nice, clean departure. Professional, you might say."

"Right." Cantra considered the side of his face. "Saw Arin's brother on the port yesterday, which is prolly what inspired the change in quarters."

"It's a good thing, so I've heard, to have brothers," Wellik said ruminatively. "Brothers in arms, for instance—" His voice faded, mouth tightening.

Cantra waited, and when she'd counted out a dozen heartbeats and he still stood caught in his brood, offering neither order nor invitation, she walked over to stand beside him.

"Take a look," Wellik said, as soft as his big voice might manage. "You're an astute woman, Pilot. What d'you make of that?"

She looked down into the tank, at the swirl and glitter and busyness that was the Spiral Arm in miniature.

At the places where the swirl was ragged and wrong. At the pattern that was taking shape out of the new darkness, as if in null reflection.

"That's not looking good, if you don't mind my saying so, Captain," she said slowly. "I'm missing a lot of what I shouldn't be off a map of this caliber."

"Real-time updates," he said, and tapped a finger against the display, bringing a certain sector of nothing up close and personal.

"Headquarters," he muttered, looking down. "Or—where Headquarters isn't anymore." He sent her a grin, hard and humorless. "We're on our own."

"Thought you didn't report to Headquarters."

"We didn't," he said seriously. "But even soldiers nourish expectations, Pilot. The expectation of the war eventually being won, for instance. The expectation that the High Command will spit in the faces of those who bought them, and take up true soldier's duty again." He sighed, and tapped the display, shrinking his particular bit of nothing back into the whole. "There are no expectations, now, except of an inglorious defeat, in which a few of us may survive to *run away*."

"Life wants to live, Captain," she said softly, and Wellik snorted.

"So it does. Speaking of which, how do your talks with the Families progress?"

"About as well as you thought they would when you put us in the position of having to deal with them at all," she answered, too tired to even snarl. "Why's it gotta be us? You got transport to spare."

He raised his head and looked at her, as bleak as she'd ever seen a man.

"We take rear-guard," he said, stark and plain. "It's our duty and our honor to protect those who are not soldiers."

"Meaning you won't have 'em in your way." Cantra sighed. "Can't say I blame you. Don't much care to have 'em in my way."

"They do not properly grasp ship protocol," Tor An surprisingly added from his vantage across the tank. "Pilot Cantra has very clearly explained ship necessities and the reasons which shape each, and I believe that Speaker Olanek has finally understood that upon points of ship's safety, the Captain is the final judge."

"She better understand it," Cantra said to Wellik's upraised eyebrow. "Because if she doesn't, she and hers can stay right here, soldier honor be damned." She sighed and raked her fingers through her hair. Deeps, she was tired. "They're supposed to come back in six hours with a viable contract, and somewhere before that, the pilots have got to have some downtime."

Wellik nodded, and moved toward his desk. "I won't keep you much longer," he said. "We did an analysis on the transitions of the ships the High Families hired. They're heading In."

Tor An looked down into the tank, then to Cantra, his brows pulled tight. "There are instances of Enemy action Inside, as well," he murmured. "These layers of darkness on the captain's map—"

"That's right," Wellik said. "They're taking bites where it pleases them. Or, as soldier-kind learns in creche, no place is safe." He picked something up off his desk. "Pilot Cantra," he said, and tossed it, soft and low.

She caught it—another logbook like the one Jela'd carried—and riffled the pages, finding them uniformly blank.

"What am I supposed to do with this?" she asked.

Wellik shrugged, and turned back to his desk. "Whatever you want, Pilot. You seemed to have an attachment to Jela's field book, so I thought you'd maybe like one of your own. It doesn't do me any good."

"Right." The leather felt smooth and soothing against her fingers. She tucked it inside her jacket and looked at Tor An, jerking her head toward the door. He took the hint, wobbling a little as he walked.

She sent a last hard look down into the tank—so *much* darkness—and followed him. Halfway to the door, she stopped; looked to the desk, and the big man bent over it, shoulders hunched.

"Get some rest, why not, Captain?" She said, easy and gentle. Comradely.

He shot her a glance over his shoulder, inclined at first to be prideful, then smiled, lopsided.

"I'll do that, Pilot. Thank you."

"'s'all right," she said and took the boy's arm. "Let's go, Pilot. Shift's over."

The journey to the inner lattices had tired the old one; the direct experience of the Iloheen's work had struck him to the core. He had returned to his body changed—as who would not be, having beheld the death of stars?—and with determination reborn within him.

"I see it," he had murmured as Rool eased him into his bed, and his lady reached forth their hands to soothe him. "I see how it must be done."

"Grandfather, that is well," she said gently. "Rest now, and recruit your strength. We shall all stand ready to do your biding, when you wake."

Perforce, the old man had slept, cocooned in healing energies. Rool straightened the quilt over the frail body, and smiled as the cat settled himself against the old one's hip.

"Well done," he murmured. "The scholar requires all the aid that we may give him."

He moved into the common room, and over to the window. This state of idle waiting—it was new, and odd. And unsettling. Here, in this form, and on this plane, he could feel the Iloheen's will gathering. Soon. Very soon.

A disturbance in the energies of the room brought him 'round from the window. He bowed, gently and with no irony intended. "Lady Moonhawk. Brother."

"Rool Tiazan," the lady answered with unexpected courtesy. "Sister. Doubtless, you are aware of the Iloheen and the progress of their work. Indeed, I should imagine that you might find the progress of their work deafening."

"Nearly so," he admitted.

"You may therefore *not* be aware that our esteemed sister has put some portion of her forces into harrying the Iloheen at their work. I assume she does this to take advantage of whatever elasticity resides within the lines, thus far from the event."

"Doubtless." He flicked his will outward, found the lines and the pattern, thought a curse, and returned to his body to find Lute smiling sardonically.

"She can ruin all, can she not?"

"Nay, I think not—all," Rool answered. "Though certainly she may introduce unneeded complexity." He turned his attention to the lady.

"I ask—your preparations are made?"

"The Weaving is complete. Fourteen templates have been crafted and stand to hand."

"Fourteen?" Lute turned to her, eyes wide. "I—Surely, Thirteen."

"Nay," she said softly. "Fourteen. You have earned your freedom, whatever that may come to mean." She slanted a cool glance toward Rool. "I thank my sister for her instruction."

He felt her move forward within their shared essence. "You are most welcome," she said. "It falls to chance now, all and each. We shall not meet again, I think, sister. Go you in grace."

"And you," the other answered.

The energies swirled—and Rool stood alone once more.

The aroma of fresh, enticing goodness hit her the second she opened the door, and by the time the door had closed and she'd crossed the room to where it sat in front of the window, her mouth was watering, her body clamoring. She could see the very pod, outlined against the window, the branch bowed slightly with its weight: the pod that had been grown and nurtured especially—only—for her.

"Right," she said, and forced herself to move away from the window, to pull the leather book out of her jacket, and put it with finicky care in the very center of the desk. That done, she she slipped the jacket off, shook it and draped it over the back of the chair. A couple of deep, centering, breaths, and finally she went to the window, leaned a hip against the wall, crossed her arms over her chest, and addressed the tree.

"Now, as I recall it," she said, her voice rasping with over-use, "Jela told you this particular hobby wasn't a good use of your resources. He was right, as far as I'm able to determine. But there's something else you have to know and think on—a being as long-lived as maybe you'll be." She took a breath, and it was all she could do not to reach out a hand and take the pod that smelled so good and looked ripe to eat.

"What you got to realize is that *humans are hard.* You just can't go shuffling their designs around, and changing them on the fly. They need study, and long thought. Planning. We live fast, compared to yourself; one tiny miscalculation, and you've set twelve generations on the wrong course. Actions have consequences—and what you want to avoid is those unintended consequences that destroy all the good intentions you ever had." She sighed. "I'm assuming, you understand, for Jela's sake, that your intentions tend to generally align with humankind's, which for the sake of this discussion we'll call 'good.'"

Across the cloudless sky behind her eyes, a dragon glided, smooth and strong, wind whispering over its wide leather wings.

Cantra nodded at the pod. "Me, now, I appreciate your care, but I'm not going to avail myself of that particular pod. I'm going to have some sleep, because I'm tired, and humans, they sleep when they're tired."

No response, save that the tantalizing aroma faded slowly 'til she couldn't smell it at all. The pod in question broke away from its branch with a sharp, pure *snap*, and landed on the dirt inside the pot.

"Thank you," she whispered, and pushed away from the wall with an effort, heading for her bed.

TWENTY-NINE

Solcintra

SHE GOT TWO hours' sleep before the kid woke her up, shoved a mug of hot tea into her hand and dragged her down the hall. There they'd found the scholar in a fever of calculation so intense he'd barely been able to wrap his tongue around a non-math sentence. In the end, he'd simply spun the screen so they could see for themselves—'quations that sent a chill down her piloting nerves, and fetched an actual gasp out of the boy.

More tea and a quick meal happened between questions, not all of which were asked before it came time for pilot and co-pilot to depart for the meeting with the client.

Nalli Olanek was before them in the conference room, attended by a man so non-descript Cantra thought he would have vanished entire, had it not been for the scroll under his hand.

"Speaker," she said, inclining her head, but not bothering to sit down. "You get the contract written?"

"Indeed." Nalli Olanek moved a hand and her companion rose, bowing with neither flattery nor irony.

"Captain yos'Phelium," he said, offering the scroll across his two palms as if it were priceless treasure. "It is my sincere belief that I have conveyed the agreed-upon duties, responsibilities and command chains accurately."

She eyed him. "Who are you? If it can be told."

He bowed again, and gave her a surprisingly straight look right in the eye. His were brown.

"My name is dea'Gauss, Captain. Account and contract keeping are the services which my Family has been honored to provide for the High."

"I see." She extended a hand, caught the boy around his wrist, and brought him forward. "This is my co-pilot, Tor An yos'Galan. He'll sit right here with you and go over those lines. If everything checks out with him, then he'll bring it to me—same like you've got outlined in that section on command chains, right?"

"That is correct, Captain."

"Good. Me an' Speaker Olanek need to take a little trip."

The Speaker's eyebrows rose. "Do we, indeed? May one know our destination?"

Cantra gave her a hard, serious stare. "I want you to have a tour of the ship," she said. "Get a good idea of what you and yours are contracting for."

Nalli Olanek frowned. "We are contracting for passage off of Solcintra and—"

Cantra held up a hand. "You're contracting to travel on a ship," she interrupted. "Ever been on a ship, Speaker?"

The other woman's lips thinned. "Of course not," she said distastefully.

"Right. Which is why you need the tour. You not being wishful of putting your folk in the way of Captain's Justice, it'll fall to you to figure out how to keep them calm and happy and out of the captain's way. And to do that, you need to see, touch, and smell exactly what you're contracting for." She jerked her head toward the door.

"Let's go. Soonest begun, soonest done, as my foster-mother used to say."

Credit where credit was earned, Cantra conceded: Nalli Olanek was tough. It was clear enough that the means and workings of *Salkithin* distressed her. By the time they'd finished the tour, and Sergeant Ilneri had delivered himself of a short lesson on slow-sleep so pat and slick she figured he must've only given it twelve hundred times before, the Speaker was pale, but she hadn't broke out into active horror, nor demanded to be brought back down to cozy Solcintra where the council of law called outlaw to any such devices as the *sheriekas* might use, and others of more normal habit to the wider galaxy. Gene selection beyond physical pick-and-choose, commercial AI, even personal comm units were either disallowed or else heavily regulated on Solcintra, and though many such devices would have given the service class an easier life, they seemed as wedded to the minimal tech as their now-departed overseers.

Seeing her charge was like to wobble a bit in her trajectory, Cantra set them a course for the galley and waved the other woman to a table while she poured them each a mug of tea.

"You'll want to be careful of that," she said as she settled into the chair opposite. "It'll be pilot's tea, strong an' sweet." She sipped, watching with amusement while Nalli Olanek sampled her drink and struggled to keep the distaste from reaching her face.

"S'all right," Cantra said comfortably. "What they call an acquired taste." She had another sip and set her mug aside, looking straight and as honest as she could muster into Nalli Olanek's cool gray eyes.

"Now's the time to say out what you think, Speaker. Your folk going to hold still for putting their lives in the care of this ship—not to say the slow-sleep?"

The other woman sighed. "Truthfully, Captain, it will be a challenge, even in the face of such an enormous catastrophe as Captain Wellik proposes. Slow-sleep—" She closed her eyes, opened them, and pushed her mug toward the center of the table.

"You understand," she said, "that I must ask this, though I believe I know what your answer will be. Is it necessary that we ride as sleepers, wholly dependent upon the—the devices that govern the operations of this vessel for our well-being?"

"Sleepers don't use as much of the ship's resources," Cantra answered. "Since we don't know where we're going, and we don't know how long we'll be a-ship, the pilots have got to calculate on the conservative side of the 'quations; we'd not being filling our guarantee of care for all the passengers doing it any other way. It ain't our intention to dice with anybody's life. Now. You heard what Sergeant Ilneri had to say about the redundant life-support systems, right?"

Nalli Olanek's mouth tightened. "I did. And I understand that he meant to convey the point that, should the device supporting the sleepers fail, the ship would be in such peril as to be unlikely itself to survive."

Cantra looked at her with approval. "That's it. Those asleep are every bit as well-protected as those of us who're going to be awake for the whole adventure. In her calculations of passenger safety, the captain makes no difference between who's asleep and who's not." She sipped tea, watching the other woman over the rim of the mug. "There ain't any High or Low 'mong the passengers on this ship, 'cept as you need to keep trouble out of my hair. I won't have it, and I don't expect to have it proposed."

"I understand." The Speaker folded her hands on the table, knuckles showing pale. "Livestock—"

"Livestock travels as embryos and Batch samples," Cantra said. "It's gotta be that way, for all those good reasons the sergeant listed out for you. The ship's equipped with reconstitution equipment. Captain Wellik states the garrison stands ready to help get those samples in order for you, if needed."

"We have samples and Batch seed, as it happens," Nalli Olanek murmured, and smiled when Cantra looked at her in surprise. "Several of the husbander Families have created a bank, as I believe they call it, in case there should be an emergency requiring that the flocks and herds be re-established." She reached for the tea mug, thought better of it, and refolded her hands. "I believe they were thinking in terms of illness—plague—but surely this qualifies as an emergency."

"You could say." Cantra finished her tea, and considered the other woman. "Some other info you're going to need. Share it or hold it—that's your call. But you need to have it, so you understand what we're likely to have before us."

Nalli Olanek snorted lightly. "We have received much information from Captain Wellik's office. Also, we have obtained those records upon which the High Families based their decision to return to the core. I believe that we are conversant—"

Cantra held up her hand. Nalli Olanek stopped, eyebrows arched delicately.

"I figured Wellik'd be free with the info of what's coming," she said. "What he doesn't have—though he should by the time we get back to the ground—is a picture of what comes *after* we make what Ilneri's calling a retreat."

"Ah. I had assumed that we would simply outrun the Enemy; locate worlds beyond the Rim, perhaps."

Grounders. Cantra felt the sharp words lining up on her tongue—and heard Jela's voice, damn' near in her ear. *She doesn't have the math, Pilot. She's never seen the Rim. There's no way she can know it like we do.*

Well. She looked down at her mug then back to Nalli Olanek.

"The Enemy's actions," she said, keeping her voice friendly and calm—"the decrystallization, like Scholar dea'Syl names it—that's creating a wave front of energy. Or, say, it creates an opportunity for that wavefront to exist. The actual math is tricky, admitted. What we're going to be doing is riding this wave of opportunity straight on out of—Straight out of everything we know, Speaker. The best the scholar can figure is that those objects and energy states which haven't been compromised by the Enemy's actions will be introduced into another—energy phase, let's call it—and then into another galaxy."

"Another galaxy," the Speaker repeated, brows drawn. "But such forces—We will be damaging existing worlds?"

"Don't know," Cantra said, which was the truth as spoken by none other than Rool Tiazan, damn his pretty blue eyes. "Never been done before. Don't know if we can do it now, though the scholar's math says it's possible." She paused then added in the spirit of being as honest with the client as was safe, "Understand, it's not a risk-free thing we're doing. The only reason to take this kind of chance is because there's no other choice."

Silence.

When it had stretched a while, and Speaker Olanek didn't look any less grim or get any more communicative, Cantra cleared her throat.

"What's good," she said, making her voice sound like it was just that. "What's good is that the initial burst—that ought to be fast. And see, what you can't tell from down here in the thick of it is that, really, most of what's in a galaxy is empty space, anyhow. The Arm's collided with other galaxies back in the 'way back, so pilot lore tells us, and mostly what happened is we moved through each other like ghosts.

"So what we'll be doing is going into a transition, almost like normal. That part'll be quick, real quick. What we might have to do in order to come to land, that might could take a while. Which brings us right 'round again to the necessity of slow-sleep."

"I—see." There was a little more silence then Nalli Olanek pushed away from the table and stood.

"I thank you for the tour, Captain yos'Phelium," she said formally. "It has been most informative. I believe we should return home—" Her face tightened, and she took a hard breath. "I believe we should return to Solcintra, and see if your co-pilot has cleared the contract for signature."

"Right you are." Cantra came to her feet, collected the mugs and set them into the washer, then led the way down the hall to the shuttle bay.

THIRTY

Solcintra
Near Orbit

THE BOY SAT the board like he belonged there, which was a good thing, Cantra thought. Ought to be one of the two of 'em knew what he was doing.

Granted, Pilot Y. Argast had checked them both out on the full board, neither stinting nor accepting less than perfect from the pilots who were going to be flying *Jela's ship*. And granted that they'd both passed muster. The boy, though, he sat his tests cool as Solcintra snow, showing confident clear through—and it weren't no bogus confident, either, not from a lad as easy to read as the for'ard screens.

Herself, she'd given Argast as much confidence as he liked, and an edge of Rimmer attitude to go with, which might've been enough to help him miss the fact that she'd damn' near bobbled twice—or maybe not, though he was respectful enough not to mention it.

"Captain Wellik sends that he's coming up, and requests a meeting with the pilots," he'd said, leaving the observer's chair with a grin so cocky he might've been a Rimmer himself.

Cantra eyed him. "He say why?"

Argast's grin got cockier. "Captain doesn't give me his secrets to hold," he said. "You're lucky he sent ahead."

Though truth told, he hadn't sent that far ahead. The tower door had barely closed on Argast's heels when it opened again and there was Wellik, trailing an honor guard and carrying a case.

"Permission to enter the tower, Captain?" he'd said, with no perceptible irony.

Cantra sighed. "Looks to me like you're already in."

"In fact," he agreed, "I am. We'll do this as quickly as possible, as none of us has time to waste." He put the case up on the board's ledge, opened it, and in short order produced about twenty-eight sets of ship keys, emergency keys, gun-bay keys, lock-up keys—

plus, as she might've known there would be, forms to sign for each set, certifying that she'd received them.

Forms signed and stowed, Wellik brought another handful of papers out of his case.

"Captain, as you are no doubt aware," he said, brisk and straight-faced, "policy requires that any vessel decommissioned from military service must retire its name. Now, I've put down on the manifests here—" he rattled his fist full of paperwork "—that *Salkithin* is being decommissioned and turned over to an appropriate agency, which intends to put it into service as a luxury cruise vessel."

The boy sneezed—which saved her the trouble of doing it herself. Wellik looked up from his paper with a frown.

"As per instructions received from M. Jela Granthor's Guard," he continued forcefully. "My office has completed the appropriate paperwork, excepting the names and affiliations of the new owners and the name of the vessel. We have, to insure compliance, provided work crew and materials." He glanced up again, teasing a single sheet of print-out from the rest.

"Before we proceed, Captain yos'Phelium, your co-pilot requested that you be given this information, since I encountered him first on the issue. He felt it was a good thing that the name of the vessel be demobilized, granting the sometimes quaint and even superstitious approach to life exhibited by the local population."

Frowning, Cantra took the paper, gave it a quick read—and then another, slower.

Salkithin—Jela's own sweet ship—had been named after a planet on which a force of less than twenty thousand soldiers had successfully held off an enemy attack until a trap could be sprung. Thing was, the planet's forces—and the planet—died with the enemy. Damn' if that didn't sound like a familiar situation.

Salkithin. Soldiers found that kind of naming important, and for herself, she wouldn't have cared. The gentle citizens of Solcintra, though—that was another matter. The boy had the right of it. And, she thought, he *did* have the right of it; he'd caught the problem before it became a problem, just like a co-pilot ought to do.

"I'm going to be meeting with Sergeant Ilneri," Wellik was saying, "and doing an inspection. I'll leave these with you—" He held the papers out to the boy, who received them with a slight bow.

"Please fill in the name of your ship, sign the forms, and have them ready for me when I'm done inspection."

He turned, sealed up the case, took it in hand, and was gone, waving them an airy salute.

Cantra glared at the blameless door. "Now, what I don't know about naming ships—" she began, and then stopped because the comm let go with its incoming message tone.

Wellik's papers still in hand, Tor An crossed the tower—communications being on the co-pilot's side of the board—flipped a toggle—

"Tcha!" he said, sounding something between put-out and impatient.

"What now? The local priests want to bless the hull and shrive the pilots?"

He turned from the board, a half-smile on his mouth.

"Nothing quite so drastic. The dea'Gauss sends that he must bring us an amended contract for review and signature."

"Amended?" She frowned. "Amended how?"

He glanced back at his screen. "It would appear that the Service Families have reformulated themselves and are now the High Houses of Solcintra. The dea'Gauss believes that an addendum putting forth this lineage will be in the pilot's interests, should there be a dispute regarding payment."

"Which you know and I know and dea'Gauss knows there likely will be," Cantra pointed out. "Not to say that Nalli Olanek ain't as honorable as they come when dealing with one of her own. But I'm betting there ain't no rules saying she's got to treat straight with a pair of *kenake* pilots. Stands to reason she'll do her utmost to short us."

The boy sighed and turned from the screen. "I believe you are correct, Pilot," he said seriously. "However, there is surely no harm in allowing the dea'Gauss to amend the contract as he suggests. It will be one more thing on our side of the trade table when it comes time to sue for our fee."

"Right you are. Tell him to fetch it on up, then." She waited while he sent the message on.

"Now," she said when he turned back to her, Wellik's papers in hand. "What will you be caring to name this fine vessel, Pilot Tor An?"

Damn' if he didn't pale, the rich golden skin going to a sort of beige—and here she thought she'd been doing him the kind of honor a well-brought-up boy from a trade clan would cherish.

"I?" he gasped. "What right have I to—Surely it falls to the captain to name her ship!"

"No hand at it," she said, laconic and Rim-wise. "And as to right—you're my co-pilot, and my heir. Says so in those papers dea'Gauss drew up between us and the Service Families. If I die on con, the ship goes to you."

"The contract—" He took a breath, color returning to his face. "The contract must demonstrate a clear passage of responsibility, for the safety of ship and passengers. However, the contract describes necessity for this one flight which we are soon to undertake. We—We cannot know that we will work well together, long-term, or that we will wish to continue our association beyond contract's end—"

"Assuming that there's anything at the end of the contract saving gray screens the pilots' last duty," she said, maybe a bit harsher than she needed to. "You saw those 'quations, Pilot. They shape up to a certain future, in your opinion?"

He closed his eyes and bowed his head. "They are the equations we are given, and when the time comes, we will fly them. I depend on Scholar dea'Syl's genius—and the skill of the best damn' pilot Jela had ever known."

And who was she, Cantra thought, suddenly tired, to snatch hope out of the boy's hands? He might even be right.

"All right, then," she said, making her voice easy and light. She crossed over and took up a lean against the pilot's chair, producing a smile when he raised his head and looked at her. "Let's take this by the numbers, if you'll bear with me, Pilot."

He moved his hand, fingers shaping the sign for *go on*.

"Right. The way it scans to me is that you're my co-pilot, and you can handle this ship. Jela's tree likes you, the cat likes you, Scholar dea'Syl likes you, Rool Tiazan likes you—Deeps, I think even Wellik likes you! Certain-sure Jela liked you, or he wouldn't never have given you care of the scholar and sent you on ahead. All those upstanding folk liking you, trusting you—that weighs with me, Pilot. I can't think of anybody within reach who I'd rather stand as my heir and carry on with my ship."

She paused, watching him as he stared around the tower, something like awe in his face. *My ship*—she could see him thinking it, he was so easy to read—and he shed a tithe of the sadness he'd been carrying with him since he'd realized his old Dejon was going to be left behind on the ground.

"Now, before you decide," she said when she'd judged he'd had time enough to feel the full wonder of someday being master of such a vessel—"before you decide, there's something else you need to know."

His attention was on her that fast, purple eyes non-committal in a face that had gone trader-bland. "Captain."

Almost Cantra grinned, which wasn't at all what she wanted to be doing at this point. Easy to read he might be, but Tor An yos'Galan was a pilot, and a trader-trained-and-raised. Inexperience, she reminded herself, wasn't anywhere near the same as foolhardy.

"If you stand my heir, there's other things that'll fall to your care with this ship, those being"—she extended her hand, fist closed, and showed him her thumb—"Jela's tree, which he honored as a comrade and a brother-in-arms. He took my oath that I'd keep it safe, and I'd expect you to take up that oath as your own."

Tor An inclined his head.

Cantra raised her first finger. "Second and last, Jela's heir will also come into your keeping, and I'll expect you to care and nurture it as you would a child of your own body."

The boy blinked. "Jela's heir?" he repeated. Another blink. "You are pregnant with Jela's child?"

"That's right." She said it as forthrightly as possible—and waited, not at all certain what to expect from—

He took three steps toward her, and she could see the shine of tears in his eyes. She swallowed, her throat tight and her own eyes suddenly wet.

"Captain, you are—You are not only calling heir, then. You are calling clan."

That came from an odd trajectory. She hadn't thought of clan, being only Torvin by Garen's say-so. But a boy from an old and extended family of traders and ship-masters—Aye, he'd think clan right enough, and most especially as he'd lost all that they'd been.

And, really, she thought, what difference? Clan served her purpose as well as heir, if it meant protection for the tree and the child.

The boy was looking—elsewhere, like he was seeing something or someone she couldn't. "Yes," he said softly, in that thinking-out-loud voice she'd already heard him use at the board. "Yes, this will be good. It *will* be good. There is strength in clan. And the contract—The contract will be properly then between clans, and less easy to ignore, come time to collect our fee." His eyes focused on her face again. "But our clan will need a name!"

Cantra felt something unknot in her chest, like maybe there'd been cargo twine around her heart, and it had suddenly come loose. But—

"Let's name the ship first, hey?" She said, keeping it light and easy. "And I'll tell you straight, Pilot, I don't know anything about starting up a clan—"

He smiled at her.

"Nor do I. However, we are fortunate in our acquaintance. The dea'Gauss is one who oversees contracts and alliances, and who understands the measuring of such things. I doubt he would refuse a request for his assistance in this matter."

And there it was again, Cantra thought. Co-pilot taking co-pilot care. The boy was sound. He'd do.

He'd have to do.

"So, we'll ask dea'Gauss to do the pretty for us. Right. Now—ship name, Pilot? Didn't you never think of your own ship when you was a kid?"

Amusement glimmered in those improbable eyes. "What, the son of a trading house and never dare dream of my own ship? I'd hardly have made pilot if I hadn't that much spark!"

True enough. She gave him an encouraging smile and set herself to coaxing him. Pretty soon she had two names: one a pure kid super-duper-hero-pilot name that he'd been slightly embarrassed to admit to, and the other a solid, sober kind of a name for a ship, with the tang of optimism about it.

"I like that," she said, meaning it. "And we'll hope it's true-named." She nodded at the paperwork still in his hand. "Fill it in, if you will, Pilot. *Quick Passage*."

THIRTY-ONE

Quick Passage

THE BOY WAS on comm when Cantra came into the tower from her latest visit to the passenger bays. She walked past the tree, lashed good and tight in its position; dropped into the pilot's chair and leaned her head back, watching him through half-closed eyes. He flicked a toggle and general audio came live.

"We've got a clean reading on all automatic transponders and passive visuals." That was Solcintra Station—which was pushing its inspection a bit, in Cantra's opinion. "*Quick Passage*, home port Solcintra, owner Cantra yos'Phelium. Active visual check in progress—Looks like you've still got a blue beacon where you should have a green at degree one-eighty."

The boy tipped his head and tapped his left ear—a sign to her that he had another party on the line.

"The crew boat suggests that your inspection is before-time, Solcintra Station," he said politely, which if it was Vachik at comm on the 'boat, took considerable liberty with what had most likely been said.

There was a slight pause, then Station again, sounding to Cantra's ear just a thought apologetic.

"Acknowledge that, *Quick Passage*. Will relay. Merely an activity report."

"Thank you, Station. *Quick Passage* out." He closed the connection, and paused with his hand over the second toggle, his nose wrinkled slightly while doubtless having his ear filled with the Deeps knew what ribald and outrageous nonsense, Vachik having taken it as a hobby to try and rattle the boy's reserve.

"As to that, I couldn't say, Pilot," Tor An murmured, not noticeably rattled. "*Quick Passage* out." He snapped the toggle and sighed, pulling the bud out of his ear as he spun his chair to face her.

"Vachik's amused by Station, is he?" she asked laconically.

Tor An stretched, putting the seams of his handsome embroidered tunic at risk." Pilot Vachik points out that Station oversteps," he said serenely. "Which it had, and now does not. How does the boarding go on?"

"Not quite a riot. It's a rare wonder what having a couple brace o'nice X Strains monitoring the intakes will do for the general level of politeness."

Nalli Olanek hadn't wanted to swallow the limit on baggage, claiming her folk would be reasonable—which they hadn't been, not by any measure known to ship-dwellers. So there'd had to be a limit set, which the captain did, and then there had to be arguments from the Speaker and her seconds, from which young Tor An had excused himself, returning some few minutes later bearing the message that Captain Wellik had approved the guards she'd requested, and they stood ready to take her orders.

That had solved the immediate problem—without bloodshed—though she figured they'd bought future grief. Stipulating there was a future. And not to say, she thought fair-mindedly, that the boy's notion had been off-course, which it hadn't.

It was turning out to be the case that Pilot Tor An had a good many useful notions in that pretty head of his.

It had, for an instance, been his notion—thinking out loud in her direction, as was his habit—that since they didn't have full-time military staffing, maybe they didn't need the extra officer-training seat there in the middle of the tower, and that maybe that seat lock and mounting block would make a better lash-point for the tree than ever they'd be able to cobble in a corner with twine and tape.

"Assuming, of course," he'd said to nothing and nobody in particular, "that the captain would prefer to have the tree ship in the tower, rather than in its own cargo-pod."

That cargo-pod idea hadn't played well to the green crew at all, and it hadn't quite seemed right to her either. She'd gotten used to having the tree in her eye, and having it mumble its pictures at the back of her head. Apparently, the tree had gotten used to her, too, and used to being part of the tower crew.

"Sergeant Ilneri and Pilot Argast report that three of our proposed back-up pilots test well," Tor An said softly. "The fourth was found inadequate and returned to port."

She nodded. "Saw Ilneri on the way back up, and he gave me the news."

He'd also insisted she take another tour of work-almost-complete, over which Jela's mates labored, as far as she could tell, non-stop. Kinda spooky, were Jela's mates, for as hard as they'd taken the news of his dying, it seemed to hearten them to know he'd last been seen trying to take someone's head off with that nasty flexible cutter of his. And everywhichone of them still talked like he was hanging over their shoulders, insisting on nothing less than perfect.

"The dea'Gauss will be here shortly," Tor An said carefully, interrupting that line of thought. "Will you wish to dress for the ceremony?"

Ceremony. All they were set to do was sign some local legal papers, but the kid had built it up in his mind into a *ceremony*, and had gotten himself dressed up proper to face it. She eyed the tunic: space black, with the star-holding dragon that'd been the chop for Alkia Trade Clan embroidered on shoulder and sleeve in gold and silver thread. He'd brushed his bright hair 'til it gleamed and even shined his boots. By contrast, she felt nothing but grubby in her leathers.

Ceremony, she thought sourly, and caught a glimmer of wing and branch from the tree.

"Right," she said, levering herself out of the pilot's chair. "I'll be a minute."

The non-descript man with the surprisingly bold brown eyes was dressed neat and respectful in pale tunic and pants. He had placed two black, silver-edged folios before him on the fold-out work table; a flat wooden box was at his right hand, and a small satchel that looked like a traveling bag sat quietly by his feet.

Looking down at the table, he touched the flat box—mayhap for luck—took a visible breath, and raised his head.

"We are ready, I believe," he said quietly. "I am dea'Gauss. I have been requested to oversee the establishment of a clan new to Solcintra and to known space, and I am recognized by the Solcintra Accountants Guild as a member in good standing."

Here he paused, very briefly, and looked about the tower before continuing.

"As required by the protocols of the Accountants Guild, I bring with me three persons of known character and unallied clan, each to witness as they will. They arrive knowing that they witness, and they declare themselves individually disinterested observers of the event at hand."

Cantra faced dea'Gauss across the work desk, dressed as formally as her small kit allowed, the boy at her side. The strangers—witnesses—stood behind them, and behind *them* was the tree, which comforted her some, even as she could feel it paying attention *real hard.* Behind the tree stood Argast, acting half as honor guard and half as pilot-in-waiting in case the ship required something during the course of the ceremony.

Meanwhile, dea'Gauss was talking again.

"In so far as Solcintra and its population have an interest in the careful arrangement of debts and balances, of property and ownership, of precedence and inheritance, of honor and responsibility, of *melant'i* and necessity, and of actions which permit the public good, it is meet and fitting that individuals join together into such groups and organizations which present the opportunity for surety in relationships and commerce. We witness here today the signing and sealing of documents representing the establishment of a particular group which names itself Clan Korval. This group…"

Cantra glanced to the side, caught the kid's eyes on her and the flicker of fingers—*acceptable course?*

Korval? Well, it was better than Valkor, the other combo possible from the two syllables deemed most propitious by means she hadn't cared to inquire into—and she had shunted the details of the paperwork to him.

She returned *clear lift!* and felt him relax beside her.

"…. has control and ownership of respectable properties, is peopled by individuals known as reliable and forthright, and has established a clear lineage and succession. Clan Korval honors the absent M. Jela Granthor's Guard as Founder and acknowledges duties, goals, heirs, debts, property, responsibility and *melant'i* deriving from the Founder."

Cantra stood, breath-caught, and damn' if she didn't feel tears prickling at the edges of her eyes—

In her head, a flutter of images: a tree dropped a pod across a thin river, that pod grew into a tree, in its turn dropping a pod…

"Clan Korval is composed of two lines until and unless the Clan shall choose otherwise. The predominant line is yos'Phelium, currently headed by Cantra yos'Phelium. The subordinate line is yos'Galan, currently headed by Tor An yos'Galan."

She blinked and sent another glance to the boy, meeting a slight smile. She'd've thought they'd share—but no, he had the right of it again. He was her heir, and his part was to support her—co-pilot to pilot. They both knew that protocol, down deep in their bones. She just hoped any of it lasted longer that them getting out of orbit and starting the transition run.

"The Clan together acknowledges the duties, goals, heirs, debts, property, responsibility, and *melant'i* of these line heads as its own, and from this day forward all within the Clan will be governed, judged, rewarded, punished, and otherwise dealt with as the Clan requires within its own written code of conduct. All actions performed individually or in unison reflect the Clan, and the Clan holds ultimate responsibility for its members. Formed in orbit around Solcintra, Clan Korval looks for council and fellowship from the Fifty High Houses of Solcintra, and the Council of the Fifty High Houses of Solcintra will honor Korval as a member, as well."

This last was spoken just a little more firmly than what had gone before, as if maybe dea'Gauss wasn't one-hundred-percent certain that the new High Council would find Korval an ornament to itself.

"Clan Korval exists," dea'Gauss said, back to quiet now. "May its name shine and its deeds endure."

Beside her, she heard a discreet sniffle, and damn' if she wasn't tearing up again herself. She blinked. Clan Korval. And Jela listed down as Founder, all right and proper. Almost—almost, she could hear him laughing…

The accountant bowed deeply—first to Tor An, then to herself. Straightening, he opened the right-most of the two black-and-silver folios.

"If the line heads will be good enough to sign here, with the subordinate line signing first and the predominant line after, we shall witness and seal."

Sign they did—first the boy, precise and unornamented. He passed the pen to her and stood to one side as she wrote out her name, the ink that same shade of purple that flickered along the far edge of the Rim.

Cantra yos'Phelium. She blinked down at the shape of it along the cream-colored page, took a breath to steady herself, and signed the second book, too.

She put the pen down, and the tree let loose with a burst of flying dragons so bright and joyous she went back a step—and bumped right into the kid, who caught her arm, and whispered, for her ears alone, and like it was the most natural thing ever—"Jela's tree rejoices. It is rightly done."

"Who'm I to argue with a vegetable?" she muttered back, and heard him laugh softly while the witnesses filed up one at a time and put their signatures down in the books.

That done, dea'Gauss opened the flat box and removed a little gizmo, which he activated and touched to her signature and to Tor An's, leaving a disk of green wax on each.

He stowed the gizmo, sealed the box, and waved a cautious hand over the wax to be sure it was cool before he closed the first book and handed it to her, with a bow so deep she feared for his back.

"Korval, I am honored."

It struck her then—and only then—that the lines she'd just signed tied her as close as she'd ever been tied in her life. *Clan Korval*, she thought, half-wildly. Kid, tree, ship and all.

She took a hard breath and centered herself, managing to return the accountant's bow with the respect he'd earned.

"Mr. dea'Gauss," she murmured; "the honor is mine."

After a series of bows and formal well-wishings, the witnesses were escorted out by Argast. Mr. dea'Gauss was carefully fitting the second signed book into an archive envelope, being fussy about seating the corners just so.

"We are led to understand that the planet itself is in danger," he said, his eyes on his task, "and thus it was only prudence that moved the High-Houses-that-were to bear the archives of Council and Law with them. I cannot reproduce the reasoning which would have caused them to destroy the secondary archives, nor was the Accountants Guild asked to render an opinion prior to this action. Communications from those who had been the Elders of the Service Families directed to the escape ships are rejected." He glanced up. "This means that the inception of your clan has not been properly recorded with those in whom authority and law invests."

"Nothing you can do, is there," Cantra said as the pause got longer, "if they ain't answering comm?"

"Indeed. However, one attempts to honor propriety and to fulfill the tasks for which one's service was engaged." He finished fussing with the envelope at last, and put his palm flat against the seal.

"The new council—they call themselves the High Houses, and thus put on a suit which they cannot properly wear. Yet, what choice had they? Lacking the archives and the law, they now stumble to create arrangements and protocols for which there exist no precedent." He gave her one of his straight looks, this one maybe not so much bold as tired.

"Though the new council has seen fit to disbar me and mine, citing our ties to the old order, I am able to report that they have acknowledged the right of Clan Korval to come among them, to treat and be treated as an equal member of the council."

He bent, pulled his satchel up onto the desk, and stowed the envelope in an outside pocket, taking care with the seal.

"It is possible that we who remain on-planet during—"

Cantra blinked, shot a question-look at Tor An, and took receipt of a baffled stare.

"Hold that orbit," she said, bringing her attention back to the accountant.

He paused with his hands on his satchel, and inclined his head, "Korval?"

"You're planning on staying on-planet, is what I'm hearing you say."

"That is correct."

She frowned at him, which he bore with patience. He looked as sensible a man as she'd ever seen, but, she supposed it might be that he hadn't been able to hold the thought of what was coming toward them—

"You understand," she said carefully, "that Solcintra won't likely exist at the end of the action Captain Wellik's told us is coming?"

"I have heard this, yes. We will, of course, attempt to lift what ships there are—"

"No." She waved the hand that wasn't full of black-and-silver book, cutting off the rest of whatever he'd been going to say.

"This ship here—You drew up the contract! This ship here is set to take on all the members of the Service Families that now style themselves High Houses. There's a place here for your and yours, never fear it, though you'll be needing to sleep—"

And what, she thought suddenly, if that were it? If dea'Gauss for all his sense and his steadiness and his firm, bold gaze was afraid of slow-sleep—

"I have not made myself plain," he said, and inclined his head. "The case is that the new council has disbarred Family dea'Gauss. We are seen as holding allegiance to those who have deserted us, and the new council would choose its own—"

From the tree came a sense of sudden, rushing wind—

The wind was real, whipping her hair and fluttering the sleeves of Tor An's tunic—and then it was gone.

THIRTY-TWO

Quick Passage

THE WIND FELL as suddenly as it had risen, leaving the one known as Rool Tiazan standing disheveled and breathless within the confines of the pilots' tower.

"What has gone forth?" he cried, as much frightened as angry, or so Tor An thought. He raised a hand and scraped the wild red curls away from his face, the black ring on his first finger winking quick and cunning as a living eye.

"Problem?" Cantra yos'Phelium asked, one winged eyebrow lifting in unmistakable irony.

"You may perhaps allow the close attention of the Iloheen—your pardon, the *sheriekas*!—to be a problem," the other snapped, less breathless now, and with anger perhaps ascending over fear. "And how could they fail to focus upon such a gaudy display of energy and—" He stopped, his gaze having fallen from the pilot's face to that which she yet held in her hand.

"I see," he murmured, and extended a hand. "May I—"

It was, to Tor An's shame, dea'Gauss who moved first and placed himself between the clan's primary and the potential threat.

"The book belongs to Korval and to none other, sir," he said coolly. "It is not for out-clan to—"

Rool Tiazan turned his hands palm up and smiled at the accountant. "Peace, peace, Ser—dea'Gauss, is it?—I—"

"Indeed it is dea'Gauss, though I stand not so high as 'ser.'"

"Ah. Forgive my lapse; I meant no discourtesy, either to yourself or to Korval. It is merely that—"

"Quiet!" Pilot Cantra ordered loudly, and perforce there was quiet. Rool Tiazan bowed with neither irony nor temper, and properly to Korval's honor, followed by Mr. dea'Gauss, who did not, however, retire from his position between pilot and *dramliza*.

"Now, here's what I thought," Pilot Cantra said briskly, and the Rim accent was more noticeable than it had been during the ceremony. "I thought I was captain on my own ship. I thought I was talking with somebody. I *didn't* think I'd set off any look-at-mes in the direction of the Enemy nor hadn't done anything more remarkable than carry out ship's business. If you got information touching on that, say it out, straight and quick."

"Captain." Rool Tiazan bowed slightly and seriously. "My information is this: as I was observing actions brought by certain of the free *dramliza* directly against the Iloheen, suddenly I was snatched, against my will, and with naught I might do to deny it, *here*, born on the wings of such a maelstrom of luck and possibility as I have never experienced. Something has altered event, noisily. Something has shifted the pattern of the lines of what will be, and the luck swirls not merely about the environs of this star system or, more nearly, this planet, but *here*," he stamped, his soft slipper waking an unlikely ring from the decking. "On this ship." He inclined his head. "I suspect that what has been bound into that book which you hold is the cause of these unexpected alterations."

He inclined his head. "May I see and hold the book, Pilot? It is necessary." He turned to the accountant. "Mr. dea'Gauss, I swear to you that I am an ally."

"He's right," Pilot Cantra said briskly. "I 'preciate your concern, Mr. dea'Gauss, but you can stand down. He's twelve kinds of twisty, and you'll do well to weigh everything he tells you, but I vouch for him."

The accountant bowed, and retired, face grim.

Tor An stepped to his side. "Thank you, sir," he whispered, "for your quick action on behalf of the clan."

That gained a startled glance, and the beginning of a smile. "You are quite welcome, your lordship."

"Nay—" he began, but there was Rool Tiazan taking the clan book into his slim hands, and he found his feet had moved him forward again, his own hand lifting as if to snatch the precious object back.

Firm fingers encircled his wrist and held him close. "Steady, Pilot," she murmured. "Let the man look."

If he looked, it was with senses other than his eyes, yet one could not but be gratified by the reverent stroke of palm across the surface of the cover.

"Yes. What we have here—" Rool Tiazan sighed. "What we have here is just such an event as cannot be predicted nor planned against. There is a purity of purpose which can only act to confound the Enemy."

He opened his eyes and held the book out across his two palms.

"It is done and done well," Rool Tiazan said, and there was an odd resonant sound to his voice, as if his words echoed against the stars. "Prosper, Korval. May your name shine and your deeds endure."

Pilot Cantra received the book properly into her hands, and inclined her head. "May that be true-speaking," she murmured, the accent of the Rim entirely absent.

"Mr. dea'Gauss," she said abruptly, and the accent was back, and thicker than ever.

"Korval?"

"Comes to me that a brand-new and hope-to-be-respectable clan like we just got through setting up's going to need somebody to oversee our contracts and 'counts. You willing to work for us?"

The man's face took fire, hope blazing in his tired eyes. "Korval, I am."

"Good," Pilot Cantra nodded toward the fold-out table. "Sit yourself down and write up the contract—short and simple, mind you, 'cause I got some other things I want you to do." She held out her fist, thumb and first finger extended. "First thing, get your family up here. Second, I want the word out on the port that this vessel is taking on passengers, whether or not they're attached to any of the so-called High Houses. Got those?"

"Yes," the accountant said, fervently. "Korval, I do."

"Then get busy," she said crisply, her hand fluttering out of its counting fist and into pilot hand-sign: *acceptable*?

Tor An smiled and inclined his head. "Most acceptable, Pilot," he said.

"That's good, too." She turned her attention back to Rool Tiazan.

"So we got the Enemy's attention," she said as if it were the merest nothing. "What'll we do with it?"

Rool Tiazan smiled. "An excellent question. Perhaps we—" His smile faded into a frown, and he lifted a finger.

"Problem?"

"Anomaly, rather. I feel energies aligning strangely—and random event approaches."

"Whatever that means," Pilot Cantra said. "You were going to tell me—"

The door to the pilots' tower slid open to admit Lucky the cat, strutting, tail high.

Cantra sighed. "Who let the cat in?"

"I did, dear Pilot Cantra." Liad dea'Syl guided his power-chair carefully into the tower. After him came a small parade. Several looked to be beggars. Others were kempt enough to maybe be panhandlers, day jobbers, pawnsters, thieves, joy-workers.

Cantra handed the clan book to the boy. "Stow it safe," she said quietly, and he moved off without comment. She went forward to meet the power-chair and its escort, Rool Tiazan at her side.

"Ser Tiazan, it is well that you are here," the scholar said pleasantly. "I have framed the last set of equations. I believe you will approve—and the pilots, as well."

"Certainly, that is welcome news," Rool Tiazan said.

"But," Cantra interrupted ruthlessly, "bringing strangers up to the tower without clearance, Scholar. I've gotta disallow that."

"Of course, of course." The old man smiled at her. "Permit this to be an unique case, if you will. They came first to me, and invoked M. Jela as their motivator. That being the case, I thought it best to bring them directly to Jela's heir for parsing."

She considered the bunch of them, huddled close to each other and to the chair, as if maybe they were having second thoughts about their chosen course—all save a tiny and trim red-haired woman with clever eyes and a gun in her sleeve.

"You," Cantra said to her. "Talk."

"With pleasure," the woman answered, standing forward and sending a quick, appraising look around the tower. She parted with a cool nod in the direction of Rool Tiazan, but her eyes lingered on the tree.

"I see that the mission was a success, after all. We had some doubts, though it was later reported the pilot had able back-up, outside."

Cantra thought back on the tale she'd finally teased out of Jela concerning that night's work—the night they'd met and everything had changed.

"This would be on Faldaiza," she said to the little woman. "And I'm thinking you're the gambler."

The other woman bowed. "Gambler, if you will, Captain, or runner-with-luck."

Rool Tiazan stirred; the woman's cool gaze touched him.

"No need, Elder Brother," she said. "We had known you were here and that others gather."

Cantra looked between the two of them. "You're counting this one as kin?" she asked the gambler.

"Soon enough, after we pass through that which comes."

"If," Rool Tiazan said, "we indeed emerge, which has not been Seen."

The gambler laughed. "Tush, O Mighty Tiazan! We who are at the mercy of the lines and the matrices, and most likely to be bruised by those winds which bear you high—we sight low, and see—somewhat. On this side of the event which your cleverness has shaped, we see strife, death, loneliness—and soon. Very soon."

"And after?" the *dramliza* persisted. "What do your small arts show you on the other side, Young Sister?"

The gambler smiled. "Why, strife, in some measure—but also life, and opportunity."

Rool Tiazan bowed, and folded his hands.

The gambler looked back to Cantra. "Captain, the Solcintrans will renounce us, for we embody that which they most fear. Elsewhere, we have learned to remain hidden, for the groundlings say we are dangerous, and perversions; they call us *sheriekas*-spawn and they kill us out of hand."

"And are you?" Cantra asked her, seeing dragons dancing at the back of her head, tasting mint along the edge of her tongue. "*Sheriekas*-spawn?"

"Captain, our talents are perhaps born of those forces which the *sheriekas* and the *dramliza* manipulate with such easy contempt. I have heard it argued thus, but we ourselves are human. Ask the Mighty Tiazan's lady if this is not so."

"She speaks sooth," Rool Tiazan said, in that voice which was not his own. "They are what we shall become, formed in a far different forge."

The gambler smiled, and leaned forward slightly, one hand out, fingers curled.

"Captain, I have with me healers, true-dreamers, seers, finders, hunch-makers, green-thumbs, teachers—treasure beyond counting for the days beyond. Grant us passage, and you may call upon us for any service, so long as Jela's tree survives to bind us."

The dragons in her head danced faster, and she'd swear she smelled salt on the air. Cantra rubbed her eyes and looked to where the boy—the head of her clan's subordinate line, and her co-pilot, she reminded herself forcefully—to where Tor An yos'Galan stood at watch, quiet and alert.

"Call it."

He bowed. "It is plain. The Founder did give his oath to work in the best interests of life, therefore we, his heirs, are bound by that same oath. And the tree, as we can see, is in favor of the petition."

Pay your debts, baby.

Cantra nodded.

"I agree." She turned back to the gambler. "You and yours'll need to travel asleep, same as most of the passengers; and give up your weapons to the armory-master, to be returned when we find safe port."

"Agreed," the other woman answered, and behind her there was a visible relaxing 'mong her mates.

"Right, then. Pilot yos'Galan here'll escort you, first to the armory, then to the sleep-rooms. He'll stand between you and hurt, if it's offered, and you'll accept his protection and his judgment."

"Agreed," the gambler answered once more, and bowed, as cocky and exuberant as if she was going for a stroll down the street.

"Pilot yos'Galan, lead on! We place ourselves wholly into your hands!"

THIRTY-THREE

Spiral Dance
Solcintra

DANCER WOKE, OPENED eyes and ears, and commenced to pull down data. The main-brain opened a window on the second screen, displaying a list of self-checks completed, and the nav-brain launched a preliminary query to the pilot for lift-times and destination strings.

The pilot sat, eyes closed, in her chair, listening to the sounds of her ship. Sitting there, fingers hooked 'round the arm rests so they wouldn't shake so much—sitting there, she supposed she'd been a trial and a bother more often than a comfort and true comrade in the years they'd been together, with Garen and then just each other. But the ship—the ship had never stinted in its care of her, not since the day Garen brought her aboard, out of her head with the pain of dying.

"Never stinted." She repeated the thought, hearing the echo of her voice come comforting and right off the familiar walls.

Despite *Dancer* could've called out to the Enemy twelve dozen times or more and brought destruction and worse down on them—she'd never done that. And as Cantra knew, deep down and personal, it was those things you didn't do, maybe more than those you did, that counted out a true comrade and friend.

A tickle at the back of her mind, and then a picture, forming slow and not so ept—and suddenly there was Jela, his face grimy and sweaty, back and shoulder muscles rigid with strain, as he struggled to lift and cut, the sending so clear she could swear she heard him breathing.

"That's right," she whispered. "You remember him just as long as you can. He'd want that, so he would."

The comm sounded and she bent forward, her finger finding the right switch without a fumble.

"*Spiral Dance*."

"Captain," said the deep rumble that was Y. Vachik, uncharacteristically subdued. "We're on the count, here."

Right. They were all on the count, now, weren't they?

"Keep 'er ready, Pilot," she said into the comm. "I'll be there directly."

She flicked the switch and opened her eyes, fingers already inputting lift and course. The nav-brain—she gave it leave to do anything it liked in the service of fulfilling those coordinates, and called up the wounded-pilot protocol. A flick of her finger set the timer—not giving herself a lot of room to tarry—and she was up out of the chair. Once the protocols engaged, *Dancer* was on her own, until the pilot took over again.

Or forever, whichever came first.

One more thing before she left—a touch of finger to fragile leaf, and a quick test to make sure the dirt-filled box gray-taped to the co-pilot's board was firm.

From the barely sprouted pod came a hopeful vision of dragons, and the scent of sea air.

"You'll do fine," she told it, and cleared her throat. "Jela'd be proud."

Then she was gone, running, as the timer counted down to lift off.

True to his orders, Vachik had kept the shuttle ready. Cantra hit first chair hard, yanked the webbing tight and gave the shuttle its office, the whiles counting off at the back of her head, and with a quarter-eye on the aux screen—six...five...four...three...two...

Dancer was up, rising hard through the busy air, and paying not the least attention to squawks from traffic control.

She was busy then, weaving a course through the mess and tangle filling all of Solcintra's air space. Everything that could hold air was up, and the sorts of pilots who might be sitting those boards didn't bear thinking on.

"Fools and cretins!" Vachik spat as she dodged them through a particularly tricksy knot-up, then pushed hard on the rockets.

Cantra stole a look at the aux screen—*Dancer* was deep in the worst of the mess...

"Message from *Springbane*, Captain," Vachik said. "They give us—almost ample time. Your screen two."

She looked and smiled grimly. "A challenge, would you say, Pilot?"

Vachik's answering grin was a frightening thing to behold. "Indeed, Captain. Shall we school them?"

"Shouldn't be a problem at all."

It was the board then, and the ship she was flying, and no time for sneak-looks at her life-that-was leaving her behind, nor even for the fading flickers of dragons, dancing on the shore of a sea long dead and dust.

"Long orbit on that ship, Captain," Vachik said quietly some while later. "Looks good—and it's well outside the crowd, now."

She sighed. "Thank you," she said and shot him a look. "Sure you won't come with us?"

"To receive such an offer from such a captain," he answered, formal and not at all Vachik-like, "is an honor which I will long recall. The commander, however, has given Jela's Troop a special unit designation, and it is there I would serve."

"Right," she said, and gave him a nod. "Looks like we're gonna beat *Springbane's* time, Pilot. Best get your kit together."

"I have everything I need, Captain, thank you."

She nosed the shuttle in and Vachik was out of the chair as soon as the docking light went to blue.

"Captain." He saluted and was gone.

She dumped out just as soon as the connect tube was clear, seconds ahead of the time *Springbane* had given her to dock, and extended a hand to kill the aux screen.

She found *Quick Passage* in her scans, did the math in her head and set the course.

At the far back of her head, dragons danced, insubstantial as hope.

THIRTY-FOUR

Quick Passage
Departing Solcintra

NOW, WHO'D'VE EXPECTED we'd be leading a parade? Cantra thought, scanning her screens and carefully not sighing.

In her head, the golden dragon glided easy on half-furled wings, beside her the jewel-colored dragonet, which the tree had settled on as its version of her co-pilot. Behind them rose dragons of all color and description, old, young, halt and hale. Some few emulated the effortless grace shown by the leaders, others were already laboring hard. Beyond the general chaos loomed a long, disciplined line of black dragons, wings steady, eyes baleful, teeth at ready—Wellik's rear-guard, that would be.

Back in real-time, the tower was crowded, not only because the pilots were presently enjoying the company of Liad dea'Syl, Lucky the cat, and Rool Tiazan, but with the sound of pilot voices.

Tor An played the local comm board like it was a musical instrument, pulling talk, catching chat large and small:

"*Quanta Plus*, have you even refribbed that thing in twenty years? But in case it helps, you've got to watch your starboard beacons, 'cause they're some out of synch!"

"Oughtn't be doing that. We just had it shopped to your home field—that is, if that's I've got *Clary Bee* talking to me."

"*Clary Bee's* here. I'm to port, actually. That's cousin Trisky talked about your synch, but it don't look like his're all that pretty, either. Port visuals fine, and signal strength right top."

"Trisky, tell your field-man he'll owe me a day-check if you see him."

"Last I saw, he was mounting somebody a new deflector union. Ought to be out here somewhere."

"*Chrono*, watch the drift. We got a crowd in a hurry comin' from behind—"

"You got it, Mom. We're set to spin to port and add some vee on a six count, if you'll scoot—"

"Ain't never seen so many holiday pilots in one place and if any of us get out of here without a hole in the hull—"

"Always an optimist, ain't you, Bondy?"

"What's that thing beside you, Rinder? Only got four beacons I can scan."

"Uncle, that's my guess."

"Right. Well, Rinder, you're safe on that side."

"But low on company."

Laughter from a bunch of ships on that, and the channels changed again.

The chatter seemed to soothe the boy and, truth told, it eased her, too, knowing they weren't traveling alone toward who-knew-what.

"Status report," Tor An murmured. "All ship systems blue; passenger bays secure, systems blue; cargo pods show balance within tolerance, systems blue."

"We're ready to go," Cantra answered. "If we knew when or where to."

"No taste for mystery, Lady?" Rool Tiazan asked lightly from his lean against the back-up comm station.

"Not where my ship's at risk, no," she told him shortly, and spared him an over-the-shoulder glare. "Speaking of, you'll be wanting to strap in. I won't have you bouncing about this tower, if transition goes as hard as it's like to, and putting the pilots at risk."

He inclined his head ironically. "Your tender care for my well-being is noted and appreciated."

"Appreciate it all you want, but *strap in*."

"Translation wave!" Tor An snapped, and—"Another!"

Cantra reached to the board, ready to hold her steady—which was small-ship reactions. The tiny disruptions generated by those three transitions weren't enough to jostle *Quick Passage*, even if they all hit at once.

"Wonder where they're thinking on going," she murmured, fingers simultaneously making the request of the tracking system.

"First was for The Bubble, looks like, second—"

"Incoming!" Tor An called.

"That didn't take long," someone sang across the bands. "What happened, forget your lunch?"

"The Bubble's gone," came the terse reply. "Ship won't swallow the coords."

She sent a glance down-board, that being the kind of news that might not set well with second chair. Besides his lips being pressed a little tighter than usual, he read calm and collected to her. Good boy.

"Incoming," Tor An said again—and this time the news was that Nolatine was gone.

"They should conserve energy," Liad dea'Syl said quietly. "Our good friend Lucky has the right of it, I think. Rest now, for we shall surely need the fullness of our resources on the far side of the event."

A quick glance showed the cat stretched out on his back across the old man's lap, thoroughly asleep with his paws in the air. She grinned and turned back to her board. The dragon parade in her head was fading, as if the tree had decided to take the cat's advice, too. Which was fine by her; she didn't want to be distracted by pretty pictures during what was likely to come next.

"Number three must've got where they were going," she said to her co-pilot.

"Else they were captured by the leading edge and unmade," Rool Tiazan murmured, and Cantra sighed.

"Full of fun, ain't you? Strapped in yet?"

"Incoming!" Tor An shouted. "Captain—a dozen—more!"

Her steadying hand was needed this time, not even something the size of *Quick Passage* could ignore the turbulence as Tor An's dozen ships—and then a dozen more, filling in at the fringes first, so the instruments told her, though the eye insisted they hit at once, each new ripple adding to the building wave of displaced energies.

The noise across the bands was terrible; worse was the carnage as ship was flung into ship, while others vanished, spontaneously translating—then reappearing, the ripple of their re-entry adding to the deadly agitation of energies.

"No!" Tor An cried.

Cantra's hands danced across the board. "We're leaving, Pilot," she said, keeping her voice firm and easy. *Just a piloting exercise, boy*, she thought at him. *Stay with me, here. There's worse to come.*

"Aye," he said crisply, and that quick he was steady, his hands moving sure and firm across his board, feeding the shields, slapping the noise off the bands down to a whisper, and doing all that a co-pilot ought—which was good, because she had everything she could do, dodging ships and shrapnel, as *Quick Passage* gathered and surged around them.

*

"Alert!"

His voice sounded strange in his ears: calm, collected, professional. His fingers moved efficiently across his board, doing what was needful while his heart hammered, and he rode his screens and scans—

"Captain—on visual, your screens six and eight—"

Objects—*Were* they objects? They glinted and gleamed in the visual tracking system, their shapes disturbingly fluid, even as they eclipsed stars and ships. They appeared to actively avoid *Quick Passage*, and scarcely registered on the radar—

"Got 'em," Pilot Cantra said, her voice so calm and easy that the pounding of his heart eased somewhat. "They don't scan like anything I've seen before. Almost look organic, close up. Keep 'em in eye and sing out if they look like changing their minds about avoiding us."

"Aye, Captain." His fingers had already brought the tracking systems up. He looked to the shields, and frowned, trying to place the low growling noise that had suddenly come on-line.

"Aha! Our noble feline would defend us from those!" The scholar cried, as delighted as a child. "Captain Cantra—an adjustment—if there is time? I have an additional factor. This should be added to the final equations, for accuracy."

Now? Tor An thought wildly. With space in chaos about them and creatures unlike anything seen or told by pilots—

"Go," Pilot Cantra said calmly. "I'm tracking."

"Yes. You will wish to multiply the final result of section seven by this number, which is a very rough approximation induced by the infinite expansion theory I have settled upon. The number is this: three-point-one-four-one-five-nine-two-six-five-three-five-eight-nine."

"Three-point-one-four-one-five-nine-two-six-five-three-five-eight-nine," Cantra sang back, fingers dancing across her board.

"That is correct," the scholar said. "Very good."

"Added, compiled and locked. Is the cat—"

"The cat proclaims his warrior status, Captain Cantra. Also, you will perhaps wish to know that Rool Tiazan is behaving—or shall I say, not behaving!—in a somewhat peculiar manner."

Tor An looked up. At first glance, it appeared that Rool Tiazan leaned as he had been, in defiance of the captain's repeated order to strap in.

On second glance, his pose was not relaxed, but rigid—and he was glowing with a pale green light…

"Captain—?" Tor An began, his heart racing into overdrive again.

"Mind your board, Pilot! I need seal readings, now!"

He wrenched his attention back to his first duty, scanning and quoting the shield strength, the seal parameters, the go-condition of life-support.

"Matches straight across. Energy level's up, but we're not at transition yet. Keep an eye on that, and tell me what you're scanning down low. I'm watching for intercept course objects, but I don't find anything—"

The ship's acceleration was constant, and Solcintra could now truly be said to be behind them rather than beneath. The rear screen was tracking the planet, but the clarity of the image was off. Tor An slapped the back-up into life.

The weird, organic objects were converging on Solcintra, melding into one enormous object, which cast a long, cold shadow along the land.

"I am my own destiny," Rool Tiazan said suddenly, and his voice seemed to reach beyond the skin of the ship, and out unto the very stars.

"I am my own destiny. Do what you will."

THIRTY-FIVE

His body leaning against the chair, he kept watch, all things great and small shining within the net of his regard.

There, *Spiral Dance* sang sweet seduction to her makers, the tree's sacrifice adding counterpoint, and sending insults of dragons.

And there—the Fourteen lay poised and secret, energies caught and cloaked, holding the secret of their Weaving close, watching the lines, and the luck, and the progress of annihilation, weighing the virtue of each passing instant.

Ships as numerous as the stars themselves rose from those planets which had yet escaped the Iloheen's kiss, equations were filed into boards, velocity was sought. Meanwhile, a taint of subtle poison drifted on the winds, which was the mark of she who would rule in place of the Iloheen. And at every front, through every level and phase, was there evidence of the Iloheen's work, the wave front sizzling with icy energies.

Nearby, the *ssussdriad* was silent, its essence folded close.

On this level, the pilots were living flame, burning bright and fierce and fast. Against their glory, the old man was but an ember, shielded by the shadow of the cat.

And everywhere, on every surface, on every level, the luck gleamed and swirled and danced, infusing every action, every thought, every breath, so that even the Hounds of the Iloheen were turned aside, and sought lesser prey.

The touch, when it came, was so elusive that it seemed at first a memory.

Again the touch, followed by a fuller presence. Within the lines and the fields of underspace it made itself known with a certain pleasing subtlety, as if it had learned somewhat of grace.

This falls to me, came his lady's measured appraisal.

Rool acquiesced and withdrew to the subordinate posture, sparing a thought for the precious lives and the dancing of the luck.

Daughter of my intent, I greet you! The hour of your destiny is nigh. It is time to take up your proper place and duty.

A fair sending it was, as the Iloheen came at them from several levels, seeking advantage, seeking to distract, seeking to measure their strength.

I am my own destiny, his lady made answer as Rool parried, expending the least energy possible, keeping the secret of their strength. *Do what you will.*

Is this how you welcome me, who made you what you are? The test that accompanied this was less wary, and too close to the plane wherein dwelt the darlings of the luck. All about, on every level, the wavefront of annihilation moved fast, and ever faster.

What peculiar arrangements you contrive for yourself! To cede dominance and submit to this prisoning of your powers! To consort with the small lives and strive to force a variant outcome? And yet—your promise is fulfilled. You are become as the Iloheen, and have earned your place among us. Open to me. I shall free you from this bondage you have accepted, and together we shall achieve perfection.

Rool felt a shift—stealthy and subtle—and tasted a stench upon the breeze. He looked to their shields, and made his reserves ready.

I am where I wish to be, and those things which I have put in order please me, his lady answered. *Begone! And trouble me no more.*

Rool felt the hated touch against his essence as she who would rule in place of the Iloheen drew him. Willingly, he released the small tithe of his power that she had bargained to gain, and severed the thread that bound them.

The wind whipped foul and hot as she struck, strongly and with surprising depth. The Iloheen made answer, yet not without taking some damage.

Again, the wind struck, and Rool increased his defenses, holding them close, intent only upon surviving this battle as the Iloheen drew its energies and—

From underspace itself, and from planes which no *zaliata* nor Iloheen had ever glimpsed, burst a vast and implacable greenness, a rage of life so potent that the terrible advance of perfection trembled, paused—

And crashed onward, consuming all and everything which was not itself.

Rool threw out what was left of his power, encompassing the fragile shell that contained the last, and best, hope of life.

Lute! he screamed against the wind. *Lady Moonhawk*!

Now, sister! The time is now! his lady's sending echoed his as they plummeted, burning, to the physical plane.

Behind them, the sphere that was Solcintra distorted, its crust crushed beneath the weight of the shadows, fireballs bounced around the tower, and alarms shrieked as moons, meteors, and comets assaulted the shielding. *Quick Passage* lurched while the pilots fought for control, for stability, for—

"Now!" Rool Tiazan screamed. "Transition, Pilots, or all is lost!"

Wild energies engulfed them; radiation shielding boiled away. Tor An slapped for back-ups, saw Cantra lean to the operation stud, as the ship staggered—

And steadied, the screens showing gray.

"Systems check!" the pilot snapped. "Vacuum check! Interior radiation check!" Ordered, his fingers moved, querying the ship. He read out the answers, hearing wonder in his own voice.

"All ship systems blue; passenger bays secure, systems blue; cargo pods show balance within tolerance, systems blue. Interior radiation within tolerances." He looked up and met her eyes.

"Vacuum check clean. We made it."

"By the skin of our teeth," she answered, but she was smiling.

"Rool Tiazan." She spun her chair about to address him, sitting bedraggled and bloodstained in the comm-chair, properly webbed in, and stroking the cat on his lap.

"Captain?" he returned, warily. Wearily.

"Thank you," she said, and spun back to face her board.

THIRTY-SIX

Quick Passage

THE SCREENS WERE gray.

Or say rather, Tor An thought wearily, the screens were *still* gray. And no way of knowing when they might reach normal space, and what might be awaiting them there. If they ever reached normal space.

The longest sustained transition known to pilots, so he had been taught, was *Moreta's* Flight, which had been the result of a malfunction of a prototype translation booster. The *Moreta* had been eighteen Common Months in transition, and when it finally regained normal space, its shields were shredded, its hull was pocked, and its pilot was dead.

To be sure, they were in somewhat better case—so far. The ship was whole, the pilots hale, if weary; the passengers content in their sleep. Those passengers who had not taken sleep were an entirely different matter, alas. It had nearly fallen to blows between Nalli Olanek and Cantra, before the Captain Ruled that the Speaker might only ask after arrival times once every six ship-days. The notion that they might yet be a-ship for such a length of time had—so Cantra had maintained, with amusement—stunned the Speaker into silence.

Twenty-eight ship-days now.

Tor An rubbed his eyes.

From the tree came an image of fog, and dragon-shapes seen dimly, gliding on silent half-furled wings.

Which was all very good, he thought, but even dragons must come to roost eventually.

The tree persisted, however, displaying once again the damp and chilly fog, the misty dragons—and a glow of light just off the right wing-tip.

Tor An blinked, looked to his screens and saw a familiar display, too long absent from the screens. He blinked again, and touched the button that opened the comm in the pilots' quarters.

"Go," Cantra said crisply, no hint of sleep in her voice.

"Pilot," he said, trying to keep the excitement out of his voice. "We have end of transition calculated in—thirty-six minutes."

A short silence, as if even Pilot Cantra had blinked.

"I'm on my way," she said then, and the connection closed.

Rool Tiazan knelt at the side of Liad dea'Syl's carry-chair, red hair mingling with white as the two of them bent over the old gentleman's tablet, muttering dark mathematical secrets to each other. The cat was curled 'round the tree's trunk, which had come to be a favorite position of his, eyes squinted half-shut.

The pilots were in their seats, poised and jumpy as newbies, both with their eyes tending to stray to the screens and the numbers that counted down, matter-of-fact and usual, toward transition's end.

"Cannon prepped," Cantra murmured.

"Shields on high," Tor An answered.

The numbers on the countdown zeroed out. The ship shrugged, the screens flickered. Cantra brought the cannon live, Tor An hit the scans.

The good news, Cantra thought, was that there weren't pirates waiting for them. The medium news was that they were the only ship within the considerable range of the scans.

The bad news was that the nav-brain beeped and quietly took itself off-line.

"Pilot?" She asked it quietly, though she already knew what he was going to report.

"We have no set north, Captain, and no confirmation from the computers of recognized beacons."

"Right. Guess we'll do it hard way, then. Find me something big and bright and far away. First, we need to know if we're in a galaxy." She keyed in her own searches, and the screens began to fill with stats as the sensors sifted local space for clues.

"I have magnetic fields we can read, Captain," Tor An said, sounding surprised. "We can pull a north from that. We are apparently in a galaxy, but we lack baselines—"

"One thing at a time," she told him, tending her own explorations. "Good amount of dust hereabouts. I'm wondering—"

"Captain, I have a star! We—We are close within a system—"

The old scholar laughed. "Why, thank you, Pilot Tor An, my son. Yes! The equations have not misled us. We should indeed be very close to a star system within a few percentage points of the mass and energy output of the average star-system with populated planets in our former galaxy." He raised a frail hand as both pilots turned to stare at him.

"I guarantee nothing, of course! I have merely done what my poor skill allowed." He glanced at his tablet. "Locate, my dears, the plane."

"Working on that now," Cantra assured him, spinning back to her board. "Star's slightly oblate; might be the bulge 'round the equator can tell us something interesting."

"No radio traffic on common frequencies," Tor An reported. "The military transceivers are entirely out of band."

"We've got a gas giant, working on mass analysis. 'nother gas bag right here, not nearly as big, but she'll do until we can—"

The in-ship comm chimed, and Cantra swore, not quite under her breath.

Tor An touched the stud.

"Tower," he said, prudently leaving the general line closed. "Yes, Speaker, the ship has entered normal space. No, we do not have an estimation of when we will—No, we do not know what sector—" He flushed, lips pressing tight. "The pilots are doing what we may, Speaker. The nature and order of our work is dictated by circumstance. We will inform the passengers when an appropriate port has been located. Tower out."

He hit the stud a little harder than was needful, and then looked shamefaced. Cantra chuckled, and grinned when he met her eyes.

"My foster-mother always said passengers was more trouble'n they was worth," she said. "I'd own she was right. You, Pilot?"

He tried to frown, but his lips kept twitching the wrong way, and finally he let the smile have its way. "I'd own she was right, too, Pilot," he said, and turned back to his board.

Quick Passage's brains were top-notch and her instrumentation was second to none. In relatively short order they were in possession of a fistful of useful facts. The larger gas giant was just over one-thousandth the mass of the star; the smaller gas giant half the mass of its sister. The giants were more than ninety degrees apart as they circled the star, but in the same plane. There was some debris, and some radio noise typical of energetic discharges. The star had a single small relatively low-energy magnetic storm on its surface, and there seemed to be no other stars within half-a-dozen light-years. So far, so good.

In-ship chimed; the boy reached—and stopped as she held up her hand.

"She's got six ship-days to stew, and we got work to do," she said. "Turn it off and mind your analysis, Pilot."

Tor An grinned. "Aye, Captain."

In the back of her head, an image formed: a white dragon, wings blazing light, rose in a lazy spiral into a brilliant sky. Cantra's fingers paused on the work-pad then she spun and came out of her seat quick. The boy was up, too, and they walked side-by-side and quiet to the power-chair.

Liad dea'Syl's eyes were closed, his head against the rest. He was breathing, shallowly. Lucky was curled on his lap, and the long, clever hands rested on the plush orange fur. On his far side, Rool Tiazan knelt, his fingers curled lightly 'round one thin wrist.

"Tell me, my friend," the scholar whispered. "Is it a fine world, and green? Will people prosper and do well?"

"It is the very finest world possible, Grandfather," the dramliza answered, his voice steady. "The land is rich and bountiful; its star is stable and gracious. Here, the tree will grow to its full height, honoring M. Jela. Here, may people prosper, do well, and be happy in their lives. You have given us a great gift, and we shall evermore be your children in gratitude."

The scholar smiled. "That is well, then," he said softly, and sighed.

In Cantra's head, the white dragon was lost in the brilliant sky, or maybe it was only that she couldn't see him through the tears.

THIRTY-SEVEN

Quick Passage

CANTRA LOOKED DOWN-BOARD to Tor An, who smiled at her encouragingly, and touched the in-ship stud.

"This is Captain yos'Phelium to all passengers. As you know, we've established orbit around an uninhabited world, and deployed probes to the surface. I'm pleased to say that the analysis has now been completed—and to our benefit. Wake-up protocols for passengers in slow-sleep will begin within this ship's hour, in rotation. Off-loading will commence within the next ship's day. Schedules will be on every public screen." She paused and looked again to the boy, who moved his fingers: *Captain's privilege.*

Right. She took a breath and bent again to the mic.

"Welcome to Liad, gentles. The pilots trust you'll enjoy your stay."

CAST OF CHARACTERS

Soldiers

Gorriti, Commander
Hanth
Ilneri, Sergeant
Jarn
Kwinz, Corporal
Lorit, Sergeant
M. Jela Granthor's Guard
Stile
Vachik
Wellik, Commander

Scholars

Ala Bin tay'Welford
Den Vir tel'Elyd
Elvred dea'San
Gor Tan vel'Anbrek
Jenicour tay'Azberg
Kal Var tay'Palin
Leman chi'Farlo
Liad dea'Syl
Maelyn tay'Nordif
Osabei tay'Bendril

Batchers

Arin
Dulsey
Fern
Jakoby

Pilots

Cantra yos'Phelium Clan Torvin
Tor An yos'Galan Clan Alkia
Y. Argast

Ships

Baistle
Light Wing
Profitable Passage
Salkithin
Spiral Dance, a.k.a. *Dancer*

Planets

Finthir
Korak
Landomist
Shinto
Vanehald

Cosmography

Deeps, a.k.a. the Beyond, *also* Outspace or Out-and-Away
In-Rim
Inside
Rim, The
Ringstars, The
Spiral Arm, a.k.a. the Arm

GLOSSARY

aelantaza —A specially-bred human
aetherium —a folded-space confinement area
Batch —humans made to order
Batcher —an individual grown as part of a Batch
carolis —next coin down from qwint
Confusion—a card game
demi-qwint —small change
dramliz —an enchantment of wizards
dramliza —a single wizard
dueling stick —a cross between a cattle prod and a stave
Edonai—Roughly "my lord" when speaking to an Iloheen
flan —next coin up from qwint
Iloheen —sheriekas
Iloheen-bailel roughly, "Lord of Space and Matter"
Kalfer Shimni —really expensive whiskey
kenake —roughly "foreigner"/"person without couth or shoes"/ "flatlander"
logic tile —he smallest component of a computational device
Master of Unmaking —the Iloheen
qwint —coin*sheriekas* —the Enemy
'skins —protective suit for pilot wear on-planet
smaly tube —used to move pallets from the port to warehouses within the city
smartstrands —computational media
Tanjalyre Institute —a school for *aelantaza*
truth-blade —a scholar's instrument of proof
world-eaters —sheriekas doomsday machines
zaliata —energy creatures

ABOUT THE AUTHORS

Sharon Lee and Steve Miller live in the rolling hills of Central Maine. Born and raised in Baltimore, Maryland, they met several times before taking the hint and formalizing the team in 1979. They removed to Maine with cats, books, and music following the completion of *Carpe Diem*, their third novel.

Their short fiction, written both jointly and singly, has appeared or will appear in numerous anthologies and magazines, including *Such a Pretty Face*, *Stars*, *Murder by Magic*, *Women of War*, *Absolute Magnitude*, *3SF*, and several incarnations of *Amazing*.

Meisha Merlin Publishing has or will be publishing twelve novels cleverly disguised as ten books in Steve and Sharon's Liaden Universe®—*Partners in Necessity*, *Plan B*, *Pilots Choice*, *I Dare*, *Balance of Trade*, *Crystal Soldier*, *Crystal Dragon*—*The Tomorrow Log*, first of the Gem ser Edreth adventures, and the anthology *Low Port*, edited by Sharon and Steve. Sharon has also seen a mystery novel, *Barnburner*, published by Embiid in electronic and SRM Publisher, Ltd in paper.

I Dare, *The Tomorrow Log*, and *Balance of Trade* have been Locus magazine bestsellers. *Pilots Choice* (including novels *Local Custom* and *Scout's Progress*) was a finalist for the Pearl Award. *Local Custom* took second place in the 2002 Prism Awards for best futuristic romance, while *Scout's Progress* took first place. *Scout's Progress* has also won the *Romantic Times Bookclub* Reviewer's Choice Award for the best science fiction novel of 2002. In 2005, Balance of Trade received the Hal Clement Award for the best young adult science fiction novel of 2004.

Both Sharon and Steve have seen their non-fiction work and reviews published in a variety of newspapers and magazines. Steve was the founding curator of the University of Maryland's Kuhn Library Science Fiction Research Collection, and former Nebula Award juror. Sharon served the Science Fiction and Fantasy Writers of America, Inc. for five years, as executive director, vice president and president.

Sharon's interests include music, pine cone collecting, and seashores. Steve also enjoys music, plays chess, and collects cat whiskers. Both spend 'way too much time playing on the internet and have a web site at: www.korval.com.

ABOUT THE ARTIST

Donato Giancola balances modern abstract concepts with realism in his paintings to bridge the worlds of fine and illustrative arts. He recognizes the significant cultural role played by visual art, and makes personal efforts to contribute to the expansion and appreciation of the science fiction and fantasy genre that extend beyond the commercial commissions of his clients. Since beginning his professional career in 1993 Donato's list of clients has continued to grow. From the major book publishers in New York to design firms on the West Coast, his commissions include companies such as LucasArts, National Geographic, DC Comics, The Free Masons of Philadelphia, Microsoft, Amazing Stories, Bantam Books, Ballantine Books, HarperCollins Publishers, Penguin, Playboy Magazine, Scholastic, Sony, Tor Books, Warner, Random House, Danbury Mint, Discover Magazine, The Franklin Mint, Milton-Bradley, Hasbro, and Wizards of the Coast.

Donato was born and raised in Colchester, Vermont. He moved to New York City shortly after graduating Summa Cum Laude with a BFA in Painting from Syracuse University in 1992 to begin his stellar art career.

Success as a science fiction illustrator has taken Donato around the world as a guest of honor at numerous events such as Magic: The Gathering tournaments in Santiago, Chile, to the Lucca Comic Book Convention in Italy, the Essen Toy Fair in Germany, and the Lisboa Comic Book Convention in Portugal. Donato is a frequent exhibitor at the Society of Illustrators and shows at many conventions around the states, including World Science Fiction Convention. He was given a Jack Gaughan Award for Best Emerging Artist in 1998, seven Chesley Awards including one for Artistic Acheivement 2002, and has been nominated five times for the Artist Hugo Award. Donato's work can also be seen in *Spectrum: The Best of Contemporary Fantastic Art*, whose juries have awarded him multiple medals from the recent Silver in Advertising Illustration in 2003 to a 2001 Gold in Editorial Art. He was also included in *Infinite Worlds*, a compendium of notable science fiction illustrators of the 20th century authored by Vincent DiFate.

In addition to a lucrative freelance career he has also taught at the School of Visual Arts, and in 1999 was an instructor at the Fashion Institute of Technology. He has served as Guest Lecturer at Syracuse University, Pratt Institute, Virginia Commonwealth University, and Pennsylvania School of Art and Design, and was a co-chair of the 1997 Student Scholarship Committee at the Society of Illustrators in New York.

Donato appears at various colleges, institutions, Magic tournaments and science fiction conventions, where he interacts with fans, performs demonstrations in oil paint, and displays original paintings. A comprehensive listing of his work, technique, and in depth biographical information is available on his website at www.donatoart.com.

Donato lives in New York City with his wife and two daughters. Any time away from his studio is spent in the museums, with his family, playing soccer, or attending various cultural events around the city.